Too much,
Too young

Too much,
Too young

The

Novel

of a

Generation

Caroline Bridgwood

Crown Publishers, Inc.
New York

Published by Crown Publishers, Inc., 201 East 50th Street, New York, New
York 10022. Member of the Crown Publishing Group.

Published in Great Britain by Random Century Group in 1991.

CROWN is a trademark of Crown Publishers, Inc.

Manufactured in the United States of America

Book design by Linda Kocur

Library of Congress Cataloging-in-Publication Data

Bridgwood, Caroline.
Too much, too young : the novel of a generation / Caroline
Bridgwood.—1st ed.
    I. Title.
PR6052.R442T66   1992
823'.914—dc20   91-20245
                                                      CIP

ISBN 0-517-58476-X

10   9   8   7   6   5   4   3   2   1

First American Edition

*This book is dedicated to my darling
daughter, Georgia Rae Alexandra: the product
of my own personal babyboom*

the **f**iftie*s*

birth

O *n e*

■

On a warm afternoon in the late spring of 1959, pregnant women are strolling around the babywear department of Taylor & Haddon, Hemingford's principal department store. Since it is a Saturday, they have their husbands with them. The men haul string bags of groceries and other small purchases, trying not to look bored by the racks of pastel-colored garments.

Jean and Les Fox are expecting their second child in three weeks' time. They already have a two-year-old son, Martin, with his grandmother for the afternoon. Jean moves between the racks of clothes in the trance of late pregnancy, not really concentrating. Her eye is drawn to a row of Bri-nylon nightdresses bristling with lemon and white lace.

"Look at those, Les."

Les frowns. "Not very practical, dear."

Jean, ever passive, sighs her agreement. "All that lace, covered in dribble. Silly, really, aren't they? Still, I suppose somebody buys them."

She sighs again and moves on, as if her bulky abdomen is being pulled by some invisible tow-rope.

"Anyway," says Les, "it might be another boy."

They smile at each other, satisfied that they have done the sensible thing.

Pamela Yardley stands between plastic pants and bibs, waiting for them to go. She too has seen the frilly nightdresses, and wants to take a closer look. Pamela is shopping alone; she doesn't have a husband.

3

Her father offered to come with her but she made some excuse, shrinking at the thought.

Pamela's pregnancy is less advanced than Jean's, but she presses her hands into the small of her back, making her bump look bigger. She loves being pregnant, is obsessed by it. She knows the contents of this department by heart, even though she has not had the money to buy more than a few items. She picks up a lemon-frilled nightdress from the rack and decides at once that it is lovely and she must have one for her baby. She takes it to the till to pay for it, groping in her handbag for the ten-shilling note her father has lent her.

Drifting along a similar route, a few paces behind, are prominent local businessman Geoffrey Noble and his wife Sylvia. They expect their first child in two months' time. Sylvia is tall and naturally slim; she wears an expensive tailored ensemble cut to distract the eye from her pregnant shape. Her feet ache in stiletto courts, she itches in gloves and a hat.

Her attention is caught, despite herself, by the little pink dresses and pram sets. She knows Geoffrey wants a boy, expects a boy. They probably will have a boy, if that's what Geoffrey wants. And she has been too shy to suggest that she might give birth to a girl, that she might *like* to have a girl first. Even so . . .

"Not much here, darling, is there?" Geoffrey wrinkles his nose slightly, strides ahead thrusting his hands into the pockets of his cavalry twills. "I think we'd be better off going to Harrods. You can take the train up to town one afternoon. Or one of the family could go, if you can't face it . . ."

This snippet of conversation is picked up by Audrey Pryce-Jones, whose baby is due at the same time as Sylvia's. (In fact, she thinks she has seen Sylvia during a hospital check-up, waiting outside the private consulting rooms to see that dashing Doctor Odell—or is he one that calls himself "Mr."?) She looks at the Nobles with admiration. She would dearly love to have bought her first layette at Harrods, but suspects that Ken would say they couldn't afford it.

"Kenneth!" she trills to her husband. "Kenneth, here a minute, my love!"

Kenneth strolls out from behind plastic pants, a fatuous grin attempting to mask his discomfort. The brass buttons of his blazer, which have anchors on them, gleam under the hard lighting. Audrey is still watching Sylvia Noble surreptitiously, wondering how much that coat dress must have cost, wishing that she, too, had thought to wear gloves....

"What's next?" He waits for her to consult the list she carries.

"Half a dozen packets of terry nappies. Harringtons."

"Half a dozen? Are you sure that's right? That's how many of the things ... seventy-two?"

"I don't know how many, you're the accountant, not me!" She smiles through her teeth, intent on having her own way. "I checked in all the books, Kenneth. That's how many they say he'll need."

It never occurs to the Pryce-Joneses that their child will be anything other than a boy. They've always done everything properly, after all. They became engaged when she was twenty-one, he twenty-seven. They married a year later and saved hard for their first flat. Now they have put their name on the waiting list for a brand new executive home, with carport. And they are going to have a little boy, then two years later a little girl. Everything has been planned.

Hemingford is an unremarkable town with a population of fifty thousand, some thirty-five miles southwest of London. At its center there are still some fine Georgian buildings, municipal offices, and one or two residential squares. But they are largely overshadowed by Victorian red brick, turned dark and dirty with age. The high street winds its way through the center of the town, dominated by the six solid stories and gleaming windows of Taylor & Haddon. Adjacent to the high street, a new shopping center is planned. There are already concrete mixers on site, and broken paving stones, and people grumble about the mess.

Past the library and the public baths, heading due south, lies St. Mark's, the area surrounding the old biscuit factory. There are flat-fronted Victorian cottages, narrow, dirty streets, and an aura of poverty left over from before the war. Those aspiring to a better way of life head north of the town to Lordswood Hill, the suburb that clings around the edges of Lordswood Park, Hemingford's chief recreation area. Public baths and municipal grayness are exchanged for the golf club, the tennis courts, and wide, leafy avenues. In the next few years these pin-neat thirties' semis will be made to look dowdy by new estates of detached houses with their sun patios and their barbecue areas, their brash, uncompromising modernity.

Hemingford Maternity Hospital is on the western edge of the town. In years gone by it had been the workhouse, and even the turquoise paint on the doors and railings cannot dissipate its dour appearance.

The Nobles' Jaguar glides past the HOSPITAL—QUIET sign and turns into the car park. Sylvia gazes in awe at the arrow pointing to MATER-NITY ADMISSIONS, but it is not time for that, not yet. They are at the hospital for an appointment with their private obstetrician, Mr. Odell. Odell telephoned Geoffrey's office and told him that there was something he wished to discuss. He would not have dreamed of telephoning Sylvia to make this arrangement: Sylvia does not pay his bills.

They are met in the reception area by Mr. Odell's secretary and shown straight into the private consulting rooms. He marches in with the tails of his white coat billowing behind him. The coat is open, revealing herringbone tweed and a gold watch chain.

"Ah, Mr. and Mrs. Noble, good of you to come...." He shakes Geoffrey's hand, gives Sylvia a brief glance of acknowledgment over the rim of his half-moons.

"There was something in your wife's last checkup that I wanted to discuss with you both."

Sylvia looks down at her handbag, confused. Geoffrey clears his throat. "What sort of thing, exactly?"

"It's nothing to be worried about, quite the opposite actually." He gestures to the examination couch. "Would you mind, Mrs. Noble. I'd just like a little feel of your tummy."

A nurse appears as if by magic and wheels screens around the couch, sparing Geoffrey the sight of his wife in her underwear. Mr. Odell bends over Sylvia's belly, pressing the ice-cold stethoscope first onto one side, then the other.

"Just as I thought ..."

He pushes back the screens with a flourish and addresses Geoffrey.

"Not one heartbeat, but two, Mr. Noble. Twins."

Geoffrey's face slowly turns pink. "Good God!"

"Can be quite a shock, I know. Taken out any insurance?"

"Yes, I did as a matter of fact, telephoned Lloyds ... you know, when we first found out that Sylvia was expecting."

"Good man. Wise move."

The nurse helps Sylvia off the couch and into a chair.

"You heard that, did you, Mrs. Noble? Two mouths to feed instead of one. What do you think of that?"

"Well ..."

"Of course, it could mean certain complications, with the birth itself. They're likely to arrive early, for a start. We're looking at another month, instead of two. And I'm afraid at this stage it looks as though they'll be on the small side."

"Oh ..." Sylvia looks nervously at Geoffrey.

"Better hope they're a couple of girls, eh? We find girls do better than boys when they're of low birthweight."

"Girls?" Geoffrey looks offended at the suggestion.

"A boy and a girl then. A boy for you and a girl for your lady wife here."

Sylvia smiles. A boy for Geoffrey and a girl for her.... Yes, that would be just perfect.

T w o

■

Jean Fox waddles out into her back garden to hang out the washing. She has left the back door open so that she can keep an eye on Martin, playing with his toy farm on the kitchen floor.

Her neighbor, Mrs. Hinsley, is also in the garden, planting seedlings in a flower bed. She points to Jean's belly with her trowel.

"Not long to go now, dear."

"No—thank goodness!" Jean makes a mock grimace at her waistline.

"What are you hoping for—boy or girl?"

"I don't mind really."

In Jean's case this is the truth rather than social platitude. A placid, stoical woman, she has spent her twenty-nine years patiently accepting whatever fate pushes her way. She does not see her own lack of interest in the baby's sex as negative. A girl would be nice. Another boy would be nice too, though.

In the kitchen, two-year-old Martin has grown bored with the toy farm and is going to switch on the radio, which is between the kettle and the bread bin.

"Not that, Martin love—you know Daddy doesn't like you touching his wireless."

Martin switches it on anyway. Jean does not bother to reprimand him. Instead she hums along to the music that floats out into the garden, Elvis Presley singing his new hit, "A Fool Such As I."

As she bends to pick up one of Les's shirts, she feels a sharp twinge of pain, low down in her abdomen. The baby seems to press

8

down lower in her groin. A vague memory stirs in Jean's mind of how things were two years ago, when Martin was born, and she realizes that this is it, that labor is starting. She waits for the wave of pain to pass, holding on to the side of the laundry basket. Then she straightens up slowly and pegs out a pair of Les's Y-fronts.

Jean and Les live at 41 Tudor Avenue, Lordswood. To get there, you pass the park, turn left into Plantagenet Drive, then take the second right, past York Way. Number 41 is on the left-hand side, about halfway down the street. It is a three-bedroomed, bay-fronted, semi-detached house, indistinguishable from all the others in Tudor Avenue. They all project the same middle-class blend of restraint and respectability, neither scruffy nor smart, prosperous nor impoverished. Few of the residents own a car. Les Fox does—a rusting dark green Wolseley. The car is too precious to be used as Les's transport to and from the factory, and is only aired on special occasions. The house has no garage, so it sits on a Tarmaced strip at the detached side of the house.

Neither Jean nor Les minds that it takes up most of the front garden; in fact they relish the prominence of this status symbol. When they first married, they never dreamed that they would own a car. Les's father was born in Hemingford and worked at the biscuit factory all his life. Les was set to do the same, and he and Jean began their married life in a two up–two down in St. Mark's. But at his mother's suggestion, Les went to night school and studied bookkeeping. The year before Martin was born, he was transferred from the factory floor to the offices, where he worked as a wages clerk. His mother then came up with another suggestion: that he apply for the more superior position of invoice clerk. This he duly did, and with the modest promotion came a salary that enabled him to buy a house in Lordswood.

It would be easy to make the assumption that Les Fox is as passive and resigned as his wife. This is not so: Les is quick-tempered, energetic, and impatient. He looks on his widowed mother as a mentor in the way that some men look to their wives. Jean doesn't mind this. She accepts the closeness between Winnie Fox and her son without rancor. "They're so alike, the pair of them," she tells her friends. "Like two peas from the same pod."

Jean gets in from the garden in time to see Winnie walking up the front path. She has taken the bus up from St. Mark's and walked from the stop at the corner of Plantagenet Drive. She visits several times during the week, but never says exactly when she will arrive, thereby giving herself the advantage of surprise over her daughter-in-law. Her excuse is that she doesn't have a telephone.

Looking through the window of the front room, Jean watches Winnie flick at the soggy pink and white blossoms that have drifted onto the bonnet of the Wolseley from the trees that punctuate Tudor Avenue's grass verges. She purses her lips in disapproval as though the car were an ornament that badly needed dusting.

Jean's heart sinks, as it always does when she knows Winnie is about to descend. Jean has few private thoughts, but one of them is that her mother-in-law can be an interfering old battle-ax.

"Still here, I see!" is Winnie's comment as Jean lets her in. The baby is a few days overdue. Winnie behaves as though a late baby is due to some negligence on the part of its mother.

Leading her mother-in-law through to the kitchen, Jean feels another contraction, but in a rare fit of spite resolves to say nothing, and to do nothing about it until Winnie has gone home again.

Winnie spies Martin crawling around on the kitchen floor.

"That child ought to be outside," she says. "He ought to be getting fresh air."

Bending down, she says in a wheedling tone, "Come to Nana, then, Martin. Come and see what Nana's got in her handbag."

"Martin, go to Nana," urges Jean, gripping the table as another contraction surges through her. Martin, a naturally shy child, turns down his lower lip.

"He's tired," pronounces Winnie knowingly. "He needs to go down for a nap. Don't you, my precious?"

Jean scoops up Martin and carries him into his bedroom, where she hangs onto the side of the cot for another contraction. Downstairs, Winnie starts doing the washing-up. She always washes up when she arrives. Even if Jean has just tidied up herself, Winnie still manages to find something to wash.

"I see you've still got the bassinet in the little back bedroom." Winnie shouts over her shoulder as she scours a saucer.

How on earth could she have seen when she's only been in the house five minutes? She must have looked up the stairs as she came through the front door. Eagle-eyed old ...

"Only you'll be wanting to put that in your room when the little one arrives."

Jean, who doesn't much want the baby sleeping in her bedroom, says: "Yes, I've been meaning to get round to it. I expect Les will move it later if I ask him."

"You have to tell him!" says Winnie. "You have to tell men these things, you know."

Jean nods. She says nothing about the contractions, waiting until Winnie has had her cup of tea and gone for the bus.

Then, reluctantly, she picks up the phone and telephones the biscuit factory. Les doesn't like her ringing him at work.

"I think the baby's coming, dear. Can you get home?"

He sounds surprised, then impatient. She imagines him pushing back his shirt cuff to look at his watch. "I'm rather busy at the moment. Do you think you can hang on for a couple of hours? Until about three?"

Jean lets out a long sigh as another wave of pain hits her. "I suppose so."

The staff of Hemingford Maternity Hospital are having a busy year. Yet another busy year. The marriage rate for the past decade has risen to twenty percent above its prewar level, and child rearing has become a national preoccupation. So many British women have responded to the postwar call to their ageless mission, that there has been a greater than expected rise in the birth rate. And the women of Hemingford are no exception to the rule, with facilities at the hospital stretched to their limit and the wards permanently full.

Sister Jennings, the senior midwife on duty at the admissions desk, answers a phone call, then puts the receiver down with a frown.

"Another one on the way, a Mrs. Fox. Sounds like she's pretty far gone. You'd better get a room ready, Staff."

Staff Midwife Gibbs complies with this request, then joins the porter on the steps to wait for the new patient.

"This must be them." The porter readies his wheelchair as an ambulance comes into sight. "They couldn't get here under their own steam, apparently. Their car had a flat battery. I ask you!"

He laughs to himself as he goes forward to help Jean Fox out of the ambulance. Les hovers in the background, annoyed and embarrassed at the Wolseley's failure.

As Jean is pushed up the ramp and into Admissions, she grimaces with pain.

"Left it a little bit late this time, didn't we, Mrs. Fox?" admonishes Sister Jennings, as she helps lift Jean onto a delivery bed and shuts the door firmly in Les's face.

Jean would like to explain that Les was two hours late coming home and then the precious, useless Wolseley wouldn't start, but she is too wretched with pain to speak.

"I think we'll have baby here by suppertime . . . oh my goodness! Staff! Staff—bring the trolley in right away, will you?"

She has lifted Jean's smock to find the baby's head between Jean's legs, ready to be born.

"This one's in a hurry to get into the world . . . one big push now. . . ."

Jean gives a heave and the baby slithers out, crying angrily.

"A girl, Mrs. Fox!"

"That's nice," says Jean weakly.

The baby is carried to the scales and weighed. "And a big strong one too—nine pounds, one ounce!"

After Jean has been cleaned up, Les is allowed in to admire his daughter and marvel at her size. They discuss names.

"I fancy Carolyn," says Jean shyly, stroking the baby's quiff of dark hair. "Carolyn Jane."

"Carolyn Winifred," Les corrects her. "We must have Winifred."

"All right then," agrees Jean. "Carolyn Winifred."

Les goes off to phone his mother. The baby is collected and taken to the nursery for the night. Staff Midwife Gibbs peers at the name label as she wheels the crib down the corridor. "Carolyn Winifred Fox! Poor little bugger."

T *h r e e*

■

Audrey Pryce-Jones is sitting at her dressing table, applying her make-up. She performs the ritual slowly, with meticulous care. Thick, pancake foundation is followed by a generous layer of powder. Her face, made rounder by pregnancy, now resembles a smooth, pale marshmallow. With a dark eyeliner pencil, she draws on slanting cat's eyes, then opens her box of block mascara and dabs the brush on the block with delicate little movements, applying several layers. The final touch is crimson lipstick, thickly applied.

Suddenly impatient to be finished, Audrey snatches up her hairbrush and pats it over her hair. She can't really brush it, due to an impenetrable layer of lacquer. She wishes Eduardo wouldn't use quite so much, but doesn't dare say anything. When she first started to frequent Eduardo's of Hemingford, she was under the care of Christina, one of the junior stylists. Now, due to the recent improvement in her social status, she is paying the extra ten shillings per session to be styled by Eduardo himself. And Eduardo has his own ideas on how "his" ladies should look. At this morning's visit, he insisted on tinting Audrey's brunette locks with auburn. Audrey hasn't yet decided whether or not she likes it—she is too busy worrying about what Ken will make of it.

She pulls herself to her feet and her pregnant stomach looms in front of the mirror. Usually trim and light on her feet, Audrey dislikes her condition. Ken says it makes her "peevish." Anyway, not for much longer, she consoles herself as she pushes her puffy feet into stilettos with pointed toes.

Only another two weeks. . . .

The shantung coat dress is a little tight now, but it is her smartest maternity outfit, so it will have to do. A hat would help. She read in a magazine at Eduardo's that a hat or a frilly neckline will help to detract the gaze from a pregnant woman's midriff. A hat it is then, a little glazed straw pillbox. But no gloves. Gloves might get dirty.

As she pushes the wardrobe door closed, she notices a patch of peeling wallpaper just under the cornice. In other places, the cabbage roses of the paper are stained with damp. Audrey grimaces. She hates this flat. Ken told her not to be so stupid when she said so the other day. He said, "It's only a flat, sweetheart, you can't *hate* it." In case he had thought her peevish she had quickly corrected herself: She didn't mean "hate" as such, she just meant it was no longer suitable for people in their position.

Ken is not yet late, but she goes to telephone him, just to remind him that he's suppose to be coming home to collect her.

"Good afternoon—Baring Baker. May I help you?"

"Mr. Pryce-Jones's secretary, please," says Audrey firmly.

Ken's secretary tells her that Mr. Pryce-Jones is not available to come to the phone at the moment, but that of course she will remind him of their appointment that afternoon. Audrey detects a certain warmth, a certain respect in the girl's voice. Her Kenneth was recently made a junior partner at the firm of accountants he joined five years ago. Audrey remembers with pleasure being introduced at a recent dinner party as "Our new partner, and his wife, Mrs. Kenneth Pryce-Jones. . . ."

They will have to start giving dinner parties themselves, just as soon as they have moved. First, of course, they will need to buy a new dining suite. Their old one only seats eight. She makes a mental note to tell Ken about it, when he comes home.

At Baring Baker, Ken's secretary, Beryl, is suppressing laughter as she speaks to Audrey. Silly woman, telephoning her husband every five minutes! Occasionally it becomes a little annoying, having to cover up for him. At the moment, if she leans far enough over her desk, she can just see her boss through an open door on the other side of the corridor. He is with young Philippa Bressel, secretary to one of the senior partners, and the two of them are seeing how many paper-clips they need to string together to encircle Philippa's waist.

"Mr. Pryce-Jones!" trills Beryl.

The paper-clip chain is unwound with much giggling, and Ken strolls back into his own office, smoothing back his Brylcreemed hair. "Your wife just telephoned, Mr. Pryce-Jones. Something about an appointment?"

Beryl takes off her horn-rimmed glasses and puts her head on one side, her smile sugar-sweet and faintly mocking.

Ken glances at his watch.

"I'm supposed to be taking her out ..." He glances back at Philippa and adds with some reluctance, "I'd better get going. Can't keep the little woman waiting, eh?"

He collects his briefcase and car keys, winks at Beryl, and sticks his head round the door of Philippa's office.

"I thought I might pop down to the golf club later. Fancy meeting me there for a wee drinkie?" He raises an imaginary glass to his lips.

"What time?" Philippa is cautious. She has heard from the other girls that Ken sometimes fails to make it over the marital threshold.

"What time would suit?"

"Eight?"

"Eight it is, in the lounge bar."

"Don't be late!"

Ken makes a mock salute and clicks his heels. "The proverbial wild horses couldn't prevent me, my sweet."

He is fond of such corny little phrases, clichés which he uses with confidence, knowing that a man of lesser charm and physical attraction couldn't get away with such drivel. He is confident of an amusing evening too, and hums happily to himself as he drives his brand-new Ford back to the flat. Audrey won't like the idea of him going out, but he will worry about that later.

When he gets back, Audrey is fussing about him being late, fussing about whether her hat looks right, peeved because he hasn't noticed her hair. She calms down once she is in the car, however. It always has a sedative effect, going out in the car with Ken. She sits there proudly, hoping that lowly pedestrians will notice how new their car is, and how handsome her husband. She turns to look at him now, the cowlick of dark hair on his forehead that will never quite stay smoothed back, the dark eyes and strong, square jaw. The male models on the front of knitting patterns look like Ken: handsome but dependable.

Ken catches her eye in the driving mirror and smiles at her. "Everything all right, my sweet?"

She flicks a stray paper-clip from his sleeve. "Kenneth, when we move, don't you think we should get a new dining suite ... ? Only we will do more entertaining, won't we? I saw something suitable in Taylor & Haddon the other day, actually, a rather nice reproduction table with twelve chairs ..."

"Do you really think we'll need twelve, darling? I would have thought ..."

"And we really ought to have some furniture fitted in the master bedroom, like Derek and his wife have—I took a peek when we were there for dinner—with those little brass handles. ..."

Ken brings the car to a halt and says with triumph, "Well, there it is!"

"It" is their new house, 9 Mount Rise. It is a detached brick house with sunporch and carport, on Hemingford's newest and most prestigious estate on the edge of the golf course. The Pryce-Joneses took out a large mortgage in order to buy the house when it was at the planning stage.

"There's no garden!" says Audrey weakly, looking at the swamp of mud and rubble between them and the front door.

"There will be, there will be ..." soothes Ken, helping Audrey ease herself out of the car. "It's just a question of laying some turf and a few paving stones. But the inside's complete. That's what I wanted you to see."

He finds the keys, lent to him by the builders, and opens the front door. Audrey waddles into the hall, looks around her, and sniffs.

"I don't know about this floor ..." She points to a scuff mark that her stiletto has made on the wood. "It's going to mark dreadfully. Especially with kiddies ..."

"You *wanted* parquet, my sweet, now you've *got* parquet. . . . Shall we take a look at the living room?"

The living room has big picture windows and a sliding patio door onto the rear mud-bath.

"They've got the fitted carpet down, look."

"Kenneth, I thought we asked for Old Gold!" Audrey's voice rises slightly. "Does this look like Old Gold to you?"

He peers at the carpet. "Sort of goldish, I'd say, yes."

"It looks more mustardy to me, Kenneth, and I specifically wanted it more golden to go with the color scheme I've got in mind. Will you . . . ?"

"It's all right, my sweet, I'll check with the builders. Now let's look upstairs, shall we? Can you manage the stairs?"

They inspect the bedrooms (four) and the bathrooms (two) and to Ken's relief everything meets with Audrey's approval. She spends some minutes praising the kitchen, with its gleaming Formica cupboards, then goes back for a second look at the living room. As she struggles with the catch on the patio door, she feels a hot wetness between her legs. Her waters have broken all over the Old Gold carpet.

"Do something, Ken!" she gasps. "Do something, or it will leave a stain!"

Ken pulls out his handkerchief and dabs at her skirt.

"No!" she wails. "The carpet!"

At Hemingford Maternity, fifteen minutes later, a bedraggled Audrey is assigned to the care of Staff Midwife Anne Gibbs, just starting the late shift. Staff Midwife Gibbs has hayfever and is not feeling sympathetic.

"So—no contractions yet?" she enquires briskly as she examines Audrey. "Lift your dress up, please. I'll need to do an internal."

"Not yet, no. Excuse me, but . . ."

"Right, well, if they don't start in the next few hours we'll have to give you a drip to get you going."

"Nurse, I was wondering . . ." Audrey tries to raise her head so she can look the woman in the eye. "Would it be possible for me to have a private room, d'you think, only . . ."

The midwife opens Audrey's notes and frowns at them. "Are you a private patient?"

"No, but you see, I ..."

"The rooms in the private wing are for private patients and consultants' wives, I'm afraid. You'll be on Ward Four."

"Only I did ask about it at the clinic and they said ..." Audrey's voice tails away as she sees the lack of sympathy on Anne Gibbs' face. She is deposited on the ward, where she struggles out of bed and pulls the screens around her. The woman in the next bed already has a baby, a very fat baby, and is breast-feeding her. Like a cow, thinks Audrey with distaste. She is going to bottle-feed, to keep her figure nice for Ken. She glances at the name label in the baby's cot before she closes the screens. "FOX" it says, then underneath, "Carolyn Winifred." She and Ken didn't discuss girls' names, only boys'. She hauls herself back onto the bed and prays for the contractions to come. She thinks she feels one, but it turns out to be wind.

Ken drives home to collect Audrey's overnight bag. When he returns to the hospital he is much relieved when Sister tells him there's no point waiting, and that they'll telephone when things are happening. That just gives him time to go home again, bath and change and meet Philippa at the golf club at eight. For a while he'd been worried that he wouldn't make it.

Audrey wriggles around on the bed, trying to get comfortable. She occasionally imagines she can feel something, but is not sure. What does a labor pain feel like? She would like to ask the woman in the next bed, Mrs. Fox, but when she peeps through the curtains, she sees that her neighbor has dozed off, with her fat baby asleep in the crib beside her. No one has told her what is going to happen, and she wishes Ken were here to ask for her. He'd sort her out, she thinks with a flash of pride, my husband. Is it on her notes, she wonders, that Ken is a partner in a firm of accountants?

Later, after they have brought her a cup of tea and she has relaxed enough to take her hairbrush from her vanity case and smooth her hair, she recalls them saying at the clinic that they started you off twelve hours after your waters broke, if nothing had happened by then. Twelve hours ... that took her up to six in the morning, so at least she'd have the chance of a decent night's sleep. And wasn't it lucky that she went to Eduardo that morning?

But Staff Midwife Gibbs returns at nine and says that she won't want to go on hanging around like this, will she? And why don't they just pop a little injection in her arm to get things moving? Before she can answer, they've wheeled her into another room and stuck the needle in her arm. Nothing happens, and then suddenly everything happens at once, the pains all climbing on top of one another in their haste to assault her body.

Never in her wildest dreams had Audrey imagined that childbirth could be so undignified. Her auburn hair is dark with sweat as she whimpers, then calls for Ken, and finally, her own mother. Then her legs are in the air, in stirrups, and they're cutting her. In a brief second of clarity she allows herself to imagine Ken's outrage—or will it be disgust?

"A nice easy birth," says a voice in the background, as she gives her final groan.

Then: "Give him to me!" she demands, before they've even said it's a boy.

At one o'clock Anne Gibbs goes to telephone Ken, but gets no reply.

"Your husband must be a very heavy sleeper!" she tells Audrey.

"He snores!" says Audrey, and giggles. She is euphoric.

Matthew John Pryce-Jones lies asleep in his cot, a perfect seven and a half pounds, pink and smooth and unblemished.

Several people have already commented on what a pretty baby he is.

Kenneth does not reply when the midwife on the early shift telephones at seven. He is finally contacted at Baring Baker that morning and arrives half an hour later bearing a sheaf of roses and as proud as if he has given birth himself.

Audrey asks why he didn't hear the phone and his answer is sufficiently evasive to stir a suspicion in her mind. But she dismisses it. Matthew is her consolation. "My little boy," she says, barely glancing at her husband, "my little man ..."

F o u r

■

Sylvia Noble is standing at the top of her elegant, curving staircase, looking down into the hall below. The door has been opened by Mrs. Moody, the daily woman, to admit one Miss Simmons, a maternity nurse (or "monthly" nurse as they are called in polite circles; their usual period of employment being one month). She has been engaged by Geoffrey Noble to take care of the twins, and in the approved fashion has arrived to settle in before the birth itself.

Sylvia looks down from on high, twisting the strand of pearls at her neck. Miss Simmons is a dry, desiccated woman who doesn't fill out her nurse's cape properly. Even her suitcases look dry and dusty. Sylvia tries, and fails, to imagine this woman handling her babies, her precious babies. Reluctantly, she goes downstairs to introduce herself and perform all the other offices of new employer.

Miss Simmons informs Sylvia that she likes her ladies to begin with a tour of the entire house. More from nosiness than necessity no doubt, since she will be spending all her time in the nursery, and cooking and cleaning are not part of her contract. Sylvia starts with the hall, with its black and white Italian tiled floor and circular skylight, to the wood-panelled study and the drawing room with its ornamental coving and handsome sash windows. She explains to Miss Simmons that the Italianate villa was built by a wealthy Edwardian businessman who wanted to move his family out of London and into the country-side, as the outskirts of Hemingford then were. Where the golf course now stood, to the southwest of the house, there had been open fields, and in all probability a delightful aspect. Sylvia talks like this at some length; she is interested in history, and likes to imagine the house as it was at the beginning of the century, full of children. . . .

Miss Simmons nods and sniffs and tuts, squinting at the family photographs in their frames, at the spines of the books, at the quality of the fabric in the drapes. She doesn't seem to be interested in history; the only question she asks is about Mr. Noble's profession. Sylvia tells her that Mr. Noble is a stockbroker, from a long line of stockbrokers, and that he goes to Waterloo every morning on the 7:53, returning every night on the 6:18.

And so on to the nursery. Miss Simmons is soon engrossed in sorting and airing the large piles of nightdresses, fluffy white towels and gauze squares. She is on familiar territory now, absorbed in her task, even humming to herself. Sylvia hovers for a while, offering information that she hopes will be useful, wanting Miss Simmons's approval despite herself. But it is as if she isn't there, and all of this process, this preparation of the house for two new lives, has nothing to do with her. Sylvia wonders if all monthly nurses are like this. There was no question of them having anyone but Miss Simmons.

"But we always have Miss Simmons, darling," Geoffrey had said in the tone that implies no further discussion will be required. He uses this tone frequently. By "we," of course, he does not mean Sylvia and himself, but his family, his three sisters and his cousins, who have all lived out their confinements in the company of Miss Simmons.

Later, when she is alone in her bedroom, Sylvia feels frightened. She has tried not to think about it all day, but now, with the evening approaching and her suitcase to pack, she must. Tomorrow she is having the babies. Geoffrey has arranged it with Mr. Odell. She will go into the operating theater and they will cut the babies out of her. It was to have been today, only tonight there is a dinner party that Geoffrey wants her to attend, so he told Mr. Odell that the birth would have to be a day later, and Mr. Odell agreed.

She attends to the final details of her packing, then struggles into her best maternity evening dress: an Empire line chiffon. Her bulky shape makes it impossible for her to lift her hands behind her back and fasten the zip herself. She considers asking Miss Simmons, but decides that such a task would not come under a maternity nurse's jurisdiction. Instead she waits for Geoffrey to come home.

"Nurse settle in all right?" he asks as he helps her with her dress.

When Sylvia says she assumes so, Geoffrey responds with a brisk "Good, good" and starts to talk about the dinner party: who will be there, the business deals he hopes to discuss. Sylvia sits silently in the Jaguar as they drive there. She doesn't want to go to a dinner party, not tonight. It seems callous somehow, to sit and exchange golf club gossip when two new lives are about to be wrenched into the world.

The dress is black tie, the formal dress giving the men license to be more pompous than usual, the women more trivial. Sylvia remains silent through the first two courses, then indicates to Geoffrey that she would like to be excused from the remainder. Amid the sympathetic murmurings of the women, he has no choice but to take Sylvia home. The other guests all shout "Good luck!" after her, as though she were about to appear in a school play, or take her driving test.

The next morning, Sylvia is lying on a metal trolley in an ante-room of the maternity hospital. She is dressed in a faded blue cotton gown, with her hair scraped back under a white cap. Mr. Odell and the nurses are also in white and pale blue, making the room seem cold despite the warmth of the sun outside and the hospital central heating. The atmosphere is cold and efficient: this is not a woman about to give birth, but a clinical event about to happen.

Anne Gibbs is rostered on theater duty that morning. "All right now, Mrs. Noble?" she asks through her mask, holding out a syringe. "In a minute you're going to start feeling a little sleepy...."

Sylvia shivers as she goes under. She feels her babies move inside her, and with a stab of fear she wonders if they will ever move again.

"Darling ..." It's Geoffrey's voice. "Darling, can you hear me?"

She can't remember. She can't remember if it's happened or not. Are they about to do it, or have they just done it? She can't remember.

Another voice: "She's coming round."

Coming round. So they must have done it, even though no time has passed.

She can see Geoffrey's face, the lips under the moustache. The lips are saying something.

"A boy and a girl, darling. Isn't that super?"

Midwife Gibbs is lifting Sylvia up on the pillows now, and she can see Geoffrey's face better. She is vaguely aware that despite the news, Geoffrey isn't pleased. But she doesn't much care. She feels too sick. She reaches dizzily for the side of the bed and vomits, missing the bowl.

Later Sylvia understands why Geoffrey is not happy. It seems the babies aren't well. They're too small, she is told, as though this is a failing on her part. And she can't go and see them yet, because she is still too weak. Too small, too weak.

When she becomes upset, they send for Mr. Odell. He sits on the side of the bed and talks to her in a gently patronizing tone. This must be what they call bedside manner, Sylvia thinks, this is what we're paying him for. The surgical blues have been replaced with the herringbone tweed suit.

"What's all this Sister tells me about you upsetting yourself, eh? We can't have this, can we? Now—you know why we . . ."

"I just want to see them. The babies."

"We explained about why we were having to deliver the babies early, didn't we?" Mr. Odell, like Geoffrey, is fond of the first person plural. "We were worried about them not growing properly. One of the placentas didn't seem to be nourishing the baby properly. So we thought we'd hoik 'em out."

Sylvia winces, which seems to amuse him.

"Now, the problem is, they're a bit smaller than we'd hoped. The little lad's only just three pounds. The girl is nearer four, which is better."

Sylvia remembers what Odell said before about girls doing better than boys, and smiles suddenly. Odell is talking about the boy, and what his chances are, but she is not really listening. The girl will survive, it will be all right.

When Geoffrey comes that evening, he asks her about names.

"The family want to know," he says. "We" again. "I thought if I came up with a name for the little chap, then you could do the same for the girl."

Sylvia is happy with this compromise, and approves Geoffrey's suggestion of Stephen Goodchild, his own middle name and his mother's maiden name. Thankfully Geoffrey's sisters have already named sons for their father (Henry) and grandfather (Horace).

"What about the girl, then? Have any ideas?"

"Amabel," says Sylvia firmly.

"Annabel? Well, why not?"

"No, Amabel. With an "m". It's an old version of the name, popular in the nineteenth century."

Geoffrey isn't interested in the attendant history. He thinks the corruption of a perfectly good English name a little affected, but he struck the bargain about the choice of names, and he considers himself a man of his word.

"Amabel it is then," he says, a little stiffly, and gets up to go. Apart from the question of their names, Geoffrey does not discuss his offspring with his wife. Their prematurity, their frailty, seem to embarrass him.

In the next few days, there are many more visitors to Sylvia's private room at Hemingford Maternity. Geoffrey's family come first, taking automatic priority; his strident sisters and boorish brothers-in-law. Sylvia's sister, Sara, is accommodated once all the Nobles have looked their fill. She is the only representative of the Chancellors, Sylvia's family. Their father has been dead for a year, and their mother, Lydia, lives on the Riviera with an Argentinian paramour. Several years earlier, the same Argentinian was the cause of the Chancellors' very public divorce proceedings, which were discussed by the columnists of Fleet Street's society pages. Sylvia had recently married Geoffrey, who behaved as though the Chancellors had only divorced to annoy him and that, had they done it before his wedding, he would have thought twice about linking his family name with theirs.

The size of the babies leaves the visitors at a loss, so the visits are kept mercifully short. There is time, however, for members of the Noble tribe to impress on Sylvia that the situation must be due to some failing on her part. ("But we've always had such *large* babies, darling.") After a week, Sylvia is allowed to go home, leaving the babies behind. She is nursed not by Miss Simmons—who waits, unoc-

cupied, for her charges, grudging them their time in the incubator—
but by a hired agency nurse.

After another week, Sylvia is strong enough to get up.

Under Miss Simmons's disapproving eye, she goes into the nursery
and sorts the babies' clothes. She lingers over Amabel's little dresses,
marvelling at the delicacy of the lace, the intricacy of the smocking.

The telephone rings and she tears herself away, with some reluctance, to answer it.

"It's me, darling," Geoffrey gives an embarrassed cough. "Odell
just phoned from the hospital. They want us to go down there. There's
a problem with one of the twins."

Geoffrey is going to take a taxi straight to the hospital, and Sylvia
must take the Jaguar and meet him there. She hates driving the Jaguar
and is usually overcautious, fearful of scratching its long, shiny bonnet.
Today she crashes the gears and wrenches the steering wheel round
bends, oblivious to the hoots from other drivers. *One of the twins . . .*
she is saying to herself over and over again. *Only one of the twins
. . .* Geoffrey didn't say so, but he must have meant Stephen. Stephen
was so much smaller and weaker than his sister, and besides, premature girls fare much better than boys. . . .

Geoffrey is already at the hospital when Sylvia arrives. His back
view is the first thing she sees when she walks into the intensive care
ward. He is talking to Odell and the ward sister. The next thing she
sees is the pair of cots, in their usual corner. One of them is empty.

Sylvia knows at once what that means, but all she can think is,
Which one? The two words pound in her ears as she walks across
the linoleum toward her husband. She assumes it is Stephen. Worse,
she hopes it is Stephen.

The nurse and Odell have seen her and hurry to meet her. It's
Amabel, they say, but she doesn't understand. Which is Amabel? The
one in the cot? Or the one in some other nameless place, on some
slab somewhere?

"Your little girl has gone, Mrs. Noble, I'm so sorry. . . ."

So that's what they meant. It's Stephen in the cot.

They are saying things about sudden breathing difficulties, about
cardiac arrest, but she doesn't really want to listen.

My little girl is gone. Her brain repeats the nurse's words.

Geoffrey puts his arm around her and he and Odell take her into Odell's office. The last time Geoffrey put his arm round her was at their wedding reception, when they cut the cake together. She wants to push it away.

"It'll be all right, darling, you'll see. We can have another baby. You'll have another little girl."

But she knows she can't, she won't. She wants Amabel, not another little girl.

"There is some good news." Odell addresses Geoffrey. "Some good news at this terrible time. Young Stephen is gaining weight well, and in a week or so, you'll be able to have him home. That'll do you both good, won't it, give you something to think about?"

It gives Geoffrey plenty to think about. The next morning he phones his old boarding school, Maidenhurst, and submits the name of Stephen Goodchild Noble for a place in September 1972.

Sylvia goes home and thinks about Amabel. On the day that Stephen is to leave hospital, Miss Simmons finds her in the nursery, folding and re-folding a pile of Amabel's dresses.

"I sorted those out to go away," she says, not unkindly. "You know, with ... I thought perhaps a charity. Or I could wrap them in tissue and put them in the attic. For the next little one—"

"No!" Sylvia snatches the clothes away and hugs them tightly. "No."

Miss Simmons leaves her alone; she has other things to think about. Clothes must be aired, a hot-water bottle must be filled to warm the crib. Stephen's arrival changes her, as though she has woken up from a long hibernation. She bustles and hurries, exuding purpose. She no longer seems thin and dry.

Sylvia is only too happy to leave her to it. But while Miss Simmons is taking supper in her room, she does sneak into the nursery to spend a few moments there alone. She takes down one of Amabel's smock dresses from the hanging rail in the wardrobe and holds it against Stephen's sleeping form. She is amazed by how girl-like the frock makes him look. He could be Amabel, she thinks. There's really no difference. No difference at all.

F *i v e*

■

Pamela Yardley examines her copy of *Woman's Friend* for the ump-teenth time. On the much-thumbed center pages is an article entitled "Your Baby's Dream Nursery," complete with color illustrations. It shows a pastel haven whose centerpiece is a lavishly frilled and draped cradle.

Pamela's aim is to imitate this room, as far as she possibly can, within the confines of her small rented flat. She has saved, stitched, pinned, and trimmed for several months, and now, two weeks before the baby is due to be born, the room is finished.

Almost finished. Pamela squints at the magazine and then back at the window. The curtains in the picture are tied back with rosettes of colored ribbon, hers hang straight. She could buy some ribbon and sew some rosettes. But can she face the prospect of dragging her ungainly body to the bus stop, catching a bus to the center of Hemingford, negotiating her way through the crowds, remembering to put the brass curtain ring on the fourth finger of her left hand so that the assistants in Taylor & Haddon's haberdashery department don't sniff and look down their noses as they call her "Madam"?

It is a difficult decision for Pamela, momentous. Her brain seems to have been affected by pregnancy, making her feel ever so slightly deranged. The smallest decision weighs heavily on her mind, and she feels she cannot endure any uncertainty. She wants the room to be absolutely perfect, down to the last detail. But she's so tired, so weary. . . . She buries her head in her hands and rubs her forehead.

There is a tap on the door, and then it opens. Without looking up, Pamela knows that it is Mrs. Gilchrist, her landlady. Mrs. Gilchrist never waits for her knock to be answered. She just comes straight in.

"Miss Yardley . . . Miss Yardley, are you all right?"

Pamela lifts her head.

"Only, I heard some banging, and I just wanted to make sure you weren't hammering nails. Nails aren't allowed; it says so in the lease: 'Tenants will please note that the use of nails is not permitted.' "

"I wasn't hammering nails. I was putting in some picture hooks. Look."

Pamela points to the framed nursery rhymes that she has hung on the walls, just like the ones in the magazine.

Mrs. Gilchrist purses her lips. "Very nice."

She has all sorts of theoretical objections to tenants making alterations to their rooms, and has been in to inspect progress daily. Nor, it is clear, does she approve of an unmarried girl spending her savings on a nursery for her illegitimate child, as if she had no sense of shame about that child's origins. However, she is shrewd enough to see the advantages of having a room redecorated without having to pay for it, so she has kept her objections to constant complaints and interference.

Pamela scowls after Mrs. Gilchrist's retreating back. She is forced to swallow her pride and her indignation because she needs this grubby four-room flat, she needs it desperately. There are few landladies willing to keep on a female tenant after she becomes pregnant. Pamela consoles herself with the knowledge that Mrs. Gilchrist is no better than she. Her father, Billy, says she used to be plain Maggie Donohoe, "a fast little Irish bit" who hung around in the Pig and Whistle and during the war ran a boarding house which in Billy's words was "no better than a bloody knocking shop!" She kept company with a series of servicemen who numbered several young enough to be her sons: "She wasn't too fussy if they was married, either!" Then she had married an officer and put on airs and graces, which did not wear off once she was widowed and forced to divide up the crumbling Edwardian villa in Wetherall Gardens into poky little flats.

Pamela decides she will go into town, after all. Not just to buy the ribbon, but to continue her vain search for childcare, for the time when she is forced to go back to work. When she became pregnant, she automatically lost her job as a secretary in a solicitor's office. But she has a good reference, and qualifications, and she hopes she will be able to find another similar job. Even if it means having to lie about her circumstances. So far no one has been able to help.

The attitude of everyone, including the welfare services, is that in such prosperous times, mothers should stay at home and look after their children.

Pamela is just hunting in the pocket of her coat for the brass "wedding" ring when there is another knock at the door. This time it is her father, carrying a large package.

"Brought a little something for the nipper," he says, and flings himself down in the armchair. "Put the kettle on, will you, love?"

Pamela goes to the stove in the corner and makes tea, glancing up every now and then at her father. He has, as ever, made himself very much at home. The jacket of his grubby checked suit has been unbuttoned to reveal a hideous mustard yellow waistcoat and a stained purple tie. Billy Yardley is fifty-one, but looks older due to the amount he drinks. His skin is liverish, his colorless hair clings to his pate in greasy strands.

"Fetch us a biscuit, love," he shouts. "There's some in the green tin. I know, because I looked in there yesterday."

Pamela feels the familiar wave of resentment wash over her. But she doesn't say anything. If she does express dissent, she always gets the same response: "But you're all I've got." And it's true: since her mother's death when she was twelve, there has been forced interdependence, with Pamela living in her father's affectionate, bullying shadow.

"Aren't you going to look at the present I've brought you? It's for that nursery of yours."

Billy heaves himself out of the chair to go and inspect the room in question, declaring it "fit for a prince." Pamela is his only child, and he makes no secret about the fact that he would prefer a boy. Pamela hopes it is, or she will never hear the end of it.

She unwraps the package and finds a musical box, a cheap, garish thing made from brightly colored plastic. Billy shows her how to press a switch and turn it into a nursery light, while the tinny rendition of the "Skye Boat Song" still plays.

"I got it down at the Pig and Whistle," he tells her with some pride. "There was a bloke selling them off cheap."

Pamela smiles and kisses his cheek, hiding her anger. Because she's an unmarried mother, and alone, she's expected to be grateful for every little thing he dumps on her. And she'll have to put the musical box on display or he'll never stop going on about it. But the thing is so tasteless, just like everything Billy procures, and it will look out of place, ridiculous, in her pastel dream nursery.

"So what have you done about the money then?" Billy shouts after her as she goes to put the ugly musical box away.

"What money?"

"You know very well what money I mean. The money that should be yours by rights from that pasty-faced coward that knocked you up!"

"I'm sorting it out, Dad, honest."

"Well you've left it a little bit late, haven't you? You should have had that money ages ago. Maybe it's time I had a go at him, or that stuck-up family of his."

"It's all right Dad, there's no need. I've already spoken to him about it," Pamela lies.

Billy grunts. "Well he'd better cough up, that's all. It's all very well you living off your savings, but what happens when they run out, eh?"

"I'll get a job."

"A job, is it?" Billy sneers into his tea. "It's simple enough to say that now, but what if the time comes and you can't get one? It's not going to be easy to work the hours *and* look after the little one. You know I'll always do my best to see you right, but the money comes and goes when you're in business like I am. You can't always rely on it."

You mean you might put it on the horses, thinks Pamela bitterly. Billy likes to style himself "a businessman," which means little more than doing the odd deal over the bar in the Pig and Whistle. Nothing illegal (or so he claims), just bits and pieces to earn himself cash in hand, which is usually invested at the bookmakers, his other haunt. Sometimes he wins. But only sometimes.

"I'll get the money from him," Pamela can no longer bear to name her unborn child's father, not in front of Billy anyway. She picks up her coat. "If that's all right, I'll be getting along now. I was just going out."

There's no point in her waiting for her father to go: he only goes when he's ready. She leaves the flat, where Billy is dozing off in the armchair. If she stays out until opening time, then with any luck he'll have gone to the pub.

Later, when Billy has gone to the Pig and Whistle and she is alone again, Pamela goes into the bedroom and takes out a shoebox that she keeps under the bed. It contains a photograph of her child's father, and a few other mementos of their brief relationship: concert tickets, handwritten notes, a kewpie doll won at a fair.

She looks at the photograph, and now she can say his name.

"Norman." She says it out loud. "Norman."

Norman Butler is twenty-three, two years her senior, and an articled clerk at the solicitors' practice where she worked. He was good-looking in a chubby, boyish way, confident and well spoken. Not exactly the public school type, but with a good grammar school education and from a respectable local family. To Pamela, who had absorbed the ideals of the Mills and Boon romances passed around the typing pool, he was the answer to a prayer.

She was the prettiest secretary in the company, so it was natural that Norman should notice her. It started with smiles and chit-chat over the filing cabinet and progressed to little notes left propped on her typewriter. Then he asked her out. They went out several times, over a period of two months. Pamela found she liked Norman a little less in reality than she had done in her imagination, but that didn't matter; he was nice enough and he still represented escape from a life in the typing pool, from Billy's domineering and erratic ways.

She told Norman about Billy, and he said, "Why don't you get a flat? You could get away from him a bit, and we'd have somewhere of our own."

Pamela misunderstood. She thought he meant somewhere for

them to live when they were married, or even engaged. She scrimped and saved to pay the deposit on the flat at 30 Wetherall Gardens, but it turned out that Norman had meant somewhere for them to go in the evening where they could be alone. Somewhere with a bed.

Pamela didn't much want Norman to make love to her, but she allowed him to, thinking that it would surely hasten her on the path to marriage. Two months later she was pregnant, but instead of rushing out to buy a ring, Norman—appalled and seemingly embarrassed—retreated to the bosom of his family, where he hid. He liked Pamela but he didn't want to marry her, had never wanted to. And when he told his parents about Billy and his drinking and his deals, they didn't want him to marry Pamela either, as though her family circumstances were all her fault.

Pamela lost her job, and everyone at work assumed that her lover must have been a married man. Because Norman didn't do anything, or say anything, no one suspected him. To Pamela, the shame would have been less if Norman *had* been married. To be pregnant by a man who was free to marry her but simply didn't want to was an ignominy that no amount of romantic fiction could have prepared her for.

Pamela hates Norman now, but feels she shouldn't. She still cultivates a grudging, sentimental attachment to him because of the child. She takes out his photograph each night and whispers his name, pretending that it is only his heartless parents who are holding him back from real love, that he will realize his mistake and come after her with a ring in his hand. . . .

She has turned out the light and is heaving about the narrow bed, trying to find a comfortable position, when there are footsteps on the stairs and an impatient knock at the door. It is closing time at the Pig and Whistle, so it must be Billy.

She lies still in bed, hoping he'll go away. He hammers harder. "Open the door, you silly little cow!"

Pamela can always recognize at once when her father has been drinking, but there is something other than the drink in his voice now. She opens the door in silence.

Billy crashes about the room for a while, pushing things off tables and shelves to the floor, swearing. Then he shouts, "You lied to me, didn't you? You lied to me! Didn't I tell you when your poor mother died, I said to you, don't ever lie to me! And what have you gone and done? You've lied to me!"

Frequently when drunk and always when angry, Billy raises the spectre of Pamela's mother, a woman he neither liked nor respected.

Pamela still says nothing, clutching her dressing gown around her protruding abdomen.

"I went to check up on you, didn't I?" Billy's face is so close that his spittle lands on Pamela's cheeks. "After I'd had a couple of pints at the Pig, I went to pay a call on those high and mighty Butlers and make sure that they were going to give you the money they'd promised you. Only they didn't know anything about it. Said you hadn't asked for anything. You stupid little cow, you haven't got the sense you were born with!"

As Billy raises his hand to slap her, Pamela feels a stab of pain, low down in her abdomen. The pain keeps hold of her, twisting through her, forcing her onto her knees on the grubby carpet.

Billy staggers back. "Come on! I hardly touched you!"

Pamela groans, then straightens up enough to say, "It's not that. It's the baby. I think it's started!"

Afterward, the only thing Pamela remembers about her labor is the way Staff Midwife Gibbs kept calling her "Miss Yardley," with a frosty emphasis on the "Miss." The other women in the ward are all "Mrs." One or two of them cast sympathetic smiles in her direction, but they seem frightened of talking to her in case something rubs off.

Pamela's baby, a girl, is small and sickly and doesn't feed well. She calls her Jacqueline. She can't think of a middle name, having anticipated a boy. Jacqueline seems oddly irrelevant, unconnected somehow with the disappointment over Norman, the loss of her job, the months preparing a Dream Nursery. Pamela is privately troubled by her feelings of disappointment and disinterest, but says nothing. After all, to whom could she speak on such a subject? The midwives would no doubt put it down to her fallen state. And she only has one visitor apart from her father, one of the girls she used to work with, who has only come out of curiosity because she herself is to have a baby at Hemingford Maternity in a few months' time.

On the second day of Pamela's stay, Sister comes onto the ward brandishing an envelope.

"Someone brought this for you. It was left at reception."

"Who?" Pamela looks blankly at the envelope.

"How should I know who he was?" Sister's tone implies she has a good idea. "A young man."

The envelope is from Norman Butler. It contains a check for two hundred pounds and a curt missive requesting that Pamela have no further contact with him or his family.

Pamela decides not to say anything about this to Billy when he visits her. He strolls in, wearing a grimy purple cravat and smoking a cigar. He has come from the Pig and Whistle, where the regulars have been wetting the head of baby Jacqueline.

"Landlord says to me, 'Congratulations, Granddad, have a cigar!' 'Don't mind if I do,' I said . . . How's the little one?' "

"All right."

Billy scrutinizes his daughter's face. "Come on, love, don't look so glum! That's a lovely little girl we've got there. A baby is a blessing, that's what they say!"

"A baby costs money," says Pamela, who is thinking how she must feed and clothe this small creature, day in, day out for the next twenty years.

"Your old Granddad will see you right, won't he, darling?" Billy knocks a clump of cigar ash into the bassinet as he reaches over to pinch Jacqueline's cheek. " 'Cause you're our little princess, that's what you are. And your mum and me are going to give you a wonderful life, just you wait and see!"

the S*ixties*

school days

S *i* x

■

Carolyn Fox is swinging on the front gate at 41 Tudor Avenue. She pushes her left foot hard on the driveway, then realigns it on the cast-iron gate next to her right foot so that all her weight is supported. The gate meets the gatepost with a satisfying clang, then swings back. Carolyn pushes off again with her left foot, and the process is repeated. As she goes to and fro she sings a song she has heard on the radio, "She Loves You" by the Beatles. She only knows the words of the refrain: "She loves you; yeah, yeah, yeah" so she sings them over and over in her high, tuneless voice.

Her mother has told her not to swing on the gate, but Carolyn doesn't take any notice of her mother. Her father would smack her if he caught her, but he's not going to catch her, because he's out at work. Behind her on the driveway is Sally, her sister, bleating to have a turn on the gate.

Carolyn is not going to let her. Sally is only three years old and stupid. Carolyn isn't. She's five, and she's about to start going to school with all the big boys and girls.

She aims a careless kick behind her, catching Sally on the leg and making her cry. Martin hears and runs into the kitchen to tell their mother. Carolyn doesn't like Martin, he's a sneak. She doesn't like Sally either, and she doesn't like her mother much at the moment, because she's always telling Carolyn off.

Jean comes out onto the driveway and wearily tells Carolyn to stop it. "Why don't you go and see if Helen wants to come and play?"

Helen lives at number 32 and is the same age as Carolyn.

Although she doesn't have any brothers and sisters, her house always seems to be in a mess. Gran says it's because her parents haven't a clue. Helen's father is the vicar of the parish church.

Carolyn skips out of the drive and continues down the street, but she's not going to Helen's house. She doesn't want to play with Helen: Helen's soppy. As soon as her mother has taken Sally back into the house and closed the door, Carolyn doubles back on herself and heads back toward her own house.

Her attention is drawn by a car pulling into the driveway of the house opposite. It belongs to Sheila Broomhall, the daughter of their neighbors. Sheila is eighteen and drives a pink roadster. Her boyfriend drives around in it too, but it is Sheila's car. Carolyn is fascinated by the car, by its gleaming chrome twiddly bits, by the smooth, pink outline of the bonnet, which looks like a piece of candy. Or the nose of the pink plastic hippo that Sally plays with in the bath.

The car comes to a standstill in the driveway, and the sound of the radio takes over from the roar of the engine: Cliff Richard singing "Living Doll." Carolyn hangs back, waiting for Sheila to climb out of the car. She wants to see what Sheila is wearing. She views the older girl as something of a living doll, a grown-up doll who always sports the latest fashions.

No one gets out of the car. With difficulty, Carolyn wedges one sandal on the chrome rear bumper and levers herself onto the boot. She catches her sock on a piece of stray metal and snags it, grazing her ankle at the same time. Tiny droplets of blood seep through the sock, making an interesting stain. She stops to examine it for a moment, then turns her attention to the couple in the car.

Pressing her nose against the rear window, she can watch Sheila and her boyfriend petting in the front seat. Their lips are sliding around together in a squishy sort of fashion. Occasionally their noses bash together, which Carolyn finds funny. The boyfriend has his hand on Sheila's leg, on the bare bit between her skirt and her fashionable knee-length boot. His fingers knead her flesh like colored putty. Sheila stops nose-bashing for a moment and turns her attention to the boyfriend's trousers. She strokes the front of them with her long red fingernails, then tries to poke her fingers down inside them, behind the zipper.

Carolyn is riveted. She presses her nose harder against the glass, increasing her field of vision. When he's bare, her brother Martin always holds his hands in front of his thingy, and her father never takes his underpants off, as far as she can tell. Now, at last, she has a chance to find out what lurks inside.

Her nose bumps against the window and the courting couple immediately turn around, in unison.

"Oi!" shouts the boyfriend.

"Bloody little brat!" Sheila climbs out of the front seat, straightening her skirt.

"Get off my car ... go on—clear off! Clear off or I'll tell your mum!"

As she scrambles down from the boot and retreats, Carolyn can still hear Sheila's complaints.

"She's a real pain, that little Fox girl, a right little nuisance. Fancy climbing up on the car like that. . . ."

Grinning to herself, Carolyn sets off for Helen's house. She doesn't have a very high opinion of Helen Croucher, who is a timid, unimaginative child. She thinks Helen is soppy. But she will go and see her anyway, because baiting Helen is better than being bored. Anything is better than being bored.

Helen says yes, she will come out to play, but her mummy says they've got to stay in the garden. They go into the garden, and Carolyn swings listlessly on the rusty climbing frame. If she climbs onto the top of the frame, she gets a bird's-eye view of the next door neighbor's garden. The vegetable patch looks particularly tempting, with its neatly hoed rows of brown soil. And the vicar's shambolic fencing has a convenient loose plank.

"Hey, Helen!" says Carolyn. "Helen! Let's go in there."

"Not allowed." Helen keeps her eyes lowered, dragging her toe around in the sandpit.

"We can go through the hole—come on!"

There follows a tussle in which Carolyn attempts to use brute force to overcome Helen's reluctance. Helen retreats, clutching her arm and snivelling, but looks on with admiration as Carolyn crawls under the plank and onto foreign territory.

All the plants in the vegetable patch look alike to Carolyn, but she is attracted by some pretty, feathery fronds that trail over the earth. She pulls one out and finds to her surprise and delight that there is a carrot on the other end. The carrot is very dirty, but some impulse makes her bite into it anyway. As her teeth sink through the musty, gritty soil and into the sweet flesh of the vegetable, something stirs deep inside Carolyn, a rejoicing of the senses at pure physical pleasure and a willingness within her to embrace that pleasure. The carrot is delicious, tasting far better than any vegetable her mother has ever given her.

Her grubby reverie is interrupted by Mrs. Croucher, the vicar's wife, anxiously summoning her back through the hole in the fence.

"Your mummy wants you home now, dear, she says your granny's coming round for tea."

Alone in the kitchen for a few minutes, Jean Fox hurries over to her handbag and gropes around inside for a packet of Embassy cigarettes. Her hand trembles slightly as she holds the lighter up to the cigarette tip, her awkward movements those of the novice smoker. She stands next to the sink, sucking in little breaths of smoke and puffing them out of the open window without inhaling.

Jean has only just started smoking and does it in secret, taking the money for the cigarettes out of the housekeeping. She doesn't really enjoy it all that much—in fact she dislikes the sour taste of the nicotine—but does it as a solitary act of defiance, because this vice is the only thing that she has to herself. The rest of her is divided between the demands of her husband, the home, and their three children. She wishes they hadn't had three now. Two was quite manageable but three is impossible. She can't concentrate on all of them at once, and it always seems to be Carolyn, the middle one, who evades her jurisdiction. But Winnie said that two wasn't much of a family, that three was a better number, so they'd had Sally. Not that Sally was naughty, not like her sister. . . .

Jean hears the children in the hallway; the clamor of argument and scuffles as someone tries to shove someone else against the banisters. With hasty, guilty, movements she knocks the loose ash onto the window-sill and stubs out the butt in the stainless steel sink. There's no time to get rid of it, she just has to leave it there, squashed in the sink.

Carolyn comes into the kitchen, scuffing her sandals on the lino. Instantly, Jean notices the torn and bloodied sock.

"Oh, for goodness' sake, *now* what have you done, girl? That's the last time I let *you* play out in white socks! Come here, come on. . . ."

But Carolyn ignores her. She stamps over to the sink and retrieves the soggy butt with finger and thumb, wrinkling her nose as she holds it aloft.

"Eeuh, *Mum!* What's this?"

"Give that here, come on!" Jean snatches the offending object and throws it into the waste bin.

"But, Mum . . . Someone's been smoking a cigarette!"

Carolyn looks up into her mother's face offering a challenge. Jean says nothing, but in that moment a silent bargain is struck: Jean won't nag her about the socks if Carolyn doesn't say anything about the cigarette.

"Come on, help me get the table set, will you? Your gran's coming for her tea and I haven't got it started yet. And fetch Sally down."

"What's for tea?" asks Martin, coming into the kitchen.

"Liver. Liver and onions."

"Yuk, liver!" complains Martin. "Liver's all made of blood!"

"And tubes!" says Carolyn. She finds the heaps of pig's liver on the chopping board. "Look, Martin, all tubes and stuff!"

"Yuk, like red boogies!"

"Red boogies!" sniggers Carolyn.

"Red boogies, boogies, red . . ."

"Will you kids stop it!" Jean snaps. At that moment, Les and Winnie walk into the kitchen, allowing Winnie to discover Jean's home in a state of disharmony, as seems to be the case more and more frequently. Winnie administers a reproach to the children, which is really aimed at Jean, then continues her conversation with her son. Les has collected Winnie on his way back from the biscuit factory and is telling her all about his work: who's been passed over for promotion, who sent which memo to whom. Winnie loves office gossip and

•

has the personal details of all her son's colleagues filed away in her brain.

To hear her talking, you'd think she'd worked there herself, thinks Jean bitterly. Les never has those sort of conversations with her, hardly ever mentions office life, except when it affects the time he gets home. And in his mother's presence he puts her on a par with the children, ignoring her, except for the occasional request for food or service.

"... So Bill Alysson comes in and says to me, 'I've told those buggers in Despatch that there's going to be an enquiry into how many deadlines they're not meeting, and discussion of the new cloakroom facilities will be suspended pending said enquiry.' And will I put the necessary paperwork into action? So I say to him, 'Look Bill ...'—Jean, love, will you get me the mustard? I like a spot of mustard with liver...."

"Is Bill the one that's carrying on with Valerie, from Requisitions?" chips in Winnie, anxious to show off her knowledge.

"That's right ... anyway, Bill says to me ... While you're up, Jean, get us some napkins, will you?"

Jean waits on the family, her face wearing its usual impassive mask. Inside, she is grumbling to herself. It's not that she wants to know about Les's office; she finds these tales rather boring. It's just that her husband sees his mother as the best one to fill the role of confidante. And it wouldn't be so bad, if Winnie were only interested in the gossip and never interfered in anything else, but all the time she is listening, her eyes are darting around the room, looking for something to criticize. She sniffs the air.

"You know something, Jean, I can smell cigarettes, I'm sure of it. Has someone been smoking in here?"

Looking for a diversion, Jean turns her attention to her elder daughter. She feels a little guilty as she does so; it's not the first time she has used Carolyn's misdemeanors to deflect attention from herself when Winnie is around.

"Come on, Carolyn, off with those socks! If you give them to me now I'll handwash them and pop them on the boiler to dry, then I can darn them later...."

As soon as the children have gone upstairs to play and Les is sitting, legs splayed, in front of the television, Winnie wastes no time in getting onto her favorite subject. She corners Jean as she is scrubbing Carolyn's socks in the sink.

"You know, you're going to have to knock the mischief out of that Carolyn of yours."

Martin is "our Martin," but Carolyn is always "your Carolyn"; her shortcomings are Jean's fault, not Les's. Winnie would never concede that the child takes after her father.

"She's not that bad," murmurs Jean.

"She's got a devil in her, that one," says Winnie sagely. "And if you don't knock it out of her soon, she'll get worse!"

"She's only little! She ..."

"Every time I come round, she's up to something. Soil all over her arms and legs today, I notice. And I'll tell you something ..." Winnie lowers her voice to an awestruck tone. "Kiddies sometimes have, well, *instincts* that you have to repress before they get out of hand."

Jean sighs. "What instincts?"

"Mrs. Broomhall opposite stopped me the other day and said she'd seen your Carolyn playing out with Martin and some of his friends."

"So?"

"She was lifting up her dress!" Winnie hisses. "Worse than that, she was pulling down her knickers and showing them her bare behind!" Winnie crosses her arms in triumph.

"You know kids," begins Jean. "They do that sort of thing."

"My lot never did! And I bet you can't see little Helen what's-her-name doing that sort of thing. No, I'm telling you, Jean, she carries on like that and she'll turn out really wild!"

Jean scrubs the socks in silence. She's not going to let her mother-in-law have the satisfaction of knowing it, but this is one of the occasions when Winnie is probably right.

S *e v e n*

■

Sylvia Noble sits in the drawing room of her Edwardian villa. She is perched on the window seat beneath a tall sash window, her long legs curled underneath her rather awkwardly. There is a tea tray and a pile of fashion magazines next to her, but she is not drinking the tea or reading the magazines; she is staring out at the end of the drive, at a procession of small figures walking past the gateposts. They are girls, lots and lots of little girls.

It is twenty to four, and the convent at the end of the road has just finished for the day. Every afternoon at this time its pupils, aged between five and thirteen, skip and scuff their way past the Nobles' house, the younger ones accompanied by mothers, the older ones dragging book-laden satchels to the bus stop. Sylvia loves to watch them. She likes to distinguish the different age groups by the way they behave, or to see if she can recognize particular girls. She likes the sound of their high, chattering voices. They make her think of herself when she was a child. They make her think of Amabel.

Amabel might well have been one of those little girls, in a bottle green blazer with gold braid. One of those pretty little straw boaters with a green ribbon. She probably wouldn't have liked the hat very much, most schoolgirls don't. They complain that the elastic cuts into the skin. Of course, St. Paul's is a Roman Catholic convent, but they take some non-Catholics too, and it is becoming quite fashionable amongst upper middle class Protestants to send their daughters to a convent school for their primary education. It must be because there's something so very reassuring about nuns, Sylvia reflects. She likes the idea of a daughter of hers being educated by nuns.

But she no longer has a daughter, and instead of buying boaters with green ribbons there will be a trip up to London tomorrow to Harrods, to buy corduroy breeches and Aertex shirts for Stephen. He is going to attend Draycotts School, a private prep school some five miles southeast of Hemingford. It will involve Sylvia in a sixteen-mile round trip twice a day in the detested Jaguar, but Draycotts is the only "suitable" school according to Geoffrey's family, so Draycotts it must be. Sylvia is not looking forward to it.

By one of those strange coincidences whereby thought seems to conjure something into real life, Sylvia's cleaning lady comes into the drawing room and tells her that the headmaster of Draycotts is on the phone.

"He wants to talk to me?" Sylvia is momentarily flustered. The financial and administrative minutiae of their life are always, without exception, handled by Geoffrey. She picks up the phone and says nervously, "Yes?"

"Ah, Mrs. Noble ... I'm just ringing all the prospective parents to confirm that they received my letter."

"Letter? ... Oh, it wouldn't have come here. My husband ... correspondence goes to his office you see, so ..."

"Righto, fine. I expect he'll be discussing the situation with you later then. Good-bye!"

"What situa—?"

Puzzled, Sylvia hangs up.

Stephen is playing in the nursery when his father gets home from work. His experience of play is limited, so his activity is very sedate compared with that of most five-year-olds. He picks up his toys and examines them, touching them gently and carefully. He takes books down from the shelf and turns the pages slowly, pointing to the words. He doesn't run and shout and make a noise. He has no daily example of such behavior, and has only ever encountered it in his cousins, of whom he is terrified. He was going to attend a nursery school; his parents had told him about it and he was looking forward to it in a cautious sort of way. But at the last moment Mummy decided she couldn't let him go, he was too "delicate," she said.

Daddy doesn't play with Stephen much, apart from pushing his train round the track with accompanying "choo-choo" noises. Instead he talks about what Stephen is going to do when he is older. He is going to go to a prep school called Draycotts, then a bigger school called Maidenhurst, then to a university at Oxford or Cambridge. Then he's either going to be a broker like Daddy, or a banker, or a lawyer. Or, if he likes, he can go into the army before he does any of those things.

Mummy plays with him, but she only plays the Dressing-Up Game.

He can hear Mummy and Daddy talking now, and from the volume of Daddy's voice, he can tell that he's annoyed.

"Bloody hell! The nerve of the bloody place!"

"The headmaster rang here earlier...."

"It's in the letter—go on, have a look.

Owing to the recent discovery of subsidence, the main school building has been declared unsafe, and the pupils will have to be housed in alternative accommodation pending major restructural work. We therefore regret that we are unable to give places to this year's new intake, but hope to be able to welcome them to Draycotts at some time in the future. We thank you for your understanding in this matter. We will, of course, do our best to assist you in finding an alternative school place for your son.

It's a bloody outrage! I've written to the chairman of the board of governors.

"They might have given us more notice ..."

"We haven't a hope of getting him in anywhere else now! We'll have to approach the local state schools."

"Oh no, Geoffrey, I'd rather not! Couldn't we get him a private tutor?"

"I don't think that's a good idea, Sylvia, not with him being an only child. The little chap needs to mix with other boys, do some sport...."

The discussion between Stephen's parents continues in this vein until Geoffrey has drained two glasses of Scotch. He then stamps upstairs in search of a hot bath. He passes the open nursery door but does not look in.

Stephen has overheard enough to realize that his destination will not be Draycotts after all, but something terrible called a "state school," which must be something like a prison. And the phrase "mix with other boys" makes him shiver and shrink back inside himself. He clutches his favorite teddy bear for comfort and sits quietly on the nursery floor, waiting for someone to come and tell him that it's time for bed.

In their own bedroom later, Sylvia and Geoffrey go through a familiar night-time ritual. Sylvia draws the curtains while Geoffrey runs a comb through his hair. Then while Sylvia is folding down the counterpane, Geoffrey fills a tooth glass with water from the washbasin in the corner of the bedroom and places it on the mat on his night table. The glass has to be in the dead center of the mat; the mat at the dead centre of the table, and he will make the necessary adjustments until the positioning is just right. Sylvia takes up her place at her dressing table, brushing out her long, fair hair and patting on a bit of cold cream, while Geoffrey removes his dressing gown, folds it, drapes it over the arm of a chair. Then he climbs into his side of the bed and opens a book. He rarely reads more than a few words—this particular work, the short stories of Rudyard Kipling, has been on the night table for over six months. But sitting there with the book is his way of passing the time until Sylvia is ready, part of the ritual.

When Sylvia climbs in beside him and shivers against the cold sheets, Geoffrey has his cue to turn out the lights. He waits a polite thirty seconds for her to warm up a little, then he rolls over and lays a heavy arm over her ribs.

Sylvia squirms and inches away.

"What's the matter?" Geoffrey whispers.

"I'm too hot. Your arm is making me too hot."

"Oh. I thought you were cold. You were cold only a minute ago."

Disgruntled, Geoffrey rolls away. He lies still on his back, as if considering another approach. A few minutes later, he renews his attack. This time he runs his fingers gently up and down Sylvia's spine. A novel move, a departure from the usual ritual. It feels quite nice. Sylvia sighs and relaxes.

Encouraged, Geoffrey tries to hook his fingers under the hem of her nightgown. Instantly, Sylvia's muscles tense and she edges away again.

"Don't," she says, avoiding his hands. "Don't, Geoffrey."

Geoffrey rolls onto his back with a loud, exasperated sigh. He waits for a minute, then says, as if it is an idea that may not have occurred to her: "You know, we're not going to be able to have another baby if you won't."

Good. I don't want one.

Geoffrey persists. "What about that girl you wanted to have? After the twins ... we said we would have another girl later."

I don't want another girl. I wanted Amabel. My baby. I want to grieve for her, but you won't let me....

"It might be a boy," Sylvia says out loud.

She intends her message to be quite clear: she doesn't want another boy. But Geoffrey, misunderstanding, presses on. "A boy then. A brother for Stephen. He's been an only child for five years now, and it's starting to make a difference. He'd benefit from having siblings now. Harriet says ..."

Geoffrey launches into his sister's view—the family view—on only children. Sylvia lies still, saying nothing. When he has run out of things to say, Geoffrey has one final try. He grasps Sylvia's shoulders and kisses her face and neck hard, more angry now than affectionate.

"I can hear Stephen," gasps Sylvia when she is allowed to come up for air. "He's probably having a nightmare, I ought to go to him."

She fumbles her arms into her dressing gown and escapes to the silent nursery, where Stephen is sleeping soundly. She waits there, stroking his cheek and murmuring endearments until the sound of Geoffrey's snores rumble through the night air.

The following afternoon, Sylvia takes Stephen out to buy his school uniform. They do not take the train to London and visit the outfitting department of Harrods, but drive into the center of Hemingford instead; their destination is the less rarified atmosphere of Taylor & Haddon.

Geoffrey has spent the morning making telephone calls, with the result that Stephen Noble now has a place at Albert Road Mixed Infants, a primary school just north of the town center. His parents are trying to console themselves with the fact that it is considered the best local school and has a wide catchment area, including the smarter residential areas north of the town. There was a place at a private day school twenty miles away, but Sylvia felt that the driving would become too arduous in the winter, and Geoffrey reluctantly agreed.

So Stephen is to be kitted out in plain gray flannel shorts, navy sweater, and blue and gray Albert Road tie. He will look very ordinary, thinks Sylvia sadly, just an ordinary little boy. She had been looking forward to seeing him in the quaint cord trousers and hand-knitted jerseys worn at Draycotts.

The children's department is full of mothers equipping their off-spring for the autumn term. Children run up and down the carpeted walkways and fight for a turn on the departmental rocking horse. Stephen shrinks from them, clinging tightly to his mother's hand.

"Do you have white Aertex shirts?" Sylvia asks the assistant. "It says on the list that he needs white shirts."

The assistant shakes her head. "We don't have much call for them, to be honest. Most people find the nylon ones are best, the drip-dry."

"What about Viyella?" asks Sylvia desperately, gripping Stephen's hand. "Or cotton?"

She comes away half an hour later, with bulging carrier bags containing shorts, sweaters, socks and ties, and the hated nylon shirts. She feels angry, cheated that he has to wear the horrible, slimy things.

"You're to tell me if they make you sweat," she tells Stephen. "You mustn't wear them if they make you sweat. We'll just have to go up to Harrods and get you some Aertex there."

Stephen nods obediently, trotting to keep up with his mother's angry stride. She slows down eventually, then lingers as they pass through Girls Separates.

"Can I help you, madam?" asks an obsequious assistant. "Something for your little girl, was it?"

Sylvia isn't sure whether she means Stephen, whose blond curls are longer than average, or some other little girl waiting for them at home.

"I thought this was rather nice," she says, pointing to a dress with "Age 5–6" on the label. "For my niece."

The dress is a green and red plaid, with smocking across the chest and a lace collar. The sort of dress Sylvia would have bought Amabel for Christmas Day with relatives, or winter birthday parties.

"And very good value too, I think," the assistant was saying.

"I'll take it."

"It'll be something for you next, won't it?" the assistant says to Stephen as she packs the dress into a blue Taylor & Haddon bag. Stephen hangs back, saying nothing.

When they get home, Mummy makes him tea, then they go upstairs together to unpack the shopping. They put the ties in a drawer and hang up the loathsome nylon shirts. Then Mummy says, "Why don't we play the Dressing-Up Game?"

Stephen doesn't want to much, but it is better if he pretends that he does. Otherwise Mummy might start to cry.

He knows what to do without being told. He takes off his trousers and sweater and stands in front of the mirror in his vest and pants. Not Y-fronts like Daddy's, but plain white briefs like Mummy wears. Mummy puts the new frock over his head, and helps his hands through the sleeves. When she has fastened the buttons, she takes out the red shoes from the secret drawer, and the red velvet hair ribbon. She brushes his hair into a topknot and ties the ribbon around it.

"There! Isn't that pretty, Amabel?" she says, looking over his shoulder into the mirror. "Don't you look nice?"

E *i g h t*

■

Audrey Pryce-Jones has spent most of the afternoon at Eduardo's, and Matthew has had to go with her so he is bored and hyperactive by the time they return to 9 Mount Rise. When he accompanies his mother to the hairdresser's salon he has to sit and look at the pictures in magazines, which he doesn't enjoy because the magazines are stupid and soppy and girlish. Matthew knows this because he hears his father sneering at the magazines that Audrey reads. So he quickly abandons looking at pictures for roaming around the salon fiddling with the various potions in bottles, picking up locks of hair from the floor and generally making a nuisance of himself.

Now that they are at home Audrey wants to make the most of the late August warmth and top up her suntan. She dons a white two-piece and gold high-heeled mules and totters out onto the patio clutching her sunglasses in one hand and one of the despised magazines in the other. She arranges herself on the swing seat, which has a fringed canopy, plus two matching loungers and umbrella. It was their Major Purchase for the house that year.

Since they have lived at Mount Rise, Audrey has introduced a policy of one Major Purchase for the house each year. The first was a new dining suite, the next an automatic washing machine, and so on. This year it was a set of garden furniture.

Soon Audrey is perusing *Twenty New Ways With Puff Pastry* while Matthew races round the garden making aeroplane noises. But she keeps one eye on her watch and doesn't allow herself to get too engrossed. She has a lot to do before Kenneth comes home. After

precisely forty-five minutes of soaking up the sun, she puts the magazine down and shouts, "Matthew! Tea time!"

Matthew ignores her and continues dive-bombing the ornamental
fish pool. Rather than waste time arguing, Audrey goes straight upstairs
and changes into coral capri pants and matching sweater. She adjusts
Eduardo's handiwork with the tip of a comb, checks her darkly tanned
face for wrinkles, then goes out to the garden again to fetch Matthew.

"Matthew, come on, darling! I want to get your tea out of the
way so that I can cook dinner for Daddy!"

Mentioning Ken usually works; Matthew looks up to his father
and is keen to earn his good opinion. However, after the trip to
Eduardo's he is in rebellious mood, and pretends not to hear.

"Matthew!"

Matthew capitulates and follows his mother into the kitchen, dragging his feet, sulky.

"... And if you think you're going to get a chocolate biscuit for
your tea after that sort of behavior, you can think again, young man!"

Audrey puts on a frilly apron and clips about the kitchen, slicing
and buttering sandwiches.

Matthew sticks out his lower lip.

"No good sulking!" says Audrey tartly, but she puts her hand on
his head as she passes, softening slightly.

"Don't be cross with me, Mummy! Please!"

Matthew flings his arms round his mother's legs and hugs her
hard. He looks up from beneath his fringe, blue eyes wide and
appealing.

"Please!"

It is a calculated move, and it works. Audrey returns the embrace
and fetches the chocolate biscuits.

Matthew has a way of getting around her, but today she particularly wants to avoid argument and get the routine of tea, bath, and
bed over and done with quickly. She's going to prepare a special
dinner for Ken, and needs time for her preparation. She leaves Matthew watching the television (last year's Major Purchase) while she
puts the finishing touches on the Beef Olive and the Lemon Syllabub,
and lays the table with the best glasses, matching candles, and napkins.

They are going to have wine for a special treat, which makes Audrey feel very continental and decadent. She has bought a boat-shaped wine basket, of the kind seen in French and Italian restaurants.

At seven o'clock, with Matthew tucked up in bed, Audrey has about half an hour to wash and change. Kenneth said he would be back at around half-past seven, though he wasn't quite sure. He let her have the car to go to Eduardo's, and is intending to get a lift home. Quite a few of his colleagues drive this way apparently, because he never seems to have any trouble finding transport on the days when Audrey borrows the car. It is her ambition that they will have two cars one day, though she is aware that this comes under the category of Very Major Purchase.

After her bath, Audrey makes up and slips into a scoop-necked rayon cocktail dress in olive green, which she read somewhere is a color that enhances one's suntan. She opens a drawer in her dressing table and takes out a small red diary. She flicks through the pages, lips pursed in concentration. There is nothing marked on the pages except a number in a small circle. The numbers correspond to the days of Audrey's menstrual cycle. She is checking them again, because she wants to be sure, beyond any doubt, that it is the fourteenth day.

Audrey finds the organization of her second child's conception an absorbing occupation, if somewhat irksome. It should have happened three years ago. That was what they had decided when they married. A little boy first, then two years later, a second child which would, with any luck, be a girl. But their plans went astray. Even though Matthew was an angelic baby who rarely cried, Audrey found she had no interest in sex at all, and managed to avoid it. As her interest renewed, and the appointed time for the second pregnancy loomed, Matthew turned into a demanding, egotistical monster, shouting for attention all night, then climbing out of his cot and roaming around the house. Disturbed nights became commonplace and Audrey felt too tired. . . .

Matthew's behavior improved once he started going to a local playgroup, but now it was Ken who had lost interest in sex. They made love sporadically, but nothing happened. After a year of this, Audrey made a furtive trip to the doctor. He told her nothing was

•

wrong and explained the intricacies of the menstrual cycle and ovulation. It would happen, Audrey was assured, as long as intercourse took place at the middle of the month. She started counting, but Ken still never seemed to be interested at the right point of the cycle.

So counting has given way to plotting and scheming—she will *make* Ken interested. She will seduce him. This is not something she has ever done before, because of course she was raised in the belief that a woman should merely look decorous whilst the man did all the running.

At seven forty-six precisely, Audrey gives her lipstick a final dab and comes downstairs. Ken will be home any minute, she tells herself with satisfaction, as she checks that the flowers and the arrangement of the napkins are in order. She takes a gulp of the wine and feels her body warming to the task ahead. With a sweet sherry in her hand, she drapes her legs over the sofa cushions in a seductive pose. At eight o'clock, Audrey goes up to check on the sleeping Matthew, then lights the candles on the dining table. Ken will be home any minute. She has rung his office to check, and they said he had left.

Thirty minutes later, she goes into the kitchen and turns down the Beef Olive, as it is starting to dry out. She twitches back the curtains and peers down the road to see if she can spot Ken's approaching figure. He doesn't come. She pours herself another sweet sherry and turns the television on, but it's only a comedy program that she has seen before. At nine o'clock there is a smell of burning from the oven, so she switches it off. In the fridge, the syllabub is disintegrating into a thin, watery pool.

Audrey vents some anger by throwing Ken's golf magazines across the lounge. She sits sobbing into her third sweet sherry, and by ten o'clock she is asleep on the sofa.

The sound of Ken's key in the front door wakes her. It is ten past eleven. Audrey snarls a reproach at him, but he walks straight past her and goes upstairs to bed. Audrey follows him and finds that he has been drinking. She winds her thighs around him and wrestles his body on top of hers, but he rolls back again and falls into a deep, noisy sleep.

■ ■ ■

The following afternoon, Matthew takes his bicycle out for a ride. It is a new bicycle; a present for his fifth birthday. Mummy has told him not to cycle beyond the end of Mount Rise, but Daddy winked at him after she had said it, which Matthew knows gives him permission to ignore Mummy. So he keeps going beyond Mount Rise, past the golf course, until he comes to the main road from Hemingford.

The traffic is busy: the Friday afternoon rush of cars streaming out of the center of the town to the suburbs. A blue car indicates that it is pulling over and stops at the curb near to where Matthew is standing. Daddy is in the car with a lady. Matthew waves when he recognizes him. Mummy said he would be getting a lift home today with one of the people from the office, because she needed the car for shopping.

Daddy hasn't seen him yet. He's talking to the lady. Now he's kissing the lady. Not lips on the cheek, like he has to give Granny, but a big sloppy mouth kiss. Like people do on television. He gets out of the car and starts walking up the road with his briefcase in his hand.

Matthew gets back on his bicycle and pedals furiously to build up speed.

"Daddy! Daddy!"

He looks up. "Oh, hello, son!" He waves his briefcase. "Come to round me up have you, eh?"

Matthew dismounts and squints up at his father's face. "Why were you kissing that lady?"

"We often kiss our friends, don't we?" Ken puts his hand on Matthew's shoulder to guide him along the curb. "We kiss them hello and we kiss them good-bye ..."

"Not like that!" Matthew is indignant. "That's how mummies and daddies kiss!"

Ken puts his briefcase on the pavement and squats down on his haunches so that his face is level with Matthew's.

"Sometimes grown-up men can have a special lady friend who they like nearly as much as a mummy, but they don't live in the same house. They just like to be together sometimes. And if they have a special friend like that, they're allowed to kiss them like a mummy too. D'you understand?"

Matthew nods slowly, absorbing this simplification of the rules of adultery.

"Good boy! Let's do a detour via the corner shop at the end of Cobb Lane and buy you some sweets, shall we? Hop on your bike!"

Matthew pedals along happily beside his father and accepts payment of a sherbert fountain and some raspberry licorice in exchange for his silence.

"We'd better not tell Mummy anything about the lady, had we? Because she'll only make a silly fuss. It'll be our secret."

Though he doesn't yet have the words to describe it, Matthew can understand that there is a chain in operation; his father can manipulate him, but he in turn can manipulate his mother, who is at the bottom of the chain, and whose willingness to give in to him is something to be despised.

"Yes," he agrees, "Mummy is very silly."

Audrey is standing at the lounge window, looking out for Matthew. He has disappeared from view, ignoring her instructions yet again. No doubt he will show up again eventually, and she will get cross with him, and he will find some way of worming himself around her, just like his father. . . .

The thought wearies her. She continues to keep watch, like a dutiful mother, but her mind is wandering. She plays the events of last night back to herself. When the morning came and Ken got out of bed to go to work, she pretended to be asleep. Speaking to him about his absence would have brought back her disappointment, and it was a disappointment she couldn't face at that time of the morning.

Now, with a rare degree of honesty, she forces herself to consider why having another baby is so important to her. There is the plan, of course, to marry and have two children two years apart. Here they are with their firstborn five and about to go to school, and not even the beginnings of a second. One of their neighbors, whose oldest is the same age as Matthew, has just given birth to her third child. But it's not just the plan: The plan has already gone so far astray that the timing doesn't matter much any more.

Is it the baby then, the business of being pregnant and having a helpless infant to care for? It can't be that: She disliked being pregnant last time, and didn't much enjoy the baby stage. No, the reason for wanting to have another child is simply to have something to think about, something to fill the empty spaces in her mind. Because the truth of the matter is that she is lonely. There—she has admitted it. She is lonely. Ken is hardly at home, and when he is, the only thing they have to talk about is the house and its contents. Matthew is scornful of female company, and besides, he's about to start full-time at Albert Road.

No sooner has she acknowledged the problem than she is forced to push it away again, because Ken has come into view, with Matthew cycling along beside him. She could never talk to Ken about how she feels, never. She knows what he would say: "You've got what you wanted, haven't you? Marriage, a nice house, a son, plenty of money. How can you possibly be dissatisfied if you've got what you always wanted?"

Audrey keeps quiet, making no reference to the abortive seduction until Matthew has gone to bed. Then she demands to know, fiercely, why he didn't return from work until after eleven when he had said he was coming home at seven-thirty.

"*About* seven-thirty. I said I would be back at about seven-thirty.

"Don't split hairs!" shouts Audrey, slamming the dinner dishes onto the draining board. "You were nearly four hours late! Four hours!"

"You know how it is," sighs Ken.

"No! I *don't* know how it is! I'm waiting for you to tell me how it is!" Audrey throws dirty cutlery into the sink.

"Well, one of the directors, John Masters, stopped me as I was leaving and said he had one or two things to discuss with me, so we went out for a couple of drinks and then he asked me to stay on and have dinner with him, and I could hardly refuse, could I? He's a director."

"I don't care what he is!" Audrey's voice is shrill, her hands are trembling. She has never shouted at Ken like this before, and she's rather enjoying it. "Couldn't you even have phoned and told me where you were? Didn't it occur to you that I might be wondering?"

"Sorry, my sweet, I didn't think."

"*You didn't think!* That just about sums it up, doesn't it! You didn't *think* and you didn't *care!*" Audrey emphasizes these words by hurling first the potato peeler, then a Pyrex lemon squeezer onto the kitchen floor. "You just take me for granted, don't you?" She picks up the kitchen timer and throws it at Ken's head. "You just assume I'm going to be here day in, day out, waiting for you, no matter what you do! Well, I'm not going to, do you hear me, I'm not going to!"

Audrey's voice cannot become any higher, or any louder, so she breaks into hysterical sobs.

"Audrey, sweetheart, don't. . . ."

Ken tries to take her into his arms. At first, she pushes him away, but he persists and finally she gives in, sobbing onto his square masculine shoulder. He murmurs soothing words into her ear until she has calmed down. Then he begins to kiss her on the mouth, with an urgency that has been absent since their courting days.

Upstairs, Matthew has been woken by the sound of his parents shouting. He has never heard them make so much noise before, and he stays awake a while, listening. Mummy is probably being silly, he decides. About Daddy kissing that lady. *He* wasn't silly about it. Daddy said he was a very grown-up young man because he could keep a secret.

He falls asleep again before Audrey and Ken creep upstairs after making love on the lounge carpet like a couple of guilty teenagers. Audrey lies awake, not knowing why she feels happy, just glad that she does, while in the deepest recesses of her body, her second child is conceived at last.

N *i n e*

■

"You've grown so much I suppose I'm just going to have to buy you another one."

Jackie Yardley is standing on a chair while Pamela inspects the hem of her skirt. Gray skirts are worn at her new primary school, and Jackie already has a gray skirt, but it is too short. The hem reveals several inches of skinny leg above the knee.

Jackie hangs her head. Mum sounds cross. It's her fault for growing too fast. Mum's always saying she doesn't have enough money to keep buying her new clothes, that she can't keep up. Mum's usually unhappy about something, and it's usually her fault.

Mum lifts her down from the chair and gives her an impulsive kiss on the cheek. She does this often: shows affection randomly and spontaneously, then retreats into moroseness. Jackie is silent; she is always silent as a result of not knowing what to expect. She has already learned at the tender age of five not to do anything that might send her mother's mood veering off in one direction or another. She keeps her thoughts to herself.

"Come on, we'll go down to Taylor & Haddon and get you another skirt, and the other bits and pieces that you need. If we go now, we should just about fit it in before I have to get to work ... Well come *on* then, child, go and fetch your coat!"

Jackie runs to fetch her coat, a grubby brown anorak, from its peg in the living room. They still live in the tiny flat that Pamela rented when she was pregnant. They are on a housing list, but no new housing ever comes. There's no hallway, so coats and shoes and shopping bags spill out all over the room—except for Jackie's little coat, which is always hung up neatly. Jackie has already been scolded in advance about the space taken up by school paraphernalia. She will have to keep her satchel and PE kit very tidy. Pamela rarely tidies up or does any cleaning. It's Jackie's job to wash up and empty the ashtrays that are always brimming with the butts that Billy leaves.

By the time Pamela has raked through the clutter on her dressing table to find comb, powder, and lipstick and delegated Jackie to go and search the living room for her shoes, they are running late and facing a hurried shopping trip. They have to take a bus, and no buses come for fifteen minutes, which sets back their expedition even further. Pamela strides up into the children's outfitting department with Jackie at her heels, running to keep up.

Pamela drums her fingers on the counter while she waits to be served, convincing herself that the assistants are passing her over for smarter, more prosperous-looking mothers. When someone finally comes to help her, she only has time to hand over her list—not the list issued by the school, but her own modified list leaving out all the extras that she can't afford. The assistant bustles to and fro between shelves and drawers, building a pile of crisp, clean-smelling clothes on the counter. She starts ringing up the prices on the cash register and presents the total figure to Pamela with a smile.

"That will be twelve pounds, five shillings and sixpence, madam."

"Oh," says Pamela faintly. She only has ten pounds in her purse. "Er . . ." She rummages through her handbag, stalling for time.

"Of course, madam, if it is inconvenient for you to pay cash, you may open a charge account."

"Oh. All right then, yes please." Pamela thinks to herself that she can put aside a bit every week, then pay it off at the end of the month and close the account.

The assistant fetches the necessary paperwork, and Pamela starts to fill in the form. She does not get very far, however. The questions all relate to some imaginary husband that she does not have: Occupation of Spouse, Business Address of Spouse, Name and Address of Spouse's Bankers.

"It's simpler if the account's put in your husband's name, then the accounts will be sent to him," explains the assistant with another smile. "Most women prefer to let the man handle the finances, we find."

"Er . . . on second thoughts, perhaps I'll just leave it. The account, I mean." Pamela is flustered, feels sure that the shop assistant and all the other customers must be staring at her ringless left hand. She puts her hands down below the level of the counter. "If I leave out the blouses, I should have enough to pay for the rest with cash. I can pick up a couple of white blouses anywhere."

"Very well, madam."

Pamela takes the gray gymslips, plimsolls, tie, socks and sweaters in their bulging carrier bags and drags Jackie out onto the street. She is hurrying again, this time to the pub. The awkwardness over her lack of a husband has upset her equilibrium and she needs a drink. They catch a bus first, then walk the rest of the way to the Pig and Whistle. Pamela doesn't like going into a pub on her own, and will do so only if she's desperate, as she is now. She does most of her drinking alone at home.

At least the landlord of the Pig knows her, thanks to Billy's long patronage of the place. Even so, she is aware of stares from the men in the public bar as she goes to order herself a port, and a ginger beer for Jackie. (The landlord is prepared to turn a blind eye to a child's presence if she happens to be the granddaughter of a regular.) Pamela is still very young, and quite pretty, even if her complexion has a dull, unhealthy look and her hair is loose and uncared for. She doesn't look at the men as she passes them. Her contempt for the opposite sex is now quite unshakeable; she wants nothing to do with them.

Pamela doesn't speak to her daughter when they sit down. She just stares into her glass between gulps. Jackie feels, as always, that it must be something that she has done wrong. She tries not to make too much noise as she sucks up her ginger beer through the straw.

"Well, well, well! Look who's here—my two favorite girls!"

The booming voice belongs to Billy Yardley, resplendent in pork pie hat and chocolate brown car coat trimmed with nylon fur.

"And how's my princess, then?"

He swings Jackie up into the air and plonks her down on the bar next to the taps. There is a large puddle of beer on the counter and it seeps through her skirt to her underwear, making a cold, damp stain. Despite her feeble attempts at concealment, her mother notices the stain when she is lifted down again.

"Oh honestly, Jackie! Your panties are sopping wet! Couldn't you have said something? A big girl like you!"

Jackie opens her mouth to try to explain, but Pamela has started to tell her father about buying the uniform, and how she didn't have enough money for all the things on her list. She grumbles about her father interfering in her life, his using her flat as a convenience, but when it suits her she takes her troubles to him and accepts whatever handouts he is prepared to give. There is an unspoken agreement between them that he will help meet the cost of keeping Jackie.

"Don't worry about that, girl, her old granddad will see her right. Won't I, my pet?"

He bends down and pinches Jackie's cheek, puffing a great gust of cigar smoke into her face.

"I'll pick up some little blouses and what-have-you for her ... you'd like that, wouldn't you, treacle? Nothing's too good for my little princess!"

After she has finished her drink, it is time for Pamela to go to work. She has not been able to get another job as a secretary. She works part-time as a filing clerk in an insurance company. This means that girls from the typing pool, some of them several years her junior, can tell her what to do.

When she goes to work, Pamela takes her daughter to Auntie Elsa's. She is not a real aunt, just the lady who minds Jackie in her own home. It is an informal arrangement, and a cheap one, costing only a few shillings a week. It is as well that the people in the Child Welfare Department are unaware of the situation, for they would hardly approve the dark, damp house as suitable premises.

Auntie Elsa is a big, sweaty woman in her late fifties, with a fondness for cheap costume jewelry. Eagle-eyed, she wastes no time in commenting on Jackie's beer-stained skirt.

"She's had a little accident, I'm afraid," Pamela apologizes.

Auntie Elsa sucks her teeth.

"There wasn't time to go home for dry clothes."

When Pamela has left, Auntie Elsa strips off Jackie's clothes and drapes them over the boiler to dry. Jackie stays in the kitchen as it is the only warm room in the house.

"Well, go on, with you, into the front room! Can't have you hanging around in the kitchen in your underclothes."

Jackie goes into the front room, which has nicotine-stained walls and a flowered carpet so dirty that the flowers are hardly visible. Auntie Elsa's elderly father is sitting in the armchair, wheezing loudly. Jackie is afraid of him, and declines his invitation for her to come and sit on his lap. Every so often he takes out his handkerchief and coughs up a mouthful of phlegm into it.

Shivering in her underclothes, Jackie goes to the sideboard and takes out a battered cardboard box of toys. They are mostly broken and grimed with dirt. There is a small solitaire board with chipped wooden pegs. This is Jackie's favorite. She lies the pegs on the carpet in three neat rows, five pegs in each row. She takes meticulous care over getting the rows straight. Then she starts to put the pegs in the board, one by one and very slowly. Each peg she puts in, she tells herself, means that she's getting closer to the time for Mum to come back and get her. She doesn't often have fun being with Mum, but at least it is better than being here, at Auntie Elsa's.

When she has put all the pegs in the board, she takes them out, lays them in their rows and starts again. She throws the odd wary glance at Auntie Elsa's father, who is making retching noises into his handkerchief.

Auntie Elsa sticks her head round the door and summons Jackie into the kitchen.

"Come on—Mrs. Everly's here to see you!"

Mrs. Everly is Auntie's neighbor, who feigns a love for children but is really a vindictive old busybody. When Jackie appears, she is already tut-tutting over Jackie's damp dress.

"Fancy a big girlie like you wetting yourself! How old are you now? Five? And about to go to school, your auntie tells me. Well, you won't have to go doing that sort of thing when you're at school, will you? You'll have to stay dry, like a big girl. . . ."

Jackie stands motionless in her underwear, undergoing this humiliation for the sin of being sat in a puddle of beer. Then she goes back into the sitting room. She can hear Auntie and Mrs. Everly exchanging their usual observations on what a funny little thing she is. ". . . So quiet and so serious, but then what a life she's had, with no father. Mind you, I've never seen her cry, not once. . . ."

She resumes her post at the solitaire board, placing the pegs on the board more rapidly this time, to make Mum come back faster, to make her ordeal end sooner.

Jackie is in her bedroom when Billy comes round that evening. The room has not been decorated since Pamela spent all her spare time and money turning it into her Dream Nursery when she was pregnant. The frills and flounces look rather tatty now; the pink ribbons that tie back the curtains are frayed at the edges. It is appropriate that the ideal room, once perfect in every detail, should now be faded and shabby. It is like a living representation of Pamela's dreams of motherhood, an ideal which she found she could not live up to. She had wanted the baby so much, but those instincts were smothered by the struggle, the loneliness, the inability to cope. She wants to be the perfect mother, but cannot, so instead she makes the child a scapegoat for everything that is wrong in her life.

But Jackie loves her room. It is like her own little house. She keeps it very tidy, which is not easy as there are so many things in it. Billy is always bringing her toys, which invariably break. She likes her baby doll best. She sings to it as she rocks it in her arms.

Billy exchanges a few words with her mother, then pops his head round the door. He is holding a large brown paper bag.

"Brought you something . . . want to take a look?"

Jackie opens the bag. Inside there are school blouses—blue school blouses.

Her lips tremble slightly when she realizes what has happened. Summoning all her courage, she says, "But the uniform list says *white* blouses, Granddad."

"That doesn't matter, princess, they won't mind you having blue. It's only a very pale blue—bit like white, really. And I'll write a letter to the teacher, explaining your special circumstances."

Jackie knows that "special circumstances" means she doesn't have a daddy. It means she's different. And they'll know she's different, because she wears a blue blouse and the other children all have white. In her mind, the two things become confused, so that she interprets what Billy says as meaning she *has* to wear another color, so that everyone can tell that her circumstances are special. A great shudder of dread passes through her. She turns and buries her head in the pillow.

"What's the matter, pet?"

"School. I don't want to go to school."

T e n

■

Monday, September 7, 1964. In the center of Hemingford, Albert Road Mixed Infants is preparing to open its gates for the beginning of a new academic year. There will be an intake of twenty-five new pupils in Miss Rudd's class, Class Seven. In the cloakroom area outside the classroom, there is a peg for each new child, with his or her name written over it in colored crayon. The girls' pegs are on the left-hand side of the room, the boys' on the right. On the left-hand side, next to each other, there are pegs labeled "Carolyn" and "Jacqueline." On the right, opposite them, there are labels inscribed "Matthew" and "Stephen."

In the Fox household, Carolyn is acting as though starting school is something she has done many times before. She has, after all, been to Albert Road most afternoons to collect Martin, and the place and its routines are already familiar.

She is simply impatient to get started, and wears her school coat and beret to the breakfast table.

"There's a name tape on everything," says Jean, "so you know which things belong to you."

"I know," says Carolyn.

"And you give the envelope with your dinner money in it to the teacher when she asks for it."

"I know."

"Little Miss Know-All, aren't you? So I suppose you know that your PE kit is in the drawstring bag, and you hang it on your peg with your coat ..."

"I know."

"There's shorts, T-shirts, and your pumps in it. All labeled."

"Pumps is a stupid word for shoes," observes Carolyn through her mouthful of Cocoa Krispies. "Why are they called pumps when they don't pump anything?"

"Well, call them plimsolls then," Jean suggests. "Plimmies, that's what we used to call them."

Carolyn pulls a face. "That's *stupid*!"

"Our teacher calls them 'daps,' says Martin. "She says, 'Come on, daps on!' "

"Daps." Carolyn tests the new word. "Daps." She gets down from the breakfast table and runs around the kitchen shouting "Daps-daps-daps, pumps-pumps-pumps, plimmies-plimmies-plimmies" until Les orders her to stop as he can't hear the radio news. Then she announces: "I'm going to call them gym shoes."

"You can call them whatever you like, just get up those stairs and clean your teeth and brush your hair ready to go!"

Carolyn thunders up the stairs to the bathroom and brushes her teeth quickly, in a hurry to get to school. She gives a brief, uncritical glance in the mirror before leaving. Her round, snub-nosed face stares back at her, brown eyes like two chocolate drops, her coarse black hair cut as short as a boy's. She didn't want to have her hair cut, but Mummy said she had to; she said it was more practical.

Jean is standing at the front door with her satchel and PE bag, and Martin is ready and waiting, excited because they are going to school in the car today. The new pupils must arrive a quarter of an hour early, so Les has offered to give the decrepit Wolseley one of its rare outings and drop the children on his way to the factory. That way he will have the car after work to pick up Winnie and bring her back for tea. She will be wanting to hear all about Carolyn's first day, and pass damning comment.

Jean feels no pang as she waves Carolyn off; in fact she is relieved to have her most difficult child out of the house five days a week. She settles Sally down with a coloring book and goes into the kitchen for a leisurely cup of coffee and a cigarette.

When the car stops outside the school gates in Albert Road, Carolyn declines her father's offer of an escort to the classroom, boasting that she already knows where it is. She brushes past his good-bye kiss and hurries into the playground with her brother, with satchel and kit bag bouncing against the backs of her knees.

Geoffrey Noble is frowning at his son, newly attired in his school uniform.

"He should have had a haircut."

Stephen's pale gold hair is curling over his collar. The question of its length was debated several days ago, and Sylvia won. She argued that Stephen couldn't cope with too many changes all at once, and that to cut off all his hair at the same time as packing him off to school would be traumatic. Geoffrey had pointed out that short hair would have been mandatory at Draycotts.

"But he's not going to Draycotts any more," Sylvia countered, with feminine logic.

That was the end of the discussion. Geoffrey knows that his wife can be very stubborn, and he can't be bothered to argue. They hardly speak to each other at the moment, while the cold war about more children continues.

Sylvia is examining every aspect of Stephen's appearance.

"I'm not sure about these wretched nylon shirts," she says unhappily, fingering the collar. "They do feel awful. You must tell me if they make you sweat, darling ... maybe I should pop into town this afternoon and try and get you some more. Perhaps Marks and Spencer would have some cotton ones. . . ."

Geoffrey clears his throat. "I'm off now. Better hurry; don't want to miss the train."

He ruffles Stephen's hair and pats his shoulder. "You be a good chap, eh?"

Geoffrey picks up his bowler hat and his briefcase and his copy of the *Financial Times* and goes out, slamming the front door behind him. He doesn't say good-bye to Sylvia. She scarcely notices.

"Now, Stephen, can you remember what to do when you need to spend a penny?"

"Put my hand up and ask the teacher."

"Good boy. And the money in your satchel, can you remember what it's for?"

"For my lunch."

"That's right. So you must be very careful not to lose it. And if any of the other boys hit you or say nasty things to you, you must tell your teacher. And keep away from any children who look dirty; they might have head lice. The ones from the council estate, especially."

Sylvia has impressed the potential awfulness of Albert Road on Stephen so thoroughly that he is now quite terrified. He stands silent at the foot of the stairs, with his satchel strap across his chest, waiting for Sylvia to get ready. She locks the bathroom door, sits down on the lavatory and sobs. She has lost Amabel, and she feels as though she is losing the other twin now. He will become a grubby, noisy schoolboy with a Hemingford accent. He'll probably say "ain't" instead of "isn't." He won't belong to her. Even with his lovely long curls he looks grown-up in his uniform. Like a real little man. . . .

And what is she going to do all day, alone in the house? She can't fill her day shopping as her sisters-in-law do. Since the twins were born, she has lost touch with most of her friends. There's a big pile of history books sitting on her desk and she once thought that she might do some writing, but somehow her frame of mind feels all wrong. She didn't discuss the matter of her empty days with Geoffrey. He would say she should have another baby.

Sylvia splashes water over her face, applies some lipstick and goes downstairs to find Stephen still standing there like a sentry.

"Ready?"

He nods, his face pale with fear.

Sylvia feels awkward about parking the Jaguar outside the school, so she leaves it in a side street and they walk the rest of the way down Albert Road. Sylvia is struggling not to think about Amabel, about how it would have been her first day at school, too. . . .

When they reach the classroom, Stephen looks as though he might be sick. He hangs back, forcing his mother to drag on his hand. She propels him into the room with a little push, then hurries away, not daring to look back.

■　　■　　■

"Matthew!" shouts Audrey Pryce-Jones. "Matthew, stop doing that! Come here! ... *Ken!*"

Matthew Pryce-Jones is getting overexcited at the prospect of starting school, racing round the house with his satchel on his back, using his new tie to lasso the newel posts at the foot of the stairs. Audrey had meant to get up specially early to get him ready for his big day, but she's not feeling very well, and hasn't even managed to crawl out of bed. Her breasts ache, and she feels nauseous. She suspects that she could be pregnant at last, but doesn't want to say anything to Ken yet. Not until she's sure.

Audrey fetches a glass of water to wash the sour taste from her mouth, picking up her comb on her way back to bed. She sits against the pillows, teasing out her hair.

"Matthew! ... Kenneth, will you come here please, dear?"

Ken emerges from the bathroom, slapping highly scented aftershave onto his chin. His hair is sleek with Brylcreem.

"You called, my sweet?"

Audrey puts her hand to her forehead in the manner of the suffering invalid. "You're going to have to run Matthew down to the school for me. I can't go—I'm feeling absolutely dreadful!"

"Can't be done, I'm afraid, I've got a partners' meeting in half an hour."

"Well, telephone Beryl and cancel it."

"Impossible, darling, you know how import—"

"Say you're going to be late then. It won't take you far out of your way. But I really don't feel up to driving."

"What's wrong with you?" Ken asks suspiciously.

"I'm just feeling very sick, that's all, I ..." Audrey decides that the only way to get the maximum sympathy is to throw caution to the wind. "Actually, I think I might be pregnant."

"Pregnant." Ken lets the word hang there.

"Well—aren't you pleased?"

Ken gives her a broad, delighted smile. "Of course I am! That's wonderful!" Inwardly he feels mostly gloom and dread. Audrey getting fat and bad-tempered again, like the last time she was pregnant. Complaining about nausea and backache. Thrashing about at night because she can't get comfortable. Then after the birth; a baby squawking all night, and spitting sick onto his shoulder, and Audrey's gourd-like breasts oozing milk all over the sheets. . . .

"Well, well, well, a father again, eh? Wait until I tell them all at work!" It occurs to Ken that Linda, the secretary he has been seeing for the past three months, will hardly be thrilled at the news.

"It's not definite yet, Ken, so better not say anything. Not to Matthew either."

"As you wish, my dear. You try to get some rest, then. I'll see to Matthew. Only he'll have to be ready to leave in five minutes. Matthew!"

Ken's son and heir is running round the kitchen with his tie round his forehead like an Indian brave's headdress.

"Have you had breakfast?"

"Yes." Matthew holds up a chocolate biscuit.

Ken laughs. "Better not let your mother see you with that! Are you ready to go?" He bends and wipes the chocolate off Matthew's cheek. "First day at school's an important day, old man. There'll be lots of new things to see and do."

"I know all about it!" boasts Matthew, full of confidence. "I know what I'm going to do. I'm going to have milk for my morning drink, and there's going to be a Wendy house, and I'm going to play in the playground all day."

"Not quite all day, there'll be some work to do too, I'm afraid!"

"I know, I'm going to do sums, and writing and everything!"

"That's my boy!" Ken gives him a mock punch on the jaw. "You're not nervous, are you?"

"*No*—silly!"

Matthew chatters happily in the car, but goes quiet when he sees the school. He pulls a face.

"I thought you weren't nervous," says Ken impatiently, looking at his watch. If he leaves now, he'll only miss ten minutes of the meeting.

"I'm not. Just don't like it, that's all."

"Well, what's wrong with it, for heaven's sake? You haven't even got inside yet!"

"Mummy said it was a big school. But it's not. It's all small."

■ ■ ■

Jackie Yardley sticks out her tongue in concentration as she fastens the buttons of her blouse one by one. Her blue blouse. The "different" blouse.

"Let's have a look at you. . . ."

Pamela is still in her dressing gown. She lifts her daughter onto a kitchen stool so that she can view her from top to toe.

"Very smart. Pity you couldn't have new shoes; perhaps after Christmas, though . . . You haven't made much of a job of your hair, have you? I'll have to plait it all over again . . . keep still."

Pamela fiddles with Jackie's fine straw-colored locks, making a worse job of plaiting it than Jackie did, leaving her with little tufty ends sticking out all over. She smooths back Jackie's fringe with one forefinger, then gives her a hard, impulsive hug. Jackie squirms in her arms, unable to breathe.

"I shall miss my little one, my baby . . . I'll collect you at half-past three for a special treat on your first day. But tomorrow I'll be working, so Auntie Elsa will collect you and take you to her house for an hour or so. All right?"

Jackie hangs her head.

Pamela turns her attention to checking the contents of Jackie's satchel.

"What on earth's *this* doing in here?"

She pulls out Jackie's favorite baby doll.

"I wanted to take my dolly," Jackie mumbles.

"You don't take dolls to school, you stupid little girl!" Pamela shouts. "What if you lose it, or some other kid pinches it? You'll be asking for another one then. Do you think the money to buy new dolls grows on trees? There isn't even enough for a new pair of shoes!"

Pamela fumbles on the table for her cigarettes, lights one. "I don't know where the hell your grandfather's got to. He should have been here ten minutes ago!"

Billy Yardley had insisted on taking Jackie to school on her first day but now, at half-past eight, he seems to have forgotten.

Pamela sucks angrily on her cigarette. "I mean, I can't take you now, can I? Not dressed like this. If he doesn't get a move on, you're just going to have to be late."

Jackie's stomach turns tight and cold with dread. She is going to be late. If you're late, the teacher tells you off. And all the other children will be on time, so she'll be different. . . .

Billy finally arrives at eight forty-five.

"Few too many down at the Pig last night, sorry. . . ."

He hasn't shaved or combed his hair, and his breath reeks. But he has dressed in his best suit, a sky blue Crimplene worn with an olive green tie.

"Come on then, princess, time to go and show them what you're made of! Kiss your mum good-bye and then we can get down to the bus stop."

The bus doesn't come for fifteen minutes. Jackie arrives at the classroom half an hour after all the other new pupils, and Billy has to go and have a word with the teacher to explain why they're late. The other children are already at the desks, and they turn to stare at Jackie. She doesn't see their faces. All she sees are school blouses: shining white school blouses.

Albert Road Mixed Infants is a one-story building constructed from grimy purplish brick. It has its own distinctive smell, of sour milk and chalk dust and overcooked cabbage. The long low buildings, including a recently built gymnasium and assembly hall, are built around two playgrounds. One is for five- to seven-year-olds, and the larger one for eight- to eleven-year-olds.

Miss Rudd's classroom looks out over the smaller playground. It has rows of low desks, grouped in fours, and a play corner near the blackboard, with Wendy house and building blocks. Educational charts and pictures cover the walls, and there is something called a Behavior Board, with a row of empty squares next to the name of each child. These will be filled in with stars of various colors rating from green to gold, or a black spot for misdemeanors.

"Stop chattering!" says Miss Rudd loudly, when the last of the children has finally found a desk. *"I said: stop chattering!"*

She raises her voice to a frightening monotone. The murmurs

and giggles stop instantly and all the children face the front with a chastened expression. Miss Rudd would strike terror into the heart of any five-year-old. She is a stick-straight, bony spinster who looks fifty but is in fact thirty-seven. Her blouse is buttoned tightly at the throat and she wears a long A-line tweed skirt and lisle stockings. The head-mistress of Albert Road could perhaps have found someone kinder and more sympathetic to introduce the new intake to school life, but she achieves such wonderful results with teaching the three R's that her harshness is overlooked. As well as being Class Seven's form mistress, she teaches math to the older children, who still fear her.

"Right. Now. That's better." Silence. "In a minute I will hand round exercise books and pencils. The books have your names on them, so there's no excuse for losing them."

"Don't know how to read my name," mumbles Matthew Pryce-Jones.

"Don't speak unless I tell you to!" roars Miss Rudd. "Now, this morning we're going to look around the school, and find out where everything is. We'll be choosing two milk monitors, who hand out the milk at break-time, and two pencil monitors, who have to collect up all the pencils at the end of day and put them in this box here . . ." She points to an old shoebox on her desk. "We don't let you keep the pencils . . . does anyone know why? Hands up if you know. . . ."

No one is brave enough to answer.

"We don't keep pencils because they're sharp and they have lead in them and lead's dangerous. . . . In a minute, I'll be collecting your dinner money. You will go to first sitting of dinner, with Class Six and Class Five when the bell goes. The dinner ladies will show you what to do. After dinner you'll play in the playground until the bell goes again. Then you come back in here. STRAIGHT away! You stay in here until home time. . . ."

At the mention of home, a few lower lips wobble.

"Does anyone know what this is?" Miss Rudd points to a lad-derbacked chair underneath the Behavior Board.

"Chair," mutters someone.

"Not just a chair, the Naughty Chair. If anyone is very badly behaved and I have to smack them, they sit in this chair for a while afterward. How long they sit there depends on how naughty they've been."

Twenty-five pairs of eyes swivel toward the chair.

"In a minute we'll be going to see where the toilets are, and to take your PE kit to the lockers in the changing room. You should all have a drawstring bag with white T-shirt, navy shorts and plimsolls—"

"Gym shoes," says Carolyn.

"I BEG YOUR PARDON?" roars Miss Rudd. *"Who* said that?"

Some of the children stare helplessly at Carolyn.

"Well, come on! . . . I'm waiting . . . I want the child who said that to put up their hand."

Carolyn raises her hand as far as her shoulder.

"What's your name?"

"Carolyn."

"Carolyn What?"

"Carolyn Fox."

"Come up here."

Carolyn walks to the front, holding her head up defiantly.

"Put out your hand."

Carolyn hesitates.

"I said put out your hand!"

Carolyn holds her palm upward and receives six sharp slaps with the flat of a wooden ruler. She winces, but doesn't cry. No one else dares make a sound.

"Normally you would sit in the Naughty Chair now, but because it's your first day, we'll give you the benefit of the doubt. Now, I want you all to fetch your kit bags and make an orderly queue ready for going to look round the toilets. . . ."

During dinner break, Carolyn visits the toilets on her own. Her hand still smarts slightly. There is a black dot next to her name on the Behavior Board. "Don't care," she says to herself inwardly. "Don't care."

She goes into one of the toilet cubicles.

"Eugh—boogies!"

There are pieces of snot smeared all over the toilet walls, dried and crusted. Carolyn takes out the crayon she has secreted in her gymslip pocket and draws a ring around each boogy.

As she washes her hands, she stares sourly at her reflection. Surrounded by a lot of other girls of all shapes and sizes, she is aware for the first time of her un-prettiness, her lack of femininity. Next to the other girls she seems big, her stocky limbs heavy and misshapen. There is one girl in particular, Jacqueline, who has a peg next to hers. Jacqueline is tiny and delicate, with long fair hair in plaits and pink plastic bobbles at the end of each one. How Carolyn covets those pigtails and their pretty-colored bobbles. So much, that she wouldn't speak to Jacqueline when she said hello. Another girl, Debbie, has pierced ears and a Sindy doll in her satchel. Sindy's got big plastic bosoms.

Well, she's going to show them, Carolyn decides. She's going to show them that she's not scared of Miss Ruddy Rudd, and she doesn't care, even if she is put in the Naughty Chair.

Jackie is offended by the boogies too, but too inhibited to acknowl- edge the fact. Her arm brushes against one, and she flinches. As she pees, she does a complicated balancing act to avoid touching them again. This is difficult as the cubicles are very narrow.

Tracing paper. They have tracing paper to wipe yourself with. Jackie doesn't understand. She stares at the hard, shiny roll. The sheets are perforated, like normal toilet paper. There are red letters printed on it: PROPERTY OF HM GOVERNMENT and NOW WASH YOUR HANDS on alter- nate sheets. She tries to use the paper, but it is crackly and uncomfort- able. She perseveres.

Some older girls have come into the toilets and they are talking and giggling. Jackie waits for them to leave. She tries to pull the chain, but can only reach the handle by standing on tiptoe and then can't pull hard enough.

She hurries out of the toilets without washing her hands. There is probably a punishment for not doing so, as well as failing to flush. But she is afraid to linger in the toilets longer in case she gets told off for that.

It seems impossible not to do something wrong, and Jackie has spent the whole day in a miserable dread of being caught doing whatever that might be. She has kept her cardigan buttoned to the neck, despite the warmth, because she is sure that if Miss Rudd notices, she will be smacked with the ruler for wearing a blue blouse.

Matthew rushes outside as soon as dinner is over, impatient to play. He roars around the playground for a while, letting off steam, but quickly realizes that no one is taking any notice of him. This is a new phenomenon. He stands still for a while, just watching, considering.

He watches the older children, making a mental note of how they behave, memorizing the words they use. They don't bash each other as much as he had expected. Instead they use shouted verbal abuse. Matthew inwardly digests such phrases as "Stinky pants!", "Pooh-pooh bottom!", and "Spazzy cretin!" He observes a game of Kiss Chase, then bullies some of the Class Seven girls into playing. A callous streak emerges even at this tender age: he swoops on any girl he can catch up with, inducing squeals of excitement, but he only kisses the ones he feels like kissing, even though the rules stipulate that you kiss anyone you catch. He cheats, in fact. The girls accept this without complaint, already aware that Matthew with his floppy chestnut hair and long curling eyelashes is the handsomest boy in Class Seven.

Matthew likes Debbie best, the girl with gold studs in her ears. She giggles a lot. He thinks the two whose pegs are nearest his in the cloakroom, Carolyn and Jacqueline, are stupid. But he kisses Jackie, because she at least is pretty.

Stephen hates the playground most of all. The screaming and shouting of the other children is deafening, demonic. Some of the older girls have drawn hopscotch squares in chalk and hop and skip over them in a relatively peaceful manner. Stephen crouches near them, pretending to be very interested in some bits of loose stone and gravel. He rubs at the slimy, itchy collar of his nylon shirt.

Mummy said she had to tell if the other boys were nasty to him. But it is the girls who have been nasty. They have laughed at his hair, calling him "Goldilocks" and "Sissy" and "Girlie." The other boys have ignored him, which is a relief.

He doesn't want to use the toilet during the dinner break. It is a urinal, and he doesn't want the other boys looking at him while he pees. He hopes there will be a break during the afternoon, a hope that gets more and more desperate as his need becomes more urgent. No break comes and he is forced to wet himself, bunching his shorts between his legs so that urine doesn't trickle onto the floor. For the last hour of the afternoon he sits motionless and silent, barely daring to breathe out lest Miss Rudd's gimlet eye spots the damp patch on his shorts.

At four o'clock that afternoon, all over Britain, thousands of babyboom children are giving their mothers their first impressions of school. Carolyn Fox demands a Sindy doll. Stephen Noble tells Sylvia that he wants his hair cut short. Matthew Pryce-Jones reports that their teacher is "stupid—and ugly." Jackie Yardley doesn't say anything much. That night she dreams she is sitting on a toilet that's cemented into the middle of the playground. Everyone is looking at her. No, worse, they haven't seen her yet, but are on the point of noticing her. There is nothing she can do to get away. Her navy school knickers are around her ankles and she covers her exposed pubis with inadequate hands.

E l e v e n

■

June 1969. It is a hot Saturday afternoon in the center of Hemingford. The new concrete shopping center, completed two years earlier, is overflowing with eager customers. They jostle one another on the walkways, their shopping bags tangling as they pass. At the center of the concourse there is a fountain playing into a concrete moat. This is the focus for idling teenagers in tight jeans and cuban heels and tie-dye T-shirts. The more daring amongst them sport bare feet and ankle bells. The girls have their skirts hitched up so that their bare legs catch the sun, though in many cases the gesture is superfluous as their skirts are barely long enough to cover their underwear. One of the boys is playing a guitar, and his friends are singing along.

"So here's to you, Mrs. Robinson, our nation turns its lonely eyes to you. . . ."

It is a pleasant enough scene, but Audrey Pryce-Jones feels irritated by it, stepping ostentatiously over the legs of one of the girls, although her path isn't blocked. She has just emerged from the hairdresser's salon opposite the shopping center, no longer Eduardo's, but Paolo of Rome with Hair by Eduardo in small letters in one corner of the window. Gone are the days of Eduardo, sauve in his dark suit and smelling of expensive cologne, calling the customers "madam." Now they are attended to by shaggy-haired young men in tight trousers with silk shirts unbuttoned to the waist to reveal gold neckchains.

Audrey has a token grumble about these changes from time to time, but really she is quite happy with the new atmosphere of the place. She enjoys having her hair caressed by Clive's nimble fingers whilst he makes discreet enquiries about her marital life and gossips about the other clients. It is not the visit to the hairdressers that has soured her mood: if anything it has been improved by Clive's ministrations. (Under his influence she has abandoned the high, lacquered look and gone for a soft, natural bob with a heavy fringe.) No; she is feeling disgruntled because she is having to spend the afternoon in town at all, when she spends most of the week shopping for the family. But tonight the Pryce-Joneses are having a cheese and wine party for some of Ken's colleagues, a surprise dropped on her two days ago, and this is the only chance she has had to buy any of the food and drink, what with having to shop for their impending holiday in Majorca, and Matthew's tenth birthday coming up. . . .

She is not even allowed the luxury of shopping on her own, but has five-year-old Tristram with her. Ken claimed that he couldn't be expected to mind both the boys, and since Matthew wanted to stay behind to watch "Thunderbirds," and Matthew usually gets his own way, here she is with her younger son, who is tired and whiney.

From the moment he was born, Tristram couldn't have been less like his older brother. In fact, their appearance is so dissimilar that when he was born, Audrey ventured to ask the midwives at Hemingford Maternity whether they had given her the right baby. At ten, Matthew is still a beautiful child to look at, golden-limbed and sturdy, with deep-set dark blue eyes and lustrous chestnut hair. Tristram, on the other hand, has a pale freckled skin and a broad snub nose that give him a pig-like appearance. His eyes are a watery gray and his hair has a sandy tinge. Despite being more tractable, he just isn't as attractive a child as Matthew, and Audrey finds herself struggling to love him.

"Come on, Tris . . ." she says, tugging on his hand to make him keep up with her. "Let's just pop into this toy shop to see if we can get Matthew's present. . . ."

Matthew has asked for a war game called Battle of Britain. Audrey searches the shelves for it, buys it, removes Tristram from the Matchbox cars, tells him he can't have a new one, and ploughs on.

She visits the center's new supermarket, J. Sainsbury's, pushing her cart briskly up and down the gleaming aisles with their squeaky clean orange and white logos everywhere. She piles cracker biscuits, stuffed olives, cocktail onions into one corner of the cart and a variety of continental cheeses into the other. The supermarket has a small Wines and Spirits section, and Audrey parks the cart in front of it and loads in liter bottles of French table wine, red and white. Only a few years earlier she would have felt wicked, depraved even, to be doing this, but now it seems quite routine. The Summer of Love, freedom marches, sit-ins, the sexual revolution have all bypassed suburban Hemingford, but nevertheless the changes brought by the sixties have influenced Audrey's thinking at a subliminal level. She is aware of a longing for new experiences to infiltrate her neat, safe life. She would like to be a little more daring. She would like to "swing."

Back in Mount Rise, Ken has commandeered the television from Matthew and is watching "Sports Grandstand." Matthew has grown bored with drawing spectacles on the covergirls of Audrey's magazines and is riding his bicycle around on the lawn, something he has been told not to do as it makes tracks on the surface.

Audrey dumps the shopping bags in the kitchen.

"Kenneth!"

From the sitting room there are sounds of a cheering football crowd and a droning commentator.

"Kenneth! ... Come here, will you, please?"

Ken appears in the doorway.

"Ken, I can hardly be expected to get things ready for the party tonight *and* keep Tris amused, now can I? Either give me a hand in here or take Tris outside and keep him out of my way!"

"All right, my dear, all right, keep your hair on ..." He gives his wife a smile that is at once sheepish and indulgent, implying that he doesn't quite understand what he has done wrong, but he is quite willing to try to humor her.

"Come on, young man ..." He takes Tristram by the hand. "... Matthew!"

Matthew appears straight away, eager to do his father's bidding.

"Fancy a game of cricket, son?"

"Yes please!"

"All right: go and fetch your bat and ball and we'll take them into the garden, show Tristram a thing or two, eh?"

With her husband and sons out of the way, Audrey dons her apron and sets about chopping celery and slicing salami. She's not looking forward to the cheese and wine party very much, even though she enjoys a chance to dress up and show off. It's only for Ken's colleagues and their wives, and most of them are a dull bunch. No swingers there. And in less than a week, she'll be doing this all over again, for Matthew's birthday party, and the house will be full of shrieking kids from Albert Road Mixed Infants, whose families she knows nothing about. Still . . .

It has occurred to Audrey recently that she ought to take advantage of her daily contact with the school to try to meet some new people, make some friends of her own. The people they socialize with now are all Ken's friends, or neighbors. There is one woman in particular who looks interesting, and Audrey knows for a fact that she must have a child the same age as Matthew because she remembers seeing her at the maternity hospital when they were both pregnant. Her surname is Noble—Audrey knows that much because she has heard a teacher addressing her—and she is very elegant and well-bred and drives a Jaguar which she prefers to park at some distance from the school gates. Audrey has said hello to her once or twice and they have exchanged nods on numerous occasions but Mrs. Noble seems a little shy. Even so, she must have a lot of interesting friends and go to all sorts of sophisticated parties which entail much more than a cheese and wine buffet in the dining room and a pile of records on the record player in the lounge.

"Matthew! In here a minute!"

Matthew comes in from the garden.

"We need to have a little chat about your party, darling. It's only a week away and we haven't even decided who you're asking yet. Have you thought about who you want?"

Matthew helps himself to a cheese straw. He shrugs. "Dunno, lots of people," he says, with his mouth full.

"Are there any special friends who will be expecting to get an invitation?"

Matthew grins, looking exactly like his father. "Dave and Keith, of course!"

Dave and Keith are the noisiest and most disruptive boys in the class, next to Matthew himself.

Audrey chops parsley and enquires casually, "What about Mrs. Noble's little boy ... what's his name?"

"Stephen Noble. He's OK. Bit wet."

"So you don't want to ask him?"

Matthew wrinkles his nose. "Not really."

"I'll tell you what, why don't you ask all the boys from your class? Then there'll be about a dozen of you, which will be enough to play some team games in the garden." She adds rashly, knowing it will be an inducement: "I'll get Daddy to organize them."

"I want girls."

"Girls!"

"Debbie Gibbons. I said if she let me kiss her, she could come to my party. And Jackie Yardley. She's pretty and Keith says she's got a crush on me."

"Matthew!" Audrey gives an exasperated sigh as she arranges cheeses on a cheeseboard. "You can't just have two girls. They'll be outnumbered and they won't enjoy themselves ..." She is thinking quickly. "I'll tell you what ... why don't you ask all the children in your class, and then you can have a barbecue in the garden?"

She does a quick mental calculation. That will be twenty-five ten-year-olds, which is far too many to control, but then some of them are bound not to come.

"Far out!" Matthew gives a whoop of joy. "A barbecue! Fab! Thanks, Mum!"

Audrey raises the subject of the birthday party while she and Ken are changing that evening.

"What?" Ken comes to a standstill in the middle of the bedroom, dressed in shirt, underpants and socks, collar up ready to receive the knitted silk tie, which is in his hand. "Have you taken leave of your senses, woman? He can't ask the whole bloody lot of them! What if they all accept? Tell him to pick out the twelve he likes best and leave it at that!"

"I tried that. He only wanted two girls."

"So?"

"So you can't have just two girls and twelve boys!"

"I don't see why not! Half their luck! ... And if I know our Matthew, he'll have asked the class flirts anyway."

"Don't be ridiculous!" snorts Audrey, tugging down her Mary Quant shift dress. "It's a *children's* party. We'll have to even up the numbers by asking them all. They won't all come. There'll be at least half a dozen who say no for some reason."

"And what if they do all come?" Ken challenges her, as he ties his tie in front of the mirror. "They'll wreck the place! Think of the damage that Matthew can do in this house and then multiply it by twenty-five ... where are my trousers?"

"They're not going to be in the house." Audrey lowers sooty false eyelashes onto her eyes with the aid of a pair of tweezers. "They'll be out in the garden, having a barbecue. We may as well use the thing, after we spent so much money on it last year. We've only used it about twice."

"That's because I don't know how to work the bloody thing properly! You'll have a smoking barbecue full of uncooked chicken and two dozen hungry children—nice work, darling!"

Audrey matches his sarcasm with an equally insincere smile and turns her back on him. Once she would have burst into tears to elicit a withdrawal of the offensive remark, but she has learned since then that what Ken hates most is to be ignored.

He goes on talking at her back.

"You know, Audrey, I've always thought of you as quite a sensible woman, but every now and then you go and do something completely stupid like this which just makes me wonder if you have a brain at all."

Audrey storms into the bathroom, grabs her bottle of Librium and swallows a couple of tablets.

"Wretched man!" she mutters, enjoying the thrill of disloyalty, then giggles as she remembers that he was delivering his tirade in his socks and underpants.

■　■　■

The superficial gloss of unity has returned to their relationship by the time the guests start arriving. Several glasses of white wine have helped Audrey to ignore Ken's criticism and she slips happily into small talk with the wife of Ken's chairman, a large, florid woman who has worn "long," and who Audrey can tell is not going to enjoy the dancing she has planned for later.

"I'd like you to met my wife. . . ." Ken has appeared at her elbow with a couple of people she has never met before: novelty indeed.

"This is David Francis, our new Personnel Manager, and his wife Diana. My good lady wife, Audrey."

Audrey smiles and fetches drinks, making mental notes as she does so. The introduction of an unknown factor revives her interest in the evening's proceedings, and she pours herself another glass of wine to celebrate. The new couple look marginally younger and less stuffy than the others. David Francis is a broad, stocky man with curling auburn hair and big, meaty hands. Not as handsome as her Kenneth, but he has a nice smile. His wife has ash-blond hair dressed in a chignon, and a pretty pussy-cat face.

Ken homes in on Diana straight away, chatting to her as if he has met her many times before, which is Ken's way. He monopolizes her until after the food is served, far longer than is necessary to be polite. This irritates Audrey, and she makes a snap decision, influenced by the wine, to do something she has never done before. She will be reckless for once: she will flirt with Diana's husband.

"So David," she says brightly, leaning on his arm, quite unaware that while to herself she seems gay and reckless, to everyone else she appears tipsy and out of control. "Tell me about yourself . . ."

This line of questioning doesn't get very far; the others are looking at them and David is embarrassed.

"Tell you what, let's start dancing . . ." Audrey suggests.

The record player is switched on, the slingback shoes are kicked off and the guests sway self-consciously to and fro to Burt Bacharach and Simon and Garfunkel. Most are ill at ease with the new "modern" way of dancing where there is no body contact, but the partners stand opposite one another waving their arms and thrusting their hips in one another's general direction.

"Oooh, we must have this one; it's one of my favorites!" Audrey trips over to the record player and scrapes the needle onto José Feliciano's "Come on Baby Light My Fire." David Francis is just edging off the dance floor, looking around for his wife and Ken, but they are outside admiring the ornamental fishpond. Audrey is at his side again, and with a devil-may-care shrug he turns back to her and allows her to pinion herself against him in a slow dance. David's arms are around her waist, his hands pressing lightly against the curve of her buttocks. Audrey, who has never danced like this with anyone but Ken, closes her eyes and rests her head against David's substantial shoulder. She allows herself a little experimental wiggle of the hips and is disconcerted and flattered to find that David has an erection.

Audrey is sufficiently sober to worry that someone might notice, so she keeps her hips pressed against David's groin to cover him up, which only adds to his excitement. His ham-like palms are sweating through the thin material of her shift.

When the song crackles to an end and the shifting feet stop moving, Audrey is forced to open her eyes. She sees Ken and Diana Francis standing at the edge of the makeshift dance floor. Diana's feline face is impassive, but Ken looks annoyed.

"There are some people here in need of a drink, my sweet," he says, with a smile that fades as he follows her into the kitchen, out of earshot.

"I should wipe that lipstick off your chin if I were you, my dear, you look a mess ..." He takes some cans of Double Diamond from the fridge and slams the door shut, adding spitefully, "and throw a bucket of cold water over yourself while you're at it."

"I don't know what you mean." Audrey pops a cheeseball in her mouth.

"Yes, you do. Showing me up like that."

"Oh come on, Ken, it's just a bit of fun. Anyway, you fancy Diana Francis, don't deny it."

"So?"

A slow smile crosses Audrey's face. "So, why don't we ask them to stay on after the others have gone? They seem like a couple of swingers to me."

"Right you are, dear!"

Ken strides confidently into the lounge and starts handing out coats to the guests who are leaving. David Francis is hunting behind the sofa for his sheepskin car coat.

"David, old man! Why don't you and the lovely lady wife stay on for a nightcap?" He reaches into the sideboard and brings out a bottle of Dubonnet. "Bring some glasses through, will you, dearest?"

So there they are, the four of them, one couple sitting on each of the two sofas.

"Nice party," remarks David.

"It's not over yet . . ." Audrey leans over drunkenly to the record player and scrapes the needle back to the beginning of the record.

"The time for hesitation's gone . . . no time to wallow in the mire . . . come on baby, light my fire . . ."

". . . We thought you might be game for some wife swapping," she says, trying to keep her tone casual, as though it's something she does every week, like going to the supermarket.

Diana Francis throws her head back and hoots with laughter.

"I'm sorry . . . some what?" asks David.

"Wife swapping. You know—Ken gets it on with Diana, you get it on with me."

David turns pale, then blushes.

"You can't deny that at our age a marriage needs a bit of excitement from time to time. A bit of spice." Audrey drains her glass of Dubonnet, then hauls Ken to his feet. "Come on, Ken, you go and sit over there with Diana. . . ."

Ken squeezes onto the other sofa between husband and wife, giving David no option but to go and sit next to Audrey.

Ken puts his arm round Diana's shoulders and runs a finger up and down one thigh.

"I suppose at halftime someone blows a whistle and we change ends." He guffaws at his own joke. Diana giggles and reaches for his crotch. Ken kneads her breast enthusiastically.

Audrey is so fascinated by this spectacle that she temporarily forgets her own role in the proceedings. David Francis is staring down at his Hush Puppies. She winds her arms round his neck and starts kissing him wetly, worming her tongue against his lips to get him to part them. It feels funny, she thinks, necking with someone other than Ken.

"I'm sorry . . ." David pushes her hands from his neck and comes up for air. "I don't feel comfortable with this, I . . ." He shrugs.

The other three stare at him. The record comes abruptly to an end, but the needle sticks in the groove, making a monotonous *thump . . . crackle . . . thump. . . .*

The door opens. "Mummy, I can't get to sleep. The noise is keeping me awake."

Matthew stands there in his pajamas. He fixes a curious gaze on Ken who is whipping his hand from Diana's miniskirt with a snapping of elastic.

"Come on, Matthew . . ." Audrey shepherds him out of the room. "Let's find you a drink."

"Yes, well, it's been nice." David Francis puts on his sheepskin coat. "We ought to be going."

"We must do it again sometime," says Ken lamely as he shuts the door behind them. Audrey, halfway up the stairs with Matthew, turns and gives him a poisonous look.

"Not if I can help it!"

"You were the one who fancied herself as a swinger, my dear." He gives her the smile of someone who has just taught a naughty child a lesson. "I should stick to housework if I were you."

T w e l v e

■

"What's that you've got there?" Jean Fox demands when she sees Carolyn taking an envelope out of her satchel. "Not another letter from the teacher about your behavior! Here, give it to me."

"S'mine. It's an invitation. Look!" Carolyn holds the white envelope under her mother's nose and points with a stubby finger. "Miss Carolyn Fox."

"Well, go on then, don't keep me in suspense! Open it!"

"It's from a boy," says Carolyn proudly.

"A boy! Here—let me look!" Jean takes the card from the envelope and reads out loud: " 'Matthew Pryce-Jones requests the pleasure of your company at a birthday barbecue . . .' " Matthew Pryce-Jones, eh? Is he the precious little lad whose mum drives a Jag?"

"No, that's Stephen Noble. Soppy Stevie."

"So where does this Matthew live then?" Jean squints at the invitation: she is short-sighted but Les scoffs at the idea of her wearing spectacles. "Nine Mount Rise . . . must be one of those big modern houses up by the golf course. Someone was telling me one of them had a swimming pool in the garden . . ."

"Mum, what's a barbecue?" Carolyn asks.

"It's something they do a lot in Australia, and America. You have a big sort of open air grill thing and you put sausages on it. I saw some in Taylor & Haddon once; they were ever so dear. This Matthew's family must be well off, anyway. . . ."

A suspicion drifts into Jean's mind, prompted by Winnie's constant warnings about Carolyn's precociousness. "Why's this boy asked you to his party, anyway? The boys don't usually ask girls along."

"He's asked everyone. All of Class Two."

"Oh. I see. Well, good luck to them."

"He's not my boyfriend or anything," says Carolyn airily. Before her mother can comment on this statement she disappears into the living room, where her father is watching Vietnam on the television. Vietnam is on every day, at six o'clock, after the "Magic Roundabout."

Jean goes into the kitchen and takes out a tin from the top shelf of the cupboard, next to the Shreddies and the Jaffa cakes that the children have for tea on Sunday as a special treat. There is money in the tin; some pound notes, but mainly coins. She starts counting.

"Eleven shillings and six ... one pound, one shilling and six ..."

The television has been switched off and from the living room, Jean can hear Les's irritated voice reprimanding the children for squabbling. She sticks her head round the door and shouts into the hall: "Martin! Take Sally upstairs and start running her bath, will you?"

She goes on counting. "... Seven pounds ten shillings, seven pounds twelve and six, seven pounds thirteen and one, two, three pennies. Seven pounds thirteen and thruppence."

Jean makes a note of the total on a scrap of paper and puts it in the tin with the money. Then she opens her copy of the Hemingford *Evening Mail* and draws a ring round an advertisement in the Holidays and Leisure column.

"Les! Come in here a minute, will you, love?" She straightens her apron nervously. "Les, I've been thinking about our holiday and—"

"What holiday?"

"Our summer holiday. The thing is—"

"We're not going on holiday this year. I thought we'd already discussed it and decided we'd put the money toward a new car." The Wolseley had been committed to the scrap heap after nearly fifteen years.

"Yes I know, love, but the thing is ... I've been putting a bit of money by each week from the housekeeping, and I've saved up enough for a week away."

"How?" Les frowns at his wife. "You can't possibly have put by enough."

"I have, it's only a caravan, but ... look." She holds the newspaper out to him. "Six berth caravan, Rhyll. Pleasant situation overlooking beach. Five pounds per week. I've saved up seven pounds thirteen and thruppence, so that's enough to pay for the caravan with some left over for food and traveling and ..."

"How are we going to get there without a car?"

"We could go on the train."

"What, with all our luggage and the kids bellyaching? Do me a favor, woman!"

Jean hesitates, looking at the newspaper advertisement again as though it will give her some inspiration. "Perhaps we could borrow a car. We could borrow the vicar's camper van. They hardly ever use it and I'm sure they wouldn't mind us having it for a week."

"If we were in a camper van, we'd hardly need a caravan, would we?" Les picks up the tin and checks the total. "Nearly eight quid. That would come in handy for the new car. I reckon we could pick up a decent second-hand one for about sixty...."

"All right," Jean agrees, but purely from force of habit. As soon as her lips have phrased the conditioned response, she realizes that it's not all right, not this time.

"Put the kettle on, will you, love? I fancy a cup of tea."

Les takes Jean's copy of the *Evening Mail* and shuffles off to read the sports pages, leaving Jean to wash the supper dishes. Carolyn is buzzing around her like a wasp, pestering her about new clothes for the birthday barbecue. Jean tells her not to be a nuisance, exorcizing some of her anger toward Les. She scoops the money back into the tin, puts the tin back next to the Jaffa cakes, and shoos Carolyn out of the kitchen.

Les is half asleep by the time Jean goes to bed. She has been tiptoeing through the children's rooms, tidying up, collecting their dirty clothes and putting them in the linen basket, washing up the dirty mugs and plates she finds lying around the place. She feels weary, bone weary from the constant effort of thinking about the children, making sure that their clothes are clean, that they get to school on time, that there is a meal on the table for them afterward, that they do their homework. She does the same thing every day, day in, day out. But that's all she does.

Jean takes a clean nightdress out of the drawer, turns her back modestly while she takes off her sweater and bra and slips the nightdress over her head. Only then does she remove her slip, girdle, stockings and panties, fumbling underneath the nightdress as if undressing in a tent. Freed from the confines of its underwear, her pale, loose belly sags forward.

"Les, I've been thinking. . . ."

"Hmmmm?"

"I could get a job."

Les heaves himself into a sitting position, twisting his pajama jacket as he does so, exposing a patch of blue-white skin and tangled black chest hair. Despite his slight build, he has abundant body hair; great dark clumps of it emerge from the sleeves of his pajamas on his wrists and the backs of his hands and the heavy growth of stubble covers his chin like a gray stain.

"What are you talking about, woman? What do you want a job for, for God's sake?"

Jean takes a deep breath. "Well, if we need the money I've saved for the car, I could go out to work and get some money saved up for a holiday. There's plenty of jobs going in town, Rita Maitland from number 37 was telling me, part-time . . ."

"But you don't *need* a job! Those jobs are for people who need them! We don't need the money! I'm earning a decent wage, I've got another salary increment due in six months. If it's only the holiday you're bothered about, you can *have* your flaming holiday. I'll take some money out of the Post Office account."

"But, Les, if I was working there'd be no need! We'd have your money, and some extra too. . . ."

"So I'm not earning enough, is that it?" Les's pale face is suffused with blood as his temper builds. "You're trying to humiliate me now, are you? What I bring home isn't enough, is that it?"

"No, I . . ."

Les has jumped out of bed and is tracing a figure of eight around the small room, his hands on his hips. "That's flaming great, that is! Everyone will be saying that Les Fox doesn't make enough to keep his family! Bloody great! Or is it that you want more so that we can better ourselves, and the kids can keep up with their friends at school and ask them back here to some flaming barbecue party!"

Jean is standing now too; facing her husband across the bed.

"No! It's not the money, Les. I'd like a little job for me. For me. It would give me something to do."

"You've got plenty to do here, looking after three kids!"

Jean turns and walks out of the bedroom. She goes downstairs into the kitchen, thinking, How odd, I've never been down here in just a nightdress before. She has never even been as far as the bathroom without dressing gown and slippers. The night air feels cool against her naked skin. She digs her packet of Embassy out of its hiding place at the bottom of her handbag and lights a cigarette, pointing its tip toward the ceiling as she draws heavily on the filter. A wave of peace floats over her. Whatever happens, she tells herself, at least I've had my say. I said my piece and then I walked away.

She goes to bed feeling quite calm. Les has calmed down too. He is sitting up in bed with the light on. If he notices the smell of cigarette smoke, he says nothing.

"About what you were saying ..." he begins.

"Yes?" Jean sounds innocent, as though she can't remember what they were arguing about.

"About you getting a job. I've been thinking we should have a family conference about it. Let's wait until tomorrow, when Mum's here for her tea, then she'll have a chance to say what she thinks."

Ah yes, thinks Jean. Winnie. She should have known that Les wouldn't miss an opportunity to get his mother on his side.

The following afternoon, Carolyn walks back from Albert Road Mixed Infants by herself. Martin is now at Hemingford Grammar School for Boys and will come back on the bus, and Sally has gone to play with one of her friends.

It is a hot afternoon and she walks on the shaded side of the street to keep the sun out of her eyes. Her white ankle socks are gray with dust, her sandals are scuffed white on the toes and her navy blue cardigan, tied loosely around her waist, is trailing one sleeve along the pavement. The straps of her satchel are looped over her shoulders, so her homework bounces heavily against her buttocks at every step. She is sweaty and tired and irritable.

Turning from Plantagenet Drive into Tudor Avenue, she is passed by Sheila Broomhall in her new yellow Mini, which she parks opposite the Foxes' house. Sheila seems very grown-up now. She is twenty-three and engaged to be married.

Carolyn watches her climb out of the car, curious as always to see what Sheila will be wearing. A great wave of envy washes over her when she sees that Sheila has a pair of bell-bottoms. They are white and cut low on the hips, exposing Sheila's tanned midriff. The fabric clings tightly to Sheila's bottom and thighs and then just below the knee fans out in jaunty little triangles, like a sailor's trousers. Carolyn has never seen such a wonderful garment. The only trousers she possesses are for the winter: a pair of sludge green stretch nylon ones with elastic loops under the feet that Jean refers to as "slacks."

She waves, hoping Sheila will notice her. Sheila raises an arm briefly, tossing back her hair as she reaches into the car for her shopping. Her eyes are thickly lined with black, and she has a red and white bandana knotted around her forehead.

In a lather of covetousness, Carolyn runs into number 41, tosses down her satchel and shouts, *"Mum!"*

Jean is in the garden, talking over the fence to Mrs. Hinsley.

"Mum, can I have a pair of bell-bottoms, Mum, *please!*"

"No you can't! Now go in and wash your hands ready for your tea."

Carolyn ignores this instruction and goes upstairs to her mother's bedroom. She roots around in the top drawer of Jean's dressing table and finds an old headscarf which she knots around her head like a bandana. Her straight black hair is too short around her face and sticks out from the scarf in little tufts. It is the wrong color too; a drab navy blue. She needs a red one. Never mind, she can get some money from somewhere and buy one.

Jean is still in the garden, discussing the merits of the new supermarket in the town center. Carolyn drags a kitchen stool up to the cupboards, stands on it, and reaches down the money tin that she saw her mother put away the previous evening. She looks at the money inside it, picks up a half crown piece, and then hesitates when she sees the slip of paper with the total written on it.

Jean sees her through the kitchen door and comes hurrying inside.

"And just what do you think *you're* doing, young lady! Go on— put that back! It doesn't belong to you, and you've got no business snooping around inside it!"

She administers a quick slap on the back of Carolyn's legs, replaces the tin, and returns to her conversation.

"But *Mum . . . !*"

Jean ignores her and continues talking.

Carolyn tells herself that her mother is just being boring, that she never talks about anything but the weather, and shopping, and the neighbors, that she's stupid and doesn't know about anything else. But beneath these reassuring condemnations, Carolyn is aware of a subtle change in her mother's demeanor. She hasn't often smacked her children and has done so in the past with a hesitancy that confirms her distress to be greater than theirs. This time she just delivered the blow and walked away as if she didn't care.

At five o'clock, Winnie telephones and says she can't come for her tea.

"It's my bunions, they're playing up something dreadful."

"Oh, I see," says Jean.

"What with that and my back . . . if Les were coming down with the car, it would be different, but getting to the bus stop, you know, with the bunions, it's agony."

There is a faint whine in Winnie's voice, the implication being that Les should keep a car for the purpose of chauffeuring his mother to and fro.

"I suppose if I had the money for a taxi, I could get a taxi up . . . but there we are, not much I can do about it, is there?"

"No," agrees Jean. She doesn't offer to pay for a taxi.

"So, explain to Les for me, will you."

"He will be disappointed," says Jean, and she means it. When Les gets back from the factory and she breaks the news, he behaves as if his mother's infirmity is a threat to his manhood.

"It's not like Mum, though, is it?" he keeps asking, wandering aimlessly around the kitchen while Jean prepares the meal. "Not like her to miss out just because of her bunions."

"She is getting on a bit," Jean points out.

"What, Mum? Nah, she's got plenty of life in her yet, Mum has. She's probably just in a huff about something."

"Maybe." Jean empties a tin of baked beans into a saucepan.

"Anyway, it means we can't have that family conference after all. Not without Mum here."

"I don't see why not," says Jean, smashing an egg hard against the side of a basin. "I'm not prepared to wait until her bunions are better, if that's what you mean. It could be forever. Besides ..." She walks round Les to put the bread board on the table. "... I don't really see what it's got to do with your mother anyway, whether I get a job or not."

"Hey, Mum, are you going to get a job?" asks Martin.

"I haven't decided yet," says Jean, ignoring the mulish expression on her husband's face. "I might do."

She carries plates of scrambled eggs and beans to the table and hands them round. "What do you kids think about it? Would you mind if you had to let yourselves in after school occasionally and get yourselves something to eat?"

"Brilliant!" says Martin. "I'm going to have Jaffa Cakes and Wagon Wheels for my tea."

"Does that mean we'll get free school dinners like Jackie Yardley in my class does, because her mother's working?" Carolyn asks.

"Course not! It means we'll be latchkey children, won't we, Mum? It said on 'Nationwide' that latchkey children are a social evil."

"What's latchkey children?" asks Sally.

"So you children think it's a good idea, do you? You wouldn't mind too much?" Jean avoids Les's gaze.

"No, especially not if you work in a sweet shop. Then we can get free chocolate!"

"Good. Perhaps I'll look around for something then. And it might mean there's some extra money for a really lovely holiday this year."

"Fab!"

Les grimaces into his baked beans, but says nothing.

"Mum ..." says Carolyn as she helps to dry the dishes. "Mum, if you have a job, does that mean we can have a rise in our pocket money? Only I need some money because I want to buy a headband."

"Now look, Carolyn!" Jean puts her rubber-gloved hands on her hips. "I've just about had enough of this! Why must you be asking for things all the time? You can't just have more money every time you want something new. What do you want a hairband for, anyway? Your hair's too short."

"Not a *hairband*—a headband, like Sheila's got."

"Headband, hairband, what's the difference?"

Carolyn thunders up the stairs and throws herself down on her bed, grinding her teeth at the hatefulness of mothers. If the shops were open she would go straight there and *steal* a headband. Then she'd get her mother into trouble, because when children get caught stealing it's their parents who go to prison. It would serve her right and Carolyn wouldn't care.

But the shops aren't open, and she doesn't have the patience to wait until they are. She goes over to the vicarage to see Helen Croucher and tells her she must part with her new red headband. Helen doesn't have the gumption to say no, so Carolyn returns home triumphant with her booty in her pocket.

She goes into the bathroom and spends half an hour trying it on in front of the mirror. The exercise is not a success. The headband is the right color, but she's still not pretty.

T *h i r t e e n*

■

Sylvia Noble is in the lush garden of her villa, weeding the flowerbeds. She is dressed in a floral print dress, which despite being bleached and faded from frequent washing still looks as elegant as it did when she bought it at a respected couture house in Mayfair. Underneath the dress her long, slim legs are bare and slightly tanned. As she bends over her trowel, her ash-blond locks, streaked with a few gray hairs, fall over her forehead.

Now, in the summer of 1969, she feels quite content with her life in Hemingford. But this has not always been the case. She reached a low point when Stephen started school at Albert Road Mixed Infants. Hated taking him there and collecting him, standing there waiting by the railings with all the other mothers lumbered with prams and shopping bags and snotty-nosed toddlers. So dreary and provincial.

She comforted herself with the fact that this was only a temporary step, that they would be taking Stephen away as soon as Draycotts was open again. But when that time arrived, Stephen, who had been miserable and nervous, was just starting to settle in at Albert Road. A new dilemma arose: should Geoffrey and Sylvia take him away when he was just settling in, because they believed that private education was better for him? How would they then feel if he became as withdrawn and disturbed as he had been when he started Albert Road, roaming the landing at night, wetting the bed?

A compromise was reached: Stephen would stay in the state system until he was twelve, then he would take up his place at Maidenhurst, and the money saved on his prep school fees would be invested for his university education (Oxbridge, naturally).

With Stephen in school all day and the prospect of more children receding into the distance, Sylvia was bored and listless and drifted away from her early resolution to use the time to improve her mind. She saw Hemingford as a prison and herself as a prisoner, treading circles around its small, drab center. She badgered Geoffrey about moving back to London until he finally agreed to consider it.

Then she joined the hospital voluntary scheme, and pushed a cart around Hemingford General, selling newspapers and boxes of notelets with birds on them. She became friendly with another lady volunteer, who introduced her to the Friends of the Everyman Theater. This involved attending cheap matinée performances and discussing them afterward over tea and sandwiches. These outings in turn produced an introduction to the Hemingford Historical Society, whose members saw educational film shows and went on bus trips to stately homes and other historic sites. Before long, Sylvia's days were completely full and she sometimes had to send Mrs. Moody, her "treasure," to collect Stephen from school and bring him home on the bus.

She found, rather to her surprise, that she was enjoying herself, that she felt happy. She had a social life other than Geoffrey's boring business contacts, which was exactly what she had intended to achieve. Oh, it wasn't anything like her social life in London before she married; most of her new acquaintances were older than herself and led quiet lives, but they were kindred spirits by Hemingford standards. When Geoffrey suggested going to look at flats in London, she told him she had changed her mind, that she didn't want to move. She thought about Amabel less frequently than before, and about Stephen even less. The Dressing-Up Games dwindled to the odd winter afternoon when she had nothing else to do.

Sylvia straightens up and checks her watch. Three forty-five. Stephen will be back from school soon. She has asked Mrs. Moody to fetch him today because she didn't want to be late back to the house. She is expecting a friend for tea. A gentleman friend.

She picks up her trowel and her basket, removes her gardening gloves, and goes into the house. Once in the bedroom, she strips off her old dress and sponges herself down at the washbasin. Then she changes into a smart linen afternoon dress, one of her shorter ones, with a hem three inches above the knee. Geoffrey frowns when she wears short skirts. He says they are "undignified."

Sylvia brushes out her hair with her Mason and Pearson brush and twists it into a French pleat. She powders her nose and adds a little lipstick, Elizabeth Arden's Hot Summer Pink.

She can hear Mrs. Moody's key in the front door, the thud of Stephen's satchel and his feet scuffing across the flagstones of the hall to the kitchen. In a minute she will go down and say hello to him, but for now she wants to have a few minutes alone to think about her friend. Major Roger Saunders.

She says his name out loud to the dressing table mirror. "Roger Saunders." A solid, traditional English name. Rather like Roger himself. Their friendship is a recent development, a result of Sylvia's attendance at the Hemingford Historical Society. They *are* friends she tells herself firmly, nothing more, but she is aware that Roger has singled her out, and she suspects that he may have a romantic interest in her. She wonders what he would think if he could see her now, taking such care to look nice for his visit. The thought sends a little shiver through her.

Sex preoccupies her thoughts in a way that it never used to. Now, in the 1960s, one can hardly avoid it. Images of human sexuality bombard her from billboards, from magazines, from the television. In the center of Hemingford there is a huge billboard which features a young girl striding out of the sea onto a palm-fringed beach, dressed only in a thin shirt that clings to her breasts, made transparent by the seawater. Sylvia can't help staring at it every time she drives past.

She suspects that she has quite a sensual nature—or would have given the chance. The trouble is, when she was growing up, one wasn't allowed to think like that. The body was something you covered up with girdles and A-line bras, ankle-length skirts.

And then there's Geoffrey. In the past two years he has ceased to make any advances to her in bed: they have tacitly, silently agreed that that side of their life is over. She sometimes wonders whether

Geoffrey finds his pleasure elsewhere, but somehow she just can't imagine it happening. Geoffrey is just so ... unsexy. But she does think about sex in the general sense, trying to imagine what it would be like with someone other than Geoffrey. Which is rather difficult because there only ever has been Geoffrey.

She hears the doorbell ring, and Mrs. Moody going to answer it. She stands up and straightens her skirt, and Stephen chooses that precise moment to come up and find her. She feels a rush of irritation as she hears his footsteps on the landing.

"Mummy, I've got something to show you—look!" Breathless from running up the stairs, Stephen hands her a white envelope.

"Quickly then, darling, Major Saunders has just arrived." Sylvia opens the envelope and reads the enclosed invitation to the birthday party of some boy called Matthew Pryce-Jones, whom she vaguely recalls Stephen mentioning once or twice in tones of awe, as though he was someone who inspired hero worship.

"You don't want to go to it, do you?" Stephen is chronically shy and hates parties of any description.

"Not much."

Sylvia is relieved. The idea of having to collect him and stand around chatting to the other mothers appalls her. All that boasting and story-capping about childbirth, gynecological problems, and the talents of their offspring. Who says women aren't as competitive as men?

"You don't have to go if you don't want to, darling." She runs her hand through his pale blond hair and smiles down at him, at the delicate features that are closer to pretty than handsome.

"Mummy, can we play at Dressing-Up?" Stephen looks wistfully in the direction of the wardrobe where she keeps her shoes and hats and scarves. It is Stephen who initiates their games these days, desperate to get his mother's attention.

"Not now, darling—I've got a guest from the Historical Society." She kisses him on the forehead. "Another time, perhaps."

Roger is waiting in the drawing room, and Mrs. Moody has already provided them with a tray of tea and shortbread biscuits.

"Sylvia, my dear! How lovely you look!" Roger holds out his hands to her and kisses her cordially on both cheeks. Like Geoffrey he is one of the old school tie brigade: Unlike Geoffrey he is chivalrous and gentlemanly in the extreme, making a point of bestowing all the old world courtesies and attentions that went out of fashion twenty years ago. In a restaurant he will pull back Sylvia's chair and push it in again under her behind, placing her napkin across her lap as though she were too delicate to unfold it. He hurries ahead of her and opens any door she might be approaching, letting her pass with a slight bow. Sylvia has the uncharitable thought that all this fuss might get on her nerves if she had to endure it all the time. Still, it is very nice on occasion, especially if one is married to someone like Geoffrey.

She sits down opposite Roger and pours their tea. "How has business been since I last saw you?" she enquires.

Roger runs an antique shop in the Parade, Hemingford's smartest street of shops. He was an officer in the Coldstream Guards during the war; something he prefers not to talk about, and he bought out his commission and set up the business with family money. He is, by a curious coincidence, a distant cousin of Geoffrey's. This doesn't surprise Sylvia, since everyone seems to have come across the Noble family in some capacity or other. She thinks it might be quite useful, though, as it means Geoffrey can hardly object to her seeing Roger.

She wonders now, as he tells her about a particularly fine walnut desk he has sold and she pours him a second cup of Lapsang Souchong, whether they will ever go to bed together. She has not quite decided whether she finds him attractive in that way, but the fact that she is thinking about it means that she probably does. At fifty-eight, Roger is some ten years older than her husband, but well preserved and trim. He has the sort of even, aquiline features that suggest he was strikingly handsome in his youth. His steel-gray hair is smoothed back from a high forehead and he is always tanned to a sort of walnut color. His dress sense is verging on the flamboyant; a theatrical version of the English country gentleman. Today he is wearing ginger suede brogues, mustard-colored cords, a bottle green waistcoat and a rather florid tie.

"I take it you and Geoffrey will be going abroad this summer?" Roger bites delicately into his shortbread biscuit.

"Yes, to Italy. We shall be staying at the Hotel Excelsior."

"Really? That's quite extraordinary ... lovely hotel, by the way, stayed there myself once or twice ... You see, I was thinking of going back to Italy myself this summer."

"Oh you must!" says Sylvia abruptly. Envisaging how a discreet romantic interlude could liven up the dreary three weeks listening to Geoffrey talk about the City, she adds rashly: "Why don't you come to Positano at the same time as us? Then we could see something of one another. You could even stay at the Excelsior."

Roger's eyes narrow slightly. "Are you sure Geoffrey wouldn't object?"

"Object? Why should he object?" To avoid looking into Roger's eyes, Sylvia starts fiddling with the tea strainer. She can feel her cheeks going pink.

Roger's hand reaches out and pinions hers to the strainer. "Sylvia, my dear ... Look at me."

Sylvia looks up, the corners of her mouth trying not to twist into a grin of embarrassment.

"Sylvia, you must realize that over these past few weeks, I have begun to care for you very much. Our friendship has come to mean a great deal to me ... I think I speak for both of us. Being in your company under foreign skies would be like a dream come true, especially if there was a chance for us to be alone, and for our friendship to become even more intimate."

Roger speaks fervently, still holding her hand, but his expression is so English, so thoroughly decent and honorable that Sylvia is not sure whether he is talking about sex or just some chaste hand-holding.

"I don't see that Geoffrey could object, you are his cousin ... a distant one I know, but—"

Stephen's footsteps in the hall, his voice calling: "Mummy!"

"Excuse me a moment ..." Sylvia goes to the door of the drawing room. "Stephen, don't you have homework to do?"

"I've done it."

"Well, why don't you run along to the shop then? Take some money from my handbag for some sweets. Go on your bicycle."

•

"I've got some sweets. Mrs. Moody gave me some."

"Well, buy Daddy some of those strong mints that he likes. Run along!"

Roger takes her hand again when she sits down, but the momentum of their conversation has been lost.

"Umm ... you could spend your holiday with us as a friend of the family," she suggests. "Though it might be better if I told Geoffrey that you had made your arrangements already." The introduction of deviousness raises their relationship to another plane and makes them both feel awkward.

"Well, I'd better be going ..." says Roger. "Perhaps you'd care to pop into the shop tomorrow morning, if you're in town. We could have a glass of sherry."

"Lovely."

In bed that night, Sylvia says to Geoffrey: "Roger Saunders is going to be in Positano this summer."

"Hmmm."

"He's even going to be there at the same time as us. Isn't that funny?"

"Funny?"

"Well, a coincidence I mean."

"Does this Saunders chap play tennis, then?"

"I haven't the faintest idea."

"Is he taking someone?"

"Taking someone?"

"To make up a four—a lady friend."

"No, not as far as I know."

"Oh. Bit bloody odd, that, isn't it, going on holiday by yourself?" Sylvia frowns. "I don't see why."

"Hmmph." Geoffrey is not interested in the subject of Roger Saunders' holiday; all he cares about is that his own holiday is booked and paid for and will go smoothly. He returns to reading his book; a biography of Winston Churchill.

Sylvia sleeps badly. The idea of having sex with Roger Saunders will not leave her mind. She tries to imagine what he would say, how he would do it. Where it will be. She mulls over these variable factors until they have blended into an obsession by the time the morning arrives.

She has accepted the invitation for sherry at the antique shop, but will they be alone there? What about the customers? And even if he were to close the shop, the back room is hardly conducive to intimacy. Just two hard chairs. Nowhere to ... she can hardly think it, it seems so strange ... nowhere to lie down. Roger is committed to being in the shop until his assistant arrives after lunch and Sylvia's afternoons are curtailed by Stephen's return from school.

As she is searching the kitchen for the keys to the Jaguar in order to take Stephen to Albert Road, she finds the invitation to Matthew Pryce-Jones' barbecue. She notices the time at the bottom right-hand corner: "4 P.M.–7 P.M."

"Stephen!" She goes to the stairs and shouts. "Stephen, come here a minute."

He comes down the stairs with his satchel, his tie straight and his blazer neat.

"Is it time to go, Mummy?"

"In a minute. I just wanted a word with you about this party. Are you *sure* you don't want to go? It might be rather fun. A barbecue. You've never been to one of those before, have you?"

Stephen shakes his head.

"And you're always telling me you don't have any friends. It might be a chance for you to make some. If you go to his party, you can be friends with this Matthew boy. You could ask him back here."

"Everyone's going to it. All Class Two. It'll be like school."

"Go on, darling, please. For me. Do it for Mummy."

F o u r t e e n

■

When Jackie Yardley gets back from school, she lets herself in with her own key. Pamela is watching Wimbledon on the television with the shabby living room curtains drawn to keep the sun off the screen.

"*Love-fifteen,*" says a disembodied voice in the darkness.

Jackie pulls one of the curtains aside. Specks of dust dance in the intrusive shaft of sunlight, floating over the piles of newspapers and magazines, the dirty ashtrays and the half-consumed cups of tea.

"What's for tea, Mum?"

"Egg and chips," Pamela replies, without turning to look at her daughter.

"Can I have it now? I'm ever so hungry."

"In a minute. I just want to see the end of this set."

Jackie hangs up her school blazer and goes into the kitchen. She ties an apron round her waist and sets to work washing the breakfast dishes, along with Pamela's lunch dishes and sundry tea and coffee cups. She wipes down the Formica counter and the small kitchen table and vinyl-covered stools, empties ashtrays and wipes them out, then rinses the wash cloth. She puts the kettle on, because her mother is bound to want some tea. Pamela has left out the potatoes, lard, and a box of eggs. Jackie knows very well how to make egg and chips, but she can't get on with it because Pamela doesn't allow her to use the deep fat fryer on her own. She goes back into the living room.

"I'll start peeling the potatoes, shall I?"

Pamela has left her post on the sofa temporarily, and has gone into the bathroom to use the toilet. Jackie knows this because Pamela has left the door wide open and Jackie can see her from the kitchen doorway. She never bothers to close the door these days, and she doesn't like Jackie to close the door on her when its her turn to use the bathroom, saying "Come on, all girls together here, eh?" And then she laughs her bitter, cackling laugh. In fact these days Pamela has lost all modesty. She stumbles around the flat with her dressing gown open to reveal her underwear, and on one or two occasions with nothing on at all. She leaves her dirty panties and Tampax wrappings lying on the bathroom floor. Jackie tidies them up.

"Mum, shall I peel the potatoes?"

Pamela pees noisily, wipes herself, and comes back into the living room pulling up her panties. "I said *wait*, didn't I? I just want to see if Billie Jean is gong to win this set. Five minutes. . . ."

But the set goes to a tie-breaker, and Pamela doesn't want to miss out. She suggests that Jackie go out to play.

"Just go out and play with one of your friends for half an hour or so, and I'll make your tea the minute you get back, I promise."

Pamela doesn't seem to have realized that Jackie has no friends living nearby. The area of Hemingford where the Yardleys live is one of large, run-down houses divided into flats. Families with children prefer to live elsewhere, on the newer estates, leaving the flats to young childless couples and the elderly.

The old lady in the basement flat, a war widow, has a geriatric tom-cat. Jackie loves animals. She sits on the grass in the small communal garden and strokes its battered fur, talking to it in a soft, crooning voice. She doesn't have a watch, so it's difficult to tell when half an hour has gone by. She tries counting to sixty thirty times over, but loses track, and about thirty-five minutes have passed by the time she goes upstairs to the flat again.

Jackie finds Pamela scraping a plate of food into the kitchen bin. She stares at the egg-smeared plate with a sinking heart.

"Left it a bit late, didn't you?" Pamela's tone is acid. "This food's been sitting here for fifteen minutes. I gave up waiting in the end."

Jackie can see the clock on the kitchen wall, so she knows that she is not very late. She knows that her mother is irrational; she has experienced this behavior often enough. Inwardly she seethes with

•

anger, with the anger that has no voice. If she was a good mother, she would have given me my tea as soon as I got back from school, she tells herself. But if she protests, Pamela will only become worse, so she eats the one remaining slice of bread and margarine in silence and goes into her room to do her math homework.

Once she is alone, she takes Matthew Pryce-Jones's party invitation out of her satchel and looks at it thoughtfully. It would be nice to go to the party, wearing a pretty party dress like the other girls. But she doesn't dare even mention it to her mother. Pamela is having one of her strange moods today, which is awkward because there is something that she has to ask her, something that involves extra expense.

Jackie has always excelled in dancing at school; her light, fine-boned frame and unusual composure have made her an ideal pupil. Now she has been asked to join the school's special ballet class. An ex-ballerina comes to teach every Tuesday, and because it is an "extra," outside normal school hours, there is a charge for the classes, payable by the term. And of course she will need the proper equipment.

She waits until her mother has settled in front of the television with a cigarette, then summons her courage and emerges from her room.

"Mum . . ."

"Hmmm?"

"Mum, I've been chosen for Special Ballet at school."

Pamela says nothing for a few seconds. Jackie waits, frozen, unable to anticipate her reaction. She never knows how her mother will react.

"Who's a clever girl, then?" Pamela screeches, throwing her arms around Jackie in a hot, smoky embrace. "You must take after your old mum! I was a good dancer myself once."

"The thing is . . . I have to wear proper ballet shoes, pink or black, and a black leotard and ballet tights."

Pamela slumps back on the sofa, inhaling viciously on her cigarette. "God, more bloody money! Never mind, pet, we'll get you some dancing kit. I'll ask Granddad to find some for you."

"No!" Jackie can't hide the desperation in her voice. "It has to come from a special shop and everything. There's one in Brewer Street. If you just give me the money, I don't mind going by myself to get them, honest. Anyway, I'll have to try the shoes on because Madame says it's important they fit exactly right."

"Madame says ..." Pamela mimics her daughter in a breathy, affected voice. "All right, I'll have a word with your granddad about it. Now piss off to bed and leave me alone. I'm tired out."

Pamela sits on the sofa for at least an hour after Jackie has turned out her light, just lighting cigarette after cigarette and blowing the smoke up at the ceiling. Then she goes into her bedroom and wrenches the wardrobe door so hard that the handle almost comes off.

"Bloody hell!" she says when she sees the dismal collection of clothes hanging on the rail. "Bloody hell!"

She pulls the dresses and skirts out of the wardrobe and flings them to the floor, tears running down her cheeks as she does so. Then she flings herself onto the bed, sobbing loudly. She has an interview for a job the next morning but she has nothing to wear. If she looks a mess at the interview, she won't get the job, but if she can't get a job, how can she afford to buy something smart to wear? Billy did give her a couple of quid to go out and buy something, but she was feeling so dreadful that afternoon she just bought the first thing she saw; a tight A-line dress in shiny cherry red rayon. When she got it home she decided that she didn't really like it and it didn't fit her properly anyway. She picks up the red dress and savages it angrily, ripping it until the zipper comes away from the fabric.

Pamela has been out of work for eighteen months now. She lost her job as a filing clerk; sacked for incompetence. She didn't tell anybody that, not even Billy. She said that she handed in her notice because the pay and the hours were so dreadful. Which was true, anyway. Since then she has been subsisting on welfare payments and the odd handout from Billy, though he doesn't seem to make as much money as he used to. She has done the odd casual job too, a day here and a day there, working in shops and cafés mainly. Jackie gets her school dinners free and she eats like a bird anyway, never seems to grow out of her uniform the way other children do. And there's no longer any need to employ a childminder. . . .

These factors balance out to mean that Pamela is hardly any worse off than she was when she had the job. It's not the money that she misses. There is something else far more important that is lacking in her life. Self-respect.

Pamela sits up and gropes about under the bed. She fishes out a half empty bottle of brandy and a cardboard shoebox. Inside the box is her photograph of Jackie's father and the other mementos. She takes a mouthful of brandy, swilling it through her teeth before swallowing it.

"Norman bloody Butler!"

She screws up the photograph and hurls it onto the pile of dresses. Then she thinks for a moment and changes her mind; for Jackie's sake she ought not to destroy the only picture she has. She unscrews the photograph, smooths it out to the best of her ability and puts it back in the box. Then she sits down on the edge of the bed and takes several more large gulps of brandy.

Pamela is aware that she has lost control of her life somehow. She is also aware that this makes her a far worse mother than she would like to be. The problem is that the loss of control dates back to the precise moment when Jackie was born, and therefore as much as she loves her daughter, she can't help but resent her in equal measure. She wants Jackie to need her, but doesn't have the energy to meet those needs. And as Pamela's self-control lessens, her daughter's seems to increase, which fuels the resentment.

Pamela's mood dissolves into self-pity and she sits on the edge of the bed snivelling for a while. It is like this that Billy finds her when he drops round after closing time at the Pig. He comes round less often than he used to since the flat is not as comfortable a place as it once was. His daughter's inability to cope makes him uncomfortable, though he doesn't care to admit it.

"Oh, Dad!" Pamela bleats when she sees him. "Dad, I don't know what's the matter with me at the moment, I really don't. I'm just so down in the dumps!"

Billy looks round at the mess on the floor, but doesn't comment.

He searches around for an ashtray and perches it on the edge of the bedside table so that he can continue to smoke his cigar while administering paternal sympathy. His movements are slow and stiff as both his hip joints are arthritic. The thin strands of hair on his bald pate have turned from gray to white, or rather yellow, because his hair and his fingertips are heavily stained with nicotine. His bulbous nose is, in Billy's own words, "as purple as a baboon's bum."

He puts his arm around his daughter's shoulders. "Come on, pet, what's the matter? You didn't get that job you were after, is that it?"

"No ... I haven't even had the interview yet, that's tomorrow. . . . I don't know what it is, Dad, just ignore me anyway. It's probably just my time of the month or something . . ."

"Come on, it must be more than that! Look at you ... look at this ..." Billy waves his cigar at the heap of clothes on the floor.

"I don't know ..." Pamela takes the bottle from Billy, who has been helping himself. "It's everything. It's this place, it's always such a bloody tip ... I've got no job, no money, no decent clothes to wear ... and then there's Jackie. . . ."

"Our Jackie? But she's such a good girl, my princess! So quiet and so helpful."

"I know, I know ..." Pamela sighs. "But at her age kids are always wanting something, it's 'me, me, me' all the time. The latest thing is ballet lessons. She's got into a ballet class at school, and she has to have special dancing kit ... I don't know, these things all cost money and I don't like to say no to her all the time—"

"Quite right! And a smashing little dancer she's going to be, too!" Billy is overtaken by a bronchitic cough that sends a shower of cigar ash onto the bedspread. "Look, you've already got enough on your plate with the interview tomorrow. Why don't I take the little one into town after school and sort her out? Just leave it all to me."

Jackie is not happy at the prospect of a shopping trip with her grandfather. This is exactly what she was dreading, what she hoped to avoid by offering to buy her dancing equipment herself. Billy won't know what to buy, or understand the subtleties that distinguish looking like a ballet dancer from not looking like a ballet dancer. And Jackie desperately wants to look like a ballet dancer. More importantly, she doesn't want to stand out. She wears a white blouse to school now, like everyone else. That's the way it has been for three years, and she doesn't even mind that she had to save up all her pocket money to buy exactly the one she wanted. Being the same as everyone else is all that matters.

So it is with a sinking feeling that she follows Billy around Woolworths that afternoon, a small, silent figure in his shambling, arthritic wake. She knows—has known for some time—that her grandfather has no idea at all about color or form, no appreciation of quality. She feels ashamed of him even though she loves him. The lining is hanging down from his velvet-collared overcoat, and his brown hat is spotted with grease marks.

They find ballet shoes, cheap ones but in the right color. Woolworths has no leotards or tights in her size, so they go and look in Taylor & Haddon, which lifts Jackie's spirits marginally; at least their goods are of decent quality.

There are no black leotards in her size, there won't be until the next order arrives. Jackie knows they could buy one at the dancewear shop in Brewer Street, but Billy has said that he can't walk that far with his dicky hips. He is already puffing and wheezing loudly.

"I'll wait, then," says Jackie. "I'll wait until the next order comes in."

But Billy has just noticed a small rack in the corner and limps over to take a look.

"Look, princess! These are them what-do-you-call-'ems—leotards—aren't they?"

They are: bright turquoise and shiny, the kind worn for gymnastics.

"These will do, won't they?" Billy takes one off the rack and examines it. "Just the job. This one's your size. I'll go and pay for it, shall I?"

"No." Jackie stands stock still, speaks in a small, firm voice.

Billy stares at her, stunned. "What did you say?"

"No. I don't want that one. It's a horrid color and I don't like it."

Billy's disbelief is giving way to irritation. "There's nothing wrong with it, my girl, don't be so silly! Now come on, I haven't got all day!"

He turns to go to the cash register, fully expecting Jackie to follow, but she stands as still as a statue in the middle of the children's department, her little pointed face white with rage.

"I want a black leotard. We're supposed to wear black ones." Still she doesn't move. Two tears appear in the corner of her eyes and start to roll slowly down her cheeks.

Billy is dismayed: the child never cries. He puts a hand on her shoulder and bends stiffly so that his face is at her level.

"Princess . . . come on, we've got to get this thing bought. I promised your mum we'd get you sorted out, and we can't go back to her empty-handed, now can we? We don't want to go upsetting her after her interview. If she hasn't got the job she won't be happy. You want your mum to think you've been a good girl, don't you?" He employs a wheedling tone, feeling confident that mention of Pamela will bring the child into line. She's so obedient, so eager to please her mother. But Jackie just cries even harder. She doesn't seem able to stop, not even when Billy capitulates and asks the assistant to reserve a black leotard in Jackie's size. She just stands there on the same spot, tears pouring down her cheeks, the whole of her thin body shaking. As her sobs grow louder people begin to notice, turning to stare as they pass, tut-tutting under their breath.

Billy is becoming increasingly desperate. He rubs the inside of his shirt collar where he is sweating profusely.

"Ssssh, *please*, sweetheart! What on earth's the matter? You've got the black leotard, haven't you? What else do you want?"

"A party dress."

Jackie interrupts her sobs long enough to make herself heard quite plainly. She is enjoying this unprecedented fit of crying. Even more surprising, it seems to be producing results. Billy is now so terrified and so anxious to return the child to her mother that he capitulates immediately and tells Jackie in a faint voice that she can choose any party dress she likes. She picks out a traditional frock of the Shirley Temple variety, made from a shiny primrose fabric that makes little scratching sounds as it moves. It has a white satin sash and rows of frills round the skirt. Jackie has never owned anything like it before and her delight shines out all over her face. Billy can't help but enjoy her obvious pleasure, even though the dress used up most of the fiver he was planning on drinking that night at the Pig.

Jackie falls back into her habitual silence on the way home, clutching her Taylor & Haddon bag to her tightly as if afraid it will be snatched. She is glad about the dress, but disturbed about the lesson it has taught her. It seems that if you keep quiet and behave like a good girl, it gives people the right to ignore you. But if you make a fuss and frighten them you end up being given exactly what you want.

F i f t e e n

■

The day of Matthew Pryce-Jones's party dawns. It is the ideal midsummer day, dry and still with a few wisps of high cloud scudding across a hot, blue sky.

At Albert Road Mixed Infants, the children fidget their way through their lessons. During dinner break, some poor unfortunate overcome by the combination of unaccustomed heat and ice cream for pudding, vomits onto the scalding tarmac of the playground. A bucket of sawdust kept in the corridor for just such a purpose is scattered over the offending pool by the janitor. This fails to dampen the smell, which wafts through the classroom windows during afternoon lessons.

At number 9 Mount Rise, Audrey Pryce-Jones starts her preparations for the barbecue. They begin with a trip to Paolo of Rome to have her hair washed and set by Clive, and while she is in the town center, she pops into the supermarket to pick up some last minute purchases, including the frozen ice cream gateau which is to act as Matthew's birthday cake. She returns to the house in the middle of the morning, and after a quick cup of coffee, dons bikini and rubber gloves and takes the transistor radio out into the garden. She sweeps the patio and arranges the tables around the barbecue, wishing she had done all this before her hair appointment, as the heat is damping her forehead with sweat and making her fringe go frizzy.

She also wishes they had a swimming pool in the garden. Not only would she have been able to cool off after her endeavors, but when the hordes of children arrived that afternoon (nineteen of the

115

twenty-five accepted), a swimming pool would have acted as built-in entertainment. She and Ken did discuss having a pool put in that year, but Ken was against it on the grounds that the only available position would be under the ornamental willow tree, so it would always be full of leaves. Audrey had countered this argument by volunteering to chop down the willow tree, but then Ken had said the weather would never be good enough to use it.

Well, Ken was wrong, wasn't he, thought Audrey as she pushed the yard broom to and fro with angry little movements. What he had meant was *he* wouldn't get the chance to use a swimming pool, because he was never at home for more than five minutes. He was supposed to be leaving work early this afternoon, to help with the party, but Audrey fully expected him to be late. Probably be dawdling at the office to chat up one of his dolly birds.

Audrey stabs at the corner of the patio with the broom. She knows that he carries on with other women. She has suspected this for quite a long time, ten years or more, but never liked to admit it to herself. She didn't like the thought that Ken, her wonderful handsome Kenneth, was anything less than perfect. But eventually it became too obvious for her to pretend any more. Audrey is a woman with an eye for detail; she notices little things. And it is the little things that give Ken away. Not lipstick on his collar, not quite as corny as that, but clichés nonetheless. Answering the phone at length, then telling her it was a wrong number. Saying he has gone out somewhere during office hours, then failing to make sure his secretary gets her story right. And working late; lots of that.

Whereas a decade ago the idea of infidelity would have been too awful to contemplate, now it doesn't bother her very much. It is not just that Audrey aspires to being swinging and sophisticated, but because she's not sure she can really be bothered to strive for the perfect marriage any more, and Ken's little flings save her having to make the effort. She is sure that they are little flings rather than love affairs. He doesn't act moody or withdrawn or stricken, he's simply away from home more than usual. Audrey finds this intensely irritating. He can do what he wants with other women as long as it doesn't interfere with her own plans.

After she has cleared up the terrace, Audrey goes back into the kitchen and prepares salads to the accompaniment of some light classical music. She makes herself a cold chicken sandwich for lunch, with a second cup of coffee, then takes a few minutes' break to paint her toenails and fingernails fuchsia pink. When the polish is dry, she telephones Baring Baker and leaves a message with Ken's secretary, reminding him of the time of Matthew's party. At two-thirty she takes the ice cream gateau out of the freezer and leaves it on the table to thaw.

At two-thirty the pupils of Class Two are just beginning a math lesson with Miss Rudd. Math is the least popular subject in the curriculum, not only because of the dry and uninspiring syllabus, but also because of its teacher. Miss Rudd, who has driven hundreds of five-year-olds to school refusal during her career, can still silence a class with a look. She loves her subject, and despises the children for their slow minds when they cannot grasp logarithms and matrices. But she can abide laughter least of all. The wrong answer to an equation moves her to contempt, but sniggering fills her with rage.

It is unfortunate, therefore, that one of her pupils chooses today to make his classmates laugh, the day of Matthew Pryce-Jones's party, to which they are all invited after school. This pupil is Keith, a fat, loutish boy who is one of Matthew's best friends. The sickening smell of vomit is wafting through the open windows from the playground, and when Miss Rudd's back is turned, Keith is miming vomiting in response. He makes a melodramatic performance of it; with a lot of heaving and eyeball rolling. The other children giggle discreetly, and some of the boys imitate Keith's retching movements. Keith is so overcome by the success of his performance that he breaks wind loudly, reducing the rest of the class to hysterical laughter.

Miss Rudd swings round from the blackboard, poised with chalk in hand.

"Who was that?" she demands in a low voice.

There is silence, apart from the faint background whine from the nearby biscuit factory.

"I'll ask you again ... who made that ... that noise?" Fat Keith has turned very red in the face, but he knows that it's worth avoiding one of Miss Rudd's canings if he possibly can. He also knows that the others will feel far too much sympathy to tell tales.

"Very well ... since none of you is going to own up, you will all be punished. Two hours detention tonight after school, the whole class."

The children exchange glances; their looks saying *"But what about the party?"*

Matthew climbs bravely to his feet and raises his hand.

"Please, Miss Rudd ..."

"What is it, Pryce-Jones?"

"Please ... it's my birthday today and I'm having a party. Everyone is invited, and if they're in detention, they won't be able to come."

"Everyone? The whole of Class Two?"

"Yes."

A flicker of a smile passes across Miss Rudd's face. If she were ever to stoop to having a favorite, it would definitely be Matthew Pryce-Jones. Even she is not impervious to his good looks and exceptional charm. Besides, she knows better than to incur the wrath of the parents, and have the headmistress examine her methods of applying discipline.

"I see. Well, since you're all taken up by this pressing social engagement, there will be a change of plan. Instead of doing the extra work in detention, you can do it at home instead.... What time does your party end, Pryce-Jones?"

"Seven, Miss Rudd."

"Plenty of time for you to do Exercises Twelve and Thirteen before you go to bed. I want them in my locker by nine o'clock tomorrow morning. And if any of you haven't done them, you will be in detention tomorrow."

Audrey Pryce-Jones is disappointed when Stephen Noble arrives at the party without his elegant, Jaguar-driving mother, but in the company of an elderly lady who must be a nanny or a housekeeper.

"She had to be at home this afternoon," Stephen says when Audrey makes her enquiry into Sylvia's whereabouts. "Someone was coming to see her. I think it was the swimming pool man. We're having a swimming pool built in the garden, on the terrace, I think."

"Oh, I see ... did you hear that, Matthew darling? Stephen's going to have a pool in his garden ... How lovely!"

Audrey makes a mental note to resurrect the subject of a swimming pool with Ken.

Mrs. Moody has brought Stephen straight from school, so he is the first to arrive, and far too early. Matthew ignores Stephen to begin with, and Audrey observes that Stephen, who is clearly an abnormally timid child, seems frightened of her son. The mention of the forthcoming swimming pool arouses Matthew's interest and prompts him to ask if Stephen would like to play his new war game. But Stephen refuses. He has his satchel of school books with him, and he asks Audrey politely it he could get on with his math while they are waiting for the party to start. He sits at the kitchen table with a glass of Tizer, working his way through exercises Twelve and Thirteen.

Every so often he looks up from his books to watch Matthew, who is swinging from a rope ladder in the garden, dressed only in a pair of football shorts. He hooks his legs through the top rung and swings upside down, like Tarzan. With his naked chest and his thighs tanned golden brown, he seems an impossibly glamorous figure to Stephen. He admires Matthew with such a passion that it makes him tongue-tied and shy. Matthew's physical beauty and confidence place him far out of reach. Besides, he knows Matthew thinks he is a "digger," the Albert Road word for a swot and a weakling.

Stephen is bright and the math exercises pose no particular problem for him. By the time the other children start to arrive, he has finished the work. Carolyn Fox is also among the first. She is brought by her mother, who is on her way to a job interview and can't afford to be late. Jean is looking exceptionally smart; she is wearing a suit and has had her hair set that morning. Carolyn is sulking. Jean feels that trousers are the sensible attire for a barbecue party, and since no brightly colored bell-bottoms have been forthcoming, this means the hated slacks with loops under the feet. They are far too hot for this sultry afternoon, and even Jean is moved to wonder whether she should have decided on a pair of shorts when she sees her daughter's flushed face. Carolyn's pink cheeks are emphasized by her red head-band, which she insisted on tying round her forehead and now adds to her general discomfort.

Nothing would have kept Carolyn away from the party; she fancies Matthew (as do most of the girls in Class Two). She racks her brains, trying to find a way to get his attention; just as difficult here as it is at school. Her plain appearance won't achieve this, so it must be her behavior instead. Subtlety will be lost on a ten-year-old boy, so she opts for the loudest and most uncouth behavior she is capable of.

She snatches a handful of crisps from the table, and after chasing Matthew round the garden, yelling like a Red Indian, she shoves them down the front of his shorts. Matthew chases her angrily for five seconds, then gets bored with the idea and runs off in the opposite direction with Dave and fat Keith. Audrey makes a mental note not to invite Carolyn again.

Jackie Yardley is one of the last to arrive, brought by Billy, who was late collecting her from Pamela's flat. If Audrey is a little put off by Billy's purple, wheezing visage and the scent of stale cigars, she is enchanted by Jackie, who is exactly the sort of little girl she would have liked to have herself. She is dressed in the yellow frilly party dress, with her soft, fair hair in a pony tail, as dainty and feminine as a doll. She lingers in the kitchen with Audrey, answering her questions in a quiet, unexpectedly low-pitched voice. Before she eats anything, she spreads a paper napkin over her frilly skirt.

After he had left his granddaughter at 9 Mount Rise, Billy Yardley faces a long walk back to the bus stop. He finds it difficult to make progress; he is walking into the sun and it seems to leap out of the scorching sky and blind him. He is perspiring profusely and the heat is making his chest close up tightly, leaving him short of breath. Before he gets to the junction with London Road, he has to sit down on a low wall and take a rest. When he closes his eyes, the sun pervades the blackness with exploding points of light.

Carolyn Fox is staring at Jackie Yardley's party dress. One half of her brain is thinking, How sissy and wet to wear a frilly baby's dress to a barbecue! While the other retaliates with, It's not *fair*! Why should she be pretty when I'm not, why should she have things that I don't have? She would be surprised to know that Jackie envies her at least as much as she envies Jackie. Jackie would like to have Carolyn's ordinary, stable family life, with a brother and a sister and a house and a garden. She would like to have Carolyn's confidence and bravado.

It is in Carolyn's nature to covet; she must have what other people have. Therefore, although she knows that a frilly yellow party dress would not suit her, and she is not even sure that she likes it anyway, she wants to get her hands on it. She lies in wait for Jackie at the top of the stairs and ambushes her on her way out of the bathroom.

"Hey, Jackie?"

"What?"

"I like that dress."

Jackie smiles, uncertain how to interpret this overture.

"I've got an idea. Something really good we could do. Something funny."

"What?"

"Let's change clothes. I'll put on your dress, and you can put on my trousers, and we can go and surprise the others."

Jackie says nothing for a moment. Carolyn is already taking off her T-shirt. She wrongly assumes that Jackie is like her friend Helen Croucher, because she is quiet. But Jackie is not so easily manipulated.

"I don't think so," she says.

"Oh, come on, don't be wet! Why not?"

"Because I don't think the dress will fit you."

This much is obvious; Carolyn is three inches taller than Jackie and nearly twice as broad.

"Oh, go on! Just to see what it looks like. You can have it back afterward."

Jackie does not want to hand over her precious dress under any circumstances. On the other hand, she would like to be friends with Carolyn.

"Okay then."

The two girls go into Audrey and Ken's bedroom, and with a lot of giggling on Carolyn's part, they undress and change clothes. Even Jackie starts to laugh when she sees Carolyn in the yellow dress. It is so tight that it can't be fastened, and her arms hang immobile at her sides like a gorilla's. The skirt ends several inches above the knee. The legs of Carolyn's slacks cover Jackie's shoes and trail on the ground behind her, and the red bandana slips down over her eyes.

When Carolyn has finished jumping up and down in front of the mirror making ape noises, and the giggling has subsided, she agrees to Jackie's suggestion that they change back again before they go downstairs. She recognizes that being seen by Matthew while she looks like a gorilla in a baby's dress will not enhance her allure. As she removes the dress she tears it slightly. To divert Jackie's attention, she says, "Hey, Jackie, we could be friends. At school, I mean. What do you think?"

"Yes please," said Jackie.

Ken Pryce-Jones still has not arrived, so the team games that he is detailed to organize have not yet begun. The children are swarming all over the garden in a chaotic fashion and Audrey is getting a headache from the heat and the noise.

Stephen Noble watches from the sidelines, admiring Matthew from afar. Matthew's mother has pleaded with him to organize a game so Matthew has devised one called Kiss Train. The train, a chain of children linked by hands on the waist, bugs around the lawn making frequent stops at different "stations." At each stop another child joins the chain, alternating boys and girls. And at each stop the first boy turns and kisses the first girl, who turns and kisses the second boy, who turns and kisses the second girl, and so on. Thus the player who does the most kissing is the boy at the head of the train: Matthew, naturally.

All the girls would like to be chosen by Matthew, but the one he selects to ride behind him is Jackie Yardley. Her yellow dress catches his eye, and because of her shyness, she is the only pretty girl in the class he hasn't yet kissed in the playground. Jackie would like to refuse this honor but can't, and the other players enjoy her discomfiture, laughing, clapping, and whistling every time Matthew turns to plant another kiss on her cheek.

All except Carolyn Fox, who is furious. She knew that Matthew wouldn't pick her, but she didn't want Jackie to be chosen, not now they are supposed to be friends. In her mind, the friendship is instantaneously dissolved. When Jackie tries to catch her eye and share her embarrassment as she chugs past, Carolyn pointedly turns her head away. By the fourth kiss, she has branded Jackie a traitor.

Matthew's father has just arrived, which means the sensible games are about to begin. If Carolyn is to claim Matthew's attention before the party is over, she will have to resort to some extreme measure. Accordingly, she disengages her hands from the waist of fat Keith, who picked her for the train, and darts off into the house. She spotted Matthew's schoolbag in the hall when she arrived, and she goes there now and removes his math books.

"Hey, Pryce-Jones!" she shouts, standing in the middle of the lawn and letting the Kiss Train wind round her. "Look what I've got!" She waves the books under his nose.

"Hey!"

Matthew pushes Jackie's hands roughly from his waist and runs after Carolyn, leaving the train to straggle to a halt. "Foxie, you fat cow, give those back! That's the work we've got to do for Rudd tonight!"

"I know!" says Carolyn, laughing. She flaps the pages in his face, then darts away from him. Stephen, who has not yet been picked for the train, intercepts her and tries to rescue the books.

"Get off, Noble, you bloody digger!" shouts Carolyn. She is far stronger than him and wrenches his fingers from her wrist. As Matthew catches up with her she breaks free and hurls the books into the ornamental fish pond.

At that precise moment, Jean Fox is leaving the offices of the Hemingford Co-operative Society where she has just attended an interview. They need an assistant manager in Catering, part time, which means someone to run the works canteen. Jean wonders whether it will be a little too like standing around in her own kitchen all day long.

Still, no point worrying about that, if she doesn't even know whether or not she will be offered the job. The man who interviewed her was very friendly, but that didn't necessarily mean anything, did it? It is difficult for Jean to know, because she has never had a job before, unless you count a Saturday job in a sweet shop when she was sixteen. When she left school, she helped her father and uncle in their small lumber business, keeping the books straight and sending out the bills, then she met Les and got married, and that was it. You automatically gave up your job when you married, in those days. The jobs were there for the men, so that they could make Britain great again. The women were supposed to stay at home and raise the children who were going to inherit all this wealth.

As Jean walks back to the bus stop she tries to picture what it will be like going out to work. Not that it's very likely she'll get the job. The more time that elapses since the interview, the more she convinces herself that she doesn't stand a chance. She began the afternoon with her confidence on a high, boosted by her gloves and her lipstick and her shampoo-and-set. She can pinpoint the moment of tailing off to when she arrived with Carolyn at the party. To the precise moment when that Mrs. Pryce-Jones opened the front door, in fact. Standing there with her suntan and her trendy geometric haircut and her skimpy dress in electric pink, she made Jean feel suddenly frumpy and middle-aged. The two women must be roughly contemporary, but Jean looks twice as old.

Well, whether she gets the job or not, she can still change the way she looks, can't she? When she gets off the bus, Jean makes a small detour to the little hair salon near the park, the place she went to that morning for her shampoo-and-set.

"Did you leave something behind, Mrs. Fox?" asks the receptionist.

"No, I'd like to make another appointment, please."

"That's fine. I'll put you down for a shampoo-and-set, then ... when would you like to come in?"

"Not a shampoo-and-set. I'm going to have it all cut off...."

But what will Les think? Her brain throws up the old conditioned response. Whatever he thinks, she tells herself firmly, he'll just have to lump it.

Sylvia Noble and Roger Saunders are in Sylvia and Geoffrey's bedroom, getting dressed.

"Was that all right for you, my dear?" asks Roger.

"Yes ... it was very nice."

As soon as she hears herself say this, Sylvia realizes how silly it sounds, but she can't think of any other suitable adjective, except pleasant, perhaps. No, pleasant is even worse. She and Roger have spent the afternoon having rather awkward sex in the silent, empty house. Awkward because of their embarrassment, and because neither of them is very good at it. Still, Sylvia expects they will get better, and less embarrassed. And it was rather nice, lying there afterward in Roger's strong, tanned arms, with the curtains drawn to keep out the hot sun, and listening to him tell her how beautiful she is, and how soft, and how he adores her.

Yet somehow the past two hours do not conform to her idea of how illicit sex would be. She puts this down to something that happened earlier in the day, and as she lies in Roger's arms she cannot prevent her mind wandering back to the incident. She was lying outside in her bathing costume, her sun-lounger positioned amongst the rubble that is to be the pool terrace. Her eyes were closed but she became aware of someone watching her. One of the builders had come back to collect his jacket.

She turned over onto her stomach and started to read a magazine. He stood still looking at her. "Nice arse," he said.

It had never occurred to her that the backside was a part of the anatomy that could be either good or bad. And later, when she stood up to go in, she saw a magazine lying on the terrace. She went to pick it up, thinking that it was one of hers, but found instead that it was a hard porn magazine belonging to the builders. Left there in full view as a provocative gesture, no doubt. Her heart pounding, she had picked it up and looked at it. Lots of photographs, color photographs, of people doing obscene things. Impossible things. One photo in particular she cannot now banish from her mind's eye. A tall Negro with his erect member thrust deep into the mouth of a young girl kneeling submissively before him.

When she and Roger are in the bathroom together, tidying themselves up before going downstairs, Sylvia cranes her neck to try and see her buttocks in the mirror.

"Roger ... do you think I've got a nice bottom?"

"Of course." He blushes a little. "Everything about you is lovely."

"What's lovely about it?" she persists.

"Well ... it's shapely, I suppose."

"Roger, could we ... what about oral sex? Would you like me to put your ... in my mouth?"

Roger becomes very flustered, though he pretends not to be. He adjusts his cravat in the mirror to avoid looking at her. "I have to say, that I don't tend to go in for that sort of thing very much."

"Oh, I see ... A cup of tea then, perhaps?" she suggests.

"That would be very acceptable, my dear, yes please." Roger opens the bathroom door for her with a small bow.

The two of them sit on the shaded terrace amongst the rubble and sip lemon tea from fine bone china. The pornographic magazine has gone now. They talk politely about the unusually hot weather and discuss the climate in Italy, where they will be conducting their ménage à trois in a month's time. Both of them pretend that Sylvia never made her impromptu offer of fellatio.

At 6:18, the time of Geoffrey's evening train home, Sylvia looks at her watch. It is a habit, something she does at that time every day without even thinking. Today it reminds her that she must soon go and collect Stephen from his party, and that life must return to a semblance of normality before Geoffrey's train reaches Hemingford. She thinks of the empty champagne bottle and the two glasses that are standing on Geoffrey's dresser in the bedroom.

Roger notices that she is fidgeting, and gets to his feet.

"Time for me to take my leave, my dear ..." He kisses her on both cheeks and then once, softly, on her lips. *"Au revoir."* He smiles. "But not, I think, *adieu* ..."

After he has gone, Sylvia would like to drift around the house, to remember and reflect, but there is no time. She finds her shoes and handbag and takes the Jaguar to Mount Rise to collect Stephen. He has patches of sunburn on his nose and cheeks and says he has enjoyed himself. He seems to want to tell her about the party, but Sylvia is preoccupied. When they return to the house, there is no need to feed Stephen, who is full of sausages and birthday cake, so she suggests that he get on with his homework and goes to sit alone in her room and worry about Roger's reluctance to engage in oral sex. Did that make him abnormal, or was it her?

Stephen can't do his homework: he realizes on the journey home that he has left his schoolbag and all his books, including the extra math exercises, at the Pryce-Jones house. But his mother is in a strange mood and doesn't seem to want to speak to him. He doesn't dare tell her what he has done, because she will be cross if she has to get in the car again and go and collect his bag. He thinks of phoning Mrs. Pryce-Jones and telling her, but the idea of doing so makes his heart pound and his mouth dry up. Instead he has to pin his hopes on Matthew bringing the bag to school in the morning.

Pamela Yardley spends the afternoon in a listless void. The Wimbledon tournament is over, and there is nothing else worth watching on the television. The flat is unbearably warm and stuffy, so she puts on her shoes and goes to sit in the nearby park. The word "park" is something of an aggrandizement; it is a scrubby patch of grass littered with dog shit, with some benches and children's swings at one end.

She thinks she had better stay out of the flat for a while, just in case Billy comes round checking up on her after he has left Jackie. She told him she would go and follow up some of the jobs advertised in last night's edition of the Hemingford *Evening Mail*. She wasn't offered the last job she applied for. She told Billy it was because they were looking for someone younger, but the truth is that she didn't even go to the interview. She had a terrible headache that morning, and persuaded herself there was no point going because she wasn't going to get the job anyway.

After half an hour, Pamela is thirsty and decides to go home. There is a note pinned onto the front door of the flat when she returns, from her landlady.

Telephone message for Miss Yardley: Your father has been taken ill, will you please contact Ward 9, Hemingford General.

This is ridiculous, thinks Pamela, Dad's not ill. She has only seen him a couple of hours earlier and he was perfectly all right. Dad's never ill. . . .

There is no phone in the flat, and she can't find the landlady to use hers, so she decides she may as well visit the hospital in person and find out what has happened. Maybe he has just tripped and twisted his ankle; he's not too steady on his feet these days. She begins to walk, and can't help hurrying, all sorts of horrible ideas occurring to her as she draws nearer the hospital. What if . . . ? She blows the last few shillings in her purse on riding in a taxi for the last half-mile.

The air in the hospital is cloying with the smell of sweat and disinfectant, making Pamela feel frightened. She is directed to the sister's office at the end of a long ward on the top floor. There are no windows, so even on this hot July afternoon, the place is artificially lit; bare light bulbs dangling from the ceiling.

"Where's Dad?" she asks the nurse. "Mr. Yardley. Can I see him?"

"Ah, yes . . . You must be Mrs. . . ?"

"Miss Yardley."

"Right . . . There are one or two things I had better explain to you before you see him. You see, he's had a stroke. . . ."

Billy is lying at a strange angle in the bed, wearing a white backless gown. His head is tilted and dribble is running from the corner of his mouth. His face is pale except for his nose, which is still purple, giving him a clownish look.

"Dad." Pamela clutches at his hand. "Dad . . . what on earth have you done?"

He tries to smile, but can't. The nurse explains to Pamela that the stroke has affected the left side of his body, which is temporarily paralyzed. It has also affected his speech. But it was a minor stroke and he will probably be able to go home in about a week.

"Perhaps you'd like to go and fetch him some things?" the nurse asks Pamela. "A sponge bag and some pyjamas."

"Yes . . ." says Pamela. She is dazed, unable to think. "I suppose I could. I would have to catch a bus from here, the twelve, I think . . . Oh no!" She suddenly remembers. "My daughter!"

"You have a daughter, Miss Yardley? Where is she?"

"She's at a bloody birthday party ... excuse my language—and there's no one to go and get her. Dad was going to go."

"I'll tell you what, you give me the name and address of the family who are holding the party, and I'll telephone them and see if something can be sorted out. I'm sure there'll be someone who can help. One of her friends, perhaps."

"I doubt it," said Pamela. "She doesn't have any." The nurse is giving her a strange look, and she feels she needs to qualify this callous remark. "She's very shy, you see, our Jackie."

Jackie has never felt so mortified in her life as she does when the phone rings in the middle of the barbecue and Mrs. Pryce-Jones tells her in front of all the others, "Jacqueline dear, your grandfather's been taken ill and your mother wondered if we could make some other arrangement for you to get home tonight."

Audrey doesn't mention the hospital as she doesn't want to frighten or upset Jackie. So Jackie imagines that her mother has been drinking, or that Billy has been detained in the Pig and Whistle. The others all stare at her and she feels her cheeks burning with shame. She hopes perhaps that Carolyn will take pity on her and offer her a lift home, but Carolyn has become cold toward her all of a sudden. It seems she was only pretending when she claimed she wanted to be friends.

So Jackie has to suffer the further indignity of being taken home by Mr. Pryce-Jones, with Matthew and his younger brother sitting in the back of the car sniggering and thumping each other. No one from Albert Road has ever seen where she lives, and she is worried that Matthew will make belittling remarks about the place when they are at school tomorrow.

He doesn't. First, it would never occur to Matthew to even notice what sort of house Jackie lived in, unless it happened to be particularly grand, and secondly, the pupils of Class Two have other things on their mind, namely Miss Rudd's extra math. At quarter to nine that morning, they congregate in the cloakroom, where coats and school-bags are hung and confidences are exchanged. There is much last-minute scribbling in the blue math exercise books, and whispered consultations about the correct answers. Then the books are deposited in the locker outside the staff room, where the teachers collect their marking, and Class Two await the verdict and sentencing during their eleven o'clock lesson with Miss Rudd.

Miss Rudd has hayfever and is not disposed to be charitable. "Twenty exercise books," she says, slamming the pile down on her desk. "And there should be twenty-four. Sarah Dent can be excused on the grounds that she is off sick today, but what about the other three?"

Nervous glances are exchanged: should they own up?

"No need to put up your hands, I have the list here . . ." Miss Rudd puts on her half-moon spectacles and reads through the register. "Stephen Noble . . . I must say, Noble, I'm surprised at you . . . Well, I'm waiting."

"I lost my books." Stephen's cheeks blush bright pink with the fib. Matthew forgot to bring Stephen's satchel to school, but Stephen dare not name him for fear of being labeled a digger and a tattletale and being beaten up in the playground.

"Detention for you then. Matthew Pryce-Jones . . . I suppose you think your birthday excuses you?"

"No, Miss. My books met with an accident, Miss."

"An *accident?*"

Matthew grins. "They were thrown in the pond at my party."

"I see." Miss Rudd shuts her mouth so tightly that her lips almost disappear. "Would you care to tell me who perpetrated this act?"

"Carolyn Fox, Miss." Matthew turns to Carolyn and gives her a look of triumph. She sticks her tongue out at him.

"Yes, well, that doesn't surprise me. Detention for you too tonight, Fox."

Carolyn grins. She's glad to be in detention, it means she will have a chance to make Matthew notice her. They will be alone together for a whole hour, except for Soppy Stevie, of course, but he hardly counts.

"There was one other offender—" Miss Rudd looks down the list. "Ah yes, Jacqueline Yardley. I had you down as more conscientious. However, as you've had no previous detentions, and I understand that there are some problems at home at the moment, you may take the extra work home with you and do it there."

Jackie half raises her hand. "Miss Rudd ... it's all right. About detention, I mean. I'll do the extra work here."

"Goody goody!" mutters Carolyn.

Jackie is only too glad of the chance not to go home. She can't face the thought of an evening listening to Pamela crying and moaning about Billy, as she did last night. And she is afraid. At the back of her mind is the terrible thought that her tantrum over the leotard might have been the cause of her grandfather's stroke, and she doesn't want to be there when Pamela makes the connection.

"Right, so the following will be in detention tonight between four and five: Carolyn Fox, Stephen Noble, Matthew Pryce-Jones, and Jacqueline Yardley."

the

S

erenties

moving on

S i x t e e n

■

Carolyn

As she enters her teens, Carolyn Fox becomes aware that the balance of power in her parents' marriage is shifting. Her father, whose wishes and opinions were dominant during her early childhood, seems to be diminishing in stature. Jean, on the other hand, gains more influence and more of a voice as the months go past.

Carolyn's adolescent preoccupation with herself is so great that for a long time she doesn't really notice this happening. She just thinks of her mother as timid and boring, with nothing to talk about except the neighbors and the weather. Then one evening when she is upstairs in her room playing her T. Rex album over and over again on her portable record player, another sound clashes with the strains of Marc Bolan singing "Children of the Revolution." It is her mother shouting. Carolyn turns down the volume knob and listens just to be sure. She is astounded, not by the noise, but by the realization that she has never heard her mother raise her voice before.

From then on, she begins to notice things more. When she thinks about the situation, she decides that two factors have contributed to Les losing ground; his mother's failing health and Jean's job. Winnie has surprised everyone, including herself, by being diagnosed as having a weak heart. She would have despised and pooh-poohed such a vague condition in anyone else, but since this is her and not someone else, she plays the part of the helpless invalid to the hilt. Les spends a lot of time at her house, doing the things for her that she claims she cannot do herself, like changing light bulbs. ("Oh, I can't, you know, not with my weak heart.") And Winnie is unable to visit Tudor

Avenue very often, so cannot undermine Jean and boost Les's self-importance by listening to his tales from the biscuit factory.

And now, in 1973, Jean has been going out to work herself for four years. She got the job at the Co-op, and was quickly promoted to manager when her qualities of calm, efficiency, and common sense were recognized. Her years as Les Fox's drudge have smoothed her personality traits to a bland uniformity, but this blandness works to her advantage. There is nothing about Jean that anyone could possibly object to, she never demonstrates favoritism or partiality, and everyone enjoys working with her. She received a second promotion to Head of Catering Services, and from there moved first to Assistant Director of Personnel and then regional Director of Personnel. By now she is working full time, leaving the children to fend for themselves when they are home from school. She has her own office now, and her own secretary too.

Carolyn thinks about the implications of these changes, but does not let them divert her for long from the chief business of being a fourteen-year-old girl, which means thinking about yourself, rock music, and sex, though not necessarily in that order. She and her girlfriends from Hemingford Comprehensive spend much of their time mooching around the shopping center in the town, keeping a weather eye on Hemingford's adolescent male population. Evenings are for going to the cinema, or discos at the youth club, or hanging around outside the fish and chip shop, with the occasional piece of homework fitted in between these activities. And when all of the above fail, Carolyn just lies on her bed surrounded by her posters of David Cassidy, Sweet, and Mott the Hoople, thinking about the heady world outside Hemingford, dreaming of escape.

She is lying on her unmade bed one Friday evening, with her record player turned up as loud as possible to drown out Martin's Deep Purple album and the sounds of argument from the kitchen. There is a disco at the youth club tonight and she wants to go, but she has the curse and her face is covered with spots; she feels and looks terrible. She wishes she were prettier, she wishes this constantly, and her inability to change how she is fills her with rage and frustration, a sort of inbuilt spitefulness against the rest of the world for dealing her such a mean share of physical loveliness. The idea that personality matters more than looks is lost on the fourteen-year-old Caroyln as it is on most of her contemporaries; this truth requires a maturity that they simply have not yet achieved. The only criterion for judgment in their man-watching escapades is how good-looking the subject is. It doesn't matter if his personality is a cross between Shylock and Bluebeard as long as he is good-looking.

Carolyn knows that she is not, and that her only hope is for her manner to be either so bumptious or so cool that she tricks boys into liking her. At fourteen she is still no more than middling height and her body is stocky and thick-set. The fashion is for girls to be fair and wide-eyed and doll-like, with their hair flicked back off their faces in neat waves. Carolyn's hair is jet black and so coarse that none of the tongs or crimpers or styling wands she requests for birthdays and Christmas can induce her hair to wave. Her dark eyes are round like currants, and even when she has plucked her thick brows into a thin, curved line, they still don't look right. Her sallow skin quickly acquires color when there is a spell of hot weather, but most of the year it just looks pasty.

Carolyn stares at the ceiling, contemplating the hopelessness of her case until she is seething inside with self-loathing. She can no longer bear to be here inside this room, with only her self-pity for company. Therefore she must go out.

She swings her legs off the bed, galvanized into action. There's always makeup, she tells herself, and the tempting fact that Johnnie Milan is probably going to be at the club tonight. Johnnie is the coolest and the best-looking of the boys who hang out there. And he's not going out with anyone at the moment, even though he's reputed to fancy Carolyn's friend Suzanne, so there's always a chance. . . .

Carolyn rummages through her wardrobe, holding up different outfits and then casting the rejects onto the floor, which is already littered with tights, socks, and scrumpled Kleenex. She decides on her Wranglers, because she knows they make her bum look good. And when you're bopping, that's important. She puts on an underwired half-cup bra that scoops her small breasts up and out, and covers it with a V-neck cream skinny-rib sweater. Carolyn is an avid follower of fashion and puts a lot of time and thought into choosing clothes. She realized some time ago that if she couldn't be pretty, she could at least be well dressed. There is only one possibility for her feet; a pair of red leather clogs with platform soles made of cork. The eighteen-inch flares drape over the four-inch platforms, obscuring them from sight and making Carolyn's legs look four inches longer.

The space on Carolyn's desk is not taken up with books, but makeup, several raffia trays of it. Any spare pocket money she has is spent on new lipsticks and eye shadows, after first consulting *Honey* magazine. She dabs liberal amounts of blemish concealer over her spots and then uses a foundation which is far too orange for her skin. Thick gobs of pearly green smear her eyelids, and her lashes are coated with blue waterproof mascara. With a brush she shades two circles of pink blusher on her cheeks and applies matching lipstick, sliding her lips to and fro to distribute the color.

The effect is faintly grotesque; the face that looks back from the mirror is the face of a child, with paint on its surface. But Carolyn doesn't see this, she only sees that she has changed her appearance considerably, which is what she intended. Besides, the youth club discos are thick with illicit cigarette smoke and lit by tacky red and orange light bulbs. In this infernal atmosphere, even the heaviest of makeup tends to fade into insignificance.

Carolyn puts her lipstick and her blusher into her shoulder bag and clumps downstairs. Her parents are in the kitchen, still arguing. Jean's voice is calm, as always, and she intersperses her comments with puffs on her cigarette. She smokes openly in the house now, even though Les doesn't like it.

"Turn that row down!" Les shouts to Sally, who is watching "Top of the Pops" in the living. "Your mother and I are trying to have a discussion here!"

Sally ignores him. Les catches sight of Carolyn through the kitchen door. "... And you look a real sight, girl! Have you seen yourself in a mirror? You're not thinking of going out like that, I hope?"

"Les!" Jean interrupts. "Can we just decide what we're going to do about this new car? I want to go and put a deposit on one tomorrow."

"Well, in my opinion, for what that's worth—not very much round here, I know—I don't think we need a new car. We've already got a perfectly good one."

"This one's going to be *my* car. Anyway, the Austin's five years old. I thought I'd buy brand new this time. A Mini, or something."

"Oh yes? And where are you going to get the money from?"

Carolyn makes sure her parents aren't looking in her direction, then rummages in her mother's handbag, transferring several Dunhill Extra Long cigarettes into her own bag.

"I'm going to get a cheap loan from the Co-op and pay it back out of my salary. I've discussed it with Mr. Bowers already. Lots of the management have car loans."

"You'll never afford the repayments!"

In response, Jean fetches her handbag from the hall. She hardly seems to notice Carolyn standing there with her duffle coat on. She takes out a printed salary slip and hands it to her husband.

"But ... but this can't be right. This says you're earning more than I am!"

"I know. I've just had a raise."

Les doesn't know what to say. To protest will just make his humiliation greater. Carolyn chooses this moment to make her announcement.

"Mum, I'm going out. Down to the youth club."

"All right."

"Oh no, she's not, Jean! You're staying right here, young lady! I said no more youth club on a weekday night until your exams are over."

"But it's Friday, Dad! Everyone else is going!"

"I don't care. I don't want you wandering round the streets afterward with a load of pimply boys, and I'm certainly not coming to collect you."

"Don't bother!" Carolyn gives her father a final insolent smirk before striding out of the house and slamming the front door behind her.

"Bloody little...!"

Jean pours herself a cup of tea and sits at the kitchen table to look at the glossy brochures she picked up at the car dealer. "I wouldn't waste your breath if I was you. I gave up on telling her what to do years ago. She does what she wants, that one."

Carolyn thrusts her hands into the pockets of her coat and walks quickly down Tudor Avenue, hurrying in case her father decides to come after her. It is growing dark and at the Broomhalls' house opposite the lights are on but the curtains are not yet drawn. Carolyn glances in through their sitting room window. Their married daughter, Sheila, has been visiting her parents for the afternoon, and is just standing up to leave. She has a child of eighteen months and is expecting a second in a few weeks. As Carolyn passes, Sheila comes out of the front door and walks down the garden path to her car, with the toddler running ahead of her. She puts out a hand to restrain him, but it is a weary, half-hearted gesture. Her coat does not fasten over her bulky stomach, which is swathed in a shapeless corduroy dress. Her hair is tied up in a loose, wispy bun, which makes her appear older than her twenty-seven years.

Carolyn doesn't stop to greet Sheila. She finds it depressing to see her former heroine looking so ill-kempt, and wants to dissociate herself from the specter of young motherhood. "I'm never going to have kids," she tells her schoolfriends frequently. "Nine months of looking fat and ugly—no thanks!" Mothers don't go out to discos and have fun. And if you're pregnant, you can hardly wear skin-tight jeans, can you?

The Lordswood Hill Youth Club is a disused prefab some ten minutes' walk away, and the thumping music can be heard around the block. When Carolyn arrives, things are in full swing, and there are already several necking couples spilling out onto the front steps. More daring physical encounters involving a degree of undress are carried out in the covered passage at the side of the hut, away from the glare of the streetlight. Several people claim to have "gone all the way" here, including Carolyn's friend Christina. Carolyn doesn't believe her. Christina would say anything to seem cooler than Carolyn, but Carolyn knows she's just a tease and she wouldn't dare. She'd quite like to boast about such a thing herself, but when she does, she intends it to be true.

Carolyn leaves her coat in the small vestibule and lights up a Dunhill to give herself something to do. She can already spot several of her friends on the dance floor, and she waves and shouts "Hi!" to them, hoping that she will attract the attention of any boy who's not yet dancing. It is less than ideal to arrive this late, because people tend to pair up very early, and all the decent talent has probably been taken. Also, they're playing one of her favorite dance numbers: "Jumping Jack Flash" by the Rolling Stones. Her foot taps out the rhythm, she hugs her arms across her chest and takes short, impatient drags on her cigarette. (She tells her girlfriends that she always inhales, but really she does so only sometimes.) If it were later on in the evening and she had had a few drinks, she would probably venture onto the dance floor alone, but to do so just after arriving would look moronic.

The music shifts gear to a slow number by Diana Ross. Carolyn wanders over to the bar to get a drink. Only cider and lager on sale, so she orders half and half of each; a rancid but potent mixture called a Snakebite. She feels self-conscious on her own; the sooner she finds someone to pair up with the better, it doesn't matter much whom she chooses at this stage, since the unwritten house rule is that you can always ditch a partner if something better comes along.

Out of the corner of her eye, she spies Johnnie Milan, dancing with Suzanne. Johnnie is wearing flared green loons and a skin-tight T-shirt that shows off his pectorals. A tiny bright red stain on his chin reveals that he has cut himself shaving, a cause for pride rather than embarrassment. His mouth is firmly locked onto Suzanne's and his hands are clenched possessively around Suzanne's buttocks, a fact that does not fail to escape Carolyn's notice.

She feels annoyed, and foolish, because she has been bragging to everyone for weeks that she is going to get off with Johnnie Milan. It is obvious that this prophecy will not be fulfilled tonight, so to save face she must make out she doesn't care. The most effective way to do this is to get off with someone else.

Carolyn goes about this in a calm and dispassionate way. She sees a boy called Julian Kay standing alone by the dance floor. Julian is dark and quite good-looking (say, seven out of ten compared with Johnnie's nine and a half). He has the disadvantage of being rather short (five feet six compared with Johnnie's six feet). The taller boys are at a premium when it comes to dancing, but as far as Carolyn is concerned, height makes no difference if you're going to spend most of the evening snogging on a beanbag.

"Want to dance?" she asks.

"Okay."

It is a slow number which soon gives way to Michael Jackson singing "I'll Be There."

> *We will bring salvation back*
>
> *Just call my name . . .*

Carolyn and Julian neck their way mindlessly through the sentimental song.

"Shall we go outside?" Carolyn breaks free to speak, wiping the saliva off her chin. "I've got some Dunhills."

"Okay."

They got out to the covered passageway and select a site out of earshot of the other couples. Not that there is anything to overhear; their conversation extends as far as asking one another where they live. They smoke the three remaining cigarettes, sharing the last one, then Carolyn allows Julian to put his hand inside her sweater while his mouth hoovers up and down the side of her neck. Julian clambers on top of her and presses against her and she can feel the hardening lump inside his trousers. That's good; it proves he fancies her. Carolyn wonders idly about the male organ in its erect state. Does it look so very different from a flaccid one? She finds the mental picture both threatening and fascinating. It still seems amazing to her that all men have one. She can't see a man without thinking about how he looks from the waist down. Not even the vicar, Mr. Croucher, in his unseductive bicycle clips. He has one too—amazing.

She and Julian grope one another a little more, then mutually decide they have had enough. There is no point going on after a while, if you're not going to go all the way, and Carolyn certainly isn't going to go all the way with Julian Kay. She thinks about that a lot too: who she will first do it with, and when. She hopes it will be soon, but it's got to be with someone she really fancies, she has promised herself that much.

Carolyn goes inside for another drink, and agrees to walk as far as the bus stop with Christina. She walks the rest of the way to Tudor Avenue alone, singing to herself.

"You and I have made a pact . . ."

At this remove, it is easier to be slushy about Julian; for a start he's taller in her fantasies. And he was quite a good kisser. She'll tell the other girls that, that he's an ace kisser. All in all she's quite satisfied with the way the evening has gone. It doesn't matter who you get off with, as long as you have "got off." That way you have something to talk about with your girlfriends. Carolyn is rather sorry tonight is Friday and there's no school in the morning. She has two cracking love-bites on her neck and she won't have the opportunity to show them off.

Since she left Albert Road Mixed Infants at the age of eleven, Carolyn has been a pupil at Hemingford's brand new comprehensive school. Her parents and her teachers had hoped that she would win a place at King Henry Grammar School for Girls, but she did not do well enough in her eleven-plus. Carolyn is smart and quick-witted but slapdash in her classwork and lazy when it comes to preparing for examinations.

Carolyn is quite happy at the comprehensive, even though most people still believe that it offers an inferior education to the grammar school. There is a mixed standard of ability in each class, and as a pupil who narrowly missed a grammar school place, Carolyn has no trouble maintaining high marks. She is good at art, and at English, expressing herself with a degree of clarity not hinted at by her conversation, which is heavily larded with slang and swear words.

The school building is brand new and modern; Carolyn likes the sense of light and space, much nicer than the dark, dusty corridors of the grammar school. There is a comfortable common room, with nylon carpet squares and Habitat chairs, where Carolyn and her friends lounge around, cadging illicit cigarettes from one another and sharing confidences about boys and sex. Carolyn imagines that at the grammar school any spare time is taken up with swotting, and conversations are all about the school play and poetry readings.

On the Monday following the disco, Suzanne is revealing to the assembled company that she and Johnnie "did it" after they had left the youth club.

"You didn't! I don't bloody believe you!"

"I bloody did!" Suzanne gives them a coy smile as she drags on the stub of a cigarette that is being passed from hand to hand. Suzanne is an attractive girl with olive skin and large, very white teeth. Today there is a new look in her eye, and it is this look that convinces her friends rather than anything she says; they can tell that she has experienced something so momentous that it has changed her.

"God, you bloody little tart!" says Carolyn, full of admiration but determined not to show it.

"You're just jealous!" says Suzanne, still wearing her knowing, infuriating smile. "Everyone knows you wanted to get into Johnnie's trousers yourself. Even Johnnie noticed—"

"No he didn't!" says Carolyn. "How could he have done? . . . How do you know he did, anyway?"

"Because he said something about it, didn't he, stupid!"

"What did he bloody say?"

"Never mind that!" Christina cuts in impatiently. "Tell us about *doing* it. What was it like?"

"Where did you go?"

"His older brother's got a flat near the biscuit factory. You know—his brother Chris?"

"Yeah, he's bloody gorgeous and all!"

"Well, he was out. We went there."

"*Well*? What was it *like*? What did it feel like?"

"Did it hurt?"

Suzanne smiles again, luxuriating in the memory. "Nope! It was bloody fantastic!" Her audience are by now quite captive. "I got into the bed, right, and then he turned the lights out and got into the bed too—"

"Were you naked?"

"Not to begin with, stupid! I had my bra and panties on. . . ."

The door of the form room opens and the school secretary comes in. There is much coughing and the assumption of innocent poses as Christina crams the cigarette butt under her seat cushion.

"Is Carolyn Fox here, please."

Carolyn raises her hand. "Yes?"

"Miss Insley would like to see you, dear. Right away, if you wouldn't mind."

"Miss Insley? Why, what am I supposed to have done?"

"If you would just come with me, dear. . . ."

Carolyn shrugs to the assembled company and follows the secretary to the headmistress's office. Miss Insley is a blowsy, untidy woman in her mid-forties who wears thick horn-rimmed glasses and has a gravelly, masculine voice from chain-smoking. In front of her pupils she keeps up a thin pretence of not smoking, which includes leaving her window wide open all the year round. This fails to dispel the odor of stale smoke, and prevents her from smelling it on Carolyn as she comes in.

"Sit down, dear," Miss Insley croaks. She smiles, so Carolyn knows that she has done nothing wrong. Nor has she done anything right, that she can think of.

"I've just had a phone call from your father. Apparently your grandmother is very ill, and has been admitted to Hemingford General."

"Oh. Oh dear."

"Yes . . ." Miss Insley clears the catarrh from her throat. "Apparently he tried to contact your mother, but she was away from her office in a meeting. So he wants you to go to the hospital to be with him."

"Me? Why?"

"I expect if your grandmother's condition is serious . . . it's usual to want your family with you at times like this."

"But what about my brother, Martin? He's older than me."

"I think he tried to phone Martin's school—he's at King Henry's, isn't he?—but the sixth-formers were away on a geography field trip."

"Oh."

Carolyn looks down at her grimy fingernails. She doesn't want to go to the hospital, not on her own.

"My secretary has arranged for a taxi to take you to Hemingford General, and you're to wait in her office until it arrives. All right, dear?"

Miss Insley is usually a rather brusque woman, and it is the gentleness in her manner that alerts Carolyn to the gravity of the situation. She sits silently in the taxi, staring out at the passing shops and houses.

"Where do you want to be dropped, love?"

"Don't know."

"I think the lady at the school said Accident and Emergency, didn't she?"

"Did she?"

"Tell you what, I'll put you down at Casualty, and there'll be a lady on the reception desk there who can help you."

Carolyn lines up at the desk for a long time, then waits a long time for Sister, who takes her to a curtained cubicle. Les Fox is sitting there alone. His tie and top shirt button are undone, he looks small and pale.

"Dad?"

Les doesn't seem to register her presence at first, then he says, "Your mother couldn't make it. Too busy with her meeting." His voice is tight, bitter.

"Dad, what about Gran? What happened?"

"A heart attack, this morning when she got out of bed. They said it was quite a big one. You know her heart's been dicky for a while now."

"Is she . . . ? Where is she?"

"They've taken her away to sort her out. She'll be all right though, girlie. Tough as an old boot, your grandmother."

Les doesn't look at his daughter as he speaks, he keeps his gaze fixed on the curtain. They say nothing until it pulls back and a nurse comes in. She smiles.

"Ah, you must be Carolyn? Could I have a word please, love?"

She leads Carolyn out into the corridor.

"What's happening?"

The nurse puts an arm round Carolyn's shoulder. The touch chills her. "Your granny died, I'm afraid, love. She was dead on arrival at hospital. It was a massive attack."

Carolyn stands silently looking down at her shoes, at her school socks that have lost their elastic and bag around her ankles. She is aware of a strange, distancing sensation as the blood rushes away from her face and her fingers and toes. The nurse leads her to a chair in the corridor.

"The thing is ... your dad seems to be having some trouble accepting it. He keeps asking when we're bringing her back, and when she's going to be better. We thought it might help if his family were here. But I gather your mum works ... is that right?"

Carolyn nods, "She didn't like Gran much anyway. . . ." She looks up, at the nurses and doctors walking up and down the corridor, at the visitors carrying bunches of flowers for their relatives. Thinks back to half an hour ago, when she was sitting in the form room talking about Johnnie Milan having it away with Suzanne.

"I'm sorry ... I can't believe this is happening," she tells the nurse.

"Would it help if you saw your gran? Would you like to?"

"Okay."

Carolyn isn't sure she wants to at all, not on her own, but feels somehow that for her father's sake, she must. They take her to a small side room, where Winnie's body is lying on a metal trolley. She still wears her own nightie and shabby plaid dressing gown, pulled open at the neck where the ambulancemen tried to resuscitate her. Medical equipment is littered about the room. The overall effect is rather untidy. Carolyn thinks how much this would have annoyed her grandmother.

It takes her a few seconds to summon courage to look at Winnie's face. Her skin is a funny shade and she looks vaguely surprised; apart from that the sight is not too terrible. It is just the stillness that unnerves Carolyn. The fact that she isn't going to move, not ever. So this is it, she thinks, the end of a person's life. It began, and now, today, it has ended. At Hemingford General Hospital. That's all there is.

She goes back to her father, still sitting in the curtained cubicle. "Dad?"

She stands next to his chair, puts her arms around his shoulders. "Dad . . . Gran's died. You realize that, don't you?"

He nods slowly, then begins to cry. The quiet sobs build up into a howl of despair. "I didn't want her to die!" he shouts. "I just wanted her to go on and on! I need her!"

Carolyn stands, dry-eyed, patting his back. For the first time in her life, she understands what it feels like to be an adult, the weight of it. For she, standing there in her school uniform, is like the parent, while her father is the child.

After Winnie Fox's death, Les retreats into himself. He builds a greenhouse in the small back garden of 41 Tudor Avenue. He potters about there in a silent, elderly fashion. His career, poised forever on the lower rungs of middle management, ceases to interest him and he applies for early retirement.

He also loses interest in monitoring his children's activities, so when the sixteen-year-old Carolyn comes to him in the summer of 1975 and says that she is taking a holiday job in a hairdressing salon, he tells her that she can do what she likes, as far as he is concerned.

Carolyn is irked by this lack of concern; it feels mildly uncomfortable having no one there to rebel against, no one to defy. But her main concern is the money, the glorious twenty-two pounds per week she will have to spend on clothes and makeup and going out.

Her job is at the hairdressing salon near the shopping center, once Eduardo's, then Paolo of Rome, and now Snips Unisex Hair Designers. She is to sweep up the locks of hair that have fallen to the floor during layering, mix the chemicals for curly perming, the bleaches for highlighting, and the tints for lowlighting. She is required to make tea and coffee for the clients and to gather up the dirty towels and take them to the laundry. Carolyn dislikes the sweeping and tidying, so she learns the workings of the front desk and becomes a part-time receptionist, leaving the other junior to do the more menial jobs. She finds that she enjoys going out to work, and that she doesn't have to force herself to do it for the money. She enjoys the warm, intimate atmosphere of the salon, the gossip, the jokes with the other girls, flirting with the male stylists. Her bright, cheeky manner makes her popular with the clients, some of whom she knew by sight when she started working at Snips. A few of them are friends of her mother's. One of them is Audrey Pryce-Jones, mother of her former adversary at Albert Road Mixed Infants.

The only thing that is difficult about going to work is getting up early in the morning after a night out drinking and dancing. These occasions are frequent, since under the new regime of laissez-faire at home, neither parent raises any objection to Carolyn staying out late during the week. She will look back on this summer as one of blissful freedom, one when she had money in her pocket and no other imperative than to enjoy herself. Her "O" level exams are a thing of the past, but the results and the decisions that come with them are still in the future.

Carolyn and her friends now disdain the youth club discos as childish; they have found something more sophisticated to take its place. A new nightclub has opened in the shopping center in the site where a fishmongers used to be. A flashing pink neon sign outside proclaims its name, Jangles, and it has a bouncer in tuxedo and bow tie, and a huge multifaceted silver ball hanging from the ceiling that sends spangles of light bouncing around the room. And there are special-effect slide projections on the walls, magnifying colored globules of oil into oozing psychedelic murals, and an ultraviolet strobe light that flickers on and off, turning the dancers' teeth, eyeballs, and white clothing into streaks of blinding blueness.

It costs five pounds to get into Jangles, which limits the number of times Carolyn can attend each week. Sometimes if they hang around hopefully in their trendiest gear, the bouncer will wave them in without paying, or on Tuesdays, which is Ladies' Night, they can get in free on the arm of a male escort.

The appeal of the place is not just its glittery decor or the sugary cocktails served at the bar, but the wide variety of lone males it attracts. The youth club disco could only offer schoolboys, here at the nightclub there are "older" men of all varieties, including flashy young businessmen in suits, and students from the local polytechnic and from Reading University, some fifteen miles away. Girls like Carolyn who are young and alluringly dressed only have to sit on a bar stool for a few minutes before someone will come and talk to them.

One night in late August Carolyn has arrived with Suzanne, but Suzanne has already found someone to dance with. Carolyn sits at the bar alone, sipping a Pink Lady. She is quite content to do this; confident that she is looking her best. The summer sun has tanned her skin to a pale chestnut color and it is shown off to advantage by her skin-tight white jeans and white off-the-shoulder top.

Occasionally a man will catch her eye, but if she doesn't like the look of him she turns away and absorbs herself in sucking up the Pink Lady through her straw, giving off "I am not interested" signals.

Then she sees someone worthy of her interest, or rather a pair of buttocks beautifully sculpted by tight leather trousers and silky chestnut hair, curling in a duck's tail against a suntanned neck. He turns around and Carolyn laughs out loud when she realizes that it is someone she knew all along: Matthew Pryce-Jones. He is in the middle of a group of friends, including an attractive blonde. They have their heads together, laughing.

Carolyn wanders over to Matthew's crowd. "Hi!"

One of the other boys turns round. "Hi," he says coldly, then returns to the conversation.

"Er . . . hi, Matthew."

Matthew looks up at her from beneath his dense, dark lashes. His skin is smooth and unblemished, the symmetry of his features perfect, almost too handsome. He is tall but with none of the gangly skinniness of adolescence, his heavy frame making him seem much older than sixteen.

"Sorry . . . am I supposed to know you?"

"From Albert Road. Carolyn Fox. Don't you remember?"

Matthew thinks for a moment. "Oh yeah. Fat Fox. I remember."

His friends snigger.

"So—how are you?" Matthew asks.

"Fine."

"Good. Right—see you around then."

He turns to smile at the pretty, over-made-up blonde, indicating that the interview is over.

Carolyn shrugs and wanders back to the bar, but she does not stop looking at Matthew Pryce-Jones.

"Who is he?" asks Suzanne, when she returns from the dance floor.

"Oh, just someone who went to my infants' school." Carolyn shrugs. "Pity he's such a self-satisfied prick."

She watches him dance and remembers how she used to feel when she watched him play football in the playground at Albert Road. She wanted to touch him then, and she still does. She is gripped by lust, sheer acquisitiveness. The fact that she does not like him is quite irrelevant. He looks up at her from time to time while he is dancing, his expression faintly puzzled.

Then she has an idea, a wild one, but where Matthew is concerned she has nothing at all to lose. If she doesn't want to, she needn't speak to him ever again. Actually, it was Audrey Pryce-Jones who gave her the idea. She overheard Audrey gossiping to her stylist on Tuesday afternoon, saying that she and her husband were taking their youngest son to visit his grandmother over the weekend. That means that Matthew will be alone at home tonight.

She grabs her clutch bag and slips out to the off-license on the other side of the precinct, blowing her last three pounds on a bottle of Cinzano. Then she climbs onto the concrete wall outside the entrance to Jangles. She waits.

Matthew leaves with his friends at midnight, including the blonde who is having to trot to keep up, wobbling on her pencil heels.

"Hey, Matthew!" Carolyn shouts. She unscrews the cap of the Cinzano bottle and takes a long gulp for Dutch courage.

"What do *you* want?"

"How about this, for starters?"

Carolyn flings her arms around his neck and presses her mouth against Matthew's, snaking her tongue against his lips. She would like to go on kissing him forever, he tastes so delicious. Warm male flesh, slightly spiced with aftershave. And he really shaves too; she can feel the slight scrape of stubble against her chin. Not like most of the boys his age.

Matthew's friends whistle and catcall.

"See you later then, Matt!"

"Looks like we'd better leave you to it!"

Laughing, they walk off in the direction of the bus stop with the disgruntled blonde in their wake.

Matthew breaks free from the embrace. "You haven't changed much, Fox. Still the same pushy little cow."

Carolyn shrugs. "Like a drink?"

Matthew takes the bottle from her and drinks, his eyes still wary.

"I thought we could have a drink, and then go back to your place."

"You're pretty sure of yourself, aren't you?"

"Suit yourself." Carolyn jumps down from the wall and starts to walk away.

"No—wait." He grabs her wrist and pulls her against him hard, kissing her greedily. Carolyn is aware suddenly that he has an erection straining against the leather trousers, she feels pinpricks of sweat break out down the length of her backbone.

"We can go back to my place," Matthew says, his voice slightly hoarse. "But you'd better be for real."

They walk back to Lordswood Hill, stopping every now and then to kiss some more—wet, dribbly, impatient kisses punctuated by swigs from the Cinzano bottle. By the time they reach Mount Rise, they have both drunk too much and the pace of their walking has become erratic.

"No parents?" asks Carolyn innocently as Matthew unlocks the front door.

"They're away." Matthew goes into the kitchen for glasses.

"That's lucky ..." She thumbs through the Pryce-Jones's record collection. "Hmmm ... Simon and Garfunkel; that old crap...."

Matthew comes back with two glasses for the rest of the Cinzano but it is an empty gesture; they go untouched. Their mouths are glued together and there is a frantic scrambling, an ominous creaking of the too-tight black leather as they hurry on to the next stage. Carolyn moans with frustration when Matthew can't undo her strapless bra with his one free hand. He resorts to two, grunting with exasperation as he rummages between her shoulder blades.

"It's a front-fastening one," Carolyn volunteers.

"Why didn't you say so before?"

"You didn't ask." Carolyn bites back the rest of her sarcastic reply as her breasts swing free and Matthew begins to knead them with something akin to desperation. Then he eases her onto her back and starts to unfasten her jeans. He eases them off, along with her panties and pushes them to one side. She doesn't much like the fact that she is lying there half-naked, with her legs splayed and her private parts exposed, but she doesn't see what she can do about it, not now that Matthew has unfastened the leather trousers and is bearing down on her.

She allows herself a moment of detached curiosity; now at last she will get a chance to see an erection. She supposes that *is* an erection, bouncing about under his shirttails looking smaller and thinner and more threatening than she had imagined.

Matthew holds it between thumb and finger and points it in her direction.

"Have you got anything?"

"Got anything?"

"You know, a French letter. A rubber."

"No, have you?"

"No."

"Oh, well. Nothing will happen anyway. Probably."

After a few seconds of suspending disbelief, Carolyn realizes that this is it, that she's doing it. It feels quite nice. Not very, just quite. And Matthew seems to know what he's doing, moving his hips rhythmically, slowly at first, then faster and faster ...

"Have you done this before?" she whispers.

"Yes—haven't you?"

"No!"

"Oh God ..!" Matthew groans. "This is a fine time to tell me!"

He loses his rhythm, and then his erection, which slides backward and dribbles out of her, a most curious sensation.

"... And look at the mess it's made on the carpet! Blood everywhere. Mum will go spare!"

They fetch carpet clearner and a brush from the kitchen and scrub at the lounge carpet dressed only in their underwear. Carolyn starts to giggle, which only makes Matthew more annoyed.

"Hey," she says, flicking her coarse, dark hair back from her forehead. "I could meet you at Jangles tomorrow night if you like. If your parents are still away we could ... you know."

"You must be joking." Matthew squats back on his haunches and laughs in her face. "After this fiasco! Anyway, you're not exactly the type of girl I go out with."

"What the hell do you mean by that?"

"Well, I prefer blondes for starters. And no guy likes girls who push it like you do."

"Oh yes?" Carolyn stands up and throws down the scrubbing brush, splashing water over Matthew's feet. "Well, let me tell *you* something, Matthew Pryce-Jones! Girls might fancy you like hell, but it doesn't mean they *like* you!"

"I don't care...."

"And I'll tell you something else! I could get any man I want to!"

As she slams her way out of the house and stumbles off down Mount Rise she is overwhelmed by the need to prove this, to herself as much as to the world at large.

Carolyn does better than she had expected by passing five "O" levels, with "A" grades in art and English. In September she reluctantly relinquishes her job at Snips and enrolls at the local sixth form college to take art and English "A" levels. Her group of friends at the comprehensive is now dispersed, some leave school to join the workforce, some stay at the comprehensive, some—like Carolyn and Suzanne—continue their education elsewhere. As a result her social life has a disjointed feel to it, and now more than ever she becomes aware of Hemingford's limitations, its drab provincialism. The once-smart new shopping center built in the early sixties now seems outdated and tawdry, its concrete walls spattered with graffiti. The Victorian buildings in the town are knocked down, boarded up, divided into flats or simply left to rot.

Nothing is happening; this is the constant lament of Carolyn and her friends when they do meet. They feel suspended between two states, childhood has been left behind, but the autonomy of adulthood is far off in the future. Carolyn despises 41 Tudor Avenue and its inhabitants for being boring and bourgeois. She stays out as much as possible, roaming the town center, being thrown out of pubs and X-rated films, moaning about how boring everything is. At the sixth form college she falls in with a crowd who hold bring-a-bottle parties and smoke dope when their parents aren't around. Carolyn tries it a few times but doesn't like the taste or the distanced, muddle-headed feeling it gives her.

The feeling that everything is happening somewhere else, to someone else, is heightened when the word "punk" explodes onto youth consciousness at the end of 1976, with "anarchy" hard on its heels.

"God, look at that!" says Carolyn to Suzanne when they are watching television at Tudor Avenue one afternoon, skiving off during a "free" period at college. A new rock band called the Sex Pistols are being interviewed, after performing their hit single "Pretty Vacant." Their clothes are ripped and dirty, their hair stands up in stiff peaks on top of their heads, they are covered in safety pins and tattoos.

"Bloody weird!" says Suzanne. "Do people really want to go around dressed like that?"

"Of course they do—look!"

The camera cuts away from the interview to a piece of documentary film showing punks on the streets of London, flicking "V" signs at the camera. The commentator explains that a new culture is dawning, and for the first time since the 1960s, the young are claiming the streets of London as their own.

"I'm going to go and live in London," says Suzanne. "Next summer, as soon as I've finished my 'A' levels, I'm going to find a job up there."

Carolyn doesn't think she can wait that long. The idea takes hold in her mind and grows like a weed, wrapping itself around all her waking thoughts. She takes the train up to London one Saturday and walks around all day until she has exhausted herself, just looking at everything. She sees some punks in the King's Road, with pink hair like candyfloss, drinking out of plastic cider bottles and being photographed by Japanese tourists.

On New Year's Day, 1977, she announces to her parents that she is leaving home and going to live in London. Now.

"You can't go *now!*" says Jean, frowning. She drags heavily on her cigarette. "You're right in the middle of your 'A' level course. Wait until you've done your exams, then we'll talk about it."

"But I don't want to wait. I want to go now."

"Why, for goodness' sake?" asks Jean. "It's only a few months, what difference will it make? And you're not even eighteen yet."

"'But it's only a few months till my eighteenth birthday, and you just said a few months doesn't make a difference."

Jean shrugs helplessly and starts leafing through a pile of papers in her briefcase. "Les—she's not going to listen to me. You tell her."

"All right," says Les, who has been standing in the kitchen door-way, trowel in hand, saying nothing. "All right, if you can't be bothered to stop her, I'll have to do it, won't I?" He addresses his daughter, but his eyes are still looking in Jean's direction. "Carolyn, I forbid you to go to London. . . . There, are you satisfied?"

"You might at least have said it as if you meant it," says Jean without looking up from her papers.

"Why don't you tell her yourself? Why have I always got to be the heavy with the kids, while you're off doing something else?"

Carolyn goes upstairs and packs her favorite clothes and records in a suitcase from her mother's wardrobe. Sally stares at her as she carries the case downstairs, but says nothing. Her mother has returned to her paperwork, her father has gone to sit in front of the television. They don't appear to notice the front door opening and then slam-ming. Carolyn takes the last train up to London, and sleeps on a bench at Waterloo Station.

The next day, she uses the accommodation pages of the London *Evening Standard* to find herself a bedsit in a flat-fronted terrace off the Earl's Court Road. There are mildewed cabbage roses on the walls, and a camping stove so clogged up with grease that it won't light. The deposit uses up all her savings, so she knows she will have to find a job straightaway.

An advertisement in the *Standard*'s jobs pages catches her eye.

Attractive young hostesses wanted for exclusive gentlemen's club, West End. Flexible hours. Dedicated girls can earn up to £300 per week!

Carolyn telephones the number and a foreign-sounding man tells her to come to the club for an interview, at six-thirty that evening. Carolyn can hardly believe her luck. Three *hundred* pounds a week. For working a few hours every evening. Because she can't bear to be in the bedsit for longer than she has to, she window-shops until it is time for the interview, wandering around in a daze staring at expensive clothes, thinking that soon she might be able to afford any of them, all of them. She'll be able to go back to Hemingford dressed like someone from the pages of *Vogue,* jewelry and all, and everyone will be amazed and she will say, "Well after all, I *am* earning three hundred pounds a week. . . ."

The club is in the basement of an elegant building in St. James Street. A fat, greasy man in a suit stops her as she goes down the area steps.

"You here for an interview?"

"Yes."

"You sure?" He looks her up and down.

"Yes."

"All right." He opens the door. "Wait over there."

Inside the club, it is very warm, and the sounds of the street outside are muffled by thick, crimson carpet. There is a lot of leather furniture and carriage lamps and mock Georgian knickknacks. Carolyn finds herself standing in a huddle with a half dozen other interviewees. They look at one another nervously; no one speaks. The other girls are all older than Carolyn and look like models or dancers. A couple of them are carrying portfolios.

The club has just opened for business, and a waitress at the bar is loading up a tray with glasses. As she turns round, her breasts loom into Carolyn's line of vision; large, shapely and completely naked. Two more girls sit at a table chatting to some businessmen; they too are naked from the waist up. One of them is almost flat-chested, the other is older and her breasts hang flat against her ribcage.

A woman with bottle-blond hair and a clipboard comes out of the office. "Who's next?"

Carolyn looks around frantically for the exit. The fat, greasy-haired man is blocking her way. Two waitresses push past him, their nipples touching his sleeve.

"I thought you were here for an interview," he says to Carolyn. "What's the matter?"

"Excuse me, I've got to go...."

"Don't tell me you didn't know it was a topless club?" The man laughs.

"It's not that, I just haven't got time to wait, that's all."

Carolyn runs up the steps and leans against the railings, gulping the cold night air in great drafts. She feels that she has had a lucky escape, as though she might have been forced to do something against her will. Then she thinks of the money. Couldn't she have served a few drinks topless for that amount of money? People do it on beaches all the time . . . But common sense tells her that "up to £300" probably means a lot less in reality, and that to earn it she would have to do more than serve a few drinks. She buys herself a pizza slice and a Coke at Pizzaland and goes back to her bedsit to wait for tomorrow.

At the beginning of January, London's department stores are enjoying their busiest period, and there is brief but intense need for extra labor. So Carolyn finds herself a job at the first store she walks into, which happens to be Harrods because it is the only one she's heard of. She is to work in the toy department, where all the assistants are under the age of twenty-five. It seems a remarkably undemanding way to spend the day; all she has to do is play with the toys as though she is enjoying herself, showing children how they work if they ask. Then, if they want to buy, she just has to take one from the pile in the stockroom and point them in the direction of a till.

The other assistants are bright, well dressed, and undedicated. They are mostly public school dropouts or university entrants on vacation or between school and a freshman year. They all have intriguing names like Cosmo and Sebastian and Tasha. Carolyn is entrusted to the care of a girl called Polly Kendrick. Polly is blond and pretty and talks in a posh, drawling voice. She has just left a private girls' school in Hampshire, but can't be bothered to look for a "proper" job.

"I'll probably travel," she tells Carolyn airily. "Australia probably. What was your name by the way? I didn't catch it."

"Carmen," says Carolyn, picking the first thing that comes into her head. "Carolyn" obviously won't do; it belongs to the old life. Besides, she hates it. "Carmen Fox."

"Carmen Fox ... brilliant name," says Polly approvingly. She wears red Kickers and a man's striped shirt over black satin drainpipes. Her right earlobe has been pierced three times, and sports a neat row of gold studs. Carolyn/Carmen makes a mental note to do the same, and to acquire some Kickers. She buys them with her staff discount at the end of her first week; they take almost all her wage packet and she can't afford to eat for three days.

Polly likes Carmen, she tells her so frequently. "You make me laugh," she says, demonstrating with her high-pitched bray. "You're such a scream."

After they have worked together in the toy department for nine months, Polly asks if Carmen would like to share her new flat. It's a maisonette actually, half of a Georgian house in Kensington. It seems her parents have a lot of money sitting around doing nothing, and they have decided they may as well spend some of it on a London flat for their daughter. A lot of well-heeled parents are following this course, establishing a parental barrier against the horrors of the capital city, while at the same time providing a useful base for their own trips down from the counties (Leicestershire, in the case of the Kendricks).

Carmen accepts eagerly. It will be far more comfortable than the grimy shoebox in Earl's Court, and although the room she will occupy in Polly's flat is not much bigger than a shoebox, it will be very cheap, which might prove invaluable. Carmen has been doing some sketching in her spare time and is thinking about throwing in the job at Harrods and applying for a place at art college.

"Great!" says Polly. "Why don't you come over this evening and meet Mummy and Daddy? They're down in town so that Mummy can measure the flat for new curtains. They'll be really pleased that I've found someone nice to share with."

If Mrs. Kendrick is pleased, then she has a strange way of showing it. She is a bullying, over-confident woman, a terrier in twin set and pearls who was once pretty but now has the tough and stringy appearance of someone who has had too much Caribbean sun. She bullies her husband, who stands quietly in the corner, she bullies Polly, and she attempts to bully Carmen, barking instructions at her from the drawing room floor, where she is on her hands and knees hemming curtains.

"The bedside table in your room is a good one, from my mother's house, so you mustn't put any hot cups of tea or coffee on it. And the bedspread will need washing at least once a week. How are you at cleaning?"

"I'm sorry?" Carmen blinks.

"Polly's hopeless. Comes of either having nannies or au pairs to clean up after her, I suppose."

"I know how to do housework, if that's what you mean. My mother showed me."

"I see." Mrs. Kendrick's look is pitying; to have a mother who does her own housework is a far worse fate than ending up a spoiled brat like Polly. Indeed, she seems rather proud of Polly's helplessness, as though it were a sign of a good pedigree.

"We are installing a washing machine ..." From her position on the carpet she raises her eyes to frown at Carmen's filthy jeans and Doc Marten's. "But perhaps I'd better see about getting you a cleaning lady too. You may need someone to help out when you have dinner parties."

Dinner parties? Carmen is feeling increasingly uncomfortable and as if he senses this, Mr. Kendrick provides diversion. He points to the sketches sticking out of her raffia basket.

"Did you do these?"

"Yes. They're just sketches."

"May I?"

He lifts one out to look at it, and while he does so, Carmen studies Polly's father more closely. He looks nice, she decides, much nicer than Mrs. Kendrick. The dark suntan that makes her look so desiccated suits his broad face. His dark hair is receding slightly from a square forehead, but he still looks younger than forty-seven. He smiles at Carmen's depiction of Portobello Road market and as he does so she notices how his eyes sort of scrunch up and disappear, and how the suntan makes his teeth seem very white.

"Are you studying art?"

"I'd like to."

"You should. These are really rather nice."

Jill Kendrick looks up, sharp-eyed, from the hems of her Sanderson floral drapes.

"Carmen dear, would you come into your bedroom for a moment? There's something I'd like to show you. . . ."

Carmen follows her.

"We inherited this fitted wardrobe when we bought the place and it *is* a bit shabby, but I think it will do. You'll need to get some soapy water and a brush and scrub the shelves down before you move your clothes into it. Do you think you could do that? Perhaps you could do the wardrobe in Polly's room too. . . ."

Carmen moves into the Kendrick's maisonette the following weekend. It quickly becomes apparent that she is not going to be seeing much of Polly, who has a chaotic social life and has recently acquired a boyfriend, a gormless Old Etonian called Tim. Tim has no job but a lot of money, and seems to spend most of it on cocaine, which he and Polly mince with a razor and then hoover up through a biro with the middle bit removed. Then they go into Polly's bedroom and giggle a lot behind closed doors. Carmen sits in the drawing room, drinking endless mugs of tea (placed on a coaster to avoid the sin of leaving a heat mark on Mrs. Kendrick's precious walnut table) and feeling awkward.

On Sunday evening Tim and Polly go out for a pizza, leaving her alone with the television.

The phone rings.

"Richard Kendrick here, Polly's father."

"Ah, yes."

"I wondered if I might have a word with Polly."

"I'm afraid she's gone out to dinner. Can I take a message?"

"I'm in town for a meeting first thing tomorrow morning, staying at my club, and I was going to take Polly out for a meal ... Have you eaten?"

"Well, yes ... well, not really, I just ..."

"Why don't you come with me instead? I could use the company."

Ten minutes later Richard Kendrick's black Saab is parked outside the hall and he is on the doorstep, elegant in a gray linen suit.

"I haven't dressed up," says Carmen, who is wearing Kickers, drainpipe jeans and a Sloppy Joe.

"That's all right," He holds open the car door for her. "I thought we'd go round the corner to the local Indian restaurant. If you like Indian food?"

"Never had it."

"I love it, so I make a point of having some every time I'm down here on business. You don't find many tandoori places in rural Leicestershire. Anyway, Jill doesn't like it."

Carmen does. The two of them squeeze into a narrow booth with purple plush seats and feast on tender marinated chicken pieces and soft, doughy nan bread, spiced lentils, and prawns.

"Polly's out with her boyfriend," says Carmen through her mouthful of nan. "Tim."

"Have you got a boyfriend?"

She shakes her head. "I'm not a virgin, though," she blurts out, and immediately feels her face turn red. Jesus! she thinks, what on earth did I go and say that for? He'll think I'm a complete idiot, or a tart, or both....

Richard Kendrick smiles, so that his sleepy gray eyes almost disappear. "I've got a confession to make," he says. "I knew that Polly was going out tonight. When I rang I was hoping to find you in on your own."

He shrugs, holding his palms upward in a rather Gallic gesture.

His message is clear; he is allowing Carmen to make whatever she likes of this statement. The ball is firmly in her court.

"Polly won't be back for a couple of hours yet," she says.

The Saab roars back along the South Lambeth Road, jumping a red light, but when they get to the flat, Richard doesn't hurry. He holds Carmen in his arms on her narrow single bed, for what seems like hours, just stroking her and touching her gently all over. He cradles her and rocks her like a baby. Finally, when she can stand it no longer, he enters her with a quick, imperceptible movement and continues to rock her, with their two bodies locked together.

This is it, thinks Carmen with satisfaction, this is *real* sex.

There are many things that she enjoys about her subsequent relationship with Richard Kendrick, her flatmate's father.

The first is quite simply that he spoils her. He is a wealthy man and he can afford to indulge her with gifts of clothes, jewelry, trips to expensive restaurants. Treats that she could not otherwise have had. Unlike Polly, she was not spoiled as a child—quite the reverse—and she revels in the new sensation of being treated as special. Richard tells her she is lovely. No one has ever said anything like that to her before. He kisses away the tears when she cries. Even her mother never did that.

And Richard takes care of her. He takes an interest in her welfare, worries if she is ill, nags her to eat well. With his encouragement she leaves Harrods and takes up a place at Chelsea College of Art and Design in the autumn of 1978. She blossoms under this care, taking more trouble over her clothes, having her hair cut at a smart salon, and losing nearly a stone to trim her stocky frame into a neat, curvaceous size twelve.

Then there is the illicit nature of their affair, the fact that it must all be conducted behind closed doors. To Carmen this is fun, a game that keeps her wanting him week after week.... She doesn't even mind having to wait in on the off chance that he might ring or visit. That's part of the game too. A sort of Russian roulette.

And keeping it from Polly. She can't help but notice the gifts and the flowers, so Carmen pretends that she has an admirer at the hamburger restaurant on the King's Road where she does part-time waitressing. And what could be more natural than Richard Kendrick keeping a paternal eye on Polly on his business trips to London? It's simply coincidence that Polly always happens to be out.

"Your father dropped by," Carmen would say casually. "He sends his love."

Richard's position as director of a large engineering firm gives him a legitimate reason to visit London, but sometimes weeks pass between trips, and when he does come he can never stay for the whole night. This permanent state of suspense, living for next week, or the week after, makes the months pass quickly for Carmen. Soon she is seeing in 1979 (on her own—Richard is detained by the inevitable family gathering) and after only a few more of their hastily arranged meetings, the leaves are beginning to appear on the trees again, and it is spring. The summer brings the inevitable frustration of Richard's month-long holiday in Saint Kitt's with Jill and the family, then the days grow shorter again and it is almost two years since the affair began. Richard's influence has matured her. She met him as a girl, but now at twenty she feels she is an adult. And as two adults, two equals, there is no reason why their relationship should not continue for another two years, another five, or even ten. . . .

"You must come up to Leicestershire with me one weekend," Polly says abruptly on a cold, dank November evening. The two girls are sitting eating rounds of buttered toast, on one of the very rare occasions when they are both in together.

Carmen is so startled that she chokes on a toast crumb.

"Why not come this weekend?" asks Polly as she pats her on the back.

"Oh, no, honestly, I'm rather busy. . . ."

"No you're not," says Polly crossly. "You've just told me you weren't doing anything this weekend."

"All the same, I'd rather not. I don't think it's a very good idea. . . ."

"Well I must say, I think that's bloody rude of you, Carmen! After all Mummy and Daddy have done for you; letting you live here in their flat for two whole years paying practically no rent, not even charging you for the cleaning lady. . . ."

And Polly harps on this theme for the rest of the week until Carmen relents and agrees to go. She justifies it on the grounds that her refusal is starting to look suspicious, but she is also curious to see Jill and Richard Kendrick at home. Most of all she just wants to see Richard.

She has only been in the house five minutes before she realizes that she should never have come. Richard is pretending so hard, that he hardly even looks at her, and he just seems so *married*. Here, in the Kendricks' restored Queen Anne farmhouse, a shrine to Jill's good taste and rigorous housekeeping, Richard has turned into a middle-aged man. He wears slippers, expensive Italian leather ones, but slippers all the same.

By the time they sit down to dinner on Saturday evening, Carmen has already decided that she will have to invent a sick relative and escape first thing in the morning. Polly chatters aimlessly about Tim, Richard is silent, and Jill grills Carmen about her life in London. She insists on calling her "dear," and takes every opportunity to make her look like a stupid little girl: asking her if she has any dirty clothes that need rinsing through, drawing attention to the fact that she picks up the wrong knife to eat her starter.

Carmen looks up from her mackerel pâté and catches Jill Kendrick looking at her contemptuously. Their eyes meet, and Carmen feels herself turn cold all over.

She knows.

It is impossible to know how she could have found out. Or perhaps she just senses it from observing Richard and Carmen together. Anyway, she knows. She's not angry either. Her expression reveals merely disdain, and distaste.

Richard comes down to London on Wednesday, and comes straight to the flat. He is wearing one of his elegant suits and looks young again, to Carmen's enormous relief. She runs to him when he unlocks the front door and clings to him.

"I'm so sorry about the weekend, darling," he says. "God, wasn't it ghastly? And I had no idea you were coming, either. Jill didn't mention it, so the first I knew was when you walked through the door!"

"It was a nightmare, a bloody nightmare!" agrees Carmen, undoing his tie.

"And the worst thing about it was seeing you there looking gorgeous and not being able to touch you! I was dying for you!"

They are both impatient this time and don't even wait to get to the bedroom, falling onto the sofa covered so lovingly by Jill in a fabric that matches the curtains. Carmen has just removed her bra when a key turns in the lock and Polly comes in. She has been sent home early from secretarial college because she caught a cold in the chill, damp Leicestershire air.

When Carmen returns from the night shift at Hamburger Heaven, the flat is empty, but Polly has left her a note on the kitchen table.

> *I'd like you and your things to be gone by the time I get back tonight (11:30 P.M.). I don't want to share my flat with a slag.*

The word "slag" is underlined several times, as much to convince the writer as the reader. There is no mention of her father. Perhaps she thought he did it against his will. Either that or he has done this before. The thought makes her feel sick.

And it is she, not Richard, who finds herself suddenly homeless on a foggy November night. Still, she doesn't intend to be here when Polly gets back and have some sort of humiliating scene. It doesn't take long for her to clear her tiny, cramped bedroom; almost everything she has ever owned was given to her by Richard Kendrick. She leaves behind the clothes that have gone out of fashion and were going to be thrown out anyway. Her worldly goods are condensed into the suitcase that she took from her mother's bedroom when she left home, and a few plastic carrier bags.

She leaves the flat at eleven o'clock, having no idea where to go. It is far too late in the day to find a place to rent, and she doesn't have enough money with her to stay at a hotel. The phone numbers of her few London acquaintances are kept in her locker at art college.

As she trudges down the South Lambeth Road, she is overwhelmed by the drabness of the London street, the absence of anything to please the eye. She passes a betting shop with opaque glass windows, a Kentucky Fried Chicken outlet with greasy paper and bits of chewed meat strewing the pavement outside, a Pakistani news agent whose shop-front is covered with padlocked metal grills after numerous racist attacks. She steers a course through litter and dog shit and piles of vomit outside the noisy Irish pub, wondering why anybody wants to live in a city that is so repugnant. Certainly, at this moment, she can't think why *she* wants to live here.

At the end of the road there is a Christadelphian church, an ugly Victorian building of drab brown brick. Inside its porch is a sheltered stone seat. Carmen huddles there with her suitcase until dawn breaks, under a Day-Glo billboard that proclaims REPENT OF YOUR SINS AND GOD'S TRUE PURPOSE WILL BE REVEALED!

Carmen does not see Polly again. She finds another flat, in Shepherd's Bush, sharing with two girls from Sheffield who work for the civil service. They are saving up to travel and have bar jobs in the evening, so much of the time Carmen has the flat to herself and spends a lot of evenings alone in front of the television, just like she did at Polly's. Only this time there are no phone calls from Richard to look forward to.

She misses him, God, she misses him! This is a new sensation for her, and a painful one. By the end of the third day she cannot think of anything, or anyone else. She tries, desperately, to clear her mind and reason with herself. So here she is, slung out of Polly's flat, living somewhere else. But she's still in London, and so must Richard be, on occasion. It needn't be the end, need it?

She does not dare phone him. Instead she goes every night to a champagne bar in Mayfair, a place they used to frequent on their rare outings. Finally she sees him. He is there on Christmas Eve, wearing a new charcoal stripe suit, talking to a pretty young girl with red hair.

She feels angry, a terrible, grieving anger that explodes in her chest and sends her running down Curzon Street, just to get as far away as possible from that sight. And she cries out as she runs. Because looking at him twirling his glass of champagne, creasing up

•

his darkly tanned face as he smiles, she realizes that for the first and perhaps the only time, she had been in love.

On New Year's Day, Richard telephones Carmen.

"Hello, darling."

Silence.

"I got your new phone number from Chelsea College."

"Oh."

"Just ringing to wish you a happy new year. A happy new decade in fact. The 1980s."

"Right. Thank you."

"You don't sound very happy ... I could come over."

"No, don't do that. In fact I'd just like you to go away and leave me alone."

"I still come down to London. We could still meet from time to time. . . ."

"NO! And don't phone me, OKAY?"

Carmen shudders as she hangs up the receiver, buries her face in her hands. There, on the table next to the phone, is the cause of her distress. A home pregnancy tester. Positive.

She knows that she must get rid of the baby, the unlooked-for result of her affair with a married man more than twice her age (and Polly's brother or sister; what a strange thought *that* is). She also knows that in central London in 1980 this is a commonplace, and relatively easy procedure. At least she has that much to be thankful for.

She goes to the Marie Stopes clinic in the West End, where they are sympathetic, but businesslike. She must make another appointment and when she comes back she must bring one hundred and sixty pounds.

Carmen's grant doesn't allow for that sort of expenditure, nor does that of her friends. The following evening she does the only thing she can think of. She goes to Hemingford to see her mother.

She finds Les alone in Tudor Avenue, watching television and smoking. He took up the habit to keep Jean company, but now she is giving it up and he is hooked.

"Where's Mum?"

"Out."

"At this time? Not working, surely?"

"No, she goes out sometimes with her friends. You know. . . ."

"Oh."

Her father seems pathetically pleased to see her. He invites her into the kitchen to watch him prepare a meager meal of tinned spaghetti on toast, offers to share it with her.

"Dad . . ."

"What is it? Did you want something, girlie?" He uses his old pet name for her, a word he hasn't uttered once since Winnie died. It makes Carmen feel sorry for him, makes her feel she should be offering help, not seeking it.

"Nothing . . . it doesn't matter. Listen, I've got to go."

As she goes to the front door, her younger sister Sally hangs her head over the banisters.

"Punk," she says. "You're a punk."

She supposes that Sally is making reference to the three gold studs in each of her ear lobes, her mock leopard-skin coat and Doc Martens. She has gone back to looking scruffy since she left Polly's flat, dressing like all the other art students: almost exclusively in black, raiding jumble sales in the King's Road for outsize men's clothes. She considers her appearance rather sober, but by Hemingford standards she must still look like a punk. People there use the word in a fearful way.

Carmen doesn't bother to contradict Sally; she knows the label has no meaning. London has taught her that you can dress as outrageously as you like and try to set yourself apart from the rest of the faceless masses, and still feel as vulnerable and ordinary inside. She remembers seeing a young punk mother in Leicester Square, pushing a pram. The bag dangling from the handles had a diaper poking out of it; she had to change shitty diapers, just like any other mother.

If she can't ask her family, Carmen will have to borrow the money she needs from a friend. She can only think of one person who would have that amount available, and she can't face the humiliation of having to ask Richard for it. Not now that she has told him to leave her alone.

•

But she does have a gold bracelet that he gave her for her nineteenth birthday. She sells this for seventy pounds, borrows forty from a fellow waitress at Hamburger Heaven and scrapes the rest together out of her wages. As the day of the appointment approches, she tries to think of it as a therapeutic procedure, one that is going to remove a growth, make her better in some way. She doesn't think of it as a child, nor does she use the word "abortion." Neither does the clinic—they refer to it as a "termination."

A doctor speaks to her briefly and signs her form, then the termination is done with local anaesthetic only, so that she can feel them doing it, feel them scraping it out of her. The pain is terrible, but she is not expected to make a fuss. She lies down for a few hours afterward, then a nurse brings her a cup of tea before sending her on her way. It is all horribly civilized.

"There," the nurse says, drawing back the curtains of the cubicle, "that wasn't so bad, was it? And it's all over now."

All over, she repeats to herself. She knows what is all over. What is over is her trusting men, caring for them. Sitting around night after night waiting for them. A good time, that's all she's going to have from now on. Three small words, which will be inscribed on her heart—should anyone bother to look—and which will be her anthem for the 1980s. Sex, fun, and money.

S e v e n t e e n

■

Stephen

Stephen Noble is in his bedroom reading *Decline and Fall*. There is a tap on the door.

"All right to come in, old fellow?"

The door opens to admit Roger Saunders. "Getting your stuff shipshape for school, I see."

"Sort of."

Stephen swings his legs off the bed and starts to stack some books into his tuck box, feeling obliged to take up some sort of activity now that Roger has intruded. It is September 1972, and Stephen is about to begin his first term as a boarder at Maidenhurst. He has spent the last two years as a day pupil at Draycotts Preparatory School, and this taste of private education has not left him looking forward to Maidenhurst. He preferred his first school, Albert Road Mixed Infants. At least there you didn't feel that much was expected of you.

"What are you reading?" Roger picks up the book from the bed and settles himself into a chair. "Let me see ... *Decline and Fall*. Evelyn Waugh, eh? Impressive stuff. I was expecting *Boy's Own Stories*, that sort of thing. Still, you take after your mother in that respect. A bit brainy."

He flicks through the pages, exclaiming over certain paragraphs, reading short passages aloud in a companionable fashion. Stephen resents the avuncular interest, even though he recognizes that Roger is a nice man, nicer than his own father in many ways. Roger describes himself (and is passed off by Sylvia) as "an old friend of the family,"

•

but Stephen knows that Roger and his mother are having an affair, and suspects that everyone else knows too. Certainly Geoffrey knows about it, but pretends not to. Stephen often wonders if Geoffrey has other girlfriends. He thinks that it would be much better if this was the case.

Stephen doesn't *mind* about Roger, inasmuch as it doesn't bother him that his mother is unfaithful to his father. In fact, his parents have got along better since Roger has been around because Sylvia is happier, and Geoffrey only cares about appearances, so if Sylvia appears to be happy with him, then that is all right. Stephen just wishes that they could all be more honest about the situation and stop pretending. Roger has joined the family for their summer holiday a couple of times and the pretence of the two separate rooms with his mother creeping up and down the corridor was just embarrassing.

And sometimes he has had a secret wish to spend more time alone with his mother, but Roger has always been there distracting her. Stephen knows that he had a twin sister who died when she was a baby, and he wonders if it would have been quite so easy for Sylvia to disentangle herself from motherhood and devote herself to her lover if there had been two of them around. Probably not. Anyway, now they are sending him away to school for nine months of the year, which will give Roger and Sylvia plenty of opportunity to sit around staring at one another moonily, the way they do.

"Ah yes ..." says Roger, abandoning Evelyn Waugh and sifting through the tuck box with S. G. NOBLE painted on its side, examining Stephen's pocket knife, snake belt, and shoe-cleaning kit. "You know, I can remember packing up for my first term at public school. I was at Wellington."

"What was it like?"

Roger hesitates before answering. "Some good, some bad. One can make some good friends, friends one keeps for a lifetime. And there's the cut and thrust of communal life, of sleeping in a dormitory with a lot of other people, not even being able to fart in private. Not everyone's cut out for that sort of thing."

He looks at Stephen; Stephen looks away. They both know that he is not the type cut out for communal living.

"The other boys will try and test you out," Roger goes on. "They always do, especially if you're the quiet type. You know, go on needling you to try and get a rise ..."

"It's just a school," Stephen interrupts him and finds his voice wobbling a bit. He tries to cram his ruler into his pencil case, but it won't fit. He pulls the zip shut anyway, leaving one end sticking out. "It's just a school, where you go learn and take exams and stuff. Daddy says all he can remember about it is the rugger."

Stephen is wondering whether his mother has sent Roger in to give him a pep talk, or to try and gauge his frame of mind. She uses Roger for that sometimes. He is aware he sounds defensive, but he goes on anyway. "I don't see why anyone has to test anyone out. You make it sound as though I should be scared."

"Well, aren't you scared?" Roger twirls Stephen's squash racket on the palm of his hand. " 'Course you are! Everyone is when they go to a public school for the first time. One thing's for sure; it's bound not to be as bad as you think it will be. I hear the places aren't as uncomfortable as they used to be in my day. Carpet on the floor of the dorm, that sort of thing."

"They don't have carpet at Maidenhurst."

"Right. Well, anyway.... Here's a piece of advice for you, one my father gave me and it stood me in good stead. Never give them the satisfaction of knowing what you're thinking."

Stephen doesn't think there's much chance of that happening. For the first three weeks at Maidenhurst, no one even speaks to him, let alone tries to read his thoughts. He is in a dormitory with fourteen other boys and is considered lucky, because this is one of the smaller dorms. The beds are arranged in two rows, facing one another, and at night the iron bedsteads creak and the horsehair mattresses rustle with every movement. As soon as the lights have been turned out at eight forty-five, the older boys egg the others into masturbatory competition, with the boy who ejaculates first claiming the victor's prize. Stephen, who has the squeamishness of an only child about bodily functions, finds this practice abhorrent and tries to absent himself in the bathroom when the ritual begins. This in turn causes comment.

"Noble's too good for the rest of us; he likes to wank in private. . . ."

In many respects Roger's warning holds true; it doesn't do to display emotion of any kind. When he first arrives, Stephen puts a photograph of Sylvia on his bedside locker. This earns him the label of "wet," and the ragging continues until he takes the photograph down, to the satisfaction of his tormentors.

The night of Halloween, halfway through the first term, brings a fresh ordeal. The first the new boys know about it is at midnight when they are woken and herded together into the boot room, having been told first that if they make a noise they are in for a good thrashing. The boot room houses the boiler and the pipes for the hot water system; it is also where trunks are stored during term-time. It is dark, windowless, and airless. The anxious third formers are told to wait their turn, and are taken one by one into an adjoining sluice. The lambs yet to go to the slaughter listen in silence. There are scrapes and thuds, and the occasional muffled scream. No one speaks. It doesn't occur to anyone to try to leave either; they are aware that some rite of passage is being conducted.

Stephen is one of the first to be taken into the ante-room. It has a high slit of a window that pulls open with a sash-cord. Through it he glimpses a streak of dark night sky before a blindfold is pulled over his eyes; an owl shrieks in the blackness. He is pushed into the center of the room and made to climb steps onto some sort of scaffolding arrangement. He ends up standing on a stool and it wobbles violently if he moves. The feeling of being about to lose his footing and fall, when he cannot see the floor below him, is terrifying.

Hands come out of nowhere and put a loop of rope around his neck, pulling it tight, with the knot against his windpipe. The length of rope is taut, and seems to be coming from above, from the ceiling.

"Right . . ." Stephen recognizes the disembodied voice as Brightwell's, his fat, bullying head of dorm. "Kick the stool away."

For some reason Stephen finds himself thinking of Roger Saunders and remembers his advice.

Don't let them see what you're thinking. . . .

As the stool is pushed from beneath his feet he forces his face to remain motionless and impassive, he clamps his mouth shut on the shout of fear that explodes inside him when he feels his legs drop and the rope—

He is picturing the noose pulling tight around his neck, the darkness and disorientation make the picture so vivid that he can almost feel it. But it doesn't happen. As the stool is pulled from beneath him he falls a couple of feet onto a table, the length of rope slackens and is baled out to allow him to land. He twists his ankle as he does so, but the pain of this is nothing compared with the relief. If performed in the daylight, with no blindfold, it would be a feeble trick, he decides. It is the pitch blackness that makes you feel as though you are about to be hanged.

The blindfold is pulled off him. In the gloom he can make out a row of grinning faces.

"Not bad, Noble, not bad ..." Brightwell extends a fat hand and tweaks the front of Stephen's pajamas. "Dry as a bone. Most freshers piss themselves when the stool goes. Perhaps you're not such a mummy's boy after all."

Acquitting himself in the Halloween ritual doesn't make Stephen like Maidenhurst any better. He still loathes the place. But life settles down into a more peaceful rhythm. The third formers get to know their contemporaries, finding safety in numbers. They recognize and gravitate toward kindred spirits, cliques form and tentative friendships are forged. Stephen is still amongst the shyest and quietest of the new intake, but he is learning to ignore the others, and they are realizing in their turn that Noble is harmless enough for them to ignore. He is a very able squash player, which is a saving grace in the eyes of the sporting clique. When this fact becomes known, he is treated more genially. The bullying stops.

Stephen spends every term longing for the holidays, but when they come they are invariably a disappointment. After the noise and bustle of school, he feels awkward in the tidy, elegant villa in Hemingford. It seems so silent. He wonders why he never noticed the silence before.

He is awkward with his parents too. They insist on treating him like an adult now, and he is not sure he wants them to. He wants the holidays to provide a lapse into the comforts of childhood, but it seems this is not allowed. Instead he has to smarten himself up every evening and sit down to dinner with his parents, listen to them pretending that everything is normal and that Sylvia is not in love with Roger Saunders.

It is Roger with whom Stephen feels most at ease now. He can talk to him about what school is really like. Geoffrey (and all his cousins and brothers-in-law too) adored Maidenhurst and thought it "a marvelous experience." His name is engraved on the sporting roll of honor in the dining room, as Captain of the First XV rugby team. Stephen has to pass it every day. Roger, on the other hand, reveals gradually that he was not happy at Wellington, hated it in fact. So Stephen tells him about the hanging game and Roger grimaces and squeezes his shoulder, and tells him that he was braver than he, Roger, would have been. There was something similar at Wellington, apparently. It involved having a candle stuck up one's backside.

In the summer vacation, Sylvia comes into Stephen's room when he is reading and sits beside him on the bed. She pats his ankle in an absent fashion.

"You'll never guess who I've had a phone call from."

"Who?"

"Audrey Pryce-Jones. Do you remember little Matthew Pryce-Jones who used to be in your class at Albert Road? His mother."

"Oh. Right."

"She wondered whether Matthew could come round for a swim sometime. She's quite an extraordinary woman, isn't she? It amazes me the way she's kept in touch all this time. Why do you suppose she does it?"

"I don't know."

"She must have some great need for Matthew to get on socially, or something. They live in one of those frightful modern monstrosities by the park, if I remember correctly. Anyway, I said that was okay. For Matthew to come over. I take it you would like to see him?"

"Not really." Part of being treated like an adult, the good part, is being able to say what you really think, and not what your parents want you to say.

"Oh. Why not?"

Stephen shrugs.

"But you used to like Matthew ever such a lot. We all did. Charming boy, even if he is a bit pushy."

"I suppose I haven't got anything in common any more."

Stephen did like Matthew. He worshipped him. But he nas learned a lot during his year away, and he knows instinctively what sort of boy Matthew will be turning into. He would be one of the loudmouths who set out to win the wanking contests after lights out.

"It won't do any harm to have him over for a swim, though, will it? I thought he would be company for you anyway. Roger and I were going to go out for a little drive. . . ."

Matthew Pryce-Jones comes round to the villa at two o'clock. He cycles over on a large gleaming racing bike, with his bag of swimming gear dangling from the handlebars. Stephen has seen Matthew at least once a year since he left Albert Road Mixed Infants, thanks to Audrey Pryce-Jones's extraordinary persistence in maintaining the friendship, and each time he is struck by how Matthew is more mature than he is. Now, at fourteen, Matthew could easily pass for eighteen. He is tall and broad-shouldered and carries himself with a straight-backed swagger that implies experience beyond his years. Two weeks of warm sunshine since term ended have given him an impressive suntan. Even the waving, collar-length hair and his thick-lashed eyes do not detract from his masculinity. Stephen feels conscious of his thin, pale limbs and his long girlish neck, which now lacks hair to cover it. His blond locks have been transformed by the Maidenhurst barber into a regulation short back and sides.

Stephen remembers how he used to think Matthew was beautiful and longed to be his friend. He still finds Matthew beautiful, but he does not consider him a friend, not even after all these years. He recognizes that Matthew is not interested in him, but in the swimming pool and the house. In short, Matthew uses him. When he learned that Stephen's maternal grandmother had a villa on the Riviera, his interest intensified, and he asked all sorts of questions about what his grandmother's name was, and what the villa was like. Stephen once considered inviting him to join them there on a family holiday, but decided that it would set a dangerous precedent. Audrey Pryce-Jones would have made sure he was invited every year thereafter, and Stephen wasn't sure he wanted that.

After a cursory grunt of a hello, Matthew strides straight round to the pool terrace and strips off his T-shirt and cycling shorts. His golden, muscled back gleams with perspiration. Stephen averts his eyes.

"Aren't you coming in?" Matthew shouts after he has dived into the water.

"No, thanks," Stephen goes to sit on a deck-chair in the shade.

"Why not?"

"It's not the same when the pool's there all the time. I can swim any time I like."

"There's no need to bloody show off about it!"

Matthew heaves himself onto the side, water streaming from his nose, and dives in again to do a length of crawl. Stephen picks up his book, but he is reading the same page over and over again. He usually enjoys sitting out here. The pool terrace, like the rest of the house, bears the hallmark of Sylvia's exquisite taste. There are rattan chairs covered with fat, floral cushions, and large terra-cotta pots full of trailing fuchsia and exotic-colored lilies and sweet-scented *nicotiana*. But today Stephen is disturbed by Matthew's presence. He wishes he weren't there.

After half an hour, Matthew is bored with splashing up and down the pool on his own, and annoyed by the fact that Stephen has his nose buried in a book instead of being rapt by Matthew's athleticism.

He scrambles out of the pool and stands next to Stephen's chair to towel himself off. A deliberate move so that water will drip all over Stephen's legs.

"Hey, come on, let's go up to your room!"

Once upstairs, Matthew falls on Stephen's carefully cataloged record collection and leafs through it, dropping records in a disordered heap on the floor.

"Crosby, Stills and Nash . . . yuk . . . Cat Stevens, crap . . . Donovan. *Donovan*, for God's sake!"

"Well, what do you like?"

"Alice Cooper. And Pink Floyd. They're brilliant."

Matthew abandons the records and starts looking at the book-shelves instead.

"How's the grammar school?" Stephen asks.

"King Henry's? Great, you know ... a good laugh."

"Oh. That's good."

"Of course, I shouldn't really be speaking to you now that you go to a public school. Everyone knows that people from public schools are real spastics."

Matthew's tone is aggressive, angry even. When Stephen doesn't respond, he goes on: "Is it true that you're all queer and spend your whole time buggering each other after lights out?"

"Of course not."

"All right, tossing each other off, then?"

Stephen blushes, unable to conceal his discomfiture.

Matthew laughs raucously. "Oh dear, touched a raw nerve, have I?"

"Look ..." Stephen stands up. "I think you'd better go now."

"Oh come on, don't be so wet ... I was going to go and have another swim."

"All right, leave after your swim then."

Matthew stares at Stephen in surprise as he goes out of the room. He waits on the landing for a while, as if hoping Stephen will come after him. Then Stephen hears him whistling as he gallops downstairs. He goes to his bedroom window and watches Matthew swim, beating up and down the pool in a powerful overarm crawl. He lies in the sun to dry, droplets of water glinting on his torso. Then he wraps his damp towel round his neck, hops onto his racing bike and speeds off down the lane. As Stephen watches him disappear from view, he knows he won't be seeing Matthew again.

That autumn there is a new boy at Maidenhurst who causes quite a commotion. His name is Nicholas Pobjoy, and he is very strange-looking. His hair is a rich dark auburn, but instead of the pinky fair skin associated with redheads, he has a dark olive complexion and black eyes. Nicholas Pobjoy is an Anglo-Indian. His father is from a distinguished Scots military family; his mother is the daughter of an Indian politician and educated at an English public school.

"A bloody nig with red hair!" is the astonished reaction of his fellow pupils at Maidenhurst. His looks are so exotic that he avoids a lot of the racist taunting handed out to the few other foreign boys; it is as if they fear he has supernatural powers.

Pobjoy's appearance is so very odd that Stephen finds he cannot help looking at him whenever they are in the same room. His eyes are drawn to the gleaming copper hair and the smooth *café au lait* cheeks. He goes on looking long after everyone else has grown used to the sight of the nig with red hair. He starts to seek Pobjoy out, to hang around the places where he knows Pobjoy might be. Even a glimpse is enough to add interest to the day. His fascination is becoming an obsession.

"What's so bloody interesting about Pobjoy, Noble?" someone asks one lunchtime when he is peering at the younger boy over the edge of his soup spoon. Stephen blushes and mumbles something, anything to allay suspicion. He is terrified that people will notice, and a fourth former's interest in a third former is bound to be considered "pervy." It is all right for the younger boys to hero-worship the captain of cricket or for the prefects to make risqué jokes about their "fags," the junior boys assigned to them as skivvies, who clean their shoes and tidy their studies. Any frustrated feelings they may be harboring can always be expunged by beating the younger boys, a centuries-old practice that remains one of the prefects' privileges. But interest between near-contemporaries is not tolerated.

Halloween falls just before the half-term holiday this year. The boys have been cooped up in the school grounds for eight weeks and feelings are running high. The hanging rite is about to be enacted and Stephen's contemporaries are all talking about it, heady with relief that for them the ordeal is over. They speculate about how the various new boys will react, who will cry, who will wet themselves, and so on. Stephen finds the whole business quite abhorrent, closing his ears and his mind and, if possible, leaving the room whenever the subject is raised. He dreams of that night again, of the slit of starlit sky glimpsed through the window, the salty smell of the blindfold that covers his nose as well as his mouth, the hollow call of the owl in the distance, the marks his fingernails make in his clenched palms.

Halloween is a Thursday. Stephen knows that Nicholas Pobjoy has a piano lesson on a Thursday in the period before lunch. He leaves his classmates queuing at the serving hatch for cottage pie and slivers of overcooked carrot and stands in wait outside the music block.

"Um, Pobjoy ..." He blocks the path of the younger boy as he emerges with his music case. "Can I have a word with you about tonight?"

"What about tonight?"

It is the first time Stephen has been near Pobjoy, who is as tall as he is. (He is only eight months younger—Stephen checked his date of birth in the school yearbook.) It is making him sweat. He can't look at those glittering almond-shaped eyes, focusing instead on the air behind his shoulder.

"There's a bit of a prank on tonight ... er, it happens every year. To all the new boys."

"A prank?"

"They take you into this room in turns and pretend to hang you. I just wanted to say that they don't really. They let go of the rope as soon as you fall. They just want to see how much they can frighten you."

He is afraid Pobjoy will ask why he is telling him this, but he doesn't. He just laughs and says, "Thanks a lot." He has a strange, high-pitched laugh.

Stephen stands shaking for a few seconds, then hurries into lunch before anyone sees him. If anyone found out about his warning the consequences would be catastrophic. A sacred code prevents anyone from breathing a word to any of the third formers. To do so would mean to risk destroying a school tradition, and the perpetrator would be punished and despised accordingly. Stephen considers it worth the risk. He couldn't bear the thought of Pobjoy standing on the stool, feeling the rope tighten around his neck, and experiencing that same suffocating fear. Besides, it is a stupid tradition, and one which deserves to be undermined.

He is curious to know how Pobjoy will make use of this forewarning, but half term comes and goes and he hears no more about it, except that the tormentors consider this year's intake "bloody brave."

Then one day he is returning from a cross-country run when he sees Pobjoy walking down to the boating lake. He is alone, and carrying a large bag.

"Hey, Noble!" he waves. "Over here!"

Stephen walks toward him, smiling shyly.

"Want to come with me and do an experiment?"

"What sort of experiment?"

"A chemistry practical." There is a wicked gleam in Pobjoy's eye. He opens the tote bag to reveal a large lump of sodium, the size of a small football.

"Bloody hell!"

"I thought I'd chuck it in the lake, see what happens."

"It'll explode, of course!"

Stephen knows from his "O" level chemistry course that when neat sodium makes contact with water it reacts violently, releasing a surge of energy. The tiny fragments handed out in the laboratory make a substantial bang.

"My cousin at Gordonstoun tried it. Said it was quite something."

Stephen follows Pobjoy to the far corner of the lake, which is surrounded by dense thicket and screened from the main school building by the projection of the boat house.

"Get ready to run!" Pobjoy opens the bag.

"No, wait a minute . . ."

It is too late. The sodium hits the water with a resounding boom, that hurls Stephen onto the muddy bank. Water and fragments of pond weed shoot into the air.

Pobjoy is on his hands and knees. "Bloody hell!"

"Jesus bloody Christ!"

After the sodium episode, Stephen and Nicholas become friends. This does not meet with anyone's approval, since friendships are supposed to be confined to boys in one's own form. But Stephen has already been put down as odd, and Pobjoy is rapidly turning out to be a law unto himself. He is a free spirit, wild and imaginative, with ideas as exotic and colorful as the subcontinent whose blood runs through his veins. He is constantly breaking the school rules and defying its small-minded conventions, but he gets away with it. It is almost as though the others—pupils and teachers alike—believe that his strange racial mix makes him superhuman. He and Stephen are referred to as Aladdin and his genie, with many coarse jokes about who is rubbing whose lamp.

Stephen does not have sex with Nicholas, though he is aware that everyone thinks they do. It is rumored that some boys "do it" with one another, but in fact information on that subject is very vague. Stephen is afraid of the idea of sex with Nicholas, so afraid that he doesn't even dare consider whether he would enjoy it or not. Nevertheless, they are very close. And in his private thoughts, Stephen admits that he loves Nicholas. He doesn't think he could ever say so.

On one occasion they come close to doing something they shouldn't. They have been running together and it starts to rain. Spotting at first, then drizzle, then an outright deluge. Nicholas suggests they shelter in the hollow of a large oak, an ancient tree alleged to have been planted by King Charles II. The trunk has been made into an alcove with a carved bench, and there is a plaque to commemorate its history.

The boys huddle on the bench, squeezing their knees together to keep them out of the rain.

"Are you going to watch the First XI play away tomorrow?" Stephen is conscious of the need to keep up the conversation.

"Don't think so. How about you?"

"Not if you're not going."

"What shall we do instead?"

"We could go into town and check out some bookshops. Buy a bottle of cider."

"Okay."

They are silent again, and Nicholas suddenly puts his arm around Stephen's shoulder and pulls him close as though he is going to kiss him. Stephen finds himself responding, the idea doesn't appall him as it should, in fact he wants it. Then Nicholas pulls away again as though he has changed his mind, and Stephen is left thinking he must have imagined it, that the embrace was just a chummy hug.

Then Mr. Barron, the Physics master, spots them while out walking his dog and waves his stick at them.

"Oi—you boys! What do you think you're up to? Get out of there, you nasty little animals!"

The two boys jump down from the bench and run back to the school in the pelting rain, with Nicholas laughing his loud, eerie laugh.

"Mummy . . ."

In the summer holiday of the following year, 1974, Stephen seeks out his mother.

"Mummy, can I have a friend to stay this hols? From school. His name's Nicholas Pobjoy, and he's very nice, you'll like him."

Sylvia sits down at her dressing table and starts to brush her hair with vague, distracted strokes. She is not really looking at her reflection. She has been even more distant than usual since Stephen has been home from school. Her face looks pale and puffy, and the warm weather seems to be making her listless and exhausted. Stephen wonders if it is what they call the "change of life," which he has heard is something nasty that mothers go through once they are past forty.

"I don't know . . ." she is saying. "I don't think it's a good idea at the moment."

"But, Mummy, you'll like him really, and he won't be any trouble, I promise!"

"I'm sure I'll like him, darling. But that's not the point. I just don't feel up to having house guests at the moment."

Stephen is angry with his mother and sulks in his room for several days, relieving his feelings by writing long tracts to Nicholas about the unreasonable nature of women. One afternoon when he is at his desk, and Geoffrey is at his desk somewhere in the City, he hears his mother calling his name. He is tempted to ignore her, but she sounds distressed.

"What is it?" he shouts from the landing.

"Stephen, come in here . . ."

He goes into the bedroom. Sylvia is sitting on the edge of her bed, clutching her lower abdomen.

"Stephen . . ." she gasps. "I want you to go downstairs and phone Dr. McCullough. Tell him I think I'm losing the baby."

The baby? Stephen can only stand there and stare at her, horrified.

"I'm pregnant," she says, speaking hurriedly before the next pain comes. "About three months. Please—just phone the doctor."

Dr. McCullough's receptionist puts him on hold while she interrupts a consultation and before he has a chance to speak to the doctor he hears his mother shouting, calling him back. He hangs up and goes upstairs.

Sylvia is standing in the middle of the bedroom, with blood dripping from between her legs, making a rash of red spots on the pale Wilton carpet.

"I don't think I can wait until Dr. McCullough comes." She adds, as though this were not obvious to her son, "I've started to bleed."

"I'll call an ambulance."

"No! Not an ambulance. I don't want people seeing an ambulance come to the house. A taxi."

"You can't go in a taxi, what about ..."

What about all the mess on the seat? He can't bring himself to say it.

"Phone Roger then, please!"

So it's Roger's baby. Of course it is. Stephen is finally aware of the extent of his mother's predicament. Part of him wants to abandon her to her fate, he feels so angry with her, but he is only too aware that she is relying on him to cope. He phones both of Roger's numbers, but there is no reply. In desperation he tries the number of his Aunt Sara's flat in Knightsbridge. He knows there is no time for her to travel down from London, he just wants someone else to be there to help him with this mess, preferably another woman. There is no reply from his Aunt Sara either. He phones the emergency service and asks for an ambulance.

Sylvia is worse. With her every movement there is a fresh gush of blood. It is soaking through her underwear and the skirt of her dress, leaving brownish red smears wherever she sits.

"Stephen, you'd better fetch me a pad."

"A pad?"

"A sanitary pad, stupid! From the cabinet in the bathroom."

Stephen stands motionless for a few seconds, trying to pin down his floating, horror-struck mind to the task in hand. He finds a sanitary pad, and as he touches it he retches. Back in the bedroom, Sylvia waves it away.

"You're going to have to fetch me a bucket."

Stephen brings a plastic bucket from the kitchen and Sylvia squats over it. She won't let Stephen leave the room, so he stands near her, unable to find a blood-free corner to sit. He closes his eyes, but he can still hear the steady "drip, drip" onto the bottom of the bucket, and hear his mother's groans. At each drip his gorge rises. His mother's body was a mysterious and secret thing, now it is terrifyingly real.

He can't bear to look at her in the ambulance, and although Sylvia screams and pleads for Stephen to be allowed to stay with her at the hospital, he is relieved when a nurse leads him away.

He goes to see his mother later. She has a private room, but to get to it Stephen has to walk through the gynecology ward. He recognizes the smell now, the smell of women and their bodies; raw and bleeding.

Sylvia looks tired and pale, but all traces of the blood are gone and she is wearing a fresh nightgown. Stephen can sit close to her and hold her hand.

"Had you told Daddy?" he asks.

She shakes her head.

"You were going to *have* the baby, weren't you?"

Sylvia sighs a deep sigh. "I wanted to. I know forty-two is considered too old to be safe, but ... I was hoping so much that it would be another girl. I felt I was being given a last chance. After losing Amabel ..."

"Tell me about her."

Sylvia has never spoken to Stephen about his sister, but he has seen the dresses in her bottom drawer, some tiny baby ones, some for a much older child. She used to try Amabel's dresses on him sometimes ... or was he just imagining that?

"There's not much to say. I didn't even hold her. Or perhaps just once ... It was all over so quickly, so suddenly. But afterward I always felt that there was something—someone—missing in my life."

"I'm sorry." Stephen looks down at his hands.

"Do you feel like that? They say bereaved twins grieve and feel the loss, even if they never knew their twin."

This is a new idea to Stephen, he considers it for a while.

"I've felt lonely," he says.

In September that year, Geoffrey and Sylvia take Stephen to his grandmother's villa in Cap Ferrat, and Nicholas Pobjoy comes with them, at Sylvia's suggestion. Stephen recognizes that this is his reward for saying nothing to anyone about his mother's miscarriage.

Roger Saunders does not come this year. There has been a marked cooling off between the lovers of late, as though Sylvia's pregnancy was a climax and now, with the baby gone, anticlimax inevitably follows.

Sylvia's mother, Lydia Chancellor, lives in some style with the same Argentinian polo player she ran off with twenty years earlier in the face of predictions that it would only last six months. At the age of sixty-two, there is a little of the faded beauty about her, and a great deal of the grande dame. Even so, she has a dry, bitchy sense of humor and is not above poking fun at herself and her life-style.

Stephen likes going to his grandmother's house, he feels free there. He is treated as an adult, but here it is enjoyable to be an adult, not stifling as it is in Hemingford. And, as he had expected, Nicholas and his grandmother have an instant rapport.

"Where *did* you get him from, Stevie darling?" she exclaims. "What a charmer! And that extraordinary coloring. He looks like the outcome of some genetic experiment. A most successful outcome, I should add."

Though he returns to the Cap many times in years to come, Stephen will always remember that particular summer holiday, in 1974, as the best of all. His parents are in a conciliatory mood toward one another, and disappear daily to go on shopping expeditions or drives along the corniche, or to lunch with old acquaintances. They offer to take the boys, but the answer is invariably that they would prefer to stay behind.

The villa is built in Romanesque style, with a terra-cotta roof and rough plaster walls washed a pale pink. There is a round tower with its own wrought-iron balcony which looks down on the roofs of the tiny hillside village below, and from which the turquoise waters of the Mediterranean can be glimpsed. The landscaped garden has a circular pool with pillars and statues around it, and is overlooked by a shady terrace entwined with bougainvillaea. The interior is cool and white; white upholstery, white ceramic floor tiles, and white walls which display Raoul's collection of modernist paintings.

Raoul, Lydia's lover, is a source of great amusement to Nicholas. Now that there is someone to share the joke with, Stephen also begins to find him funny, and wonders why he never noticed this before. Raoul is seventy years old, lean and muscular with skin baked to the color of gingerbread after years on the polo fields of South America and the beaches of Europe. His white hair is swept back from his forehead in a bouffant style and his chest sports a thick white mat, which is always on view since his customary dress in the daytime is a pair of tight, skimpy shorts. Raoul has a toy poodle which he carries about in the crook of his arm in the French fashion. It looks odd on such a tall, athletic man, as does the leather handbag which dangles from his wrist on a strap.

Despite his years with Lydia, poor Raoul has no grasp at all of the subtleties of the English language, and his speech is littered with malapropisms and mispronunciations. When Nicholas enquires how old the dog is, he is told "She is 'alf-past three."

Raoul is well known locally as a chaser of anything dressed in a skirt, something to which Lydia turns a blind and benign eye. Certainly Aimée, the maid-of-all-work keeps a wary eye on his movements when they are in the same room together.

Stephen and Nicholas have adjoining rooms, but they convene in one room or the other after they have retired and talk into the small hours.

One night, when Nicholas is perched companionably on Stephen's bed, leaning back against the pillows, they hear Raoul wandering the corridor singing an aria from *Turandot*. When he is drunk, which is frequently, he berates Lydia and the poodle in Spanish and then lapses into opera, usually Italian.

The boys start to laugh when they hear him.

"You'll never guess what I saw in Raoul's dressing room today," Nicholas whispers.

"What?"

"A can of hairspray. That's how he makes his hair stand up like that. It doesn't even move when he dives into the—"

The door opens and Raoul wanders in, his knees sagging. He stumbles about in the dark, finally seeing the two figures on the bed.

"Oh, *pardon*, I have the unjust room. . . ."

He wanders out into the corridor. Both boys are silent for a while, wondering what conclusions Raoul will have drawn from seeing them on the bed together, hoping that he is drunk enough to forget about it the next day.

"I wonder if he was looking for Aimée's room." Stephen breaks the silence finally. "She won't be safe if he is."

"I think Aimée would rather it was you."

"What d'you mean?"

"I've seen the way she looks at you. She goes bright red in the face and gets all embarrassed. It must be your blond hair. I think French women go for that sort of thing."

Stephen finds the idea distasteful. Aimée is a coarse, thick-set girl with a fine line of down on her upper lip. She doesn't shave her armpits and her personal odor suggests that she doesn't use deodorant either.

"Come off it, Nicholas! She's twice as old as I am! She's more likely to be interested in my father than she is in me."

"But would you, though . . . if she, you know . . . would you do it with her?"

"God, no!"

"Why not?"

"I don't like the way she smells, that's why." Stephen thinks privately that he doesn't like the way any women smell, but he doesn't dare say as much. "Have you ever . . . you know, with a girl?"

"Only kissing. French kissing. With tongues."

"Was it, you know . . . what was it like?"

"There's quite a knack to it actually. You have to make sure your faces are pointed in opposite directions, otherwise your noses bash together. Look, like this: I'll show you."

Nicholas places a hand firmly on Stephen's shoulder and pulls him forward until their mouths are touching. Stephen can just feel the tip of Nicholas's tongue, pressing softly against his lips. They begin to part instinctively.

Then Nicholas breaks away and laughs his high-pitched, barking laugh. Confused, Stephen scrambles from the bed and walks out of the bedroom and along the cool darkness of the corridor. He has an erection, and he doesn't want Nicholas to know. Or was that what Nicholas wanted?

He steps outside onto the terrace, and his brain churns with a welter of questions, fears, and longings as he looks down on the blank reflection of the pool.

Nicholas does not accompany the Nobles on holiday the following summer, because they go to the hotel in Positano again, but he does in the summer of 1976, when they return to Lydia's hillside villa.

By this time Stephen and Nicholas are in the upper and lower sixth form at Maidenhurst, a state of affairs that allows them a little more freedom, but not much. Their persisting closeness has become a matter for comment, not so much among the other boys, who have grown used to Aladdin and his genie (or the Lone Ranger and Tonto, as they have been named more recently), but among the masters. Casual homosexual encounters are one thing, but a love affair is quite something else, and not to be tolerated. It smacks of bohemianism, of some sort of decadent regime along the lines of E. M. Forster.

Accordingly, Stephen is summoned to the head master's office; he is considered to be the more responsible of the two.

Mr. Emrys Hopwood, MA (Cantab.) is wearing his academic hood and gown to reinforce his authority and instill some sort of resolve. He presses his fingers together in a church steeple, speaking as though reading aloud from a school prospectus.

"Whilst we encourage the boys to make friendships—friendships which in many cases will last for the rest of their lives—it is probably not a good idea for two boys to seek one another out to the exclusion of everyone else. Hardly in keeping with our aim to cultivate the good all-rounder. Eh, Noble?"

"No, sir."

"I understand from my staff that you and Pobjoy see a great deal of one another."

"Yes, sir."

"Do you have anything else to say on the matter?"

"Well, it's quite hard not to, sir. We're in the same house. And we do a lot of the same sports."

"I think we both know what we're talking about here, Noble. I don't suppose you're entirely ignorant of the ways of the world, and I know I'm not. What I'm talking about are certain immoral acts, things which used to be illegal in this country until fairly recently. Are you with me?"

"Yes, sir."

"Well—has anything of that nature gone on between you and Pobjoy?"

"No, sir."

"You're quite sure about that?"

"Yes, sir."

"Good. Because you see, Noble, if I were to hear that any boy in this school had been found to be doing that sort of thing with one of his fellow pupils, I would be obliged to expel both of them immediately. And of course I would have to tell their parents why, which would be deeply unpleasant. Are you still with me?"

"Entirely, sir."

Stephen is telling Mr. Hopwood the truth—at that time he and Nicholas are not lovers. But they are to become so, on that second summer holiday in the south of France. It is on a hot night when they have been for a midnight swim in the pool, and then finished off a litre bottle of the local wine, a crisp but rather coarse *rosé*. A drunken hurdle race over the garden sprinklers follows, leaving them collapsed on the damp grass in a panting, laughing heap. And then it happens.

Without any trace of self-consciousness or deliberation, they go from laughing to kissing. Nicholas moves behind Stephen, reaching forward to caress his chest, then Stephen feels Nicholas entering him. It is as simple as that: a strange, painful sensation, so strange and wonderful that in only seconds he is drained, shattered by an orgasm. Is this really me? Stephen wonders as his shudders subside and the lawn sprinkler drenches his naked body with its rhythmic spray. Is the person who wanted that *me*?

· ■ ■

He is not sure whether they made too much noise with their laughter, or whether it was some other noise, but the next day his parents seem to know about it. Perhaps they are aware of the electric tension between Stephen and Nicholas, some way in which they just seem *different*. Geoffrey stomps off angrily after breakfast to go to the golf club, and remains angry for the rest of the holiday. If he speaks to Stephen he is polite but curt and he doesn't address Nicholas at all, referring to him in the third person as "your friend."

Sylvia, on the other hand, seems upset. On at least two occasions Stephen finds her in tears and the tone she uses with him is either resentful or pleading. Some insecurity is awakened in her and she spends much of her time writing long letters to Roger Saunders, driven to rekindle the relationship which has all but died away. Neither of Stephen's parents says anything directly or indirectly on the subject of homosexuality. They are far too frightened by the idea and besides, it doesn't happen to people like them.

Though nothing is ever said, it is clear that Nicholas is no longer welcome in Hemingford, nor is he invited to join the Nobles on their trip to Cap Ferrat in the following summer of 1977. Nicholas has just left Maidenhurst for good, dropping out of his "A" level course, and Stephen is to return for one more term to take the Oxford University entrance examination.

Nicholas makes no overt reaction to the Noble family's withdrawal of hospitality, and it occurs to Stephen that Nicholas might be assuming that the two of them will be going away together to some other destination. He seeks out Nicholas on the last day of term and finds him in the boot room, stuffing cricket pads into his trunk.

He sits on the edge of Nicholas's trunk and looks down at his hands.

"I can't believe this is really it. The end of our school days."

Nicholas gives Stephen's thigh an affectionate clap. "Come on! You should be glad! I thought you couldn't wait to get out of this place! Anyway, it's not the end for you. You're back next term to sit that dreary exam."

"It's the end of us being here together though, isn't it?"

Nicholas squats back on his heels, looking up at Stephen's face. "What's brought all this on?"

"I was wondering what you were going to do this summer. You haven't said."

"Spot of relative-bashing," says Nicholas cheerfully. "I'm going to New Delhi to see my aunts and uncles and all the cousins I haven't seen for years. Should be good fun."

He laughs, to make his point. Stephen says nothing, looks down at his hands again.

"Cheer up! I'm not going to be gone forever! I'll be back in England in the autumn, probably, and I'll see you then."

But Stephen is aware that beneath the question of the holidays lies the deeper, more urgent matter of where their relationship can go from there. He loves Nicholas with the overwhelming clarity and single-mindedness of first love, and yet he feels constantly sick with guilt. To have a teenage love affair with a member of one's own sex can be forgiven and forgotten but to pursue it into adult life is to take it onto another plane. He finds himself reluctant to do this when he knows it will distress his family; he has been raised, after all, to be a good boy, not to be a trouble or a nuisance to anyone.

And then he thinks of women; chiefly of his mother and her sad distractedness when he was young, and her miscarriage and the ward full of swollen and bleeding female bodies and he is not sure that he wants that either. . . .

He would like to know what Nicholas thinks, but when it comes to laying bare the inner self, Nicholas practices an Oriental inscrutability, or just laughs in that maddening, evasive way of his. He flies off to India with nothing resolved and Stephen goes to the villa on the Cap with Sylvia and Geoffrey and Roger Saunders (recently reinstated as "old family friend") and mopes about wishing he were in New Delhi. He worries about whether and when Nicholas will come back; he said in the autumn, but he also said only "probably."

Nicholas Pobjoy is not mentioned by anyone, except Lydia, who enquires in private after his health.

"Never mind," she says, patting her grandson's hand with her liver-spotted one. "Delightful boy. I'm sorry he couldn't be here this year."

There is a tension in the air which is not just the result of Sylvia and Roger being together again. Roger comes into Stephen's room one evening when he is writing to New Delhi and tries to raise the subject of Stephen's relationship with Nicholas. He tries to make his manner that of the seasoned man of the world, but it comes out as merely awkward. Stephen realizes that he is acting on Sylvia's instructions and says nothing.

Just before Christmas, Stephen learns that he has won a scholarship to University College, Oxford, to read a joint honors degree in French and philosophy. He will take up the place in October 1978, and during the year in between he will either find a job or travel; it is a popular belief in the 1970s that one or both of these pastimes will confer maturity and experience on the pre-university student.

Stephen favors the former option. He is almost nineteen and has never had gainful employment of any description. Besides, Nicholas is working, as a messenger for a London record company. If Stephen were to find a job in London, then they could certainly see a lot of one another, perhaps even share a flat.

It is no doubt with this thought in their minds that Sylvia and Geoffrey promote the benefits of travel, and present Stephen with a check for a thousand pounds with which to travel round Europe. He sets off alone with his belongings in a brand-new blue nylon rucksack, a present from Roger. He takes the boat train from Victoria and goes first to Paris, then to Dijon and from there to Switzerland and Germany. He stays in cheap, but respectable hotels, visits the obligatory sights and spends long hours sitting in street cafés doing preparatory reading for his course at Oxford and writing dutiful postcards home to his parents. He is solitary, but not lonely. In fact after the crowded communal life of Maidenhurst he positively relishes his own company and the complete anonymity of being alone in a foreign city.

But he misses Nicholas, quite terribly. Then in June, just before Stephen's money is running out, Nicholas leaves his job in London and joins Stephen in Italy for the last few weeks of his tour. By mutual consent they head for the red-brown domes and scorching blue skies of Florence, where they stay in the quaint old-fashioned comfort of the Pensione Quisisana, near the Ponte Vecchio. They have a small room at the back of the building, and from the slanting attic window they can just glimpse the roof of the Duomo.

Their sexual relationship resumes there with an intensity and lack of restraint that would have been impossible at the villa in France, under the same roof as Stephen's parents. Stephen tells himself—and Nicholas—that this was not what he intended by inviting Nicholas to join him abroad, but it has little effect. Thus, as well as enjoying himself, he loathes himself too, for his lack of restraint. He loves Nicholas, but wishes he could do so in a distant, intellectual way.

Two weeks of sexual oblivion lead to exhaustion; the weather is hot and humid, the city dusty and beginning to fill with its crippling burden of summer tourists. Nicholas announces that he is going to head off to the Greek island of Mikonos and try to find a job in a bar. He describes the island to Stephen one evening as they sit opposite Santa Croce sipping glasses of grappa, and his eyes glow as he describes the nudist beaches, the free availability of drugs, the gay party scene.

Stephen declines to join him, though he doesn't say what he is thinking: that Mikonos sounds appalling. His public school education has left him with a streak of inbuilt hypocrisy that has him shuddering at the thought of an open, promiscuous homosexual community. After Nicholas has left he cannot face the three-day train journey home, so he spends his last hundred pounds on an air ticket from Pisa to Gatwick and flies back.

He arrives in Hemingford unannounced to find his parents in the middle of a small supper party. Instead of being annoyed they seem delighted by his bursting in halfway through, unkempt, with two days' growth of beard and clothes that have gone unwashed for months.

"How marvelous!" says Sylvia, uncharacteristically gushing after an aperitif and three different wines. "We were just telling the Griffiths all about you, weren't we, Geoffrey?"

The Griffiths are Sir Roland Griffiths and his wife Delia. Sir

Roland is the chairman of Geoffrey's firm of stockbrokers, and Stephen vaguely remembers meeting him at the firm's Christmas children's parties when he was a child.

"... And this is our daughter, Alison."

He ought to remember meeting Alison, too, but he doesn't. She is a girl of outstanding plainness: tall and angular, with pale fish eyes and awkwardly large hands and feet. Her mouse-colored hair is swept back from her oval forehead with a child's velvet Alice band and she wears no makeup on her pale skin, seeming younger than her nineteen years.

"Alison is starting university in the autumn, too, at Girton in Cambridge. Isn't that a coincidence? She was just saying how much she would like to meet you...."

Alison smiles uncertainly.

"... and here you are!"

"Yes, here you are!"

"Give the lad a glass, Geoffrey!" says Sir Roland expansively, waving an arm from the depths of the sofa. He is both immensely tall and immensely stout, and seems to have been wedged firmly between the sagging seat cushions. "Let's drink a toast to the return of the prodigal son!"

"To the prodigal son!"

"... the prodigal son!"

Stephen stands in the circle of raised glasses, his sunburnt face flushed with embarrassment. "Er, perhaps I should just go and have a bath and change...."

"And here's to a successful summer holiday!" Delia Griffiths raises her glass.

"We've asked the Griffiths to join us at Grandmama's this August," Sylvia explains. "And the best part of it is that Alison can come too! So you'll have some company of your own age. We thought it would be a nice idea."

Alison and Stephen have been set up by their parents in the most bald and calculating fashion, answering their mutual need for suitable companionship for their offspring. Sylvia and Geoffrey are desperate to rescue their son from Nicholas Pobjoy's influence and any girl will do, even one as unlikely to cast a sexual spell as Alison. The Griffiths, who are very "social" are embarrassed by their daughter's gaucheness: She has never once been asked out by a boy and doesn't seem inclined to rectify the situation.

This mutually satisfactory arrangement is only too obvious to Stephen and Alison, who ignore one another resentfully for the first few days of the holiday at Lydia's villa. Resentment that is fueled on Stephen's part by the fact that Alison has been put into Nicholas's old room. For her part, Alison seems to dislike the superworldly Lydia and to be terrified of Raoul.

Then one morning it strikes Stephen how ridiculous this situation is. He is sitting on a sun-lounger on one side of the pool with his head stuck in a book; Alison is sitting on a lounger on the other side of the pool, with her nose equally firmly stuck in her own book.

He lays down his copy of the poems of Baudelaire and approaches Alison's chair. He notes, with approval, that she is reading the poems of Robert Browning.

"Would you like to come for a walk?"

Alison lowers her book to look at him. She is wearing a floppy sunhat to shade her face, so he can't see her eyes. She has broken out in pale freckles all over her body, and the skin between the freckles has turned a pale, rosy pink.

"I don't really think I want to." She speaks in a tense, measured tone.

"Look," says Stephen patiently. "If we're going to be pushed together like this, then we may as well try and get something out of the situation."

Alison pushes back her hat so that he can see that she is smiling. "Let's go for that walk then."

And so Stephen discovers that Alison is not nearly so gormless as her parents' treatment of her would imply, and Alison finds that Stephen is not as unapproachable as she feared. In fact, they discover that they like each other quite a lot, which is not surprising given all they have in common. They are both only children, both shy, both love literature and hated their boarding schools. Their new friendship becomes a source of pleasure, but they conceal this from their parents so as not to give them the satisfaction of feeling they have achieved their aim.

Stephen resumes his habit of swimming late in the evening after the others have gone to bed, and on several occasions Alison joins him. They sit next to one another on the edge of the pool with their bare legs turned ghostly white by the underwater spotlights.

One night they drink a bottle of Listel rosé, and the wine loosens their inhibitions a little. Alison confides how her greatest fear about going up to university is being the only girl in the college who doesn't have a boyfriend.

"... And yet I'm afraid of the men, too. There'll be ever such a lot of them you see, they outnumber the girls by about four to one. I wish I knew what it was like to have a brother, or I'd been to a co-ed school."

Stephen sighs.

"D'you worry about that too? About failing with the girls?"

He nods slowly, looking straight ahead.

When they go back into the villa, Stephen bids Alison goodnight outside the door of her bedroom.

"Um ..." She pauses, seeming to want to delay their parting. He feels her pale, freckled hand on his wrist, thinks of Nicholas's dark skin.

"Why don't you come in with me? We could ..."

Stephen pushes her hand away gently. "I don't think that's a very good idea." He kisses her cheek. "But thanks, anyway."

On October 9, 1978, Stephen goes up to Oxford to begin his new life as an undergraduate.

He settles into it more quickly than he had expected to. In college life he anticipated some of the horrors of Maidenhurst, the lack of escape from one's peers, competitive posing, and victimization of those who are different. But here in liberal-minded Oxford, he discovers, undergraduates are expected to carve their own niche and not take too much notice—outwardly at least—of what other people think of them.

Stephen's scholarship entitles him to some of the best rooms in the college. They are at the top of a staircase on the main quad looking out over the bustle of the high street; a small bedroom and a large sitting room with an adjoining study annex. Though the undergraduates have done nothing to deserve the privilege, and show little appreciation, the old system of college servants still persists and at nine-thirty each morning there is a knock on the door and a gnarled Oxonian called Fred, Stephen's "scout," appears in the doorway wearing a gray steward's jacket and holding an ancient Hoover. He is there to clean the room and make the bed, and clicks his false teeth impatiently if Stephen is still in it.

This rarely happens, as the only reason for rising late is a late party the night before, and Stephen doesn't attend many of those. He rises early, feeling great exhilaration at having an empty day stretching away before him, and the freedom to fill it exactly as he wishes. Lectures are optional for students in the Faculty of Arts; the only commitments Stephen has are three hour-long tutorials each week, for which he must write an essay.

Stephen enjoys this independence; he is rapidly discovering that he is good at being on his own, resourceful when left to his own devices. However, such autonomy disorientates many of the students, who have spent all of their eighteen or nineteen years being told what to do, and they flounder around, spending too much time in the pub, or the library, or simply wandering about the city. Many of them solve the problem by hastening into a relationship. This is not necessarily with someone of the opposite sex—being gay is acceptable at Oxford, fashionable even. During the freshman year there is a rash of undergraduates "coming out." Stephen is not coming out, he has every intention of staying in. He enjoys his work and hides from the issue of his sexual identity by studying hard, spending hours in the wood-paneled, fusty rooms of the Bodleian Library.

His gentle, self-effacing nature makes him popular, and almost despite himself he makes friends. One of his best friends at University College is Ben Woodrow. Stephen suspects that Ben is probably gay, but the two of them go around with a crowd of both sexes, and Stephen avoids discussing Ben's preferences.

Then, at the beginning of Trinity term in 1979, Ben asks Stephen to go to a party with him. Oxford is wearing its spring colors, fresh, green, and thick with horse-chestnut candles and apple blossom, and the students are in festive mood. There are always more parties in May and June than at any other time of year.

"It's a toga party," says Ben. "A rite of spring. At the Piers Gaveston."

"Oh, I see. Listen, Ben, I'm not sure I can go. I've got this essay. . . ."

The Piers Gaveston is Oxford's most decadent dining society, formed by a group of well-connected young men and women, bright young things, whose gatherings are rumored to include outrageous behavior and depraved acts. Their parties are the focus of great interest, to the extent of featuring in full-length articles, with color pictures, in the Sunday supplements. It is no coincidence, either, that the society is named for King Edward II's partner in sodomy.

"Come on, Stephen . . ." Ben wheedles. "It's going to be great fun; there's a wine fountain apparently, and banqueting tables, and live music. . . ."

Stephen's curiosity gets the better of him. He rigs together a toga from two bed sheets and a laurel headdress from some shrubs in the college gardens and walks down the high street to the function rooms of the Oxford Union, where the party is being held. This being Oxford during term time, no one gives him a second glance.

He is appalled and fascinated by what he finds. A dimly lit room, fogged with cigarette smoke and reeking of sour wine is crammed to bursting point with semiclad bodies. Stephen trips over the legs of two who are entwined underneath a table. They are both girls. People are dancing, some of them men with men, smooching like heterosexual couples at a high school hop. Stephen stands next to the food table and peers through the smoke, taking it all in. A couple of girls ask him to dance; he declines.

Ben has vanished into the crowd, but he reappears at Stephen's side some minutes later, his lips and teeth stained indigo with cheap red wine.

He puts his arm round Stephen's shoulders and tries to steer him into the mass of swaying bodies. "C'mon, let's dance."

Stephen stands his ground, resisting being pulled. "No, Ben."

"Why not, for fuck's sake? What are you being so coy about? You are gay, aren't you?"

"I think you've made a mistake." Stephen pulls free of Ben's grasp and fights his way through the crowd, bursting out of the hot, choking atmosphere and into the cool air of the lane outside. He takes long, deep breaths of it, drenching his lungs.

It is after midnight when he gets back to his room, but he turns on the lamp in his study and sits down at the desk, still dressed in his sheets and open sandals. He thinks of the male participants at the party with a shudder; the hot greediness of them. Their freedom of expression is all about sex, not love. It is love that Stephen wants.

He picks up a sheet of headed college paper and writes. "My dearest Nicholas ..."

Stephen has all but lost touch with Nicholas since Italy. He is back in London, drifting from job to job, mistrustful of the rarefied life-style of Oxford undergraduates. But Stephen misses him with a pain that runs right to the depth of his being, he thinks of him constantly.

He sets down his pen and looks at the three words on the paper. *My dearest Nicholas* ... The problem that he was facing when he left school has crystallized now: he must make a commitment. He must decide how he is going to live the rest of his life, either as a gay man or as a straight. Because of the permissive society in which he has grown up, there is at least a choice. Stephen feels he should be grateful for that, although it does not make the choosing any easier.

He stares at the letter for a few moments longer then screws it up and selects a fresh sheet.

"Dear Alison ..."

E *i g h t e e n*

■

Jackie

Jackie Yardley is lying in the bath, reading, when her mother comes into the room. Pamela is holding a full teapot in her hand. She smiles down at Jackie, baring her teeth. Then she tips the steaming tea all over Jackie's legs, scalding them. The boiling liquid and the tea-leaves swirl around in the water, turning it dark brown. Jackie tries to protect herself with her book, but the book has floated away. The water is turning from brown to red, blood red. Jackie screams but her mother has gone from the room.

The scene changes: they are now at a party. Jackie is following Pamela, pursuing her. She sees her with her back turned, talking to an unknown man. Her father, perhaps? Jackie calls out to attract her attention. Pamela turns her head slowly and the look on her face is one of sheer scorn and contempt. . . .

Jackie wakes before the alarm, sweating. She often has dreams like this. Their common theme is that her mother hates her. They have been so vivid of late that Jackie is beginning to wonder if this is true. Is there hatred there, beneath the indifference and the pathetic need?

There is little opportunity for her to toy with this disturbing idea. It is 1973, and at the age of fourteen Jackie is studying for her "O" levels at King Henry Grammar School for Girls, sister to the boys' school, and taking sole responsibility for the running of two households.

It is five-thirty when she wakes up, but she does not bother rolling over and returning to sleep. There is too much to do, and the alarm would be going off in thirty minutes anyway. She creeps into the bathroom, barefoot so as not to wake Pamela with the slap-slap of her slippers on the linoleum. She washes her face, cleans her teeth, and brushes her hair back into a sensible ponytail. All these movements are mechanical and efficient; the result of long years of having to get the business of caring for herself over and done with as quickly and unobtrusively as possible.

In that respect she neglects herself; she does not look unkempt, but she does look worn out. Her figure is slender and petite, with no spare flesh at all on her fine-boned frame. Her gray eyes are enormous in her small, pointed face. Her hair is a warm golden color and floats about her face in wisps if left to hang free. In fact Jackie would be very pretty if only she did not look so tired all the time.

When she has dressed in her school uniform of white blouse, pleated gray skirt, and maroon and gold tie, she collects up a bundle of dirty underwear from the linen basket in her room and rinses them all out by hand, hanging the row of damp panties on the radiator in her room. She pulls a chair in front of them so that Pamela won't notice. Doing the laundry is supposed to be her mother's area of responsibility but she forgets, and Jackie does not like to trust her underthings to Pamela anyway, she would rather take care of them herself. But she has to hide the evidence as her mother is so sensitive about any suggestion of incompetence or failure.

Once her laundry is drying and while it is still quiet, Jackie sits at her desk and checks through her homework, finished off at midnight the night before. Then she cleans up the sitting room, emptying full ashtrays, dusting and picking up rubbish from the floor, just as she has done for the last five or six years of her life. She checks the kitchen cupboards, makes a brief note of groceries that are low in supply, and puts the list into her satchel.

Jackie then boils the kettle and sits down with a pot of tea and a slice of toast. She dare not put the radio on for fear of waking her mother and they cannot afford a daily newspaper, so she munches her toast in complete silence. She always enjoys this time: the quiet, the chance to sit with her own thoughts. She remembers the dream. It seems odd that her mind should insist that her mother is angry with her when the only person Pamela expresses anger against these days is Billy. She and Billy have not spoken for two years, not since Pamela borrowed some money from her father and then spent it all on drink. They had a row about Pamela standing on her own two feet, and after that Pamela has refused to go and see Billy in his house. His poor health prevents him from visiting the flat.

After she has eaten her toast, Jackie washes her own cup and plate and sets the table ready for Pamela's breakfast, leaving the empty teapot ready beside the kettle. Then she puts on her blazer, shoulders her satchel and sets off to the bus stop. It is twenty to eight. Pamela will not surface until at least nine o'clock.

It is Thursday, which means she has double physics followed by math. After the morning break she has a free period, then German. When the bell rings to indicate that it is time for lunch, Jackie slips away from the herd of chattering girls queuing outside the canteen. She collects her purse and her list and leaves the school by the front gate. Strictly speaking only sixth formers are allowed out in their lunch hour, but nobody sees her. Her name is on the list of pupils who bring their own packed lunch to school. In fact Jackie rarely has any lunch at all; there is no time.

There is a small Gateway foodstore in the street adjacent to the school, and Jackie goes in there and buys groceries: bread, milk and margarine, tinned ham and baked beans. Her slight body tilting a little under the weight, she carries the shopping bag along a circuitous route of backstreets and alleyways, until fifteen minutes later she reaches Billy's house. He lives in a bay-fronted, pebble-dashed semi, neglected and unadorned, with grimy net curtains and a plastic donkey in a sombrero on the windowsill of the ground-floor room.

Inside, all is dark and quiet. Billy has fallen asleep in the sitting room, in front of the gas fire. He starts when she comes in, then smiles.

"Hello, Princess!"

Billy Yardley is an invalid now, and has been since his stroke. No one knows how long he will survive. Jackie sometimes wishes he would die now. Not for her sake, but for his. He is completely housebound, and the house is so grim and depressing. At least it is clean; Jackie makes sure of that.

"How are you feeling today, Granddad, all right?"

"Not so bad, sweetheart, not so bad. Mrs. Phelps, that so-called Home Help, was here earlier."

"Oh. Is she any good?" Jackie goes through into the kitchen and puts the kettle on, starts making a plate of sandwiches.

"She's a pleasant enough soul, I suppose." Billy rummages for his handkerchief and blows his large, purple nose. "She tidied round a bit, but she's not much good at that. Not like you are. She offered to give me a bath."

"And . . . ?"

"I said not to bother. I was hoping you would give me one."

"Oh Granddad!" Jackie hands him the sandwiches then checks her watch. "I haven't got time! I'll have to get back to school in a minute."

"Oh. I see." Billy's face crumples in disappointment, just like a child's.

"Maybe tomorrow, though?"

"All right, tomorrow." Billy watches his granddaughter as she goes back into the kitchen. "I don't suppose I could have a little snifter of something to wash these down?"

"No, you can't! You know what the doctor said about booze."

"Just thought I'd ask. . . . You're a great kid, you know that, Princess. I told you your old granddad would always take care of you, didn't I, but now it's you who's taking care of me. That reminds me, how's your mother?"

"The same."

"Stubborn cow."

Jackie leaves a plate of food ready for her grandfather's evening meal, then goes upstairs to make his bed, tidy up his dirty clothes and put his dressing gown and pyjamas to warm on the radiator. Billy can manage to get himself upstairs, but only just. Jackie thinks that they will soon have to bring his bed down into the front room, a step that Billy is reluctant to take because he knows it marks the end. After that there's only hospital or death.

Jackie hurries back through the dingy streets and into school, her carrier bag full of her grandfather's dirty linen. Then it's double

French and netball, then home to the flat, a tedious journey which involves taking two different buses.

Pamela spots the bag of washing instantly.

"You've been to see him, then?"

"Yes."

"How is he?"

"Why don't you go and see for yourself?"

This provokes no response at all. Pamela merely turns her head back to the television screen.

"He's the same," says Jackie.

"Oh."

Jackie takes Billy's clothes down to the launderette, as Pamela doesn't like to see them drying around the flat. At least it is warm there, and she can sit and read her English lit. texts uninterrupted. When the clothes are washed and dried, she takes them home again and leaves them in a bag by the front door. She will be going back tomorrow. And the day after.

Pamela is in one of her catatonic moods, sitting motionless in front of the television, smoking. Jackie makes baked beans on toast for the pair of them and takes her mother's through to her on a tray.

"Mum, I was thinking ..."

"What?" Pamela frowns.

"I thought I could do some decorating here in the flat. My room could do with it—"

"I thought you liked it." Pamela's tone is accusing. "I chose that stuff specially for you."

"But Mum, that was fourteen years ago! It's baby stuff! Anyway, I could start in here if you like. Brighten the place up a bit."

"There's no point," says Pamela through her mouthful of beans. "The landlord probably wouldn't allow it. Anyway, we don't know how long we'll be here."

Jackie's mother has said this frequently over the years, and here they are still in the same scruffy two-bedroomed flat with no likelihood—no hope—of ever moving anywhere else.

After years of long experience, Jackie knows exactly when to abandon a subject and say nothing. She clears away the dishes, washes up and sits down in her room to catch up with her school work. It is nearly midnight before she turns out the light. Pamela is still watching the television. It has been a typical day.

Many girls in Jackie's position might have resented the time spent at school, or at the very least found it difficult to make the commitment that their studies demanded. But Jackie loves the grammar school, everything about it: from the ugly, pointed Gothic windows to the smell of beeswax on its polished wax floors and the gray felt bowlers the pupils wear in the winter. She does not even mind the heavy workload, reveling in the school's academic tradition and its reputation for producing first-rate exam results. The day she learned that she had won a place there was the happiest in her bleak life.

King Henry's is her sanctuary from the present, a place where she can escape from the burden of her domestic routine. It is also her stake in the future, because by working hard she will guarantee herself a place at a university, and from there a good job. The school can provide her with an escape, from her mother, from the flat, from Hemingford itself.

It has not given her much of a social life, not because she is unpopular, but because she feels that she cannot reciprocate or follow up any friendship outside school hours. She cannot invite friends back to her home; shame prevents her wanting them to see the flat, or to meet Pamela. And it is difficult for her to join the other girls when they go out into the town together to shop, or to discos. Pamela has funny turns if Jackie is absent from the flat too long, and besides, she has nothing to wear. Literally. She only has her school uniform, one dress and a couple of sweaters. Billy used to buy her clothes, ugly, tasteless ones, but he is no longer "earning." And Pamela has hardly any money at all, certainly not enough to pay for a teenager's clothes.

Jackie worries long and hard about the lack of money. This worry in turn spurs her to even greater dedication to her studies, because good grades will mean a good job and that will mean plenty of money. She intends to have plenty of money, always.

Her own contribution to the household budget is from a paper round which she does on Saturday and Sunday mornings. Most of this is spent on food. Pamela does occasional casual work and claims social security and the statutory child allowance. Fortunately they have a protected tenancy at the flat and the meager rent is subsidized heavily by an allowance from Hemingford Borough Council. Otherwise they would have to live in Billy's house. Pamela would probably opt for homelessness in the face of this option, which would mean Jackie being taken into care. Could being in care possibly be worse than her life as it is? she wonders, as she tidies the same old mess every day, and shops and cooks and cares for Billy. But it might jeopardize her place at King Henry's, her passport to a new life, and that would be the worst thing that could happen.

So she does not pursue the issue of redecorating the flat, in case it leads to their being evicted. As long as there is money for food and heating and her school uniform, she will survive the next four years somehow. She has never been on holiday, or left Hemingford at all, except for a day trip to Hastings when she was nine and her fellow pupils at Albert Road were heading off to Italy or Majorca.

The other girls in Jackie's form are very much in awe of her single-minded dedication to study. They do not despise or dislike her for it, for the grammar school is after all a monument to the middle-class ideal of bettering oneself through good teaching and individual effort. There are many intelligent, hard-working girls in Jackie's class, with their sights set high. But they recognize that Jackie's need for results is in a class of its own. Her seriousness would be all right if she did not seem so very *old* with it. She carries herself like an adult; albeit a small and undernourished one. The assumption of responsibility for her mother and grandfather has stripped her of any youthfulness and prevents her from being one of the crowd.

She does have one close friend: Helen Croucher. Helen is also excessively serious, though not as mature as Jackie. Her sobriety is generally put down to the fact that her father is a vicar. Helen lives in a nice, ordinary suburban house with a garden and a mother and father. In this sense she and Jackie are worlds apart. What they have in common is their aptitude for study, though in Helen's case it is learning for learning's sake, unprompted by the burning need to get on in life. They lend one another books and compare notes on homework, and on the rare occasions when Pamela is working, Jackie goes round to Helen's house near Lordswood Park and studies with her in her room. Mrs. Croucher lights a fire for them and brings them in a tray of tea and buttered toast and Jackie has to quell her feelings of envy and force herself to view the visit as a chance for extra work, and not a taste of another, more kindly life.

Helen has covered for Jackie on a couple of occasions when she has had to sneak out of school to visit Billy. She cannot quite conceal her disapproval, or her curiosity about the situation.

"Surely you can do *something?*" she whispers to Jackie when they are in the changing room getting ready to go and play hockey. "I mean, your mother really shouldn't be letting you do everything. Can't you try talking to her?"

"It wouldn't do any good."

"But she's your *mother*, Jackie. I mean, if it were my mother—"

"But it's not, is it?" Jackie tugs viciously at the laces of her hockey boots. "Your mother's different."

"I don't believe there isn't *someone* who can help, though. What about a social worker or something?"

"Look, Helen, it's a lot more complicated than you could possibly realize. You'll just have to believe me when I say it's better if the situation stays as it is. For now."

And so it does, until the summer of 1975 when Jackie takes her "O" levels. She manages well with the extra workload of exam revision, because unlike most of her classmates she is not troubled by the distractions of boys and parties. Boys are starting to feature more prominently now that she and her contemporaries are sixteen. And the topic that provokes the most discussion is the dance with the fifth formers of King Henry's Boys Grammar, a joint celebration of the last of the exams, and the impending end of term. Everyone is going.

"I'm not going," says Jackie to Helen. "I can't stand that sort of thing."

"How d'you know, if you've never been to a dance before?"

"I just know I won't like it."

She can't bring herself to mention the two real reasons—one, that she has not spoken to a boy since she left primary school (unless you count one of the paper boys, who is twelve) and two, she (literally) has nothing to wear.

Finally she is convinced, not because of any argument Helen has to offer, but because if she is going to go to university eventually and then get a top job, she will need some practice in talking to the opposite sex. She scrapes together some money from her paper round and buys herself a cheap T-shirt with a sequined butterfly on the front. And Helen lends her a pair of flared jeans which are too loose round the waist and too long; they have to be pinned up at the bottom into bulky, ungainly hems. Neither she nor Helen have ever worn makeup, but Helen buys some from Outdoor Girl at Woolworths, a metallic gray eyeshadow that makes Jackie's eyes look even more enormous and hollow than they already are, green waterproof mascara that smudges, and a pink lipstick that neither of them applies very well.

Jackie hates every minute of the dance. The girls congregate at eight o'clock in the school assembly hall, decorated for the purpose with balloons and streamers and posters of 10cc and the Who. They stand close together like so many penned sheep, giggling and whispering and comparing clothes and jewelry. Then the King Henry's boys arrive in a coach and are corralled in through the door at the other end of the hall. The two herds stand and stare at one another: sheep and goats. Then one brave boy asks a girl to dance and the sheep and the goats gradually mingle together into an animated blur. The air becomes thick with sex and competition.

Jackie knows how to dance, because for years Pamela has sat in front of "Top of the Pops" on Thursday night, watching the studio audience hopping and jiving. But she does not know how to talk to boys, so she does not dance. Instead she hovers behind the table where the drinks are laid out; fizzy orange and, for the very daring, dry cider.

There is a boy who keeps looking at her from the dance floor. His gaze makes her uncomfortable. She looks down at her hands, then busies herself rearranging the rows of plastic cups on the table.

He comes over to her. "Are you in charge of the drinks?"

"No."

"Then what are you hiding behind here for?"

She looks up and he is smiling at her in a good-natured fashion. He is of medium height but broad and heavily built, with a pleasant, open face, light brown hair waving back from his forehead, wide-set green eyes and a full, generous mouth. Not really *good*-looking, she decides. Nice-looking, though.

"I'm Robert Jones. Rob."

"Jackie Yardley."

They shake hands solemnly.

"Come and dance."

She shakes her head. "No, no thank you."

"Don't be silly, come on!" He pulls her onto the floor, still smiling. He never stops smiling.

Rob compliments her on her dancing, then when the music changes pace and the other couples become locked firmly together from the lips down, he shows a hesitant Jackie how to slow-dance.

"That's it, put your arms round my neck but keep them loose, don't strangle me! Relax!"

Jackie relaxes, and as she does so finds to her amazement that she is enjoying herself. So much so that she scarcely notices when the dance comes to an end and the hall begins to empty. She looks around everywhere for Helen but can't see her. She must have already left.

"I'd better go. . . ."

"Give me your phone number and I'll ring you. We could go out some time."

Jackie is thrown into confusion. "No, I don't think . . . we haven't got a phone." She feels her face turning red.

Rob gives her his easygoing smile. "So? Give me your address and I'll call round some time."

"Honestly, I'd rather not, I . . ." Jackie is starting to stammer. She takes a deep breath and says, "I live alone with my mother and she's very strange about things like that, I just . . . she doesn't like meeting people and the flat's too small, really. We don't have a nice house or anything . . . And there's Granddad . . ."

"Look." Rob puts his hands squarely on her shoulders and looks her in the eye. "I don't mind about any of that, it's hardly your fault where you live, and anyway, it's you I'm interested in, Butterfly ..."

"What? ... Oh, I see."

Rob is pointing at the sequined butterfly on her T-shirt. "It suits you. You're like a butterfly. A pretty, delicate butterfly."

Jackie can't look at him, not now he has said that. "Listen, I'd really better be going. I'm late as it is."

He scribbles on a piece of paper and hands it to her. "Here's my phone number then. You could always ring me."

Jackie was counting on a lift from Helen, and didn't bring any money for the bus. She has to walk the four miles home, getting back an hour and a half later than she told her mother she would. When she sees two uniformed police officers on the landing outside the front door of the flat she assumes that Pamela has panicked and called the police out to search for her.

"Miss Yardley?"

"Yes?"

"We need to speak to you ... it would be better if we could come inside for a moment."

Jackie unlocks the door and leads them into the darkened flat. The television is off, which means Pamela must have gone to bed.

The policemen take off their helmets and sit down heavily on the stained, fraying sofa. "We've got some bad news for you, I'm afraid, love. It's about your father."

"My *father?* But ..."

The older of the two policemen pulls out his notebook. "You are Miss Pamela Yardley? Flat B, 30 Wetherall Gardens?"

"Oh no, that's my mother. I'm Jacqueline Yardley."

"I see. Beg your pardon ..." The policeman makes a note on his pad. "It's about your grandfather in that case. Is your mother in?"

"She's sleeping."

"Don't wake her just yet. It might be better if you break it to her."

And he tells her as kindly as he can that Billy Yardley has been found dead in the gutter, a few streets away from his home. Apparently he was on his way to the Pig and Whistle for a drink.

■ ■ ■

Pamela is having a nervous breakdown.

After Billy's funeral, Jackie notices that her mother does not change her clothes for a couple of days. The two days stretch into three, then four, then five. She does not wash her hair either. When Jackie prepares food for her she just sits and stares at it until her daughter spoons it into her mouth as if she were a baby. For the last few days of the summer term, Jackie takes to returning home from school at lunchtime to care for her, just as she did with Billy. She knows that this cannot go on for much longer. Then on the day school finishes for the holidays, she comes home to find that Pamela has rampaged around the flat, smashing things, throwing food at the walls, tearing up her clothes. It is almost a relief for Jackie to find her like this. Now she can legitimately stop managing by herself.

She telephones Pamela's GP, who comes round immediately, gives Pamela an injection, and takes her to Hemingford General. He says that her mother will be sedated for quite a while and there is little point in Jackie coming to the hospital. So she stays behind in the flat. It is strange being there on her own; there have always been the two of them, she and her mother.

Term is over, there is no more studying to do. Jackie occupies herself tidying up the mess. She starts with the kitchen, where the damage is worst. This takes her an hour and a half, then she turns to her mother's bedroom. There is an old cardboard shoe box on the bed whose contents have been ripped up and shaken across the room like large petals of confetti. They seem to be photographs, mementos of some sort. Curious, Jackie starts to piece them together, but is interrupted by a ring on the doorbell. She bundles all the pieces of paper back into the box and puts it into the wardrobe.

Her visitor is a young woman called Miss Prentiss, who describes herself as a psychiatric social worker. She has come from the hospital to talk about Pamela. They sit down together at the kitchen table.

"Now, Jacqueline, how much do you understand about your mother's condition?"

"Has she gone mad?"

Miss Prentiss smiles the smile of the well-informed professional. "Not mad, no. But she is very ill. I've not had a chance to talk to your mother myself, but to behave as she did, she must have been very unhappy for a very long time."

Jackie is worried by this. "Should I have called the doctor sooner?"

"I'm sure you did what you could, no one's blaming you. Sometimes these things can be very hard to spot, they happen so gradually. And then something triggers a breakdown ... in this case I think it was your grandfather's death."

"Will she get better?"

"Probably. But mental illness is like any other illness, it needs the correct treatment. And the best place to do that at the moment is in hospital, as an in-patient. So your mother will need to be away for quite some time."

"In an asylum?"

Miss Prentiss smiles again, and shakes her head. "No, not an asylum. Your mother's very lucky, we've just opened up a brand-new center to treat people with her sort of illness. It's a nice modern place with private rooms instead of wards. A bit like a hotel, really. She'll receive excellent care and counseling, and there are lots of facilities for her to use her time creatively when she's up and about."

"Oh." Jackie tries to imagine her mother using her time creatively, but cannot.

Miss Prentiss turns her attention from the subject of Pamela's welfare to Jackie's. Where will she be living in the meantime, she wants to know, and with whom?

"What about your father?" she asks.

Jackie makes no response.

"Have you lost contact with him?"

"My mother wouldn't talk about him." She can't bring herself to say to this neat, confident woman, who wears a diamond engagement ring on her left hand: *I don't even know who he is....*

"What about other relatives? Or friends?"

Jackie realizes that she must say something to satisfy the woman, so she gives Reverend Croucher's name. Miss Prentiss promises to telephone him and "make arrangements."

■   ■   ■

Jackie is quite content to stay with the Crouchers for a few days, but it is always her intention to return to the flat as soon as the fuss has died down. She does not like the idea of leaving it empty; it makes her feel insecure, as though she will return and find it gone. Miss Prentiss has assured her that the rent will continue to be paid until such time as Pamela is well enough to return, but Miss Prentiss is part of the system and Jackie doesn't entirely trust the system.

The Crouchers are not happy about Jackie going to live in the empty flat, but she fobs them off with a tale about a neighbor who is going to keep an eye on her. In reality, none of their neighbors have become friends, few have even spoken to her. The other flats in the building are on short lets, and tenants come and go too often to care.

To begin with, Jackie misses her mother, misses having someone to say hello to first thing in the morning and wish her good night last thing in the evening. But she becomes accustomed to the solitude quite quickly, and what follows is a blissful period of independence and freedom from drudgery.

First, she spring-cleans the flat from top to bottom, then buys a cheap can of pastel paint in Hemingford's Wednesday market and paints the sitting room. She cannot afford any new ornaments or furniture, but she buys fresh flowers for the flat and puts them in milk bottles and jam jars. Once the tone of her environment has been raised somewhat she feels charged with energy and decides she will pass the time until school starts in September by getting a job.

Casual jobs are in plentiful supply at that time of year, and she has no trouble finding work. Indeed, it is so easy that she wonders why her mother always claimed that finding a job was difficult. Jackie has no skills and no experience, but she is offered a job as a shelf-stacker at the supermarket in the shopping center, and if she is willing to work late shifts, she can take home a princely twenty-eight pounds each week. There is a subsidized canteen at the supermarket, so she need spend no more than five pounds each week on food, and she saves bus fares by rising early and walking. So at the end of each week, she has at least two crisp ten-pound notes to put into the music box that Billy once gave her.

Seeing that pile of money grow gives Jackie a pleasure and a satisfaction she never dreamed possible. She lives for the end of Friday afternoon when she is handed the small buff envelope with "J. Yardley" written on it, and she hurries straight home to put the new notes into the pile, to count them and count them again.

She sees Helen occasionally and visits her mother twice a week, but otherwise her only company is her fellow shelf-stackers. On a few occasions she catches sight of her old adversary from Albert Road, Caroyln Fox, who is working at the hairdressing salon in the shopping center. Carolyn wears platform shoes and a long leather coat; Jackie thinks she looks very tarty. She does not want to have to talk to her and explain her circumstances, so when she sees her she pretends not to recognize her. Apparently Carolyn lives in the same street as Helen Croucher. She and her friends from the comprehensive school hang around at Jangles discotheque and talk about nothing but boys.

She has resolved to save most of the money, but at Helen's prompting she does allow herself to spend some on clothes. It is strange to go shopping for clothes after years of never having any. She spends five pounds on a new pair of Brutus jeans, and three pounds on a gauzy cheesecloth top with batwing sleeves.

Trying out her new finery in front of the mirror in the flat, it strikes her how wasteful it is to buy new clothes and have nothing to wear them for, no one to see how splendid she looks. Her makeup is applied much better these days too; some of the girls at the supermarket have been giving her tips.

So it is only now that she goes to her chest of drawers and takes out the slip of paper with Rob Jones's number on it, though it is not as if he has slipped from her mind. In fact, she has thought about him rather a lot.

They arrange to meet in town at the Pizza Parlor. Jackie has never had a pizza before, nor wine, which she reluctantly agrees to try. Rob tells her that she will like the white more than the red, and he is right. Before the pizzas have even arrived at the table, Jackie has told him about Pamela's breakdown. She made a decision before coming out to mention it as soon as possible, get it out of the way. Rob is very sympathetic. Of course, he has a nice, normal family. His father owns a garage, his mother is a housewife, he has a younger brother, Gareth, and a sister, Susie. They are all close, they "get on really well," as Rob puts it. But then how could Rob be so pleasant and confident, so eternally cheerful without a family like that?

"So, what are you going to spend all your hard-earned cash on?" he asks, as they bite into the hot, gooey triangles of pizza.

"I'm saving it for the moment. There's a sixth form skiing trip on at the end of December. My friend Helen is trying to persuade me to go on that, though it seems a bit extravagant to spend it all in one go . . ."

"A trip? So you might be away this Christmas?" Rob looks distinctly put out, hurt even.

"Don't worry, it's only for a week," says Jackie and then they laugh at themselves: here they are already behaving as though they're a couple. Rob orders more wine and they laugh some more.

"This is fun, isn't it?

"Yes it is," says Jackie, meaning it. She feels relaxed, just like she did when they danced.

"We could do it again tomorrow."

"Another time. But not tomorrow, I'm due for another visit to my mother."

Pamela Yardley is an inmate at the Mayflower Center, a new and experimental psychiatric hospital built by the Hemingford Health Authority with funds from a massive government grant. It is an attractive, single-story building on the edge of the town, set in its own grounds, which have been landscaped and filled with flowering shrubs. Numerous sliding glass doors give access to the gardens and admit light to the comfortable carpeted interior. The staff wear informal white overalls and white shoes in the American style; the atmosphere is relaxed, friendly, intimate even.

On Jackie's first few visits, Pamela seems distant and confused but tranquil after the massive doses of antidepressant drugs she is receiving. She sleeps a lot, as much as fourteen hours in twenty-four. Then she undergoes a course of electroconvulsive therapy, and there is a gradual improvement in her general demeanor. The doctors explain to Jackie that the simulation of a controlled fit, or convulsion, often helps sufferers of severe depression, though it is not fully understood how this is achieved.

By the end of the summer Pamela is up and dressed and leaving her room to spend time with the other patients, whose company she seems to genuinely enjoy.

"We had an old-time dance evening yesterday, it was ever such fun!" she tells Jackie on one of her visits.

Jackie is amazed; she has never thought of her mother as a social being, one who is capable of making friends. And yet with increasing frequency she arrives at the Center to find Pamela chatting to the other inmates or busy with some activity or other. There is a television room, with a set switched on constantly, but Pamela is too busy to watch it, she says. One week she has been painting in watercolors, the next playing badminton, the week after that a course in first aid is added to the growing list.

A natural consequence of all this socializing is that Pamela starts taking an interest in her own appearance again. There is a hairdressing salon at the Center, staffed by volunteers, and Pamela becomes a frequent visitor to have her hair washed and set and her fingernails manicured. She gives up smoking, and she starts to make clothes for herself in the sewing class. Jackie often arrives to find her wearing a new blouse or skirt, made in bright colors and cheerful floral prints.

Pamela seems to enjoy her daughter's visits, but not to depend on them. Jackie gradually forms the impression that if she failed to turn up, her mother would not be upset. She talks eagerly to Jackie about her new life and the people in it and the way her days are spent, but the boundaries of the Mayflower Center mark the limit of her interest. She rarely asks Jackie about her own life, about the flat, or her new studies in the sixth form of King Henry's, or even whether Jackie is managing all right on her own. She just seems to assume that Jackie will be all right.

The doctors are delighted with Pamela's progress, they are confidently predicting a complete cure for the depression that has haunted her since Jackie's birth. Jackie sees only that she has lost the old mother, who had no time for her, and is gaining a new mother who will have even less time for her.

This feeling is strengthened by the advent of Don. When Jackie arrives to visit her mother, she often finds her in the company of one of her many friends. Increasingly, the friend she is with is a man called Don Anderson.

"Don and I are partners in the dancing classes," Pamela tells her daughter. "Everyone has the same partner for the whole course of lessons, and me and Don are together, aren't we, Don?" She gives his arm a squeeze. "He's a real devil on the dance floor!"

Anyone less devilish than Don would be difficult to imagine. He is nearly twenty years Pamela's senior, a small, stout, sheepish man in his late fifties. Don has been mildly deranged since the death of his wife two years earlier. He always smiles at Jackie in a friendly fashion but speaks very little to anyone. Pamela, on the other hand, is transformed in his presence into a giggling, simpering flirt, someone less recognizable as Jackie's mother than the drugged, sleeping figure of her very earliest visits.

The regime at the Mayflower Center allows the inmates to leave on day release, to visit friends and relatives. The frequency of these outings is built up gradually to help patients adjust to their return to the real world. Pamela begins to mention trips out with Don, shopping mainly, or to walk in Lordswood Park. At no time does she suggest that she might visit Jackie on one of her days out. As the days darken and winter approaches, Jackie raises the question of Christmas.

"I thought we ought to decide what we're going to do now," she says, while her mother gets on with hemming a bright scarlet blouse. "Then I can start to make plans. Matron told me that you can have two days away over Christmas."

"Well, yes, but not everyone takes them. Do they, Don?" The ever-silent Don shakes his head. "You see, there's so much going on here, that not everyone wants to. There's a roast turkey lunch, and carols round the tree on Christmas Eve—"

"And the blessing of the crib."

This is the longest sentence Don has ever uttered in Jackie's hearing.

"… And the blessing of the crib, yes, that's right. And then on Christmas Day itself, Don and I have been invited to visit Don's son and daughter-in-law. Haven't we, Don?"

"I see," says Jackie.

"What about you?" Pamela adds, as an afterthought. "What will you do?"

"I'm going away with the school," says Jackie, making an instant decision. "To Switzerland."

The next morning she gets to school earlier than usual, goes straight to the school secretary's office, and puts her name down for the last available place on the skiing trip. It costs one hundred and sixty pounds, all of her savings.

If asked to convey her first impression of Switzerland, Jackie would be unable to. She is simply in shock, albeit a very pleasant sort of shock.

The expedition leaves the day before New Year's Eve. Jackie has spent Christmas Eve alone, catching up on some school work, and Christmas Day at the Crouchers' house. This is a bleak celebration for Jackie, although the family do their best to make her feel at home. She finds she misses Billy more than she does Pamela. He was always so cheerful at Christmas, full of festive spirit, usually the alcoholic kind.

The flight to Geneva is an ordeal for such an inexperienced traveler. Jackie feels queasy and terrified throughout, sucking end-lessly on green boiled sweets and not daring to move lest she suffer the indignity of needing the waxed paper sick bag.

Then there is the bus journey to the resort of Verbier, and finally the mountains themselves. To someone who has never been further afield than the south coast of England (and then only once), who has not even seen a hill, the sight of the snow-clad Alps against a sapphire sky is dizzyingly spectacular, almost too spectacular. The first time she sees them she has to look away, blinded, disbelieving. And then there is the village, with its picture-book prettiness, and the Chalet Rosa where they are staying, with carved wooden shutters and balconies like an illustration from the Heidi stories. All this before she has even set foot on a ski slope.

Sixteen girls from the sixth form at King Henry's have taken the trip, accompanied by the games mistress and the geography mistress, who is single and sporty. They are all staying in the same chalet, sharing two or three to a room. Jackie is sharing with Helen. They have a small room under the eaves, with a sloping ceiling and a round window that looks out onto huge icicles hanging from the underside of the roof. Jackie pulls back the curtain on her first morning and simply stares.

Being on skis provides another shock, the shocking discovery of the nearest possible thing to actually flying through the air. Three of the girls have skied before, the rest all start together on the nursery slopes. Jackie, who once excelled at dancing, is supple and wiry and light on her feet. This natural aptitude, combined with her customary single-mindedness mean that she is soon moving up from the beginners' class to the intermediate class, leaving Helen behind. Helen is clumsy and uncoordinated; she has no sooner struggled to her feet than she is falling over again.

When the novelty of waking up to brilliant sun and snow has worn off, and clumping around everywhere in heavy boots and swishing waterproofs seems second nature, Jackie realizes that skiing holidays are not so much about the sport as about the social life. There is a milk bar in the center of the village where people congregate during the day, in an atmosphere fogged with steam from their outsize bowls of hot chocolate and the drying-out of damp ski clothes. In the evening the centers of attraction are the pizzeria and Charlie's, a night club frequented almost exclusively by English skiers. They provide night-time haunts for the giggling, whispering group of King Henry's girls, eyeing the boys from a well-known Roman Catholic college in the north of England.

By the third night the two groups begin to merge, assignations are made, and a pairing-up process begins. Jackie is not interested in pairing up, and when Helen develops a crush on a Catholic boy called Michael, she is disapproving.

"We're here to ski," she says firmly. "Not to mess about with boys."

"Oh, *Jackie!* Don't be such a spoilsport!"

Helen is disappointed: it transpires that Michael's best friend, Andy, has been admiring Jackie from afar.

"He's ever so nice, and he told Michael he thought you were the prettiest girl in the group. He wants us to make up a foursome."

"I don't want to be part of a foursome. I just want to ski. That's why we're here. Anyway . . ." She blushes. "What about Rob Jones?"

"But you've only been out with him a few times and he hasn't even kissed you! It's a bit pathetic if you're going to let that stop you having fun!"

No one is more aware than Jackie herself that having fun is not her forte. She also knows that it is a skill, a sort of conditioning that she has never acquired. As she trudges up the hill to the cable car, with her skis on her shoulder, she doubts whether she ever will be any good at having fun. It is probably too late.

And as she watches couples meeting up at the ski lift—including Helen and Michael—she can see that there are distinct advantages to being in a pair. The boys carry the girls' skis and poles for them, find them seats in the overcrowded mountain restaurants, and prevent them being crushed in the queues for the cable cars. Women or girls alone tend to be ignored, or pushed past, thus losing their rightful place in the queue. Older couples with children leave them at home, or in a resort crèche, and head off *à deux*. The system is not designed for loners.

If Rob were here . . . she finds herself thinking constantly. If Rob were here I would have fun. The times she has spent with him have been the only fun she has experienced. Absence starts to make her heart grow fonder and fonder until she is thinking of him in a sentimental way that is quite new to her. In her mind he is assuming a quite unjustified importance in her life, an almost heroic stature. There are a lot of attractive young men around but none of them seems . . . well, as *nice* as Rob Jones, somehow.

When she is flying down the trail at full speed, however, Jackie is not aware of anyone, or anything, except the icy air in her face and the rush of snow beneath her skis. Then she falls, her first bad fall. She loses both her poles, and one ski comes off and shoots away down the slope. She straightens out her twisted limbs and fumbles to remove her other ski, but the clasps have caked with snow and her fingers are too cold to unfasten them. She has no way of reaching the missing ski unless she walks down the trail and even that will be perilous as the slope is steep and its surface icy. All she can do is sit tight and hope that someone eventually stops to help her. The likelihood of this happening is diminishing as the sky is blurring into a white-out.

Finally a skier stops beside her with a flurry of snow.

"D'you need a hand? It's Jackie, isn't it?"

The skier is Andy, the one who has been admiring her from afar. His freckled face is eager, his fingers reassuringly skillful as he unclamps her remaining ski.

"I was watching you. That was quite a fall you took, wasn't it?"

Andy goes down for the other ski, then carries them both, and her poles, to the café where he finds her a seat and buys the reluctant Jackie a hot chocolate.

"We could meet tonight. In the village. I'll take you for a *glühwein*."

"Thanks, but I don't think I should. I've got a boyfriend you see, back in England."

"Looks like you and Andy have got together, then?" Helen says as the two girls trudge down the snow-packed steps of the chalet.

"No, we haven't," says Jackie firmly. "He carried my skis back for me, that's all."

She spends the rest of the holiday conscientiously avoiding getting paired off. She will go out with a group, but that is all. And with the spending money she saves she goes to the pharmacy in the village and buys the season's most prized ski accessory: mirrored glasses in colored frames. When she first saw them she desperately coveted them, not because she liked the way they look, but because they would make her look like everybody else. Ever since her Albert Road days she has been desperate to conform, and if she is not going to pair off like the others, she will at least wear the right thing. She buys two pairs: pink frames for herself and blue ones to take back for Rob.

In the summer of 1976, just before Jackie's seventeenth birthday, Pamela Yardley is discharged from the Mayflower Center.

She has known about this for some time, but leaves it until the very last minute to tell her daughter. Jackie (who has already been informed of the date by the nursing staff) interprets her mother's secretiveness as a reluctance to leave the place that has sheltered her for nearly a year. Yet her mother does not seen dismayed by the idea of resuming her place in society; she is cheerful, bright-eyed.

"There won't be time to do much in the flat," Jackie says on her last visit. "But perhaps I could take the curtains down in your room and give them a wash? I've already washed the bedspread and the table runner. . . ."

"No need to go to any trouble, I shan't be staying in the flat for very long."

"Oh? Why not?"

"Don and I are getting married!" Pamela looks at her intended and giggles. "Aren't we, Don?"

"I see. Well . . . congratulations."

"So I'll be going to live in Don's house afterward. The wedding's in six weeks, we've booked it already. You will come, won't you?"

The invitation is issued as if Jackie were a casual acquaintance or a neighbor.

But what about me? I'm your child, what about me . . . ?

She can't say it.

"What about the flat?" she asks.

"I don't know about that. We'll have to see."

So Pamela becomes Mrs. Don Anderson, at Hemingford Register Office. She wears lilac chiffon and the gold wedding band she always wanted. The ceremony is on the afternoon of Jackie's birthday, but somehow this seems to be forgotten in the fuss. The other guests are all from the Mayflower Center. Don accepts the congratulations silently and does not make a speech. That honor falls to the Center's consultant psychiatrist.

Jackie finds the wedding depressing. Still more depressing is the news that she will be going to live with Don and Pamela at Don's house.

"I suppose you'll have to" is Pamela's comment when she hears that the Council will no longer be paying the rent on the flat, and that Jackie has no means of claiming this benefit for herself.

The newlyweds spend a honeymoon weekend in Eastbourne.

Jackie does not allow herself to imagine what this will be like. Instead she goes back to the flat in Wetherall Gardens, to pack up their belongings and say good-bye. She sits for a long time in the room that has been hers since she was a baby, the room that Pamela decorated with such care when she was pregnant. The same frilled curtains hang at the windows, tied back with their graying ribbons. Jackie never did get round to redecorating this room, and she is glad now. The task Pamela completed seventeen years ago was the first and possibly the last constructive thing she did for her daughter. Jackie wants to look at it now, and remember. She takes one of the once-pink ribbons for a memento, everything else she leaves in place, taking only three suitcases of clothes and personal items. The flat was let furnished; even the salt and pepper pots did not belong to them.

Don's house is a modern semidetached on a housing estate on the eastern extremity of Hemingford. The development was reclaimed from waste land in the late 1960s; it is bleak and windswept and lacking in vegetation of any kind except for the rows of thin, straggly trees that give the estate its name: The Poplars.

Don is very house-proud, and inside everything is meticulously clean and comfortable. But it is tiny. Jackie's presence makes it seem cramped, as though there were one too many dolls in a dolls' house. Downstairs there is a narrow hallway leading to a combined lounge and dining room. A door leads from here into a galley kitchen too small for two people to stand in at the same time. Upstairs there is a small front bedroom and an even smaller spare bedroom at the back, which is to be Jackie's.

Don and Pamela leave her up there for a while on her first evening, to unpack and settle in. The room is so narrow that if she sits sideways on the bed, her knees are touching the opposite wall. The bed is covered with a turquoise and white flouncy nylon bedspread. There is a bright turquoise wall-to-wall carpet and chocolate-box pictures on the walls in cheap gilt frames. It is as well that Jackie has few clothes; she just about fills the narrow melamine wardrobe and the tiny chest of drawers.

When she has unpacked she goes downstairs and offers to help with the supper.

"It's all right, dear," trills Pamela, "Don's taking care of it."

It is as well that Don knows how to cook, because Pamela certainly cannot. And since there is only room for one person in the kitchen, Pamela busies herself with setting the table, fiddling with napkins and fancy raffia table mats. She seems happier if she can ignore Jackie and pretend she is alone with her new husband, so Jackie sits quietly in the lounge, in a dark red armchair with an antimacassar on the back. She stares at the patterns on the carpet, swirly shapes in shades of marmalade and burnt caramel.

Then Pamela calls that supper is ready, as excited over Don's toad-in-the-hole as most people would be over a banquet. She exclaims with delight over the battered sausages and soggy runner beans, and Jackie feels bound to mumble her agreement. Don does not say much, but Pamela chatters away, addressing Jackie as "dear" which was something she never said before she was ill. As soon as supper is over the dishes are cleared away and Pamela insists on washing them. There is still no room for Jackie in the kitchen, but she stands in the dining room, next to the kitchen door, and dries the wet plates Pamela hands to her.

Then she goes upstairs to her room and gives in to tears for only the third time in her life. The first time was when Billy tried to buy her the wrong leotard, the second when his coffin disappeared through the curtains at the crematorium.

I *will* get away from here, she tells herself. A sense of determination is all she is left with, so that will have to be enough. I will get away from here one day, and have a *proper* home. . . .

Weekdays are not too bad. Jackie rises before her mother and stepfather, eats breakfast at a table that has already been laid by Don the night before, and leaves for school. She has a shorter journey now, but leaves earlier than is strictly necessary because she prefers to have the house to herself for a while. She returns from school as late as possible, and after a meal prepared by Don she excuses herself and does her homework in her room until bedtime. In outward respects the routine of her life has changed little, except that she has less shopping and cooking to do. But in the old flat she could be herself, there was no one watching her, she could relax. At The Poplars she feels perpetually on her best behavior. If there is a silence she feels she ought to fill it with conversation. This problem is most acute at weekends, which are at best dull and at worst deeply uncomfortable.

The only bright spots are when she sees Rob, who always manages to cheer her up, simply by being so cheerful himself. Their dates have to be confined to weekends to allow Jackie time for her studies. Nothing, but *nothing* could deflect her from her ambition to do well in her exams, not even Rob Jones. But it is generally accepted by her friends and his that the two of them are "going out." They go to films or for a pizza, sometimes to his house for a meal. Rob never comes back to The Poplars with her; the place is too tiny for them to have any privacy. They are at the kissing stage now, but Rob never tries to do anything else. He says he respects Jackie too much, and that they will only go further when she wants him to.

Jackie hears Don and Pamela talking when she is upstairs in her room, but in her presence, Don barely utters a word. He has found himself a job, as the caretaker of the local bingo hall, and this takes him out of the house between ten and four each day. Pamela is at home all day, not watching television as she used to before, but tidying up and having coffee with the neighbors. She has put a lot of effort into getting to know the neighbors at The Poplars; she praises the place as having "real community spirit."

The neighbor Pamela sees most of is Trish, the lady who lives next door. According to Pamela, the two of them are popping in and out of one another's houses all day, just like the cast of a detergent commercial. Trish sometimes pops round in the evening, when Jackie is studying in her room. Then one evening she comes round during supper, and Jackie is sitting at the table eating Don's cottage pie.

Trish stares. She seems genuinely nonplussed to find a third person in the house.

"This is Jackie," says Pamela. "She's staying with us at the moment."

And that is all she says. Not "This is my daughter Jackie" or "I'd like you to meet my daughter, Trish." Just, "This is Jackie," as though she were a transitory acquaintance. It is clear from Trish's reaction that Pamela has never mentioned her at the cosy coffee mornings.

And Pamela seems embarrassed. Jackie thinks about it in bed that night. The worst thing is that she cannot really blame her mother, or even feel angry. Pamela has had an unhappy life, and it only seems natural that she should want to forget it, wipe the slate clean, and start afresh with the new. Jackie does not begrudge her a second chance. The trouble is that she, Jackie, is a solid, living part of the old life, the unintended result of a liaison with some man that Pamela has not even *named* for the past eighteen years.

And that unnamed man is her father. Jackie has felt curious about him in the past, of course, but from her earliest years was party to Billy and Pamela's conspiracy of silence. It was deemed better if he was never mentioned, and she was used to just having a mother and a grandfather. The teachers at school warned the rest of her class not to tease Jackie about it.

Now she *needs* to find out about him. Suppose, just suppose he was in a position to welcome her into his family, to give her a real home? He might even be rich, and childless.

She knows she will not find out by asking Pamela. The response would be distress, or anger so extreme that she might become ill again. And her birth certificate gives no clue. She saw a copy of it when she acquired a visitor's passport for Switzerland, and under the father's details there was just a blank. The father of an illegtimate child has to give written permission to have his name entered, or to register the birth himself.

Jackie has a feeling that some clue may lie in Pamela's shoe box of shredded memorabilia, which she packed with Pamela's clothes when she left the flat. Most of the old clothes have been thrown away or replaced. It is possible that Pamela did the same with the shoe box.

She and Don go out every Tuesday evening, to an old-time dancing night at The Poplars community hall. On the next Tuesday, Jackie leaves her studies and searches their room with trembling hands and a pounding heart. She finds the shoe box at the back of a drawer and takes it back into her room. Her mother ripped up the contents when she had her nervous breakdown, so she spends the first few minutes trying to piece the scraps together.

There is a photograph of a young man; handsome, with a confident, engaging smile. A small plastic doll, of the sort won at funfairs.
Some tickets, to cinemas and concert halls dating from the autumn
of 1958, the year before she was born. Some notes, addressed to "P."
and signed "N". And a piece of paper with her mother's handwriting
on it. A name, written over and over. Norman Butler. And then, below
that: Mrs. Norman Butler. She had been practicing the signature.

So Norman Butler was the name that was never named. A
resoundingly ordinary name. Jackie knows that her mother lived and
worked in Hemingford before her birth, so the chances are that Norman was a local boy. He could have moved away, but there is a
reasonable possibility that he hasn't. Jackie puts the box and its contents back in her mother's drawer and goes downstairs to look in the
telephone directory. There are a lot of Butlers, but only two N. Butlers.
One of these is a Miss Butler. The other is listed as N. M. Butler and
has a Hemingford address and number.

Norman Butler—solicitor, freemason, and keen amateur golfer—is
returning home from work. He parks his company saloon car in the
driveway of his large, comfortable house, situated conveniently near
to Hemingford Golf Club. The house was built of brick in the late
1920s, with a gabled roof and porticoed porch, screened from the
road by a tall privet hedge. He gathers up raincoat, briefcase, and
umbrella and goes in to his wife, Marian, and his sons, twelve-year-
old Alan and ten-year-old Simon.

Jackie is watching him from the other side of the road. It is dusk,
so she cannot easily be seen. When the car door opens, her instinct is
to close her eyes. She hears the gravel drive crunch beneath his feet.

Then she opens her eyes and looks. She sees a man in early
middle age, not very tall, and with a spreading waistline from too
many directors' lunches. His reddish gold hair is thinning, but his
features are still good; he looks like any other handsome man going
slightly to seed. Can that be him? Jackie wonders, with a stab of fear.
Can that really be him? He turns round to take his briefcase out of
the boot of the car and she ducks out of sight, afraid that he might
see her.

But she *is* going to see him, isn't she? That is what she is here for. She had planned to find the place, and if "he" was in—she can't bring herself to think of him as her father—to speak with him. She decides she cannot go in now, not immediately after he has returned from work. There is plenty of time; she told Pamela she was going to spend the evening studying at the Crouchers' house.

She waits twenty-seven minutes, looking at her watch frequently, then she cannot stand it any longer. She walks up the crunching gravel drive and rings the doorbell.

"His" wife opens the door. "Yes?"

"Could I speak to Mr. Butler, please?"

The woman looks puzzled, surprised, but she smiles and ushers Jackie into the hall. She is a pretty woman in her late thirties, with ash blond hair in a short, neat club cut. She wears jeans and tennis shoes.

"Norman! Norman, there's someone to see you!"

Jackie turns her head to the right; through the open door to the drawing room she can see the two boys, playing Cluedo. They give her a brief, uncurious glance and turn back to their game. His sons. Her brothers.

He comes into the hall in his shirtsleeves. He was in the middle of changing, his shirttail is hanging half out over the waistband of his suit trousers.

"Yes?"

Jackie glances at his wife, still standing there smiling. "Could we talk in private?"

He leads her through into the study, stands in front of the desk, waiting for her to try and sell him double glazing or life insurance. Jackie knows that it is him. She recognizes the young man in the photograph. She sees her own eyes in his face, the shape of her eyebrows, her unusually long ear lobes. She shivers.

"I'm Jackie."

"I'm sorry ... Jackie...?"

"Jackie Yardley. Pamela Yardley's daughter."

"Sorry?"

"Your daughter."

He looks at her for a moment. He must recognize her, too, because he seems to accept this statement.

"I see."

He does not ask her to sit down, to take off her coat. She struggles on. "I thought I ought to come and see you. I mean, I wanted to come and see you. Just to say hello really, and find out—"

"Look ..." His voice is firm, but he is trembling, his forehead breaking out in perspiration. "Look, this isn't a good idea. Doing this. Surely you must realize that?" His voice becomes higher, angry. "I mean, you must have known that I would be married with a family of my own. Marian ... my wife ... *She* doesn't know about this—"

"I'm sorry, I ..."

"What do you expect me to say to her—'Oh darling, I forgot to tell you, I had a child before I met you?' I didn't even know whether you were a boy or a girl, for God's sake, the hospital wouldn't tell me. I just left the money and ... Pamela and I hardly even knew one another...."

"Oh ..." Jackie wants to run out of the room, to disappear. She wants the clock to go back to before she came. "I didn't know ... I suppose I just wanted to find out ..."

There are footsteps outside in the hall. Norman lowers his voice again. "I can't do this ... I have a good job, a wife, and two young children. We have a happy home, and that's the way I want it to stay. I'm sorry."

Jackie stares at him, hating him.

"When you've had a chance to think about it, I'm sure you'll agree it's for the best."

With this platitude, Jackie's father ushers her out. His wife is within earshot, so he says loudly, "Thank you, but we're not interested," pretending that she is an unwanted saleswoman. Saleswoman, daughter; what's the difference?

Jackie is too resourceful to let her anger and disappointment fester and grow. She does not brood. She wanted to know about her father and now she does; he is an unremarkable member of the middle classes, a source of neither pride nor shame. The future still lies before her, and she does not need a father to get on in life. She just needs to know what she wants, and to work hard to get it.

So on returning from her visit to Norman Butler she decides two things: one, that she will say nothing about the matter to Pamela, or anyone else and two, she will make the most of her situation for the time being, until she is in a position to change it.

She concentrates on studying for her "A" level examinations, which are to take place in the summer of 1977, and at The Poplars she is as quiet and unobtrusive as possible, helping around the house when necessary but making no demands other than a room in which to sleep and study. Her mother and stepfather in turn start to relax a little in her company, Don holds the occasional conversation with her, even seems to become attached to her in his silent way. He asks her if she would like a pet, and at Christmas presents her with a goldfish. It swims around its bowl while Jackie sits in her room working; like her it makes no noise and causes no trouble.

When the "A" level results arrive in August 1977, no one is surprised when Jackie gets straight A's in Latin, history, and economics. And no one is more delighted than Rob, who takes her out for a special celebratory dinner at La Madonette, Hemingford's smartest restaurant.

"So, what's next, Butterfly?" he asks as he pours her a glass of sparkling white wine, the nearest thing to champagne that he could afford. "A scholarship to Oxford or Cambridge?"

Jackie shakes her head. "My teachers at King Henry's want me to sit the entrance exam this autumn, but that would mean deferring my university entrance until the autumn of next year." She laughs. "I've no intention of spending another dreary year at The Poplars with Don and Mum and the goldfish, thank you!"

"It would give us another year together ..." ventures Rob.

"Anyway, I don't want to study classics or philosophy and end up as yet another arts graduate with a vague, useless degree. I need a more practical and relevant qualification if I'm going to be sure of a high-flying career."

"So ..." Rob stabs a fork into his peppered steak. "What have you decided?"

"I've accepted a place at Sussex, to read economics and business studies."

"For three years?"

"For three years. I leave for Brighton on the first of October."

Rob's smile falters momentarily. "I'm going to miss you like hell. Anyway . . ." He takes her hand and forces the smile back. "I'm very, very proud of what you've achieved. Well done."

"And what about you, Rob, what are you going to do?"

"I'm going to be joining Dad at the garage; he's promised me a partnership when I'm twenty-one. And I expect Gareth will join us too, and we'll be able to expand a bit. We're hoping to go into used-car sales."

"What—here in Hemingford?" Jackie frowns. "I mean, don't you want to get away from home, travel or something? Haven't you ever had any ambition to get away from Hemingford, move on?"

"But why should I? Hemingford is my home."

Rob's existence proves very convenient while Jackie is at university. Having a boyfriend in her hometown gives her the perfect excuse to devote all her time to her work, and the pursuit of the first-class degree she wants so badly.

"I don't think I should go out with you," she says to her admirers, just as she did in Switzerland. "You see, I've already got a boyfriend."

She keeps a photograph of him on her desk as a permanent reminder of this, and she looks at it while she is reading her texts on Keynesian theory, smiling fondly at the image of Rob's face. He sends her flowers and whimsical cards with pictures of butterflies on them, which she sticks up on the wall of her room. And Jackie writes letters back to him, squeezing them in between lectures and seminars and essays on "The Importance of Venture Capital in Britain's Manu-facturing Industry." They are long, chatty letters, full of campus gossip and descriptions of university life which she knows Rob reads until he knows them by heart.

She also knows that they describe an existence very different form his own, working long hours in his father's business, longing for Jackie's return. She does return to Hemingford for brief visits during the vacations, but these days she feels like an alien from outer space when she is with Don and Pamela, so she spends most of the vacation on campus, preparing for the next term's work. When she does see Rob, they go out to films and for pizzas, just like they always used to. And Jackie enjoys being with him, just like she always used to.

Sex poses a problem. The problem is that everybody is doing it, except for Jackie. She can't help but be aware of it; the condom machine in the students' union common room, the not-so-discreet scurrying from room to room that goes on at night.

Losing one's virginity is one of life's hurdles that Jackie feels she ought to get over, before it becomes an embarrassment. And she would far rather lose it to Rob, whom she loves, than to anyone else. So she starts to plan her campaign. First, there is the question of when it will take place. She decides on the weekend following her last exam. The end of the summer term will be upon them, and the campus will be in a celebratory mood. So she starts taking the pill at the beginning of that term, allowing two months for its protection to become completely effective. There must be no risk at all of unwanted pregnancy; Jackie knows only too well how much that can sour one's life.

The next question is where. It cannot be in her room in the hall of residence; the walls are paper thin and the beds hard and narrow. The occasion must not be sordid or illicit, Jackie could not tolerate the idea of anything like that. It must be done properly. So she writes to Rob to suggest that he take a weekend off and come down to the coast to visit her. And when she meets him at the station in Brighton, she tells him that they are going out to dinner at the Grand Hotel. She is so parsimonious with her grant money that she can afford it.

"A five-star hotel, eh?" says Rob, raising his glass of claret to hers. He is looking uncomfortable in a collar and tie and an old suit borrowed from his father. "What next?"

"Well actually . . ." Jackie bends nearer and whispers so that the other diners won't hear. "I've booked us a room upstairs."

"You mean . . . ?"

"You said you'd wait until I was ready. Well, I'm ready."

"I see." Rob laughs. "Well, I wish I'd known. I could have studied *The Joy of Sex*. Then I might feel I know what to do."

"You're bound to be nervous. We both are. That's the wonderful thing about it—we're well and truly in it together."

Their nervousness is dispelled somewhat by the gourmet meal, and the freshly turned down four-poster warmed by a roaring log fire. It seems quite obvious to start by undressing and caressing each other, and after that everything is easy.

"Was I all right?" Rob asks anxiously afterward.

"It was lovely." Jackie flexes her limbs on the warm sheets like a cat basking in the flickering light of the fire. "Lovelier than I thought it possibly could be."

"I expect that's because we're so close." Rob tucks the blankets around her and then lies beside her, stroking her shoulder.

"I love you, Butterfly."

"Shhh!" Jackie puts a finger to her lips. "You're only saying it because we've just made love."

"No, I'm not!" Rob puts his hand under her chin and turns her head so that she is facing him. "I loved you before this. I always will love you, Jackie."

"Don't," she says, turning her face away again. "Don't say things like that."

When Jackie graduates in the summer of 1980, it is Rob who comes down to Brighton to collect her, loading all her possessions into his car, an old Morris Minor that is his pride and joy.

Good old Rob. He is full of chat on the journey back, mainly about the thriving family business, moving to larger premises now that his younger brother Gareth has joined them.

". . . And did I tell you about my sister, Susie? She's landed herself a really good job as a legal secretary with a firm of solicitors in Hemingford."

"Oh. Really?" Jackie frowns, shivers slightly.

"What's the matter with it?"

"Nothing. That's what my mother used to do before she had me, that's all."

"Is it? I never knew that. Well, what an amazing coincidence."

"Yes."

"You and Susie will get on brilliantly, I know it. When we get engaged ..."

"We're not going to get engaged."

They are on the outskirts of Hemingford now, coming to a stop at a red light. Rob continues to grip the wheel hard. His face has gone pale. In five years this is the first time that Jackie has seen him look unhappy.

"But I thought, I just assumed ... I've even bought the ring. It's in my jacket pocket, you can look if you like. I was going to give it to you when we got back."

Jackie takes the box from his pocket. The ring inside is a diamond solitaire, small but perfect. Jackie looks at it for a few seconds, then puts it back.

"It's over, Rob. I don't want to rot here for the rest of my life, like my mother."

"But you could work in London and commute ..."

"No! You don't understand ... I don't want that sort of life. I need something new. Anyway, you say you love me now but you're only twenty-two. Will you love me in ten years time, or twenty?"

"Jackie, of course I will, listen ... JACKIE!"

The car has stopped at another set of traffic lights and Jackie opens the passenger door and jumps out. She walks back to The Poplars, goes straight to her room and flings herself on the bed, crying.

Five minutes later the phone rings.

"Jackie, this is ridiculous. I've got all your belongings here in my car."

"I'll send a taxi round for them."

"Surely we can sort something out?"

"No, please. I don't want to."

She hangs up, digging her fingernails into the palms of her hands. The pain is excruciating.

When the phone rings again it is Helen Croucher, Jackie's old school-friend, newly graduated from Girton College, Cambridge, and in Hemingford for three weeks.

Grateful for the distraction, Jackie agrees to see Helen the following week. They meet in Parkers, a new wine bar in the center of town, all stripped pine floors, bamboo chairs and potted palms. When Helen walks in, Jackie thinks how frumpy and middle-aged she looks with her hair in a bun and wearing an Indian cotton skirt and baggy cardigan. Jackie spent very little of her grant on going out, so there was always plenty left over for spending on clothes. Besides, she has always been so neat in her habits that she couldn't bring herself to dress the part of the scruffy student. She wears her hair in a sleek, layered cut, and her fluffy angora sweater coordinates perfectly with the cords tucked into her boots.

"So," says Helen, once they have broken the ice and started on their second glass of Piesporter Michelburg. "You split up with good old Rob Jones on the day you leave Brighton. And after all those years. You two seemed so ... *so close*. I expected to see you walk in here with an engagement ring on your finger."

"No," says Jackie, looking down at her naked fourth finger. "I was offered the ring all right, but I turned it down."

Helen sips her wine in silence while she takes all this in. "Don't you believe in marriage?" she asks cautiously.

"Oh yes. I'll get married. But not yet. I've got to get my career underway first. Then I'll think about marriage. Probably in my mid-twenties."

Helen cannot help herself staring at Jackie, this new Jackie who seems so different from the timid girl who arrived at the grammar school eight years ago. But then again, perhaps not so different. She was single-minded and ambitious then, she is still. The qualities were in childlike guise before, that's all.

"But it won't be Rob you marry."

"No." Jackie shakes her head slowly. "I ... Rob means—*meant* so much to me ..." She takes a gulp of wine because she can feel her voice start to falter. "But he's not the right one for me to marry. I don't want to become a Hemingford housewife, and that's what Rob would want."

"How can you be sure? He might surprise you."

She shakes her head again. "I just know."

Jackie does not say so to Helen, but she already knows exactly what her husband will be like. She can picture him. Tall, handsome, and dashing. And they are going to have two children, born roughly two years apart. They will have a boy first, then a girl. She has already picked out their names: Jamie and Emily. And she will be the most loving mother possible (as well as the most effective business-woman), with children who are rosy, flaxen-haired, and quite, quite perfect.

N i n e t e e n

■

Matthew

When the alarm clock rings in Matthew Pryce-Jones's room in 9 Mount Rise, he throws one of his pillows at it, knocking it onto the floor, and pulls the other pillow down tightly over his head.

He does not go back to sleep, he is not even particularly tired, he just enjoys his ritual rebellion at the idea of getting up and going to school. Eventually he hears his parents moving about their bedroom, and then the hum of his father's electric razor coming from the bathroom. His eight-year-old brother, Tristram, thunders up and down the landing. Matthew gives in and climbs out of bed.

His prized possession is a large transistor radio, smothered with smiley stickers and Roadhogs, which you can send off for free with gasoline tokens. Everyone has them; stuck all over their satchels and schoolbooks. Matthew tunes the transistor to Radio One and turns the volume up loud so that the DJ is shouting and the music crackles into a fuzzy blur.

"And now, here's one for all you rock fans, Deep Purple and 'Smoke on the Water' ..."

"Fantastic!"

Dressed only in his Y-fronts and socks, Matthew snatches up his tennis racket and dubs his own solo over the whining lead guitar riff.

"*Smoke* on the water, and fire in the sky, yeah ..."

The door opens and Ken comes in.

"Oh, hi, Dad!"

Ken starts to speak but is drowned by the music. Matthew turns the radio down a fraction.

•

"I'm off now," says his father.

"Oh, right. See you this evening." Matthew waves his hand dismissively.

"Your mother's still in the bathroom. When she comes out, will you tell her that I shall be a bit late getting home tonight?"

"How late?"

"Well, that rather depends, old son."

Ken winks, and Matthew gives the required response, which is to laugh. His father is a bit of a lad, even now. He's also a bit of a fool, too, if he still persists in hanging around the younger secretaries at Baring Baker, oblivious of his thickening waistline and graying hair.

Tristram is in the bathroom now, so he bangs on the door of his parents' bathroom until his mother comes out.

"Oh, Mum! You look nice!" Matthew has no compunction in stretching the truth in order to get his mother into a good mood. Although she is dressed in a coordinating sweater and ski-pants set, Audrey has not yet applied her makeup and her cheeks are greasy with face cream, her eyes puffy from sleep.

"Thank you, darling." Audrey's smile is uncertain.

"Dad said to tell you he'll be back late tonight."

"Oh. How late?"

"He didn't say. Mum, can I borrow a fiver?"

"What do you need it for?"

"Oh, you know, just things. Books and stuff."

Audrey sighs. "My handbag's next to my bed. You'll find a couple of five-pound notes in my purse."

"Thanks Mum!"

Matthew whistles cheerfully as he shaves himself. At thirteen years old, he does not really need to shave, but he read somewhere that if you ran a razor over your face every day, it would encourage the hair growth. It's difficult to know whether it is working, but he certainly has more stubble than most of the boys in his class.

After the ritual shave, which ends with a generous splash of his father's cologne, Matthew dresses in his school uniform, helps himself to the five pounds from his mother's purse, and thunders downstairs.

On his way through the kitchen he grabs the piece of toast that Tristram was about to butter.

"Hey!" Tristram protests. "That was *my* toast! Mum, Matthew's nicked my toast!"

But Matthew is already heading for the back door with his satchel slung over his shoulder and the toast between his teeth.

"Bye!" he shouts, with his mouth full.

"Matthew ...!"

He does not stop, so Audrey has to run after him into the garage, where he is swinging one long leg over the saddle of his racing bike. Most of the boys at King Henry's go to school by bus, but Matthew likes to cycle. It gives him the independence to come and go when he is ready, and the stamina created by several miles of hard cycling each day gives him an edge on the sports field.

"Matthew, you haven't forgotten about going swimming, have you? I rang Sylvia Noble and she said that you could go round and have a swim with Stephen after school."

"I might," says Matthew, settling himself in the saddle and freewheeling down the drive. "If I feel like it."

Matthew Pryce-Jones is undoubtedly a fortunate child. He has health, brains, and good looks; moreover, he has inherited his father's smooth charm and his mother's pushiness.

At home, he rules the roost with ease. Ken Pryce-Jones admires his son, and flatters himself that he can see his own, younger self there. In consequence, Matthew has little trouble persuading his father to see his point of view. From the day of his birth he has been able to get around Audrey, simply by being beautiful. Skilled wheedling and flattering reinforce his position as a demigod in her eyes. And Tristram does not stand a chance against his older brother, for at every point of comparison he comes off worse. He is plain, pudgy, and destined for Hemingford Comprehensive, since his performance at school is too weak to win him a place at King Henry's.

Matthew, on the other hand, tells everyone that he is going to be a brilliant brain surgeon, and they believe him. He is top of his class academically and socially, too, being bigger, brighter, and more

•

full of persuasive bullshit than the others. Even the teachers have to admit that he has leadership qualities, and while some of them are reluctant to like him for his cockinesss and overwhelming belief in Matthew Pryce-Jones, they all agree that he will do well and go far.

He arrives at school in a cheerful frame of mind, having changed the five-pound note for coins at the news agent he passes on the way. He uses this money to pay off his gambling debts. A few months ago, he was the founder of the school poker game which meets regularly in a disused shed behind the physics lab and plays for real money. Betting and gambling of any kind are strictly against the school rules.

"What's that, Pryce-Jones?" The eagle-eyed games master, patrolling the changing rooms before assembly, sees Matthew handing Fat Keith two fifty-pence pieces.

"Just some money I owe him, sir." Matthew smiles innocently. "I borrowed some off him yesterday, to buy my mother some flowers on the way home. It was her birthday."

"I see."

The master walks away, satisfied, and the other boys laugh admiringly. "Your mother's birthday! God, what an absolute porker!"

It is only the first of many lies that Matthew will tell during the day. He has very little use for the truth, believing that if the lie is credible and convincing enough to be passed off as gospel, why bother with the real thing? If people want to accept invented facts, then let them. It does no harm.

It is a hot afternoon in July, cloudless and dusty, and Matthew decides that he will go for a swim after all. He allows his mother to maintain this rather weak social link with the Nobles, because he looks on them as a useful source of research. He wants to know more about how rich people live.

He cycles over to the Nobles' house after school. Stephen is alone there with the cleaning lady, Mrs. Moody. His mother has gone out; Stephen says he does not know where. Matthew thinks this is strange. It is impossible to imagine Audrey disappearing without telling Matthew where she would be. But then, the Nobles are strange anyway. To Matthew this seems part and parcel of being members of the upper class. Stephen is also wet, as well as strange. He is already on holiday for the summer, as he goes to a private prep school and private schools have longer holidays.

The two boys swim for half an hour, then Mrs. Moody brings them a glass of milk and biscuits. Matthew does not want to swim any longer. He can out-swim Stephen easily, and thrashing up and down the length of the pool with Stephen puffing in his wake has little appeal. He tells Stephen he needs to use the bathroom and leaves him practicing his crawl at snail's pace.

Inside, the house is cool and still. Mrs. Moody is closeted in the kitchen, peeling vegetables and listening to the afternoon play on Radio Four. Matthew treads silently on bare feet. The black and white tiles of the hall feel icy cold, they make him curl up his toes. In front of him, the staircase stretches away in an elegant curve. The mahogany handrail has been polished that afternoon, the pungent beeswax and lavender smell has lingered. The roof of the hall is a dome, with an ornate circular window at its center. Craning his neck backward, Matthew can see an arc of bright blue sky.

This villa is so different from the house in which Matthew lives. It is not just that it is bigger; the doors and windows, the proportions, the things in it—all of it is different. Matthew looks around the wood-paneled library, touches the wood to see if it is real. So many books, they could not possibly read them all. Ken and Audrey have three shelves of paperbacks on the landing and they think that makes them intellectuals.

The drawing room impresses Matthew most. It has tall, narrow sash-windows framed by watered silk curtains and an Adam fireplace with a marble hearth. He walks slowly around the room, touching the furniture and the expensive knick-knacks on the side tables. His mother likes to collect ornaments, but they are not like these. Audrey buys little glass animals and china shepherdesses.

When he sits down on the sofa, he does so in a slow, deliberate manner, as though he has all the time in the world. He is pretending that this house is his, that he has always lived here. This is easy to do, for Matthew has a rich fantasy life. He needs to extend the boundaries of his existence in his imagination, to feel that he is a bigger and better person than the son of an accountant living in a detached modern house in the suburbs of an insignificant small town. Like telling lies, fantasizing makes him feel powerful.

As if to prove the point to himself, he walks over to one of the tables and helps himself to an exquisite silver pillbox. With this souvenir in his pocket he goes out to the pool again and tells Stephen he is going home.

When he returns to Mount Rise, Audrey is keeping a meal ready for him in the oven. She fusses around him as she used to fuss round Ken when he returned from work in the early days of their marriage. She fetches knife, fork, and napkin and lays a plate of fish fingers, chips, and peas in front of him.

"Did you have a good time?"

"Okay." Matthew loads up his fork. "Mum, can we move?"

"What do you want to move for?"

"I just thought it would be better if we bought a bigger house, that's all."

"We're going to build an extension in the spring, remember? With two more rooms. So we won't need to move anywhere bigger. Anyway, what's wrong with this place? A lot of people would have their eyeteeth to live in Mount Rise, believe me. And have you any idea how much houses like this cost?"

The next day Matthew takes the silver pillbox to school and sells it to his friend Murray for three pounds, using the money as stakes in the poker game.

Matthew wants to have sex.

He has already told his friends that he has done it, lots of times, garnishing these stories with a rich seam of detail from the soft porn magazines Ken keeps in the garden shed. By the time he is fifteen, however, he decides it is time he did it for real. Apart from the consideration of his status amongst his peers, he is curious, the sort of overwhelming curiosity created by hormones.

In the autumn of 1974, he starts to look around for candidates. King Henry's School for Girls is considered a traditional hunting ground. Although the two schools are run separately, they share sporting facilities and hold joint social events for fifth and sixth formers. But Matthew knows instinctively that the girls who attend these events would be far too prudish and clean-living to go the whole way. Sure, he could easily pick up a girl from the comprehensive at one of the discos or pubs in town, but that would be too anonymous. When it comes to bragging about it afterward, he can only milk the situation to the full if his friends know the girl involved.

Then inspiration strikes.

"Tell you what," he says over cottage pie and runner beans in the school canteen. "I bet I could have her."

Fat Keith gapes, his bean-laden fork poised halfway to his mouth. "What—*her?* Miss Bennett? Busty Bennett? You are joking, aren't you?"

Matthew shakes his head. "No, I'm not. I'm deadly serious."

"Busty" Bennett has just arrived at King Henry's for a term's practical teaching assignment as part of her course at Hemingford College of Art. She is twenty-two, short, plump, and pretty in an ingenuous way. She is also shy and self-conscious and finds it hard to look any individual boy in the eye.

"How the hell are you going to manage that?" asks Murray, licking mashed potato from his knife.

"I'll ask her out, how else?"

"We'll need proof that you've done it, Pryce-Jones. We know what a bullshitter you are."

"Fine. I'll bring back her panties for you to sniff."

Matthew approaches this new project with the sort of confidence that ensures success. Art is not his best subject, but at the next lesson, he makes a great show of trying hard. The class have been assigned a still life to draw, and they are seated in a semicircle around a lemon, a trout, and a couple of earthenware jars, squinting over the top of their easels and holding up pencils to try to measure the horizontal axis.

Matthew hangs back when the bell rings and the others troop out of the art studio.

"Miss Bennett . . . ?" He frowns intently a his watercolor rendition of the trout. "I don't think I've quite got the perspective right."

'Let me see . . ." Miss Bennett bends over his shoulder and examines the canvas. Matthew inhales her female odor; mingled Revlon's Charlie and chalk, washing powder and sweat. When she catches him looking at her, she steps back, looking distinctly flustered.

"Ah, it's your jars . . . you haven't taken into account that they are some way behind the fish, therefore they ought to appear smaller, relatively."

"I see . . ." Matthew measure's up his pencil against his oversized jar and then holds it out at arm's length, as he has seen Miss Bennett doing. "I really want to get this right. I've decided I'm going to take art 'O' level, you see."

"But I thought your 'O' level subjects were already decided and it was too late to change?"

"I thought I'd do it when I'm in the sixth form," says Matthew quickly. "As an extra to my science 'A' levels. I'm going to be a doctor, you see. A brain surgeon."

"I see." Miss Bennett is genuinely impressed, if only by his utter certainty.

"The thing is . . ." Matthew throws down his pencil with a flourish and stands up to put his blazer on. He is much taller than Miss Bennett, towering over her. "I thought you might be able to help me with the art thing. I need to be a lot better at it before the head will let me take the 'O' level. I thought you could tell me what I'll need to do to be good enough. After school."

"After school . . . what, here?"

"No, I thought we could meet in town. I'll take you out for a drink."

He flashes her a smile that is simultaneously engaging and businesslike.

"Well . . . it's very kind of you, er . . ."

"Matthew."

". . . Matthew, but teachers aren't supposed to associate with pupils outside the school grounds."

"But it's not as if you're really a teacher, though, is it? You're here to learn yourself. That sort of puts us in the same boat. And we wouldn't be 'associating,' I'd be seeking your advice."

"All right. You've talked me into it." She smiles.

"Great! I'll meet you by the fountain in the shopping center at eight o'clock!"

Matthew grabs his satchel and sprints down the corridor to his Latin lesson, which is already in progress. He slips into his desk, mouthing "Sorry" at the frowning teacher. When the teacher has turned back to the blackboard, he rips a page from his exercise book, scribbles on it and screws it into a paper pellet, which he tosses on to Fat Keith's desk.

Keith opens it and reads: *"It's in the bag, mate."*

"Dad."

"Hmmm?"

"Can I borrow a tenner?"

"Ten pounds? That's rather a lot of dough, old son. What do you need it for?"

"There's this girl, you see ..."

"A bird, eh? Chip off the old block, that's what you are!"

"... I'm taking her out on a date, and I thought it ought to be me who pays."

"Go on then—take a tenner. But you'd better not tell your mother where you're going. You know she doesn't want anything distracting you from your studies. She's got her heart set on you being a doctor, she really has."

"Cover for me, Dad?"

"Of course I will. I'll tell her you've gone to study at Keith's."

"Thanks, Dad. You're a mate."

Matthew arrives at his rendezvous late and out of breath, but this only adds to his attraction. His face glows with color and vitality, his newly washed chestnut hair flops over his forehead.

Miss Bennett blushes when she sees him. She has abandoned the conservative skirt and blouse that she wears to work, and is dressed in jeans and a red bomber jacket. The combination of clothes and heavier makeup make her appear much younger; the two of them could be contemporaries.

"Where would you like to go?"

"I don't mind, as long as it's quiet. Somewhere we can have a quiet drink."

Matthew just wants there to be drink, lots of it. Miss Bennett wants him to make love to her, naturally, but she may not become aware of this fact while she is still sober. Her shyness and sense of professional integrity may continue to stand in the way until she has been plied with large quantities of alcohol. They go to Pizza Parlor in the shopping center and Matthew orders a large carafe of house white before the waitress has even brought menus.

"Drink up!"

"Thank you . . ."

Miss Bennett sips demurely, lowering her eyes rather than looking him in the face.

"I'm not sure how I can help you with your artwork, Matthew, not by doing this. If you really want to improve your drawing skills, you can only do so by practicing, over and over again. Something like getting perspective right just needs to be practiced."

"The thing is, Miss Bennett . . ." (God, how ridiculous, he's about to screw her and he doesn't even know her Christian name) ". . . if I'm going to make a stab at the 'O' level, I'd like to know what sort of things the examiners are looking for . . . drink up, I'll pour you another glass . . . I need to know which bits of my technique to brush up on."

"In that case, we'd do better to get out your portfolio at school and look at some of your past work. That way I could get an idea of your weaknesses."

"Great idea! Why don't we go now? When we've finished the wine, I mean."

(That would be a brilliant twist to his story, rogering Busty Bennett on the art room floor.)

"We can't possibly go now. Apart from anything else, the art studio will be locked."

"Don't you have a key?"

"The school gates will be locked."

"Oh. Of course. Have another glass of wine. I'll order another carafe."

"Look, Matthew . . ." Miss Bennett looks up at him, and her cheeks flush deep pink with embarrassment.

Time to come clean.

"Miss Bennett, you know as well as I do that I haven't asked you here to improve my chances of getting an 'O' level in art. I find you very attractive, that's why I asked you out, and I think if you're honest you're attracted to me, too."

"Yes, but . . . I work at your school for a start."

"But no one at King Henry's knows you're here tonight. I haven't told anyone. And we're not likely to bump into the headmaster at Pizza Parlor, are we?"

"No. But you're so much younger than me, and . . ."

"Miss Bennett . . ."

"Karen."

"Karen, I guarantee you that for every glass of wine you drink, the age gap between us will appear to shorten by one year."

Miss Bennett smiles, and pours herself another glass. Matthew's mind leaps forward to the next stage of his plan.

"Do you have your car, with you?" he asks, when their meal is over and the second carafe of wine emptied.

"No, I walked. I couldn't drive after all this wine."

"Never mind, we'll get a taxi."

"Where are we going?"

"I want to show you something."

They hail a taxi in the high street and head out of the town in a northeasterly direction, past the rolling greens of the Hemingford Golf Club. They come to a halt outside the Nobles' imposing Italianate villa.

"That's my house. That's where I live."

"It's beautiful."

Miss Bennett's tone of voice gives Matthew all the proof he needs that women are impressed by that sort of thing.

"There's a swimming pool too, at the back."

"Gosh, how lovely!"

"Yeah, it's okay," he says. "Not a bad house, I suppose. I don't think about it much really."

"Are your parents in?"

"No. They're both abroad. They travel a lot, keeping tabs on their investments, that sort of thing."

"Oh." Miss Bennett peers up at the windows. "The lights are all on."

•

"The maid."

"Oh, I see."

"That's why I'd better not ask you in. But I just wanted to show you. Because you're special."

"Oh."

"Do you want to come for a walk?"

Now that he has dragged her all the way out here, Matthew does not have the least idea where they are going to go, or how she will get home again. He feels the evening slipping away from him. It's past ten o'clock and he hasn't even kissed her yet.

They walk into the grounds of the golf club, despite the signs saying NO ADMITTANCE, and sit on a bench on the edge of the fairway. In the distance, the lights of the clubhouse gleam brightly. The late September air is cold and damp, and Miss Bennett begins to shiver.

"You're cold." Matthew puts his arm round her and kisses her on the lips. He recalls a line from a film he once watched, and uses it. "God, but you're lovely!"

She sighs, and closes her eyes, inviting more.

Matthew is anxious to get onto the next stage of the proceedings. He uses a line he read in a steamy paperback of his mother's about a plantation in the American South.

"See how much you excite me!" He cups Miss Bennett's hand around his erection.

"Matthew, I . . ."

"Ssssh. . . !"

He pulls her down onto the grass of the fairway. Damp, brown leaves cling to their clothing. She shivers violently as Matthew undresses her, and with more luck than judgment plunges himself into the dampness between her legs. The heat at the core of her body produces a sensation so intense that Matthew thinks he will swoon with pleasure.

"My God!" he shouts. "My God, you're brilliant!"

She claws at him, trying to pull him closer, tugging at his shoulder, his neck, his hair. He groans and slumps on top of her, pressing her head back into the damp grass.

The sensation he was experiencing has faded and gone. His member has begun to shrivel and it slips from Miss Bennett's body. So that was it. That was sexual intercourse. Rather good, really.

It is cold, so neither of them wishes to prolong the embrace, Matthew realizes as he watches Miss Bennett zipping her jeans that it is too late to take her panties as a trophy. He would not dare to ask her, not now. She would be offended and he would not want to do that to her. She is too nice, Miss Bennett. He still cannot think of her as Karen.

The next morning he raids his mother's drawers for a pair of her skimpier underpants, sprays them with her perfume and parades them in triumph round the fifth-form common room. The other boys complain there are no stains on them. Matthew says that Miss Bennett ripped them off too quickly.

Her discomfiture in art classes is the final proof they need. Matthew decides to do the decent thing, and transfers from art to woodwork.

"We've got some new neighbors," Audrey Pryce-Jones tells the family over supper the following summer. "And, Kenneth, you'll never guess who they are."

"Who?"

"The Francises. David and Diana Francis. They came to that party we gave five or six years ago. D'you remember?"

"How could I forget?" They exchange glances. "David left Baring Baker a couple of years ago to work for one of the big insurance companies and I haven't seen him since."

"Well, you will now. They've bought number 5. After they'd been round the house with their surveyor they came to say hello, and that we'd soon be neighbors."

"That should please you then, shouldn't it?" Ken returns to his copy of the *Daily Express*. "As I recall, you were pretty keen to get to know them better."

"*I* was? That's rich! You made a beeline for Diana the minute they walked through the door!"

Listening to his parents bickering like this, Matthew is intrigued.

He decides he ought to go and check over these new neighbors. Once the removal van has been and gone, and the "Sold" sign has been taken down from number 5, he waits for a hot afternoon that has all the residents of Mount Rise out in their gardens, and he circles slowly round the house on his bicycle.

They have a smart car: a Rover with a sun-roof. There are pretty curtains at the windows and lots of stylish new furniture, framed prints and posters on the walls. Mr. and Mrs. Francis are in the garden. He is a big, beefy man running to fat, with striking auburn curls. His wife looks a little younger than Matthew's mother, in her late thirties perhaps. She is wearing a large sunhat so he cannot see her face, but she has a lovely trim figure, with long shapely legs. She watches Matthew circling in front of the drive, and he thinks he sees her mouth curving upward in a smile, beneath the shadow cast by the deep brim of her hat.

There are no children in evidence, just a small, yappy lapdog that runs around and around the garden, imitating Matthew's circling movement.

Matthew thinks that perhaps this Diana woman will be a friend for his mother. She needs a few friends about the place. She is going a bit loopy of late, probably with boredom. She ought to get herself a job, then they would have twice as much money and they could live in a better house, drive a better car, go on better holidays. But she doesn't. She just drifts around the house, changing into a different outfit every five minutes. Or she races around like a whirlwind, doing nonessential household jobs and moaning about Ken.

If she's not in the house, she's always at the hairdressers in town, the place that used to be called something else but is now called Snips. She seems to have her hair done every other day now, even when it does not need it. The hot weather does little to improve her temper or her sanity. She spends the whole of term time when the boys are at school complaining that she is lonely, and now they are at home for the holidays, she does not seem to want them around, and is always trying to get them out of the house.

As Matthew cycles slowly back to number 9, he sees his mother coming out of the side gate and walking toward him.

"I'm not mowing the lawn," he shouts. "It's Dad's turn."

"I wasn't going to ask you to mow the lawn," says Audrey tartly. She has been sunbathing in the garden and has thrown a towel beach wrap over her bikini. Her skin is very brown, it is always very brown. Her hair—for the moment—is tinted honey gold and cropped very short in a gamine cut. It gets shorter and shorter at each trip to the hairdresser. Very soon there won't be anything left. But that won't stop her going.

"I was just popping over to ask David and Diana if they'd like to come over for a meal one night ... Yoo-hoo, Diana!"

Matthew watches his mother talking to the Francises over their garden fence. It is David Francis who comes to speak to her; Diana carries on watering the tubs of flowers. His mother is laughing with David Francis, giggling and putting her head on one side. Flirting. Matthew does not like it.

A few afternoons later, Matthew comes in from the garden and finds his mother hastily hanging up the telephone receiver.

"Who was that?" he asks.

"No one."

"No one?"

"A wrong number."

Audrey takes a comb from her handbag and stands in front of the mirror in the hall to tidy her hair.

"I'm just going out; I shan't be long. Keep an eye on Tris, will you?"

"Where are you going?"

"Just to the hairdresser."

"Oh."

Matthew watches his mother's car pull out of the driveway and disappear from view at the end of Mount Rise.

"Tris! Go next door and play with Christopher for a while. I'm going out for a bit."

Matthew jumps onto his bike and cycles into town. He wants to find out; he wants to know for sure. He simply cannot bear the idea that his mother is one step ahead of him in some sort of game. He parks his bicycle in the central concourse of the shopping center and walks to Snips. The front of the salon is a full-length plate of smoked glass, through which the stylists and their clients can be seen, sitting in rows between the pot plants and framed prints of pouting hairdressers' models. And there is his mother, in the middle of the row of chairs. There is a dryer over her head, obscuring most of her face, but he recognizes her handbag, on the floor next to her feet, and her shoes. Kevin, the stylist, a camp young man with a hairdryer dangling from his belt, is handing her a cup of coffee.

And there's another surprise: Carolyn Fox is at the desk. He didn't know she worked there. So *that's* how the crafty little cow knew he would be on his own in the house that night a couple of weeks ago ... He does not want Carolyn to catch sight of him, so he turns away quickly and walks back to his bike.

His mother has won this round, but Matthew is still not satisfied. He watches her carefully in the days that follow, and becomes convinced that she is in the throes of some sort of intrigue. She tries to use the phone when she thinks no one will overhear her, she jumps when the doorbell rings, and when she mentions over breakfast one morning that she is having her hair set for the Francises' dinner party that evening, she turns bright pink.

Matthew knows he only has to wait. And sure enough, she walks into a trap of her own making.

"Matthew," she asks, affecting nonchalance, "Will you be going out on any afternoons this week? Only if you are, and it clashes with my going into town, I shall ask Moira if Tris can go and play with Christopher. You know how he hates trailing round the shops with me."

"I thought I might go over and see Keith one afternoon." Give her time to set up a rendezvous ... "On Thursday, perhaps."

"Right, I'll ask Moira."

On Thursday afternoon, Audrey deposits Tristram with the next door neighbors and spends a long time getting ready to go out. She is waiting for Matthew to leave.

He watches her putting on her makeup, leaning against the doorframe with his arms crossed. He smiles at her.

"So . . ." says Audrey.

"So?"

"You're off then." She glances at her watch, presses a tissue against her mouth to blot her lipstick.

"Yes." He straightens up slowly, lazily. "I suppose I had better get going. I'll see you later."

Matthew rounds the corner of Mount Rise on his bicycle, circling like a vulture, backpedaling slightly to maintain momentum. God, this is fun! He keeps up surveillance for half an hour, counting the cars turning into Mount Rise. Three, including David Francis's Rover. As if he could miss that.

He cycles slowly back to the house, very slowly, enjoying his advantage. He takes his bike round the side of the house, parks it against the garage wall and goes in through the open kitchen door. His mother is still in the house.

On the kitchen counter there is a bottle of white wine, opened and two-thirds empty. The cork and the foil wrapping have been flung impatiently to one side, the cupboard that stores the wine glasses is still open.

Matthew walks to the foot of the stairs. He can hear voices from upstairs, laughter. He kicks his shoes off and walks up. The door to his parents' bedroom is ajar. He pushes it open with his bare foot.

Audrey is lying on the bed in her petticoat, with a glass of wine in her hand. Her lipstick is smudged. Next to her, naked, is Kevin, the hairdresser from Snips.

Matthew turns and runs down the stairs.

"Matthew . . !" Audrey comes after him, struggling to get her arms into her negligée. "Matthew, darling, come back! I can explain, honestly!"

Matthew tells Ken what he has seen, that same evening. He has no hesitation in doing this. Since his father persists in the role of aging cad, his dignity is imperiled already. He cannot allow it to slip any further. Besides it would be terrible if Audrey were to leave home. She might insist on selling the house and dividing up the money, and then they would be much worse off.

"Bloody hell!" says Ken, when Matthew tells him. "I mean, bloody hell, *Audrey!*" He rubs his hands to and fro over his face, as if he is tired. "And with a poncey bloody hairdreser. That's what gets me, you know, she couldn't even pick a real man!"

"What are you going to do, Dad?"

"I'll talk to her. Tell her what's what. I'll tell her I'm not going to bloody put up with this sort of thing!"

Ken maintains a rugged silence over supper, while Audrey is artificially bright and chatty, her voice straining with the effort of sounding normal. Matthew knows they will not talk until he is in bed, so he excuses himself early, then sits on the stairs to listen.

He fully expected his mother to be contrite, ashamed, to plead for forgiveness. (He expected her to ask him, Matthew, for forgiveness too, and that he would grant it in a high-handed manner.) But his mother is the one who launches the attack.

"I *warned* you!" she shouts. "Didn't I? I told you I was sick of being taken for granted. Of taking care of the kids and the house and then sitting on my backside waiting for you to show up. It's bad enough that you're not around to lend me a hand occasionally, without the humiliation of ringing you at the office and finding that no one knows where you are because you're out making an idiot of yourself with some typist or other!"

"Audrey, listen—"

"Well, I'd had enough! If you can't beat them, join them, isn't that one of your mottos? If it's good enough for Ken, then it's good enough for me, I'll go out and have a little fling of my own. And do you know something, Kenneth, this afternoon was the first time I'd ever ... and even then we didn't get as far as ... It seemed to be the simplest thing in the world for you to forget you were married, but it took me months, *years*, to pluck up the courage, and even then I didn't get as far as doing it. I made a complete mess of it; isn't that *pathetic?*"

And Audrey bursts into noisy tears.

"Oh my dear, I'm so sorry...."

Matthew is horrified. His father is apologizing. This was not how the scene should have gone at all. He retreats in disgust, and soon afterward hears his parents coming upstairs. For the next hour they make love noisily. Matthew is mollified. At least his mother will not be going anywhere now.

"We thought we'd go away for a few days," Ken announces over breakfast the next morning. "Just the two of us."

He looks over at Audrey who is smiling into the scrambled eggs. "Your mother could do with a break from you two."

"We thought you two were old enough to take care of yourselves," Audrey says. "Is that all right, Matthew? Will you take care of the house?"

"Sure. I'll take care of the house."

"You should have a party," says Fat Keith. Ken and Audrey have left for five days in the Channel Islands. "We could have a real bash. Mike knows lots of girls from the comp, and my brother's got some mobile disco equipment."

"I might," says Matthew. "If I feel like it."

The hot spell continues. For the time being he is content to spend as much time as possible in the garden, soaking up the sun. He gives Tristram a pile of Ken's porn mags to keep him quiet, pours himself a rum and Coke and lies in Audrey's chair lounge listening to the radio.

"Hi."

Matthew opens his eyes and promptly closes them again, dazzled by the sun. He was drifting off into a pleasant doze.

"Sorry, have I woken you up?"

He opens his eyes again and finds himself looking straight at the navel of Diana Francis. She is wearing a cheesecloth shirt knotted under her bust and a pair of denim cutoffs. Her stomach is a lovely shade of brown, a rich copper color.

"The sink's blocked, and I was going to ask your mum if I could borrow a plunger."

"Mum's away, I'm afraid, they both are."

"Oh. Sorry to bother you then."

"No bother." He gives her his most charming smile. "I know where Dad keeps the plunger. I'll go and get it for you."

He returns from the garage and holds it out to her.

"Thanks. I'll get David to see to it when he gets back from work."

"I'll come over and do it for you, if you like. I'm always unclogging the sink for Mum."

"Thanks."

She stands next to him in the kitchen and watches. Matthew notices how brown her bare feet look against the white floor tiles. He finds he cannot look at her without his eyes straying to her naked stomach. She does not seem to mind him looking at her.

"Would you like a coffee?"

"Not coffee. A cold drink."

She pours him a chilled beer and they go through into the sitting room.

"I'll put some music on if you like. We've got Abba."

He pulls a face.

"Don't you like them? I thought they were the "in" group."

"They're all right if you're middle-aged, I suppose." He catches her eye. "Sorry, I didn't mean ..."

"That's all right." Diana laughs. "I suppose we are very out of touch with what teenagers listen to. We don't have any children to keep us informed."

"Are you sorry? About not having children?"

She shakes her head firmly. "No. It was a deliberate decision. David was quite tempted, I think, but I couldn't face the whole business of getting fat, and having stretch marks...."

Matthew's eyes move involuntarily to her flat, brown midriff.

"... and getting up in the middle of the night. I know children can be lovely, but ... we have a different sort of life-style."

"Oh." Matthew sips on his beer. There is a long silence, which starts to make him feel uncomfortable. Diana is sitting on the sofa with her legs folded, tailor fashion. She is very still.

Then she says abruptly: "I was watching you, you know. That first day after we moved in, when your mother came over to ask us round. You were out there on your bike, wearing just a pair of shorts. Nothing on your top half. And I was looking at your body as you cycled past and thinking, I don't know how old he is, but he's absolutely beautiful."

The silence resumes. Still she does not move.

Matthew puts his glass of beer down. "Diana, I mean, Mrs. Francis..." He is reaching out his hand, rendered helpless by his need to touch her.

"Would you like to go to bed?" she asks.

"Have you done this before?"

"Yes. Yes, I have."

"Who was she? Or was there more than one?"

"Two. A girl I picked up at a disco. And the first one was an older woman."

"Like me."

"Not that much older. Twenty-two, I think."

She laughs. "That's young!"

"She was my teacher."

"Oh, I see. An older and wiser woman, then."

"How old are you?"

"Thirty-seven. Ancient."

"You don't look it. I mean, you look younger than she did. Her body was all soft and squashy. Yours is all sort of hard."

She laughs. "Come here, I want to eat you."

"With your mouth?"

"Yes, with my mouth. Didn't she use her mouth, your teacher?"

"No ... um!... Oh my God, Diana! Oh! You're beautiful, you're fantastic ... let me put it in you, please!"

"Not now, later."

"Can I use my mouth on you, then?"

"Now you're talking ..."

Matthew is in love. He lies awake all night with an unrelenting erection, his skin crawling with desire. He has never known anything like this before, he just wants to be still making love to her and to go on doing so, endlessly.

His bedroom is hot, airless. He throws off all his covers except for a sheet, he opens the window wide, but sleep eludes him. At five o'clock, unable to lie still, he goes down to the kitchen and rests his forehead on the cool tiles.

"Diana, God, Diana ...!"

The next morning he watches for David Francis's car to drive past. At the earliest opportunity, he goes to see Diana. She is in the garden, pruning standard rose trees. Her dog, lying in the shade, growls.

"Oh, hi!" Her tone is casual, she only gives him the most fleeting of glances before turning back to her task.

"I had a terrible night."

"Oh?"

"I couldn't sleep a wink."

"That's a shame."

Diana is dressed in a bikini top and white shorts, with a plastic sun visor over her head; the sort that tennis players wear. Matthew bends over and kisses her naked back.

"You know why I couldn't sleep? Because I wanted to fuck you, that's why!"

"Really?"

"Can we go to bed?" Matthew's hands stray round to the front of Diana's body.

She straightens up and places a canvas gloved hand over his. "I don't think it's a very good idea, Matthew, honestly."

"Why not?"

"It's just ..." She shrugs.

"Oh go on, *please*! It won't take long." He presses her hand on his fly. "Feel!"

She laughs. "How could I resist that?"

They go upstairs. Matthew is impatient, pushes Diana onto the bed, takes charge. Afterward, with her brown hair clinging damply to her forehead, she smiles her pussy-cat smile. "Well, you're certainly learning!"

Matthew is overwhelmed by his conquest, he has to tell someone about it. He rings Fat Keith.

Fat Keith is incredulous. "You did *what?* You mean this woman actually gave you a blow-job? Honest to God?"

"Honest to God."

"You're making this up!"

"I'm not, I swear. She's insatiable. I think I'm in love."

"Oh, come off it! Don't bring love into it! Sex is sex, isn't it?"

Matthew intends to find out. He returns to number 5 the following afternoon, after the most frustrating few hours of his life. David Francis goes into work late that day, leaving the house at eleven-thirty. As soon as he has left, Diana's white Mini backs out of the driveway; she is going shopping.

Diana returns at five past three. At eight minutes past three, Matthew rings her doorbell.

Diana lets him in and they go upstairs and make love, but Matthew is aware of a certain reluctance on her part, and afterward she tries to hurry him on his way.

"Why can't I stay?"

"Because I have other things to do, that's why. Haven't you got any little friends of your own age to play with?"

Matthew is stung by this sarcasm, but he does not dwell on it. His father has told him often enough that that's just what women are like, bitchy. That's their nature. He prepares to wait out the next two days. It is the weekend, and David Francis will be at home. Matthew keeps watch on their house, and when David is inside he circles mournfully around Mount Rise on his bicycle, looking at Diana. She spends the whole weekend gardening. In fact she spends all her time gardening—except when she is in bed.

The following day, Monday, Ken and Audrey are due to return from the Channel Islands. Because he does not know precisely when they will return, Matthew details Tristram to wash the breakfast dishes and tidy up, and goes over to Diana's house as early as possible.

She does not greet him with warmth, indeed she seems positively irritable, pushing his hands away when he puts them round her waist.

"What's wrong?"

"Just don't, Matthew, that's all."

"But why not? I only want to make love to you. I thought you enjoyed it. You *did* enjoy it."

"I know, but . . . Come and sit down."

Diana leads Matthew into the sitting room, and lights a cigarette for herself.

"Can I have one?"

She shakes her head, then gives in. "Oh all right, one won't hurt ... your parents are back today, aren't they?"

"Yes."

"Well, obviously we can't go on like this once your parents are back. Can we?"

"Why not?"

"David and I are their friends, for God's sake! And your mother worhsips the ground you walk on. If she knew I'd seduced her precious son ..."

"But they won't know. We won't tell them. And they go out quite a lot. We could still meet."

Diana stubs out her cigarette. Her voice becomes hard. "Look, Matthew, it's over. It was fun, but it's over. End of discussion."

"Oh go on, Diana, *please* ..." Matthew is aware that his voice sounds whiny. He is not going to whine. He sucks on the end of his cigarette instead.

"I've treated you like an adult, Matthew, don't let me down now." She tries to look him in the eye, but he turns his face away. "We've had a nice time, but it wasn't going to go anywhere. Knowing when to quit is the first rule of love affairs, you're going to have to learn that some time so it may as well be now."

"Well, fuck you!"

Matthew stubs out his cigarette and leaves the room. For a few seconds he stands in the hall, but she does not come after him. He goes out of the house, picks up one of her terra-cotta flowerpots and throws it at the garage door. It explodes in a shower of soil and geraniums.

He screams, at the top of his voice: "FUCK YOU, YOU BITCH!" Matthew telephones Fat Keith.

"I blew her out."

"You did what?"

"I blew her out. Chucked her. Dumped her. Finished with her."

"You're crazy! What did you do that for? All that hot sex. Anyway, I thought you were in love."

"Sex, Keithie boy, that's all it was. And knowing when to call it quits is the most important rule of the game. The first thing you've got to learn."

For the following two years Matthew finds himself under great pressure at school. It is a pressure he had not anticipated, imagining that he could ease himself through by charming the teachers and exerting his brain as little as possible. But he has decided that he wants to be a doctor, and he does not want to do so in a provincial fashion. He wants a place at one of London's top medical schools, and to win it, he is going to have to work very hard.

The headmaster summons all the upper sixth in turn for an informal "chat" about career choices.

"I see you've put St. James's Medical School first on your list of choices, Pryce-Jones."

"That's right, sir. It's the best."

"I'm aware of that. I also know how much pressure there is for places."

"I think I can do it, sir." Matthew graces the headmaster with his most charming smile.

"Unfortunately, this is one situation where confidence alone won't do the trick. You are going to need good grades, Pryce-Jones, the best. Three A's, if you're going to have any certainty of a place."

Matthew smiles again. "Three A's it will have to be then, sir."

"Well, wait a minute, let's see what we have here ..." The headmaster leafs through Matthew's term reports. "You'll have to make sure you work on any weak spots. In your case, it seems to be your biology practical work, dissection and so on. I must say I'm rather surprised about that, because I thought you wanted to be a surgeon. I would have thought to be good at cutting people up you would need to show a bit more finesse in your biology practical work."

"Finesse!" Matthew repeats this to his friend Murray afterward, spitting the word. "Finesse! What would that stupid old fart know about being a surgeon? I don't need finesse, I just need a bit of luck with the biology practical question."

"And we won't know about that until the day of the exam, unfortunately. Murray wants to go to medical school too.

"Unless ..."

"Unless we find out what they're giving us for the practical a day in advance...."

"You don't mean .. ?"

"Why not? It would be so easy. The exam starts at nine o'clock, so the lab technicians have to get it all set up the day before. Don't you remember when we did our biology 'O' level? They went round laying out those chicken feet for us to draw."

"Yes. And then they locked the door of the lab, so no one could go in and take a peek."

"But they had obviously forgotten what big windows the biology lab has."

"They'll draw the curtains."

"Of course they will. So we can't see in. But that doesn't mean we can't *climb* in."

"You mean .. ?"

"The first rule of life, Murray, my boy, is that if you can't get what you want by hard work, then get it by cheating."

The more Matthew thinks about this scheme, the more feasible and the more desirable it seems. If he can just boost his practical work by a few points, it could make the difference between an A for biology or a B. So he plans with great care, telling himself that the effort he is putting into cheating should alone earn him an A grade. The evening before the exam, he returns to school at dusk. He has already ascertained that Bob, the janitor, will be there. Like many others, Bob is prey to Matthew's charm. Matthew has sat in his room and smoked sour-tasting roll-ups on many occasions, putting up with Bob's boring monologues because he is a useful person to have on his side. In the past, his friendship with Bob has saved him having to pay for several broken windows and a new tire for the French master's car. On this occasion, when he bangs on the side entry gate and tells Bob that he has forgotten some important books for his revision, he is admitted straight away.

The biology lab has one whole wall of windows. Normally these give a panoramic view of the playing fields, but tonight they are obscured with full-length black-out curtains. But Matthew guesses that the lab assistants will have been forced to leave a window open to keep the room cool. He is right but it is one of the upper windows, too narrow to climb through safely. He waits until Bob is sweeping the classrooms, then fetches his folding steps and with the aid of a coat hanger, pushes back the catch on the lower window.

He cannot switch on the light in the lab, but pulls back the curtain slightly so that he can see the places that have been laid, in a neat row, for the candidates. The topic for examination is the dissection of the earthworm, and the worms have been laid out in glass Petri dishes. Matthew makes sure that the biggest, fleshiest worm is in front of his place, then goes home and studies the anatomy of the earthworm until one-thirty in the morning. He forgets to draw back the curtain, but on the day no one seems to notice.

In the middle of August, his exam results are posted to Mount Rise. He has an A in biology, an A in chemistry and a B in physics.

St. James's Hospital Medical School was prepared to offer Matthew an automatic place on the strength of three grade A's in his exams. Now he is requested to attend an interview with the dean. Matthew knows that his future career rests on a twenty-minute impression of his personality. This thought elates him. If anyone can change their life through the brief exercise of charm, it is Matthew Pryce-Jones.

"Here for an interview, sir?" asks the medical school porter, who is excessively cheerful, like the porters in films about hospital life.

"That's right."

"Third door on the right, at the end of the corridor. And good luck, sir."

"Thank you."

Matthew smiles. This is the first time in his life that he has ever been addressed as "sir." This is what it is going to be like from now on. Respect and admiration coming at him from all sides. Everyone thinks doctors are wonderful. Particularly women.

Professor Sadler, the Dean, is a large, handsome man wearing a bow tie and a wool sweater. He nods at Matthew, points to the chair opposite his desk, and commences the interview without any of the jocular preamble Matthew had expected.

"So, tell me why you want to be a doctor."

Matthew forces himself to look humble. "I know this may sound trite, sir, but I would consider it an honor to be a member of a profession that is dedicated to healing people."

"I see." Professor Sadler raises his eyebrows. "And what do you consider are the qualities necessary to be a good doctor?"

"Compassion. Patience. Sensitivity. A good intellect."

"And which of those do you possess, Mr. Pryce-Jones?"

"I think I have all of them, to some degree."

Professor Sadler looks straight at him. He is waiting for Matthew to back down, to become embarrassed, to retract some of this hyperbole. Matthew smiles back at him.

"I see from your application that your particular interest is surgery.... Do you come from a medical family?"

"My great-grandfather was a doctor." This has little impact; he had better invent a more immediate relative. "And my uncle is a surgeon. Orthopedic."

"Really? What's his name? I may have come across him."

"Er, Ballard." Matthew gives Fat Keith's surname; he likes his lies to have a humorous touch. Well, why not go the whole way, now he's started. "Keith Ballard. He's in private practice now. In Harley Street."

"Really?" Professor Sadler looks directly at Matthew again, not quite believing him. He waits for Matthew to become flustered, to try to retrace his tracks. Matthew does not. He looks directly back at the Dean, daring him not to offer him a place.

A letter confirming the offer arrives by first post the following morning. Matthew goes to London to start his six years of medical training one month later. For many students, the beginning of this process is daunting. For Matthew, it is heaven. His parents are beside themselves with pride, and have swelled his meager grant with an allowance from their own savings. He has a cheap room in a hall of residence, right in the center of London with all the capital's attractions on his doorstep. His social life is wonderful. He falls in with a fast, ex-public school crowd who hold frequent parties and go out every night to punk rock concerts in the Roundhouse or the Marquee, and jazz clubs in Soho.

And more than anything he has ever done before, being a medical student is like a game of make-believe. Matthew only has to don a white coat and walk down the corridors of the hospital for porters and cleaners to nod respectfully and nurses to blush and giggle. He becomes a bigger, better person simply by assuming that role.

In fact there is only one thing lacking before Matthew feels he has everything he needs to make his new life an unqualified success. And that is Graziella Buscowicz. She is a first-year medical student, half Italian and half Polish but raised in London. Her name alone is exotic enough to give kudos to her consort, but she also has the looks to match, a lush, breathtaking beauty. Tall and graceful, her sable hair falls in thick waves down her back, and she has the most exquisite Slavic cheekbones. Her beauty is alluded to in the medical school Christmas revue:

> *Graziella, Graziella.*
> *Make some man a happy fella . . .*

All of the male medical students would like to go out with Graziella Buscowicz. Most of them would not even dare try. For the few braver ones who do, the answer is a polite no. Graziella is more interested in her studies. She wants to be a neurosurgeon, a speciality in which no woman has ever succeeded at St. James's. The hospital only has two female surgeons and one of those is a nun.

Matthew asks Graziella for a date. She says no more politely than she does to most suitors, because Matthew is widely recognized as the most handsome student in his year, and has been voted Pin-up Boy 1978 by the nursing staff. He is charming, and also very determined. He asks Graziella again. And again. He goes on asking her out once a week, at the Monday morning anatomy lecture. Finally she says yes.

Graziella admits defeat with a good grace. She goes to dinner with Matthew at an Italian restaurant on the river in Pimlico, then she allows him into her bed. It is the first time for her, and she is frightened.

"Shh . . . relax, enjoy it! There's nothing to it. . . ."

Matthew is profoundly grateful for his experience with Diana Francis. There could be nothing worse than winning a date with Graziella Buscowicz and failing to perform in bed. The humiliation of it! As it turns out, the situation is quite the reverse. Matthew's experience and confidence penetrate Graziella's defenses like a knife moving through butter. She falls into a sort of sexual trance, she cannot get enough of him. It is accepted in the medical school that they are a couple, the undisputed king and queen of the first year.

Matthew likes Graziella. What he likes most about her is the effect that she has on men wherever they go. They stare at her and give him frankly envious glances. He cares less for the fact that she is reserved and withdrawn, prone to Slavic moodiness. She wants to be alone with Matthew in her room, listening to classical music and discussing medicine. He wants to go out to parties and clubs and show her off.

When the first batch of preclinical exams comes round, the pace of Matthew's social life is forced to slow down, temporarily. Everyone is studying, some harder than others. Matthew puts in a couple of hours work each evening after his supper, then goes to the pub with his friends to sit drinking Irish whiskey and moaning about the hard life of the medical student.

On one of these occasions he goes to Graziella's room after closing time, hoping to lure her away from her books and into bed. As he expected, she is still working, her long hair gleaming under the light from her desk lamp.

He lifts the curtain of hair and kisses the back of her neck.

Graziella give his hand an absent squeeze, flicks her hair back over her shoulder. "One minute, Matthew, I just want to finish this."

He picks up one of the textbooks on her desk.

"Anatomy? But we took our anatomy paper on Tuesday."

"I know."

"What's this for then?"

"The anatomy prize. There's an extra exam next week for people doing the prize."

Matthew frowns. "Why didn't I know about this?"

"There was a notice about it on the medical school noticeboard." She shrugs. "Anyway, it's optional. No one has to do it."

"So why are you doing it?"

"Professor Sadler suggested it."

"Sadler?" Matthew pours himself a glass of red wine from the bottle on Graziella's desk, and sits down on the bed. "Let me see if I've got this right. Sadler called you in to tell you that you should go in for the anatomy prize, but he didn't say anything to me. . . . But we've both got the same marks in our course work."

"I know . . ." Graziella spins her chair round to face him. "But Sadler said he thought I had a particularly good chance because I obviously performed well under exam pressure."

"How does he know that?"

"From my 'A' level results, I suppose. I got four A's."

"Four?"

"I took zoology as well as biology."

"Oh. I see." Matthew sips his wine thoughtfully. It had not occurred to him before that Graziella was cleverer than him. The idea makes him distinctly uncomfortable.

"There's no reason why you shouldn't enter for the prize too. It's not too late." Graziella reaches out and strokes his thigh with circling, teasing movements. "Are you staying here tonight?"

"No, I don't think I will. I'm rather tired."

The St. James's Medical School Anatomy Prize for 1978 is awarded to Graziella Buscowicz, who comes first out of the eight prize applicants. Matthew Pryce-Jones comes fourth.

The week after the exam, it is the hospital ball. Graziella waits for Matthew to buy them two tickets, but he does not. He does not mention the ball. In the end, she raises the subject herself, catching him in the corridor outside the doctors' mess.

"Sorry, Graz, I'm in a terrible rush."

"Matthew, I just wondered about the ball. Whether we were going to get tickets."

"I thought it was rather a waste of money. Anyone worth their salt can just stick on a tux and crash it. Simple."

"But I thought we would go together, as a couple."

"Look, I'm in rather a hurry . . ."

Graziella blocks his path. "We need to talk, Matthew."

"All right, later. I'll come over."

Matthew goes to Graziella's room that night. There is a bottle of wine open on the table. She has been waiting for over two hours.

Matthew declines the glass she offers him. "The thing is, Graz, it's time it was over."

"Over?"

"I don't think it's a good idea for us to go out together any more."

"But, Matthew, why not? What on earth have I done wrong . . . ?" Her voice cracks slightly, she fumbles in her pocket for a Kleenex.

"Come on, Graziella, let's be adult about this. It was fun while it lasted, but now it's over. It wasn't going anywhere. And the first rule of relationships is knowing when to quit."

"It's the anatomy prize, isn't it?"

"That has something to do with it, yes."

"But, Matthew, that's stupid! One of us had to do better than the other. If you had won I wouldn't finish with you! Why on earth does it matter?"

Matthew says stiffly: "Well, if you must know, I find it humiliating to have a girlfriend who lords it over me, trying to score points—"

"*Scoring points!*" Graziella laughs through her tears. "How ridiculous and pompous you are! If it were the other way round, it wouldn't pose a problem, would it? But the plain truth of it is that you can't handle the idea of a woman being smarter than you. You find that too threatening!"

Graziella is laughing openly now. "You know, Matthew, I feel sorry for you, I really do. All I can suggest is that you go and find yourself some little doormouse who's so dumb she makes you look like Einstein. Because that's all you want from a woman apart from sex, isn't it? Someone to make you look good!"

Matthew wastes little time in taking Graziella's advice. Three days, in fact. On the night of the hospital ball, he and his friend Jonathan dress up in black tie and climb into the functions room through the window of the men's cloakroom. They stop to check their appearance in the washroom mirrors before joining the fray.

"Nurses!" Johnnie says to his reflection. "Wall-to-wall nurses. Let me at them!"

Matthew adjusts his tie. "It's not really the same though, is it, when they're not in uniform? I'm going to find myself a nice, mature consultant's wife. An older woman with a bit of influence."

"And a bit of experience! You should save the consultant's wife till last and work your way through a few nurses first. Break a few hearts, after having yours decimated by the incomparable Graziella."

Jonathan plays an imaginary violin.

Matthew laughs. "And the rest! Tell you what, let's suss out the best-looking girl in the room and see how long it takes me to pick her up. You can time me."

They go to join the dancing, ignoring requests to show their tickets.

"How about her? She's fairly easy on the eye." Matthew points to a girl in a blue taffeta ball gown. She is petite and pretty, with a glowing pink and white complexion. It is a safe, Anglo-Saxon sort of prettiness, very different from the luscious beauty of Graziella Buscowicz.

"That's cheating! That's Lucinda McIver!"

"What about her?"

"Well, she's not exactly your run-of-the-mill St. James's nurse. She wanted to meet unattached young men and it was a toss-up between the debutante circuit and nursing. She's got a soft heart, so nursing won. Now she's just waiting to meet Dr. Right, and the lucky bastard's going to be able to retire and live off her loot."

"She's well off then?"

"Fucking loaded! Money coming out of every pretty little orifice. Her old man is the head of the McIver brewing family."

"I see." Matthew smiles broadly, then checks his watch. "Well, come on, what are you waiting for? I reckon I've got thirty seconds on the clock so far."

He walks up to Lucinda McIver and extends a hand. "Hi, I'm Matthew Pryce-Jones. Would you like to dance?"

the

e

ighties
_____

c o m i n g   h o m e

T *w e n t y*

■

Carmen Fox wakes at twelve minutes past eight. She opens her eyes slowly, tries to yawn but cannot because her mouth is too dry. She drank too much last night. A vodka and tonic in the bath before leaving home, two gin and tonics before the meal, then half a bottle of Medoc. And a large brandy.

There is a rustling sound under the duvet and an arm appears, making Carmen jump. She had forgotten that there was someone in the bed with her. She looks at him now, still asleep. He looks as if he might be quite handsome, but his mouth is open. She wonders what his name is.

They didn't do anything, or at least, if they did it was a quick in and out before lapsing into a state of deep unconsciousness. They were both too drunk for memorable sex.

She met the man at a dinner party at a friend's house. (Home-made guacamole, chicken cooked with grapes and cream, followed by chocolate mousse.) Her friends are into dinner parties in a big way at the moment. Eight for eight-thirty is the norm, though it is accepted that some people will not show up until nine. If they are not lucky enough to have a dining room, then they erect a large table in the sitting room, and borrow chairs. There are usually between eight and twelve guests, all single and almost all unattached. Everyone brings wine, so there is far too much. The meals are rowdy and good-humored, few formalities are observed. Afterward, if the guests still have the strength, games might be played, charades, consequences, or "Are you there, Moriarty?" which involves hitting one another over the head with rolled up newspapers.

Carmen finds that dinner parties are a good way to meet men, whom she may or may not see again. Last night's is stirring now, stretching his arms and yawning. She dumps a mug of instant coffee on the table beside him.

"You're going to have to hurry, I'm afraid. It's twenty-five past eight. I'm already running late for work."

He groans, stretching. Then stares at her curiously.

"Hi . . . ?"

"Hi," says, Carmen briskly. "The bathroom's off the hall. The water's hot, if you want a shower. You don't have time for a bath, I'm afraid." She sits down at the antique pine washstand that acts as a dressing table, brushes her hair and starts applying makeup.

"Oh God . . . !" He groans again with great emphasis as he swings his legs over the edge of the bed. "I feel bloody grim. Got any paracetamol?"

Carmen hands him two tablets.

"Cheers . . ." By the way did we . . . ?"

"I don't know. I think probably not."

Carmen goes back to making up.

He watches her from the bed, looking at her reflected face in the mirror. "Are you doing anything later? This evening, I mean. We could meet for a drink or something."

"Sorry. I've already got a date."

"Some other time, maybe."

"Maybe."

Stephen Noble picks up the telephone and dials.

"Hello, Alison?"

"Hello?"

"It's me, Stephen. I'm in London, so I thought I'd give you a ring. I'm just down from Oxford. Are you . . . ?"

"Down from Cambridge? Yes."

"Odd that, isn't it, the way we're described as being 'down.' We ought to say we've left, now that we're down for the last time."

"Mmm. But no one ever does, do they? They don't talk about having left Oxford or Cambridge."

"No. Funny, that."

"So . . ."

"So . . ."

There is a pause. Alison asks: "Where are you living now?"

"I'm staying with my aunt at the moment, my mother's sister. She has a flat in Knightsbridge. Beaufort Gardens."

"Oh, that's nice."

"Yes. And you?"

"Still living with my parents, for the time being. Until I get some research work sorted out, at least. Have you managed to arrange yours yet?"

"Yes, I have, as a matter of fact. I've got a research fellowship with the University of London. So I'll be staying here for the time being."

"Congratulations, that's wonderful . . ." Another pause. "I did enjoy your letters so much, when I was in Cambridge."

"And I enjoyed yours too. Shall we meet? That was the reason I was ringing, really."

"I'd love to."

"Would you like to go and see a film? There's a Buñuel on at the Lumière tonight."

"That would be super."

"Fine. I'll pick you up at seven-thirty then."

Jackie Yardley is going for a job interview. Not her first job, if you count stacking supermarket shelves and other things she did to earn money in her university vacations. But her first *real* job. Her first job as a graduate.

Her friends from Sussex all went to lots of job interviews. There is a shortage of jobs for university graduates in Britain, so they have spread their nets wide, applying to as many as fifty companies with the hope of being interviewed by a handful and offered employment by two at the most. Jackie has only applied to one company. She did her research thoroughly and picked out the company she most wanted to work for. She chooses Munro Willis, a massive chain store empire with outlets in every high street in Britain. They have a comprehensive graduate training program, which enables recruits to rise rapidly to the top of the retail management pyramid.

Jackie is asked if it isn't a little risky putting all her eggs in one basket, considering only one possible career. But she has great faith in the power of tunnel vision. If you work out exactly what you want, and concentrate all your efforts on obtaining it, then your chances of success are much greater than with a "bran tub" approach, groping about blindly and grabbing hold of the first thing that comes up.

This may be the last time she stands here like this, in the tiny bedroom of her stepfather's house at The Poplars, Hemingford. Because if she gets the job—*when* she gets the job—the first thing she will do is find herself a place to live in London. Now that she knows she is about to leave, about to escape Hemingford at last, being in this dolls' house does not seem quite so terrible. She feels quite benevolent toward Don and Pamela. They have been acting sad, but she knows they will be quite relieved to have her gone at last.

She adds the last-minute touches to her appearance—earrings, a pearl necklace and lipstick—and goes onto the landing to look at herself in the full-length mirror. She is wearing a suit, the first she has ever owned. It is navy blue, with gilt buttons on the jacket and a tailored skirt. Underneath it she wears a pale pink silk blouse with a soft bow at the neck, like the ones Lady Diana Spencer wears. On her feet are pumps with high heels—but not too high. Her hair is smoothed back from her face and held in place with a pair of tortoiseshell combs.

She checked the fit of the suit meticulously when she bought it, making sure she would be able to sit comfortably with her legs crossed at the ankles. When she took the suit home, she practiced this pose. In fact she has rehearsed the whole interview in her mind.

"Your application really is most impressive, Miss Yardley," they will say, and she will give them the faintest smile of acknowledgement. "Three A's at 'A' Level, and a first-class degree in business studies. . . ."

Jackie looks at her reflection in amazement. She can see no trace of that shy, frightened little girl who turned up for her first day of school at Albert Road Mixed Infants. Do we leave those other selves behind, she wonders, or are they always with us, lurking in corners where they cannot easily be seen?

■   ■   ■

"Quite a view, isn't it?"

"Bloody fantastic."

Matthew Pryce-Jones nods his agreement. He and another house guest are leaning on a wall of the terrace at the McIvers' country retreat in Hampshire. Below them stretch stepped lawns and an elaborate topiary in the shape of chess pieces. Peacocks strut up and down the paths, trailing the great weight of their tail feathers.

Matthew's fellow guest is a friend of Lucinda's brother. His father is the Duke of Glencoffrie, which makes him an earl. He owns a large chunk of Scotland.

"Where do your people live?" he asks.

"In the country. Not far from London."

"Oh? Where? I might know them."

"It's Berkshire, actually. Near Hemingford."

"Don't know round there. Nice place?"

Matthew puts his hands in his pockets, shrugs. "Quite small, really, only a few acres. Nothing exciting—you know the Home Counties. Not a patch on Scotland."

"But this place isn't half bad though, is it? And handy for Town. Lucky Lucinda!"

"Yes, quite. Lucky Lucinda." Matthew turns round and looks through the French windows at the girl in question.

"Hear you're a doctor."

"Well, not quite. I'm still training."

"Got long to go?"

"I'm halfway there. I've done the three years preclinical, and I'm just starting the three years clinical. They're letting us loose on the patients at last."

"Fantastic. Bloody fantastic. I admire you chaps, I really do. . . ."

Matthew is bored. He looks back through the open window, hoping to catch Lucinda's eye. He and Lucinda have been going out for over two years. Up until now, this has suited both of them. Lucinda has had a built-in escort for any and every outing she cares to go on, from trips to the cinema through to big London charity balls and a cruise around the coast of Sardinia on McIvers' yacht. In return she

•

has turned a blind eye when she suspects that Matthew has slept with another woman. Which he does, frequently.

And Matthew gains an entrée into Lucinda's world, the world of the super-wealthy industrialist who knows everyone and owns everything. He suspects that this state of affairs will not last for much longer. For a while it seemed that Lucinda was content to wait for Matthew to marry her but perhaps now she is realizing she could do better. She has been indifferent of late.

Matthew does not want to lose Lucinda, not until he has found a viable alternative. He is in love with her life-style. The time he has spent with Lucinda's family has proved to him how much easier life is for the rich, and in consequence how much more enjoyable. As a doctor he is never destined to be rich, not unless he establishes a hugely successful private practice.

Lucinda looks up and smiles at him. He smiles back, winks and mouths "Shall we go upstairs?"

Lucinda shakes her head, mouths "Not now," and returns to her conversation with the Earl of Glencoffrie's girlfriend. Matthew strolls off to mingle with the peacocks and look for the very attractive girl who was sitting opposite him at lunch.

T w e n t y - o n e
■

By 1981, Carmen has been living in London for four years, and has achieved a degree of prosperity and security she would not have thought possible when she spent her first night in the city on a station bench.

After completing her course at Chelsea College, she found herself a job designing catalog layouts for a mail-order fashion company. The salary is generous, and she can afford to rent her own flat in Notting Hill Gate, which belongs to a junior diplomat away on a long posting. The flat is very small, but pretty and comfortable. She has a wide circle of friends now, all single like herself, and a busy social life. There is no permanent boyfriend in her life, but plenty of opportunity for sexual intrigue. That is the way she likes it.

But Carmen no longer enjoys her job. The work is repetitive, her colleagues are conservative, there is no opportunity for her to express her personality, which is confined and frustrated. She knows that she is not a good enough artist to make a living in a more creative way, so she must change direction completely.

It does not take her long to decide that she will pursue a career in television. This, after all, is the young people's medium of the 1980s, a booming industry with a seemingly unquenchable need for personnel under the age of thirty. She will have to start at the bottom, as a secretary perhaps, but in such a fast-moving medium that does not rule out the possibility of a rapid rise. Carmen brushes aside impatiently the question of her lack of qualifications. Initiative and enthusiasm are bound to carry more weight.

She starts combing the Media Appointments section in Monday's *Guardian*, applying for vacancies in television companies. The replies are always rejections on the grounds of her lack of a degree or any formal secretarial qualifications. So with the next job she applies for—personal assistant to a senior news journalist at Thames Television—she lies on her application form, awarding herself respectable typing speeds and shorthand. After all, it's not a *complete* lie to say that she can type. She has used a computer keyboard in her current job, and the letters are all in the same place, aren't they?

A week later, she is requested to attend an interview at Thames Television's headquarters in Euston. She thinks carefully about what to wear and decides on a very informal approach in keeping with television's new, young image. She wears jeans and baseball boots and earrings in the shape of telephones.

Her appearance gives her confidence. This is not Carmen Fox dressed up as a successful secretary, nor is she about to put on some sort of act. She is simply going to be herself. She breezes into the interview, plonks herself down in a chair, and sits back, relaxed.

The man facing her over the desk is the journalist she has applied to work for, Alexander Cairns. He has spent several successful years as a BBC foreign correspondent and has now moved into documentaries. In his mid-forties, Cairns has thinning sandy hair and craggy features. Not my type, thinks Carmen. Definitely not my type.

He asks Carmen about her interest in television and she answers at great length, discoursing on her favorite shows, applauding the experimental new formats on youth programs, deploring the predictability of the BBC. Cairns does not interrupt her, though he nods from time to time, or raises his eyebrows.

Finally he says: "Miss Fox, I can hardly fault your enthusiasm, but I have to be sure that your secretarial skills are up to scratch too." He glances at her application form. "What you say here certainly sounds all right, but I do need someone with experience. There is quite a volume of routine paperwork to be processed."

"Oh, don't worry about that, that's no problem." Carmen grins at him. "I could cope with all that."

"We'll see." Cairns's smile is amused, but skeptical. "Janet, my temporary secretary, will be in touch. And now, if you don't mind, I have another candidate to see...."

The girl in question is waiting in the outer office. She is very tall, with long fair hair tied back in a velvet bow. She wears a jacket with a pleated skirt and low-heeled pumps, and looks every inch the efficient personal assistant. Carmen glances at her neatly typed c.v., which is on the edge of Janet's desk. She can just see the name in block capitals, PENELOPE CLARE MAIDEN.

"So it's just between the two of you now," says Janet, winding a sheet of paper into her typewriter.

"Really?" Carmen blinks. "Just ... her and me?"

"That's right. He only wanted to see you two. He's very fussy about the sort of person he wants, is Mr. Cairns...."

Janet's phone rings and she disappears from the room in answer to a summons from the voice at the other end of the line. Carmen picks up the c.v. from her desk and reads. Penelope Maiden certainly has some impressive qualifications; educated at a well-known public school, has worked in television before, *and* she has all sorts of wholesome hobbies like horse-riding and embroidery.

Damn, thinks Carmen. And I came so close, too....

When she gets back to the flat Carmen sits by the phone with a can of lager in her hand, brooding. At five fifty-nine, just as the switchboard is about to shut down for the night, she phones Thames Television and asks to be put through to Janet.

"Hello, this is Penelope Maiden." She makes her voice all high and breathy. "I'm just ringing to say that I'm not interested in the job with Mr. Cairns after all. I'm frightfully sorry to have wasted his time, but I've given it some thought and I've decided to look elsewhere."

The following afternoon Carmen gets home a little earlier than usual. She has invited a man round for a drink, someone she met at a party the previous week, and she needs time to tidy the flat. She rushes out to work every morning and leaves it looking as if there has been a contained explosion in the place.

There are really only two rooms, the bedroom and the open-plan living and dining area, so it is difficult to stop clothes straying into the living room and mugs and plates into the bedroom. She puts away all her clothes and shoes, hangs up her coats and washes up all the pieces of crockery she can find. When the rooms have been cleared of debris, the place looks quite respectable, quite "grown-up." It has polished wood floors with Chinese rugs and the only furniture in the sitting area (unless you count the hi-fi) are two large white sofas covered with pink and blue cushions, and a lamp-table with a huge ceramic lamp on it. The sash-windows look out over the leafy square below, and since the flat is on the third floor, the view is of the tops of the trees. In the summer they give the light in the room a greenish tinge.

She is just staring into her wardrobe in despair, wondering why she has a rack full of clothes and nothing to wear, when the phone rings.

"It's Janet here, phoning from Alexander Cairns's office. He'd like to see you again, and I wondered whether you could make five-thirty this afternoon?"

Five-thirty? Carmen squints at her watch. That gives her forty-five minutes.

"Yes, I should think I could. Just."

She is already stripping off her jeans and T-shirt as she hangs up the receiver. She is not going to take any chances this time, which means there is only one thing she can wear: a Calvin Klein suit made of softest mole-gray suede. It is not the sort of thing that she could normally afford, but her best friend Ros has contacts in the fashion industry, and has access to a source of half-price remainders by top designers. Ros was at Chelsea College with Carmen studying fashion design, and now has a bright future ahead designing for a large chain store company.

When she walks into the front office, Janet greets her with a smile, a slightly knowing smile that implies that she is party to some decision that Carmen is not yet aware of.

I've got it! I must have got the job....!

She walks into Alexander Cairns's office with a distinct swagger. He in turn smiles broadly and holds out his hand.

"Nice to see you again, Carmen . . . or should I say Penelope?'

"What. . . ?"

"Janet recognized your voice. It wasn't difficult given that Miss Maiden had telephoned five minutes earlier to give me some information missing from her application. Oh, and she calls herself Penny by the way."

Carmen slumps down in the chair. "Oh, I see."

"You haven't got the job, I'm afraid. That went to Miss Maiden, as a result of her superior qualifications. But I haven't brought you here to rub your nose in it. I asked you here to tell you that I can't help admiring your cheek." He gives her a wintry smile. "It is, after all, just initiative by another name. And I wanted to let you know that I've found you another job, if you'd like it."

"You mean here? At Thames? Even after I?"

"Yes. There's a position coming up in New Program Development. It's actually a better job in as much as it will involve you in some audience research and could lead on to other things."

Carmen shrugs. "Mr. Cairns, what can I say?"

"Nothing. Just work hard and don't pull any more stunts like this, and you should go far." He shuffles through his papers, indicating that the meeting is over.

"So . . ." Carmen stands up, straightening her skirt. "See you around, then."

"I doubt it."

T *w e n t y - t w o*

■

"The trouble with Renoir ..." Alison Griffiths wrinkles her nose at one of his paintings "... is that he's so preoccupied with painting cute children or fat, naked women. And I don't like looking at either."

Stephen Noble is standing in front of the pink, rounded buttocks of Renoir's mistress. "Neither do I!" he says fervently, and shivers. "How did they get to be so overweight?"

He looks approvingly at Alison's figure. She is pencil-slim, and dresses in loose, layered clothes that conceal rather than reveal the figure. Today she is wearing a pair of tailored wool trousers, a Japanese padded jacket and a black felt hat with her hair tucked underneath it. The hat adds a cheeky, feminine touch to what would otherwise be a rather severe outfit.

They link arms and stroll out of the Hayward Gallery and onto the terrace that looks across the Thames.

"I shall miss you when you go back to Cambridge," says Stephen. "I must confess, I've been rather lazy. I've allowed myself to rely on your company rather than making any new friends."

Alison smiles. "I haven't gone yet! There's another whole week before term starts. And we'll see each other at dinner tonight."

"Ah yes. Dinner tonight."

Alison has been spending her long vacation at her parents' gloomy mansion flat in the Boltons (their other home is a gloomy seventeenth-century house in Wiltshire). She has secured a postgraduate place at her old college and will be returning for the beginning of the Michaelmas term. By way of a farewell, Sir Roland and Lady

Griffiths are taking her out for dinner. Stephen has been invited and so have Geoffrey and Sylvia Noble. Six of them. Three couples.

A table has been booked at Le Gavroche. Stephen is wearing a suit for the first time in months, Alison is in a black silk dress and pearls. Both of them are uncomfortable.

"So ..." Geoffrey Noble slips his fish knife into an exquisite navarin of lobster and monkfish. "Have you enjoyed your time up here in town, Alison?"

"Well ..."

"It's been *marvelous* for her having Stephen around!" gushes Delia Griffiths. "They've been all over the place, doing things together. I should think Stephen will be quite lost when she's up in Cambridge again."

"Yes, it's a pity she has to go back to Cambridge," observes Sylvia.

"Yes," says Stephen.

"Still, Cambridge isn't very far. Only fifty minutes on the train, I gather. Hardly any time at all."

"No."

"You and Geoffrey have just got back from France, I hear?" Sir Roland belches discreetly and pours himself another glass of Chateau Margaux. "Your mother's place, was it?"

"Yes. We usually go there."

"I know Alison absolutely *loved* her trip out there," says Lady Delia.

"Well we'd love to have her back some time. Perhaps next summer?"

"It would be nice if it could be arranged for when Stephen's out there ...?"

Stephen and Alison are drowning in an ocean of parental approval, unable to speak or move without doing the right thing. And every topic mentioned is intended to link them in some way, to bond them as a couple.

After the meal, Sylvia and Geoffrey go back with Stephen to Sara Chancellor's flat for a nightcap. Stephen's aunt is away on a cultural tour of China.

"Very good of Sara to put you up like this," says Geoffrey, helping himself to malt whisky from her crystal decanter. "Especially since the place isn't big enough to swing a cat."

"Well, it was never intended to be a permanent arrangement," Sylvia points out. "Have you thought of where you might move to, Stephen?"

"Not really. Aunt Sara said I could stay here as long as I like. And she's away such a lot, we're hardly ever both here together."

"Ah, but she might sell," says Geoffrey quickly. "She did say something about selling, didn't she, dear?"

"Yes, I think she did, now you mention it. . . ."

"In that case, I expect I'd find somewhere in a college hall of residence. Or I could flat share."

Geoffrey leans forward on the sofa, resting his hands on his knees. "You do realize, Stephen, that there is some money set aside from my parents' estate for you to buy your first home. When you settle down and get married, of course."

"I see."

"It's quite a substantial sum. Enough to buy a decent flat, or about half the amount you'd need for a house—at today's prices."

"I had no idea," says Stephen. That's very generous of you both; thank you."

"Of course, we haven't said anything about it before because we thought ... well, that was before ..."

"It's only what any parent would like to do for their child if they have the means," says Sylvia quickly. "To see their son or daughter set up in their own place in London. I should think the Griffiths have got some similar arrangement for Alison, for example. For when she gets married. She's their only child, after all."

"Yes. Quite," says Stephen.

Well, why not, he thinks, lying in bed that night. If they're going to make such an obvious suggestion, why not take them up on it and reap the benefits?

If he is going to have to share a home with someone at some point in the future, he would rather it was Alison than anyone else. They have the same interests and he feels comfortable with her. And if he is to live a straight, conventional life, he has more chance of succeeding with someone he really likes.

He turns the idea over and over in his head all night, and the more it takes root, the more obvious the advantages. As soon as he has eaten breakfast, he telephones Alison.

"Can we meet? There's something I need to ask you."

"We're having lunch together tomorrow; can't it wait until then?"

"No. Meet me outside the Science Museum at ten o'clock."

Alison is waiting for Stephen when he arrives. She is wearing a beret and a man's trenchcoat. She looks anxious.

"What's wrong? Has something happened?"

"No ... well, yes, I suppose it has."

He takes Alison's hand and they walk into Kensington Gardens, as far as the Albert Memorial. It is a perfect autumn day, clear and fresh, with a pale blue sky and the sunshine making the browning leaves glow russet and flame and gold.

"Sit down."

Alison sits on the steps of the monument.

"I'd like you to marry me."

Before she can speak Stephen says all in a rush: "I've thought about it all, and it would work, it really would. My parents have promised me half the cost of a London house when I marry, and I'm sure yours would contribute something. We could get somewhere really decent and turn it into a proper home. We both have similar tastes, and like looking for books and pictures and antiques and things. We could get somewhere quite near Liverpool Street, and then you could commute up to Cambridge on the train. You wouldn't need to go into college every day; you could do a lot of your research work from home. There are plenty of libraries in London. And it would be our own place, just the two of us with no one to bother us."

Alison makes no response for a few seconds. Then: "You haven't said you love me."

"Well, of course. . . ."

"It's all right, the answer's 'yes.' "

■ ■ ■

2 9 0

No foursome of prospective parents-in-law could have been more
delighted than Sylvia and Geoffrey Noble, Sir Roland and Lady Griffiths. An announcement is placed in the *Times* Court and Social pages,
and wedding preparations begin. Stephen and Alison want to get married as quickly as possible, but Lady Delia insists that she needs at
least six months to make the necessary arrangements, and sets the
date for the last Saturday in March, 1982. The wedding will be at the
village church in Wiltshire and the reception for the three hundred
guests in a marquee in the gardens of the gloomy old house. A marquee is de rigueur, even though it will probably rain and the guests
will be wading about in a sea of mud. It is explained to Alison that
the color of the marquee's interior is of vital importance. The white
lining can be striped with pink, yellow, peach, or blue, and that color
will dictate the color of the flowers in her bouquet and headdress,
and the color of the frocks for the five bridesmaids.

Alison chooses yellow, because her mother has told her that
yellow or peach are most appropriate for spring brides. She is then
whisked off for a preliminary consultation with one of London's most
patronized society dressmakers. Alison has no idea how she should
look; she lets the dressmaker decide, trailing backward and forward
to tedious fittings. All the sizing and measuring makes her feel like
an object of barter, an asset that her parents are selling off. They have
already handed over to Stephen a very large sum of money for the
purchase of the new home, and Stephen has found a small, but classi-
cally proportioned Georgian house in Canonbury. House-hunting and
choosing things for their new home are the only enjoyable aspects of
being engaged.

"I can't face this, can you?" says Alison when she returns from
her third fitting. "I've had Mother going on and on about whether
bridesmaids should carry posies or baskets, and who's going to do
the photographs, and where the cake is going to be cut. And I'm
afraid I don't care."

"The wedding is the worst part of the whole thing," agrees Stephen. "But the point is that we're not doing it for us, we're doing it
for our parents."

"Exactly. They're being too greedy. They should just be pleased that we're getting married at all, and leave the rest to us. Can't we just, for one last time, do something that *isn't* going to be approved of?"

"You mean . . . ?"

"Yes. Let's elope."

The completion of the house purchase takes place on 1 December. A week later, Alison and Stephen are married at Chelsea Town Hall, in the presence of two witnesses. The bride wears a black velvet dress and carries a bunch of Arum lilies.

"Mrs. Stephen Noble . . ." Alison is looking at the printed name at the head of her new correspondence cards. "It sounds very mature, doesn't it?"

The cards are a present to Alison from her mother-in-law, arriving in a green and gold Harrods box, with the finest layer of tissue between each card. The gift is proof that the two of them have finally been forgiven for running off to a register office. Sylvia and Geoffrey minded least, relieved that the marriage had gone through before either of them had had a chance to change their minds. Sir Roland and Lady Delia made a big fuss about being cheated of their day of glory, and sulked for a while, but they could only be glad in the end that they had married off their plain, shy, unmarriageable daughter.

"Once these have gone in the desk, that's it—the last of the wedding gifts have been put away. What a relief!"

Alison is kneeling on the floor in the drawing room of their new house. It is a sunny room, with walls painted butter yellow and bookshelves built into every available space. The wooden floor is stripped and waxed and covered with a dark red turkey carpet, a wedding present from Raoul and Lydia.

"I'll go and make some supper." Alison climbs to her feet and dusts down her trousers. "I've bought a couple of trout, is that all right?"

Stephen follows her into the kitchen and watches as his wife lays the trout in a baking tray, parboils and slices potatoes for *pommes frites* and puts mange-touts in the steamer.

"For someone who doesn't know how to cook, you're doing a wonderful job."

"Well, it's only fish. There's nothing to it really. I couldn't cook anything really fancy—you know, dinner party food."

"I'm very glad to hear it. It means we'll be spared having to hold dinner parties. I hate them."

"Funnily enough, so do I." They both laugh.

Stephen takes a bottle of chilled Chablis from the fridge and pours them each a glass. This ought to be a relaxed, intimate moment; two newlyweds in the kitchen of their first home, preparing a meal which they will eat alone. Yet there is the faintest tension in the air, a frisson of unease. Alison looks up several times from her task to try to read the expression on Stephen's face. He expects her to speak, but each time she thinks better of it and turns back to the stove.

Finally she says: "Stephen, I ... It's been eight days since we moved in here and we still haven't ..." She sighs. "You know what I'm trying to say." She gulps down a mouthful of Chablis.

"You mean we haven't made love." Stephen examines his finger-nails. "I'm sorry, I've just been so tired, and with the tension of the move and everything ... Unpacking. We've been so late to bed every night."

"I've put everything away now. There's nothing to stop us going to bed early tonight."

Alison smiles at him shyly. He kisses her. "Tonight then, I promise."

The trout are consumed in near silence. After the meal Stephen fusses over clearing away and washing up, delaying. He says he needs a bath and lies in the tub until the water turns cold, looking at his watch at five-minute intervals. Alison lies in bed reading, dressed in a plunging silk satin nightdress given to her for the purpose by Lady Delia. As if she knew that her daughter would need help to lure her husband into bed.

Stephen seems put off by the slipperiness of the fabric, by the intensely feminine combination of Miss Dior and lily of the valley talcum powder. He kisses her mouth awkwardly, then strokes her through the nightdress with monotonous, dutiful movements. After some thirty minutes of this, Alison plucks up enough courage to try to impart some life into his resolutely limp penis. She fails. Stephen cries in her arms.

"Shhh," she says, rocking him in her arms like a baby. "It will be all right, I know it will."

The end of April and the beginning of May 1982 are unusually warm, more like midsummer than spring. Alison Noble spends as much time as possible studying at home, and in the afternoon she takes to sitting in the garden with a book. The garden is walled on all three sides, making quite a suntrap.

Stephen returns from the university one afternoon to find her there, sunbathing topless on a towel on the lawn. She sits up as soon as she sees him, and covers herself with her shirt.

"How was college?"

"Not bad. Did you get much work done?"

"Quite a bit."

"Oh, that's good."

They lapse into silence. Alison fastens the buttons on her shirt.

"Shall I make us some tea?" Stephen offers.

"That would be nice."

Once Stephen is inside the house, Alison relaxes again. They can no longer sit and be comfortable together, the way they could before they were married. Silences have to be filled, before they become too awkward. They are very kind and considerate to one another; outsiders remark on how well they get on. But their marriage has still not been consummated. They tried for a while, but after repeated failures on Stephen's part, the attempts stopped, by mutual consent.

Stephen is happier with this arrangement; he would prefer the two of them to live together as companions and friends. But it matters to Alison, who has assumed, of course, that she and her husband would be lovers as well as friends. It turns out that they do not, after all, want the same thing from the marriage.

Stephen comes back into the garden with a tray of tea. He pours a cup for Alison and hands it to her. "I'll just drink this, then I'll go in and leave you to your sunbathing. I've got some reading to do."

"Fine."

"I see there's a new Lloyd-Webber musical opening in the West End. Shall I try and get tickets?"

"Yes please, that would be lovely."

"Perhaps your parents would like to come with us?"

"We could ask them."

"We're seeing them for dinner next week, aren't we?"

"Yes. Tuesday."

"Well ..."

"Do you mind if ..."

They both speak at one.

"Sorry, go on."

"No, it doesn't matter." Alison picks up her bottle of sun lotion and starts to dab some onto her legs. Stephen watches her rub the cream into her pale, freckled skin. Her movements are deft, rhythmical. He was going to go back into the house to work, but the sensation of the sun on his back is so pleasant that he feels disinclined to move.

"I think I might stay out in the garden for a while, if that's all right with you."

"Yes, of course." Alison rolls onto her stomach, pushing her shirt up discreetly so that her back is exposed to the sun.

"I could put some lotion on your back if you like."

"It's all right, thanks."

"It's no bother, really. You don't want to burn."

"Okay."

Stephen pours a puddle of lotion onto Allison's back and begins to spread it around in ever-widening circles, making sure every inch of flesh is covered. He becomes quite engrossed in the task, closing his eyes and managing by touch alone. Her skin feels delightfully warm and firm. He moves his hands down further, encompassing her narrow hips and the curve of her buttocks just above her bikini.

He coughs to clear his throat. "You could turn over if you like. I'll do your front."

Alison rolls over without a word. Her eyes closed, she is smiling slightly. Stephen drips another pool of lotion into her navel and dips his fingers into it. He traces his fingers slowly over her hipbones, and then up under her shirt to her small, girlish breasts. She shivers, and goose pimples break out on her skin.

"I think I'd better go inside."

"Come to bed, Alison. Please."

She knows better than to express surprise, allowing him to lead her silently up the stairs to their cool blue and white bedroom. Stephen makes love to her as though he is in a trance. He feels inside as though he is a different person.

This time it is Alison who cries, and Stephen who holds her. They lie there for a long time, until it is dark. Then they go downstairs, ravenously hungry, and make omelettes and salad. The evenings are cool, so they light a fire in the drawing room and sit on the turkey carpet in front of it, drinking cognac and listening to Bach. Stephen feels at peace, in harmony with himself. I *can* change, he tells himself. I can be different. It's only a question of attitude.

Alison drapes her husband's arm around her shoulder and cuddles into him with a contented sigh. "Just think of all the time we've wasted," she says. "Never mind, from now on it's always going to be like this."

They watch the fire die out, then clear the dishes quickly, eager to return to bed. As they are putting away the last few plates, the phone rings. . . .

"Who would be ringing at this time of night? It's nearly eleven o'clock."

Stephen goes to answer it. Alison notices his surprise when the caller is identified. The way his cheeks pale and then turn bright red. He hangs up with a look of disbelief.

"Who was it?"

"And old friend of mine called Nicholas Pobjoy. I haven't seen him for years, and it turns out that he's living just round the corner." Stephen is staring down at his hands in a distracted way.

"So? That's good, isn't it?"

"Yes ... yes, I suppose it is. Anyway, he said he might come round tomorrow evening. Is that all right?"

"Of course it is, silly!" Alison kisses him gently on the mouth. "Any friend of yours is a friend of mine."

When Nicholas arrives for dinner the following evening, Alison assumes that he is on his way to a fancy-dress party. He wears a pair of baggy orange harem pants under a crimson silk kaftan, and a purple sequinned skullcap on his vivid auburn hair. She is so dazzled by his appearance that she does not notice how grubby Nicholas' garments are, and how they give off a faint odor of stale sweat and patchouli.

"Nicholas, I'd like to introduce my wife, Alison."

Nicholas bends low, takes Alison's pinky-white hand in his golden one and kisses it. When Stephen sees how she blushes he turns away quickly and busies himself with fetching drinks.

He would like to stare at Nicholas throughout the meal, the way Alison does, but of course he does not. He takes every opportunity to leave the table, to fetch and carry and tidy up, thereby avoiding being drawn fully into the conversation. He feels more comfortable in the kitchen, leaving Nicholas Pobjoy alone with his wife.

"Well, what did you think?" he asks when Nicholas has finally left, after heavy hints, at half-past one.

"Does he always dress like that?"

"No ... I don't know really. Perhaps he does now."

"Well, he's certainly different, isn't he?" Alison gives a self-conscious little laugh. "I think he's the most unusual person I've ever met."

T *w e n t y - t h r e e*

■

Jackie Yardley is a success. She excells in her job as management trainee with Munro Willis, and she loves her work with a passion that surprises even her most dedicated colleagues. Her office hours are from nine to five-thirty. Jackie arrives at seven-thirty and has cleared her desk by nine, ready to start making phone calls. She never leaves the office before six; more often it is eight or nine. There is ample time within these hours for her to complete the work in her job description, so she creates more work. She analyses company accounts and reports in detail, looking for areas of potential profit-ability and writing out her proposals. She scrutinizes the layout and content of competitors' stores to find fresh inspiration.

This regime leaves little time for a social life, but Jackie does not mind in the least. She does not know anyone in London apart from the people at Munro Willis. There is sometimes time for a drink with her colleagues, or a meal with some of the girlfriends she has made at work, before going home to her flat and collapsing into bed. She finds that she must exist on little sleep, because her brain is too full of figures, ideas, and Munro Willis company policy for her to switch off.

During her first few months in London she receives frequent letters from Rob Jones, forwarded by Pamela. She throws them away, unanswered, and eventually he confines himself to an impersonal exchange of cards at Christmas. Jackie is glad. It is better if they forget one another.

Since she rarely goes out and has no hobbies or leisure activities, it is easy for Jackie to save money. She realizes the benefits of owning property and sets aside several hundred pounds each month until she has enough money for the deposit on a flat. She finds one in a newly-converted house in Pimlico, takes out a mortgage of thirty thousand pounds and moves in with no possessions other than a bed, a fridge, and her personal computer.

Jackie's dedication is so remarkable that promotion inevitably follows. After only six months her traineeship is brought to a premature end and she is given executive status on a new development program that aims to give customers "a complete shopping experience." Jackie is the only graduate recruit singled out for such a move. The others watch her as she moves into her new fourth-floor office, whispering, envious.

Jackie knows that it will not be long before she meets the man she wants to marry. She has had one false start: a man called Jeremey Chambers who works in the accounts department. He is very attractive, very bright, very smooth, but he quickly grew bored with Jackie's working hours, and broke off their relationship. Next time she will be more ruthless.

To fit her specification, the man must be a few years older than Jackie, university-educated, good-looking, and ambitious. She is on the alert, therefore, when a man roughly fitting this description joins the Munro Willis management team. He is a high-flyer recruited from the top rungs of another company with BNG Holdings, which owns Munro Willis.

"Have you seen him yet?" Pat, Jackie's secretary, asks as she puts a pile of letters on her desk. "He's ... *mmmwah*!" She kisses her fingertips. "Gorgeous! A hunk. He's tall and dark, with lovely twinkly blue eyes, and he's wearing this fabulous suit...."

"Really?" Jackie continues reading the company memo in front of her.

But at lunch time, she goes down to the personnel department and looks at his file. Her job on the new project gives her access to information about the company's manpower resources, so no one questions her.

His name is Gregory John Maitland. He was born in 1953, so he is twenty-nine, six years older than Jackie. His father is an advocate at the Scottish bar. He went to a private day school in Glasgow, and then to Edinburgh University, where he won a first-class degree in French and business studies.

The details are perfect. Jackie scans the page for the most important information of all.

"Marital Status: Single."

She goes back into her office, and her hands are trembling with excitement. She looks out of her window and sees Gregory Maitland arriving in his company BMW for his first management meeting. The personnel director is waiting on the steps to greet him. Jackie watches them shake hands. She knows from that handshake that this is the man. He is polite and yet commanding, giving the briefest shake before bounding up the steps, taking them two at a time while the personnel manager puffs along behind. Observing the formalities, yet eager to get on with the business in hand.

Jackie spends the next few days wondering how she can make Gregory Maitland notice her. The offices are buzzing with unattached females, some of them very personable. There is no reason why she should stand out.

"Force him to notice you," says Ros. Ros is a friend of Jackie's who works on the design team. She is worldly and experienced and full of useful pieces of advice for Jackie. "Never let a man see you with face cream on," is one of Ros's gems. "Once he's seen you smeared in grease, the relationship has had it."

"What do you think I should do?"

"Try and fix it so the two of you are working together. That way he's got to give you attention. Go to him with questions. Pester him."

Jackie's chance comes when she and Gregory Maitland are both to sit in on the same resources management meeting. Jackie usually wears the minimum of makeup at work, but on this occasion she shades her eyelids to make her eyes look larger and more lustrous, and applies several coats of mascara.

"You look nice," says Pat. "What's different? Is it your hair?"

"No, I don't think so."

"Must be for old Gorgeous Gregory, eh?"

"Don't be ridiculous! I'm going to the meeting to discuss the introduction of a new Munro Willis credit card."

She watches Gorgeous Gregory surreptitiously when she can do so unobserved. He stands up when he wants to make a point, tossing his floppy dark hair back from his forehead and thrusting his hands deep into his pockets. His red silk tie is twisted round so that the label is visible. Jackie reads it and is impressed: Hermès.

After the meeting, Jackie follows Gregory into his office, clutching the notes she made.

"Jackie Yardley." She extends a hand and gives his a brief, businesslike shake. "You mentioned cash inducements to promote the credit card, and I've got a couple of ideas of my own in that line. I thought you might like to take a look."

She gives Gregory her notes, written in a neat schoolgirl hand.

He runs his eye down the list. " 'An annual fee offset by a discount of ten pounds for every two hundred spent with the card' ... These look interesting. Can I get back to you?"

"Sure."

Jackie goes back to her office and waits. She has an hour's worth of paperwork to do, and manages to spin it out for three hours.

At half-past six Richard Conybere pops his head round the door of her office. Richard is one of her fellow graduate trainees who asked her out persistently during her first months at Munro Willis.

"Fancy a drink, Jackie?"

"No thanks, I've got some more work to do."

"Oh go on! We're only going to the wine bar down the road. You can come back here later if you like, to finish off."

"No, really. I'd rather work through." She gives Richard the briefest glance before picking up her dictaphone and starting a memo to Pat.

Richard shakes his head in disbelief. "What is it with you, Jackie? You've got to unwind sometime or you'll just turn into a machine. All work and no play, makes Jackie a dull girl."

"I'll come to the wine bar with you another time, I promise. I just can't make it tonight."

"Got a secret assignation with the boss, eh?"

Jackie blushes.

"Thought so . . ."

Ten minutes later, her patience is rewarded. The tall, dashing figure of Gregory Maitland blocks her doorway. He waves her notes at her.

"Got a minute to discuss these?"

"I think so."

"Care to discuss them over a drink?"

Jackie vetoes the wine bar, where her friends will be speculating on her character defects. They cross to the other side of Oxford Street instead, and head for a champagne bar in St. James's.

To Jackie's delight, Gregory is happy to dismiss their discussion of the new credit card after endorsing a few of the points she made. They talk instead about Scotland, and the relative merits of Glasgow and Edinburgh.

"Did you know," Gregory says interrupting her self-conscious attempts at casual conversation, "you've got the most sultry eyes I've ever seen?"

Jackie Yardley and Gregory Maitland are to be married in the autumn of 1984.

Or at least, that is what Jackie decides. She makes the decision long before the subject of marriage is mentioned, after only a few dates. Gregory is perfect: dynamic, strong, masculine, a high-earner. They can have a perfect life, combining careers, travel, a lovely home and children.

Their courtship is colored by Jackie's obsessive desire to do everything right. She buys recipe books and pores over them late at night, making elaborate and fussy shopping lists that will give her all the ingredients she needs to cook the right meal. Later, when they have a fund of mutual friends, she agonizes over lists of dinner guests, juggling seating plans to get them absolutely right. Paradoxically, the more time passes, the more Jackie's fear and anxiety increase. She is afraid lest Gregory become discontented with her and decide to end things before there is any commitment between them. Deciding that

Gregory is right for her has not made *her* content, for she lives in terror of losing him.

The first few times she mentions marriage, Gregory procrastinates. "Why change anything?" is his stock response. "We're happy the way we are now, aren't we?"

"Yes," Jackie always replies, fear starting in the pit of her stomach: Is he about to ditch her? So the subject is dropped.

By the end of 1983, when they have been seeing one another for over a year, Jackie is becoming desperate. She knows she must wait for the right time to broach the subject. She waits until the night of the Christmas party held at the Café Royal for Munro Willis's senior personnel. Gregory is in a good mood. He has had a few glasses of champagne to celebrate the fact that he is being head-hunted by Amecorp, an international communications network.

"Will you take the job?" Jackie asks him as they stand shivering on the wet pavement in Piccadilly, waiting for a black cab.

"Of course." Gregory flags down a cab and opens the door for Jackie. She settles herself in the back seat, pulling her cashmere wrap tightly around her bare shoulders. "It's a brilliant opportunity. They're offering me a junior directorship. I could be on the board by the time I'm thirty-five."

The taxi trundles through the rain-soaked streets, sending sprays of water onto the windscreen as its wheels churn up the puddles. The reflection of street lights gleams on the wet surface of the road. They are heading for St. John's Wood, where Gregory has a flat. It is Friday night, and on Tuesday, Friday, and Saturday nights, they sleep together at Gregory's flat. On Monday and Wednesday they sleep together at Jackie's flat. Sunday and Thursday are days off.

"I'll be getting a much bigger salary at Amecorp," says Gregory, as he unlocks the front door of his flat. "I'll be able to sell this place and get somewhere bigger."

The flat is stylish and well designed but very small. Jackie goes into the bedroom, which is almost entirely taken up by the king-size bed. She sits on the edge of the bed, kicks off her black suede stilettos and pulls her cashmere wrap from her shoulders. She is wearing a Thai silk dress in metallic blue. The bodice is strapless, revealing her shoulders and back. Her eyes, large and luminous, shine out of her small pointed face.

"You're beautiful ..." Gregory sits beside her on the bed and kisses the nape of her neck. He starts to unzip her dress.

But Jackie cannot relax. "If you leave Munro Willis and go to work at Amecorp, we'll see a lot less of one another." She pushes Gregory's hands away and turns round to face him. "Maybe now would be a good time to think about living together all the time. Especially if you're thinking about selling this place. I could sell my flat too and we could buy a house."

"You mean you want to get married?"

"Yes."

"I don't know, Jackie ..." Gregory takes her hand and runs his fingers slowly up and down her wrist. "I'm not sure that you're ready for that sort of commitment."

"*I'm* not! Don't you mean you're not! I'm twenty-five in the summer, of course I'm ready!"

"What I mean is, I'm not sure if you really love me enough."

Jackie stares at him dumbfounded. "Of course I do! We've been together all this time. Why else would I have stuck around, if I didn't want to marry you?"

"Give him an ultimatum," advises Ros. "Tell him it's marriage or nothing."

"I don't know what's the matter with him," Jackie grumbles. "When I mention marriage he makes out the problem's with my degree of commitment. But I'm the one who's ready for marriage."

"Men never are," says Ros. "Or they don't know they are. You just have to give them a bit of a push."

So when Gregory phones on Monday evening to ask what time he should come round to Jackie's flat, she tells him not to come round.

"Why on earth not? What's the matter with you?"

"I've told you how I feel. I don't want to get stuck in a relationship that's not going anywhere. If you want to stay single, that's your decision, but I have other priorities."

"So it's marriage or nothing."

"Yes. Good-bye, Gregory."

When Jackie hangs up, her heart is pounding and her palms are sweating. She is more terrified than ever now, terrified that he will call her bluff. For ten days, she hears nothing from Gregory. They avoid one another assiduously at work.

On the tenth day her office telephone rings at eight o'clock in the morning, just as she is sitting down at her desk.

It is Gregory.

"All right," he says. "You win."

The engagement ring is a diamond solitaire, marquise cut, set in a band of platinum and diamond chips. It cost fifteen hundred pounds. This seems a great deal of money to spend on a ring, but Jackie reassures herself with the fact that jewelry is a good investment.

She must have read that somewhere, or heard someone saying so; she certainly has not learned it from experience. Pamela never had any jewelry, not until she met Don Anderson and he bought her a wedding ring. And a sapphire eternity ring from H. Samuel. There was no engagement ring, since the period of their betrothal was spent in a psychiatric hospital.

Jackie is not sure how to represent all these facts to Gregory and his family. She has never lied to Gregory, but she has been either vague or silent on the subject of her parentage. Once they are engaged she decides that she should tell Gregory she is illegitimate. Rather than being put off he is intrigued, as though illegitmacy adds an extra, fascinating dimension to her character.

Jackie also worries about whether she should invite Don and Pamela to the wedding. By convention it should be Don and Pamela who are the host and hostess, but Jackie uses Don's recent ill health as an excuse to take the arrangements on herself. She is relieved when Pamela rings to say that Don will not be well enough to travel on the day, and that she must stay with him. She suspects Don and Pamela are relieved too.

The wedding takes place on the first Saturday in October 1984. The ceremony is at a church in St. John's Wood near Gregory's flat, (where they are to live until the have found a house), followed by a reception at Claridge's. Jackie looks delicate and ravishingly pretty in a frothy Gina Fratini dress (paid for with her annual bonus from Munro Willis). Gregory looks dashing in his father's morning suit. The select gathering of fifty guests—mainly colleagues and Gregory's family—agree that they look the perfect couple.

The honeymoon is a week in Venice. Gregory had booked two weeks on a houseboat in Kashmir but Jackie told him that she could not possibly take a two-week stretch away from work, not with the busy Christmas period approaching.

Jackie is surprised to find that Gregory expects her to place less importance on her work now that she is married. She tells him so over dinner at the flat in St. John's Wood.

"*You're* not any less interested in your job, are you, now that we're married?" she challenges him over their heat-and-serve lasagne.

"No, of course not. But it's hardly worth scrambling to the top of the corporate ladder if you're about to go off and have children."

Jackie looks at him blankly.

". . . Well, we are going to have children, aren't we? You said you wanted them."

"Yes, I do. A boy and a girl would be nice. But I'm not going to stop working. You're not expected to these days. There's no reason why I shouldn't be a mother *and* get to the top of the corporate ladder."

"I see. So you believe it when *Cosmopolitan* magazine tells you you can have it all, do you?"

"I know what I'm capable of."

"I see." Gregory frowns, takes another mouthful of lasagne. "Well, if you're superwoman, then you won't have forgotten about tomorrow night, will you?"

"Tomorrow night?"

"The company dinner. At Amecorp."

Jackie fetches her handbag and consults her personal organizer. "I'm sorry, Gregory, I can't. Not tomorrow night. It's the annual stock control meeting of all the divisional managers. It'll go on until eight, at least."

"But I've told the chairman you're coming! They're expecting to meet you! I'm going to look a right lemon, aren't I, if I have to go in there and say 'I'm sorry, but my wife had something more important to do this evening than to meet all of you!' "

"Gregory, it's my job! I'm sorry too, but I can't just drop everything to go out to dinner with your colleagues. You've worked at Munro Willis, you know the situation."

Gregory thumps the table with his fist, making the knives and forks rattle and the wine bottle slosh a pale pink pool onto the tablecloth. "God damn it, Jackie, I expect you to give some thought to *my* situation! I've got a career too, remember, and I'm expected to have a supportive wife behind me!"

Jackie shrugs her shoulders, implying that the situation is beyond her control.

"Jesus Christ!" Gregory picks up a side plate, part of the dinner service that was his parents' wedding gift, and smashes it against the wall.

Jackie does not react, save for a cold, reproachful look as she bends down and starts picking up the broken china. As she straightens up, Gregory hits her, a hard, glancing blow across her cheek.

Jackie stays still, but her mind races at breakneck pace. She is afraid, not of physical violence, but of the alternative. What if he leaves me? she thinks. What will people say? Will I become just like Mum? And after everything I did to get here. . . .

"I'm sorry!" Gregory is saying, trying to pull her to her feet. "God, I'm sorry, what can I have . . ."

"It's all right." Jackie dusts herself down. "Let's just forget it happened."

T w e n t y - f o u r

■

Lucinda McIver telephones Matthew Pryce-Jones.

"Matthew, hi! It's Lucinda."

"Lucinda! Well, what a nice surprise. I haven't heard from you in ages."

"I know, sorry. You know what it's like ... listen, there's something I want to ask you. Are you working tonight?"

"No, I'm not, for once."

"Can I come round to the flat then?"

"Sure, if you like."

"Great. See you later then."

Matthew hangs up the receiver, puzzled. He and Lucinda formally ended their relationship some two years ago, but have remained friends. They decided that with the pressure of Matthew's final exams, and the punishing hours worked by a junior houseman, they would simply not see enough of one another.

Or, rather, Lucinda drew this conclusion, and Matthew had no choice but to agree. He anticipated her thoughts and was the first to suggest the split, thereby saving himself the humiliation of being "chucked." But he misses the grand country weekends and exotic holidays. Misses Lucinda occasionally, too.

She looks very well when she arrives; sleek, tanned, glowing with health. She must be getting some good sex from somewhere, Matthew decides, his hackles rising at the thought.

"God, this place is a mess!" she says, flinging herself down on the sofa and kicking off her shoes. "And it smells!"

Matthew shares a hospital-owned flat with three nurses. Sharing with nurses is generally thought by doctors to be a bit of a wheeze. The idea is that the nurses, being female, do all the shopping, cooking, ironing, and cleaning up. Matthew's flatmates have all been doing a stretch of night shifts, however, and left to his own devices Matthew has no idea how to look after himself.

He clears away a bottle of stale milk and offers Lucinda a glass of Spanish red wine, long since turned acid. She accepts it, sniffing it before she drinks.

"I wondered if you might like to come to Africa," she says casually. "If you're not doing anything else this summer. I'm going over there with some friends. Kenya."

"When?" Matthew does some mental calculations.

"About six weeks' time."

"That's rather short notice."

"It is, yes. We only just got the idea. We're going to fly to Nairobi, take the train down to Mombasa, and then go up to Lamu Island and hire a catamaran. We need a fifth person to pay for the boat hire."

"How much is it going to cost?"

"About eight hundred pounds for the whole thing."

This figure represents more than a month's salary for Matthew. "I don't know ... it's a great idea, I just don't know if I can afford it."

Lucinda shrugs. "Well, think about it. And let me know, okay?"

Shit! thinks Matthew after Lucinda has left. I should never have said I can't afford it. Lucinda will just think I'm fucking pathetic. She won't ask me anywhere again. He thumps his fist on the table in frustration. Money. Like everything else in this life, it all comes down to money.

"Bloody junkies!" says the Casualty nurse with feeling. "They cost the NHS a fortune!"

"Quite," says Matthew. He takes the hypodermic from the nurse and empties the contents into the backside of a heroin addict going through cold turkey. Five milliliters of methodone, a very expensive heroin substitute.

"How many of these do we get a week?" she grumbles. "I don't know how many wasted mongrels like these I've had to sort out, and before you know it they're back again, the same ones. You find them wandering around looking for the place where we keep the drugs too, hoping to try and nick some of the stuff."

"In Amsterdam the government goes round handing this stuff out to addicts to keep them going," says Matthew, writing down the treatment in the patient's notes. "They go round on a bus handing out methodone and syringes."

"Well more fool them ..." The nurse gives Matthew a clipboard. "You'd better sign for this little lot then, Dr. Pryce-Jones."

The heroin addict's friends are waiting for him outside the cubicle.

"Hey, Doctor!" one of them mumbles when he sees Matthew. "You got any of that good stuff for me?"

Matthew holds out the empty syringe. "All gone, I'm afraid, squire."

"Pity. I'd give you good money for it."

Matthew sits down beside him. "How much is one of these things worth on the market then? Just out of interest."

The junkie examines the empty syringe. "Five mils ... Two hundred quid. Maybe three, if someone was desperate."

"I see." Matthew thinks about this as he sits in the doctors' mess drinking a cup of coffee. The germ of an idea is already growing there. The odd hypodermic of smack is hardly going to make much difference to the hospital's budget, he tells himself. And if it ended up with addicts who were really desperate for it, he would be doing them a good turn, in a way. Wouldn't he?

The problem lies with taking the stuff without anyone knowing. Sister keeps the keys with her at all times, and the dangerous drugs cupboard can only be opened with her knowledge. Sister does not like Matthew. She is a small, gaunt woman with a haircut that resembles a helmet. She never laughs when Matthew tries to kid her along. He supposes it is because he doesn't fancy her in the slightest, and she knows it.

He will never get the keys without her knowledge, so the drugs must be taken openly, legitimately. That in itself is almost impossible.

Dangerous drugs must he administered by a doctor, who in turn must sign for them in front of a member of the nursing staff. The nurse must count the drugs before handing them over, make sure the new total in the cupboard tallies with that in the paperwork. In addition, the doctor must write down the name of the patient who will receive the drug, and what it is for.

Almost impossible. But not quite. Suppose ... Matthew carries on thinking through his scheme when he goes back to the flat, lies awake all night until he has ironed out the details. Suppose he takes out a drug for a genuine patient and a genuine purpose, but does not administer all of it? There are many patients coming through Casualty who required heroin analogues. Not just junkies, but those who need powerful pain relief.

Matthew has his first opportunity to test his theory the very next day. He likes to think of it as an abstract idea, a form of research, rather than a crime. At nine o'clock in the morning, a heart attack victim is admitted, needing urgent pain relief. Matthew sends the nurse for a two milliliter ampoule of heroin, signs for it in the usual way and dispenses it. He hesitates slightly as he squeezes the syringe. Suppose the man suffers? Then what? He will watch, wait, make sure the patient is all right. If not, he will receive more heroin. He half empties the syringe. The nurse is still in the cubicle, but she has her back turned, cleaning up. He puts the syringe, with the remaining heroin still in it, into the pocket of his white coat.

Later that same day, he treats the victim of a traffic accident. The woman has internal injuries; Matthew prescribes Omnopon, a pain-killer combining heroin and morphine. Once again, he pockets half a syringeful of the drug. This time the pain relief is insufficient. He prescribes another dose, tops her up and pockets another half syringe. He leaves the hospital at the end of the day with his white coat over his arm and three valuable hypodermics in the pocket.

He works this system for several weeks, taking home between five and ten half-used hypodermics every week. In a good week he makes five hundred pounds. He follows one of the junkies leaving the hospital and arranges to use him as a fence for the stuff. It means that Matthew receives less than the street value, but spares him having to go into Piccadilly and peddle it himself.

It works best when Matthew's "research" leaves the patient short of pain relief. The patient's obvious discomfort is the perfect alibi; no one questions him when he signs for a second dose. So the patient gets the treatment he needs—in the end—and Matthew makes twice as much money.

And the patients love him; oh, how they love him! The need to watch and observe the effects of his prescribing means that he must be exceptionally attentive.

"Quite the blue-eyed boy, aren't you?" says Sister drily. "I've had old Mrs. Williams in cubicle six singing your praises up to the skies. You're 'that lovely Dr. Pryce-Jones,' for whom nothing is too much trouble." She looks at him sharply. "And all for a pensioner's broken hip-joint."

"You know me," Matthew says flippantly. "I have a reputation for keeping the ladies happy."

Sister does not laugh. She never does. But he sees that she is watching him closely when they are both attending a road crash victim that afternoon. Matthew stitches the patient's wound, then reaches for a hypodermic full of Omnopon. Under Sister's unwavering gaze, he empties the whole dose into the man's thigh, and throws the empty syringe into the bin marked DANGEROUS WASTE.

He already has two half-used syringes in the pocket of his white coat. And though he tries to avoid her, the crash room is crowded and chaotic and he cannot help brushing against Sister as he moves around the treatment area. The syringes click against one another.

She freezes, draws back.

"Careful!" Matthew jokes. "I prefer to save the body contact until after working hours!"

But he is scared. He saw the look in her cold eyes and he is more scared than he has ever been in his life.

He expects something the next morning, but there is nothing. Sister is on duty, but she treats him with her usual contemptuous cool. He makes sure he keeps away from the dangerous drugs cupboard, wondering if this in itself will be suspicious.

By the afternoon he has convinced himself that he was imagining things and that the woman was just behaving that way because she is middle-aged and sex-starved and can't admit that she wants his body. He has a male patient with a mild case of renal colic, gives him half a hypodermic of Omnopon and slips the rest into his pocket.

He finishes work at six-thirty and leaves the hospital through the main door into the Accident and Emergency department.

He is stopped at the foot of the steps by Mr. Gadby, the chief administrator of St. James's.

He smiles; polite, respectful even. "Dr. Pryce-Jones. I wonder if I might have a word with you?"

"Of course." Matthew tries to look puzzled, but realizes that there is little point. They have got him.

I'm done for....

"We're doing a security check to try to account for some missing drugs. Would you mind showing me what you have in your pockets?"

Matthew takes keys, wallet, pen light and bleeper out of his jacket pocket.

Mr. Gadby points to the white coat, slung over his arm. "And in there?"

They hold a sort of tribunal. The consultant surgeon in charge of St. James's Casualty department is present, as is Professor Sadler, the Dean of the Medical School. At first Matthew thinks that Professor Sadler might be there to defend him, but it becomes apparent that this is not so. He is there to make an introductory speech, which is a sort of apology, since he is the man who admitted Matthew to St. James's in the first place.

"... In response to the stock question about medical connections in the family, Mr. Pryce-Jones told me an outright lie." Professor Sadler looks directly at Matthew as he speaks. Matthew looks straight back at him. "Harmless enough, you might think. There must be many would-be doctors who are tempted to embroider the truth in their admission interview. But Mr. Pryce-Jones insulted my intelligence by inventing a surgeon who does not exist. He should have known that I could easily check this information in the *Medical Directory*. He may well have an uncle called Keith Ballard, but there is no such orthopedic surgeon."

Professor Sadler looks around the assembled dignitaries. "You are asking yourselves, why, if I knew that the boy was dishonest, did I admit him to St. James's in the first place? I was certainly concerned that he might be untrustworthy. But I could also see that he was keen, and intelligent and personable. I thought he had the makings of a good doctor. I am gratified at least to see from his exam results and personal reports that he was indeed promising to be an excellent doctor. All the more shaming that he should throw away this chance in order to make himself some money.

"I was prepared to put that initial lie down to an impulse. A spur of the moment indiscretion. No doubt Mr. Pryce-Jones thought that the fictitious uncle would never be mentioned again. The fact that the name Keith Ballard has come back to haunt him seven years later should impress upon him the maxim 'Be sure your sins will find you out.'

"In case that lesson is not struck home by the measures of my colleagues here are about to take."

Matthew already knows what those measures will be. The fact that Professor Sadler refers to him as "Mister" rather than "Doctor" tells him all that he needs to know. He is struck off the register and disbarred from practicing medicine again. The hospital does not want publicity under any circumstances, so Matthew will be allowed to leave quietly if he does not create any fuss or speak to the press.

When asked for his defense, Matthew makes none. He could concoct some elaborate story, make a plea for pardon. But now he wants to go. He has indeed learned something from the experience: He likes making money. He is just glad that the hospital have not fouled up his plans by calling the police.

Lucinda McIver telephones.

"Matthew, I've just heard! Jonathan told me. I told him it *can't* be true. It's not, is it?"

"Yes." Matthew props the receiver under his chin and continues stuffing his clothes into a red nylon grip.

"You bloody idiot!"

"Lucinda, give me a break, will you? If you've phoned to lecture me, you may as well hang up."

"Have you got somewhere to live?"

"I'll crash at Johnnie's for the time being. I've got to vacate the flat today."

"How ghastly! And what are you going to do?"

"I'll find something, don't worry. Britain is about to go through a financial boom, in case you hadn't noticed. I'll just head on down to the City. They certainly won't care about my dubious history there. Probably improve my chances."

"I hope so, for your sake."

"You couldn't winkle out a few contacts for me could you, Lulu? For old times' sake."

A pause. "Okay. But Daddy had better not find out. He'll have a fit. Perhaps your parents might be able to help you out?"

Lucinda has never met Matthew's parents. He was always careful to make sure she did not have a chance. From the things he has said she imagines them to be substantial property owners, with resources of their own, both social and financial. She does not know, therefore, that Matthew's disgrace would break his mother's aspiring suburban heart.

"Perhaps. I'll call them."

Matthew does phone his parents, as soon as Lucinda has hung up.

"Mum, hi. How are you ...? Good stuff. And the old man ...? Good ... Listen, I've got something important to tell you. I've decided to give up medicine. ..."

T *w e n t y - f i v e*

■

Carmen Fox is bored.

She is not bored during the working day; in fact her career could be said to be progressing smoothly. In her three years at Thames Television she has progressed from secretarial work to research and from there to the position of production assistant.

It is when she leaves work that she is bored. No one wants to do anything exciting any more. All her girlfriends seem to be in serious relationships, which gives them a cast-iron excuse not to go out and have fun any more. And all the men she meets (and sometimes sleeps with) are boring too, intense creative types who take themselves too seriously. She wonders if she should be looking for a serious relationship herself, but somehow the idea does not appeal. It means going to the supermarket together on a Saturday morning and opening a joint savings account and having Sunday lunch with one another's parents. No, she does not want any of that, thank you! Fun, sex, and money, that is what her life is supposed to be about.

It is a cold, damp Saturday morning, and a whole weekend in London looms ahead of her, uncommitted. Her diary is quite empty for both days. Yes, she meant to do something about it on Thursday night, but she didn't get back from work until half-past nine, whereupon she finished off a half-drunk bottle of Chianti and fell asleep.

Time to get on the phone, now, sort out a few things to do to keep her out of mischief until Monday morning. Carmen makes herself a large cup of coffee and takes it back to bed, cradling the phone in one hand and her red leather Filofax in the other.

"... Ros, hi! Just wondered what you were doing this weekend. I thought maybe we could meet for lunch or something ... You're going shopping with Pete. How about this evening then ...? A dinner party ... I suppose it will go on pretty late, won't it? Tomorrow then ...? Okay, we'll leave it that you'll give me a call if you're free."

Carmen hangs up and dials again. "Beverly, hi! Just wondered what you were doing this weekend ... You're going away ... to Alastair's parents' place ... Right, well in that case it doesn't matter. I might catch up with you next weekend ..."

It is always the same: Saturday morning is too late. Plans have already been made. Well, that might rule out the fun and the sex, but there's always money ... She climbs out of bed and takes an account book from the drawer of the pine dresser. There are seventeen hundred pounds in the account, saved over the last year and a half since her salary rose considerably. Some of it was earmarked for an exotic holiday in some far-flung hot spot, the rest was waiting for a rainy day. Well it's raining now; she can see the big spots starting to appear on the window pane. She goes into the bathroom and jumps under the shower, singing "Hey, big spender!" at the top of her voice.

Carmen takes the underground to Knightsbridge and goes to Harrods. She heads straight for the Designer Room and buys the most exotic garment she can find: a Bruce Oldfield cocktail dress made from sequin-encrusted black organza. The sort of dress at which the Princess of Wales would not turn up her nose. She buys some Manolo Blahnik shoes made from black and silver suede and a sequinned evening bag. Then she goes upstairs to the beauty salon and has a facial, a manicure, and a haircut, with lowlights in a color called mahogany. This brings the total spent to twelve hundred and fifty pounds.

Carmen takes her new mahogany tinted head and her valuable merchandise into Hyde Park. The rain has stopped and there are the usual strolling lovers, Arab children with their nannies, and Japanese tourists consulting guide books. She finds an empty patch of grass under a horse chestnut tree and lies down among the fallen leaves and empty conker cases. She stares up at the sky for a while, wondering what to do next.

After a while the damp and cold beneath her become too great to tolerate, so she gets up, brushes the leaves from her expensively coiffed hair and strolls off with a little wave to the gaggle of curious Japanese who are watching her.

Back at the flat, Carmen looks at herself in the mirror. She has never looked so well groomed, her skin clear and peachy, her hair immaculate. If I had just met myself, she decides, I might think I was beautiful. It certainly seems a crying shame to keep all this gorgeousness to herself. So she runs a hot, scented bath and soaks in it for several hours, turning the tap with her big toe from time to time to add more hot water. Then, when the patch of sky outside the bathroom window has turned from gray to black, she dresses and goes out again.

The tapas bar in the Brompton Road is a familiar haunt. In fact Carmen quite often comes here to drink alone when she is bored. The bar is always packed on a Saturday night, so the likelihood is that she will not be alone for long. Sure enough, by the time she is halfway through her second bottle of Rioja, she is joined by a young Irishman, a graduate of Trinity College, Dublin, who has just come to London to do some postgraduate work. He tells Carmen that he finds the English unfriendly, and has not yet got to know anyone in the city.

"Don't worry about it," says Carmen. "Have another glass of wine."

"I just did."

"Another one then ..." Carmen drains her glass and starts on the next bottle. "We should do something, you and I. Fancy going out dancing? The Roof Gardens or somewhere? Come on, we'll get a taxi ..."

She drags her companion out onto the street and they wander aimlessly, passed by cabs that don't stop when Carmen whistles and shouts at them.

"Bloody taxi drivers! Never mind, we'll walk. Or run, let's run!" She starts to trot down the street with the bemused Irishman at her heels.

"Listen ..." She stops and puts her arms around his neck, toppling against him drunkenly. "Why are we even bothering? Let's just

•

dance here, in the street ..." She sways from side to side. "Come on! You're not even trying ... !"

But he is less drunk than she is and disentangles himself, half embarrassed, half amazed.

"Suit yourself! I'll dance by myself then!" Carmen scrambles up onto the bonnet of a parked car, and jives on the spot, rocking the car up and down on its suspension.

"Get down, the coppers might see you ...! Jesus, but you're crazy, so you are!"

"I'm just having a little fun ... What's wrong with everyone in this city, for God's sake!" She jumps down from the car and puts her arms round him again. "We could always go back to my flat."

She is only half serious, aware that she is far too drunk to do anything and not really caring. The Irishman successfully flags a cab and drops her off outside her flat. She staggers up the stairs, throws open the front door and collapses gratefully onto the sofa, feeling the blackness close in around her.

The ringing in Carmen's head blurs into the insistent ringing of the phone. It is Sunday afternoon. She crawls from the sofa on her hands and knees and picks up the receiver.

"... Lo?"

"Hi, Carmen, it's Ros."

"Oh ... right."

"Are you okay? You sound funny."

"I was asleep, actually. You woke me up."

"*Asleep!* At this time? It's half-past one!"

"Hangover. I was out last night."

"Oh, I see. Sorry. I was just ringing to tell you that Pete and I won't be around today after all."

"That's okay. I feel like I'm brain-dead anyway."

"But I did want to say that I'm having a drinks party next Friday and I want you to be there."

"A party! No one has parties any more, do they? I thought we were all too old."

"Do me a favor, Carmen, and spare me all that self-pitying crap about how boring we all are. Just make sure you're there on Friday!"

■ ■ ■

Carmen will *not* go to the party, she decides. It will only be full of couples having depressingly serious relationships. Then at seven o'clock on the Friday evening in question, she changes her mind, for economic reasons. She needs an excuse to wear the Bruce Oldfield dress and the rest of the finery she bought at Harrods. The dress looks wonderful. It *feels* wonderful. She catches a cab to Ros's flat and arrives late, making an entrance.

Ros comes to check up on her after about an hour. She links her arm through Carmen's. "So—tell me it's not so dull after all."

"Only if you'll tell me who that hunk is. I've been drooling at him from a distance all evening."

Ros laughs. "That sounds more like the Carmen we know and love! But I'm sorry, he's taken. A newlywed, what's more. That's his wife over there."

Carmen stares. "My God, it is ... How weird! It's Jackie Yardley!"

"You know her?"

"We were at infants school together, twenty years ago! Well, she's certainly done all right for herself, hasn't she?"

"We work together at Munro Willis, but perhaps I only mentioned her as Jackie Maitland. Come on over, and I'll reintroduce you?"

Carman shakes her head firmly. "No thanks, I don't feel in the mood for an old school reunion."

But Jackie has already seen her and is on her way over.

"It's Carolyn, isn't it? Carolyn Fox?"

"Yes. Except I'm called Carmen now. I didn't like Carolyn."

"Oh."

They smile at one another, forced social smiles, but are at a loss for words. Jackie knows that Carmen will be thinking that she's changed, no longer the weedy underfed little waif she was. Carmen wonders if Jackie will think that she dresses in Bruce Oldfield dresses all the time, and therefore has a lot of money.

"So what are you doing now?"

"I'm a senior manager at Munro Willis. How about you?"

"I work for Thames Television."

"Really? You must meet my husband. He's in the media business too. He works for Amecorp. I expect you've heard of them?"

The introduction of Gregory into the conversation eases the awkwardness they are both feeling. He and Carmen discuss the communications business at length. She finds him open and articulate; she likes him. She likes Jackie too, as much as it is possible to like someone whose ideals and attitudes are so different from one's own.

After the party, Carmen thinks no more of this chance meeting. Then Jackie telephones her and asks her to dinner at her new house in West Hampstead.

"Gregory said I was to be sure and ask you round some time. He thinks you're great."

Carmen accepts the invitation, out of curiosity as much as anything else. Jackie and Gregory's house turns out to be very much what she expected: handsome turn-of-the-century red brick in Compayne Gardens, painted in pretty pastel colors with a solid oak fitted kitchen and good taste wherever you look. It is a pleasant evening and she enjoys the company of husband and wife, yet Carmen feels uneasy.

"How was dinner at the Maitlands?" asks Ros the next day.

"I don't know ..." Carmen pulls a face. "Jackie's so fixated with doing everything *properly*. She showed me every corner of the house and seemed to really mind what I thought of it. I wouldn't give a toss what she thought about my flat."

"Well, she's certainly got everything, hasn't she? When he worked at Munro Willis they used to call them the Golden Couple."

Two days later, half an hour after she has returned from work, Carmen answers the door to find Gregory Maitland on her doorstep, clutching briefcase in one hand and portable phone in the other.

"I had a meeting near here. I thought I'd drop by and say hello." He adds, "I got your address from Jackie. She suggested I should come."

This all sounds innocent enough. It *is* innocent, so why does Carmen feel the need to keep glancing at Gregory over her shoulder as she pours him a Scotch? She feels on edge, much more so than she did at the house in Compayne Gardens.

Yet Gregory is a perfect gentleman. They make pleasant conversation for an hour and then he says good-bye, hesitating only fractionally as he gives her a peck on the cheek.

"I'll give your love to Jackie."

"Do that."

Three days later, Gregory drops round again. This time there is no mention of a meeting nearby.

"Coming round here last time did me so much good. I hope you don't mind me being here again."

"What do you mean?" Carmen pours herself a drink and sits down opposite him.

"I find it difficult to go straight home after work. I need to have time to relax, unwind a bit. Being here really helped me with that."

Carmen sips her drink without comment.

"I'm only telling you this because you're such a good friend of Jackie's . . ."

"I'm not. We hardly knew one another really."

"Because you seem sympathetic then. There are problems in my marriage. Things I can't really explain."

He makes an attempt at a helpless shrug, but bewilderment sits uneasily on such a powerfully attractive man. Carmen just looks at him, trying to unravel the puzzle; at his boyishly handsome face, the lock of dark hair that falls over his forehead in such an appealing manner, the expensive Italian suit and silk tie.

"I think you should try and explain."

He sighs, a long, heartfelt sigh. "I get so wound up, so tense. And then I go home and I take it out on Jackie. Which isn't fair, because she's been working too, just as hard. It's like I have to get angry with someone, or something, and it ends up being Jackie. I can't help myself; she just makes me angry."

"Does she get angry with you?"

"No. That's half the problem. I wish she would, but she doesn't. I've never seen her lose her temper."

"Does she know you're here tonight?"

"No."

"I thought not."

I know what will happen next, thinks Carmen, and it does. Gregory has two more drinks, then he sits next to her on the sofa and starts to kiss her. She would like to resist him but finds herself feebly swept away like the heroine of some steamy novelette. And Gregory is so confident, so sure, so *impassioned,* just like the hero of the novel. Only he's the husband of someone who counts herself a friend.

Only once, thinks Carmen, as they go into the bedroom and he lowers his body onto hers. Just this once, for a very special treat. Because he's so gorgeous and I've been so lonely.

When he leaves, she kisses him very thoroughly and says: "I hope you made the most of that. Because it's never going to happen again."

But it does, many times. Carmen considers she is being blackmailed at some level. Because Gregory tells her that his relationship with Jackie is very much improved. If he comes round to Carmen's flat and makes love to her, he doesn't get angry with his wife when he gets home. So it's a form of social work, really.

And he tells her that their sex life is no good, naturally, that Jackie is cold and clinical ... "too organized."

"If it weren't for you, I don't know what I'd do to her. I frighten myself sometimes, I really do."

So Carmen is doing Jackie a favor. She tells herself this as she digs her fingernails into the smooth skin of Gregory Maitland's back. Saving her marriage, in fact. Because if it weren't for this—this voluptuous lovemaking—Gregory would take his bad mood out on his wife.

He comes to her flat most weekdays, at about seven o'clock. It is a routine; he rings the doorbell, she hands him a drink as she lets him in, they go to bed. She is shocked, therefore, to open the door with Gregory's favorite drink in her hand and find Jackie Maitland standing on the doorstep.

"Carmen, can I talk to you?"

Oh shit, there's going to be a scene, thinks Carmen. She's going to confront me. Or she's going to say Gregory's having an affair, and do I know who it is.

"I need to talk to someone, Carolyn. Sorry, Carmen." She laughs self-consciously at the slip.

"Here—have a drink." Carmen hands her the cocktail meant for her husband.

"I'm sorry to dump this on you, only with you being such an old friend. . . ."

"Don't kid yourself, Jackie. We weren't friends. Not really. Most of the time we couldn't stand the sight of one another, as I recall."

"No!" Jackie speaks vehemently. "I wanted to be your friend. Very much."

"Okay. Well, none of that matters now."

"No. Anyway, you're the only person who knows both Gregory and me who doesn't work with one of us."

"Really?"

"Yes, really. And I've been so . . . I'm worried about the way he's been behaving."

Carmen's heart sinks. "What do you mean?"

"He's been hitting me."

Carmen stares. "Oh no . . . Oh my God, no. When . . . ? I mean, when did this start?"

"Just after we got married, he slapped me once after an argument about work. But it was an isolated incident. It didn't happen again for a while. But then recently . . . he gets really abusive . . . It's been almost every night, after he gets back from work." Jackie does not cry. She just stares down into her drink as if she would like to drown in it.

"Oh my God, I'm sorry . . ." Carmen sits beside her and puts her arm round Jackie's shoulders. Still she does not cry. "I'm so sorry. That's terrible."

Carmen Fox, you stupid bitch, how could you be so dumb? How could you possibly kid yourself you were doing her a favor? Look what you're done. . . .

She soothes Jackie with platitudes. She even suggests (hating herself) that Jackie might try showing some anger in response.

When Gregory comes the following evening, she tells him she won't be seeing him again.

"Has Jackie said something to you?"

"Yes. But not about us." Carmen sits down on the white sofa with a drink in her hand. She does not offer one to Gregory.

"Oh shit."

"Exactly. She told me you'd been bashing her around."

Gregory does not reply. He stares out of the window. Then he goes to sit next to her on the sofa and puts his arms round her. "Carmen ..."

"I'd like you to go now."

"But don't you understand? Without you, things are going to be even worse."

"Oh no!" Carmen shakes her head. "You won't persuade me that way. I don't understand what your problem is, I just know I don't want to be involved. I shouldn't have got involved in the first place."

She pushes Gregory away and stands up. He stands up too. And then he hits her.

"You shit!"

Carmen hits him back, as hard as she can. Into that one action she puts all the anger she has ever felt against men, all her long-buried disappointment over Richard Kendrick. The blow sends him reeling across the room. She closes her eyes until he has gone.

T *w* *e* *n* *t* *y* - *s* *i* *x*

■

"How long is Nicholas going to be staying?" Alison Noble asks as she and Stephen wash and dry the supper dishes.

Stephen answers with a shrug, picks up a saucepan, and begins to dry it. Then he says: "You don't like him staying here very much, do you?"

"It's not that . . ."

Alison thinks how their spare bedroom looks at the moment. Nicholas's exotic but grubby clothes flung into corners. The bed unmade, smelling sourly of sweat and stale aftershave. His Sony Walkman and cassettes strewn across the carpet. Sketch pad and pencils spread out on the sofa. Empty ashtrays filled with the rancid butts of his French cigarettes. Nicholas's high maniacal laugh, which she hears from upstairs as Stephen and Nicholas sit up talking late into the night.

"It's not that I don't like him," she says. "You know I do. It's just . . . I don't know whether it's a good thing for *him*, staying here indefinitely, with nothing to do."

When Nicholas first reappeared in Stephen's life, he had a flat close by, in Islington. He used to drop round quite often in the evenings but was happy to be part of a threesome, entertaining Stephen and Alison with tales of his life in India. As a couple they were different when Nicholas was around. They seemed livelier, more colorful, more adventurous. She suspected that Nicholas dropped round quite often during the day, when she was up in Cambridge, but she didn't mind this as long as it didn't distract Stephen from his studies.

Then, after about a year, things changed. In the summer of 1983, Nicholas lost his job at the record store in Oxford Street for repeated lateness. And with no income, he lost his tenancy of the flat in Islington a month later. Stephen offered him their spare room, rent-free.

And living with Nicholas has turned out to be very different from receiving visits from Nicholas. He is not house-proud, a slob by Alison's standards. She dislikes cleaning up after him, or nagging Stephen to clean up after him. But for Alison a far worse problem is the fascination he exerts. When they are in the same room, however resentful she feels, she is mesmerized by him. And she catches him looking at her a lot too, especially when she kisses Stephen or shows any physical affection. The tension between the three of them is starting to make her feel very uncomfortable.

"I mean, what's he going to do with his life?" Alison asks as she stacks the clean plates in the cupboard. "He's well educated and obviously very bright. Why has he decided to drop out?"

"He's in a bit of a mess at the moment. All sorts of things have gone wrong for him, not just losing the flat. He's fallen out badly with his parents."

"Why "

"They don't approve of him."

Alison pretends to be very engrossed in sorting out knives and forks. "Is he gay?"

"Yes. At least, I think so; I'm not sure."

The conversation ends there, even though there are many more questions Alison would like to ask. But when they make love that night there is anxiety in the way she tries to arouse her husband, goading him to a climax.

Stephen returns from college the following afternoon to find Nicholas reading the paper on the drawing room floor. He has lit the fire and stretched out on the carpet with his cigarettes and a mug of coffee. He does not get up when Stephen comes in, just greets him with a wave and his customary mocking smile.

Stephen finds that he can cope as long as he does not look into Nicholas's eyes. He makes a great show of unpacking his books and putting them away, and as his back is turned toward the desk he says: "I think you're going to have to find somewhere else to stay."

Nicholas laughs and drags deeply on his cigarette. "The wife been giving you a hard time, has she?"

"It wasn't her idea."

"But she's very twitchy when I'm around, isn't she? Why do you think that is?"

"Actually, I think Alison's put up with the situation very well." Stephen's voice is tight with anger. He stacks and restacks his books in meaningless piles. "I don't think you have any right to criticize her."

"Alison does have a lot to put up with, I agree. She has to put up with you masquerading as the contented husband, for a start."

Stephen stays where he is, in front of the desk, too angry to turn round and look at Nicholas. Little drifts of Nicholas's acrid cigarette smoke catch at his nostrils. His voice trembles slightly as he says, "We *are* contented, I don't have to pretend. It's just not something you'd understand. You've never had the urge to try and create something good, all your urges are destructive ones. You just want to destroy."

"So you want what she wants, do you? Are you sure you know what that is? She looks decidedly frustrated to me. I don't think she's getting fucked often enough."

Stephen grips the edges of the desk.

Nicholas blows smoke up at the ceiling. "Come on, who are you trying to kid? Playing at being straight. It's never going to work. You're shitting yourself with fear the whole time that you're going to lapse. You'll end up like those sad middle-aged men in raincoats watching little schoolboys play soccer."

"*Shut up!* Will you just shut up! This is what I want, don't you understand? It's what I *want.*"

"Stephen—look at me."

Stephen turns round. He looks directly into Nicholas's eyes. Glittering, almond-shaped eyes, with irises so dark they are almost black.

Hungry, yearning eyes.

"Come here."

Stephen goes to him, kneels on the floor next to him. Nicholas

328

puts a hand on his arm, spreads out his fingers, sinks them imperceptibly into Stephen's flesh.

Stephen looks down at the fingers on his forearm. Smooth, golden brown flesh. Long fingers with elegant oval-shaped nails. Alisons's hands are pale and puffy, the skin freckled and the fingernails stubby and chewed.

"Oh, Stephen ..." Nicholas sighs. "I've been so fucking jealous. Seeing you with Alison, the two of you touching. I think for a while she thought I was looking at her ..." His fingers continue their gentle kneading movement up and down, up and down ... "Remember Florence? Remember how good it was?"

Stephen shudders.

"In a moment I'm going to kiss you. Then I'll make love to you. And you're going to allow me to do it, because you want me to."

"All right!" Stephen pulls Nicholas toward him. "All right. Just once. But afterward, please ... just go, all right? Go away and leave me alone."

Stephen and Alison are making a farewell dinner for Nicholas.

He announces, quite suddenly, that he is going, and now that it has happened Alison feels sorry. She feels as though the whole episode has been brought to an unsatisfactory conclusion, and as she prepares the meal she feels even more tense than she did before. The shadow of unfinished business hangs over the proceedings.

She has made a special effort with her appearance tonight, dressing in a turquoise silk cheongsam that her father bought on a business trip to Hong Kong. It has a demure high collar, but clings to her body and is slit generously at the side, Suzy Wong style, to reveal her slim thighs.

"Well!" says Nicholas. He stands in the doorway of the kitchen, cigarette in hand. "Don't you look a sight for sore eyes!"

Alison is bending down to put the lamb in the oven. She gives an embarrassed laugh as she straightens up, never quite knowing what to make of Nicholas's compliments. She suspects he is laughing at her, but the expression in his eyes is so intense....

"I'd rather you didn't smoke in here, Nicholas." She starts taking saucepans out of the cupboards with a great clatter. "Not over the food."

Nicholas stubs out his cigarette in a saucer and moves a few steps nearer. The kitchen is so narrow that it is impossible for Alison to move around without brushing against him. He is wearing a pleated Oriental sarong, and beneath it his legs and feet are bare. Through his thin T-shirt, Alison notices the outline of his chest, rising and falling. He is surprisingly muscular for someone who never exerts himself.

"You could help," she snaps, feeling hot and flustered. "With the vegetables or something."

"So you need help?" Nicholas takes hold of her pale wrist, imprisons it in his. He starts to stroke her forearm with one finger.

"Nicholas, don't ..."

"You don't want me to do this, is that what you're saying?"

"Yes." Alison's face is so hot she can feel her cheeks burning and a pulse throbbing in her forehead.

"All right." Nicholas takes his hand away abruptly and holds it up in a gesture of retreat. "All right, I'll stop."

"No ...! I mean ..."

"I think you want me to do it." Nicholas grabs her, fiercely this time, and sinks his mouth into her throat, sucking at the edge of her collar. His hands move up under the slippery silk and press between her legs.

"You're wet, you poor frustrated little cow!" He pushes her underwear to one side and enters her angrily, thrusting against her until he climaxes. Then he withdraws abruptly and walks away. Alison clings to the edge of the Formica worktop, staring at him helplessly.

"But you're gay ..." she wants to say. She opens her mouth, but no sound comes out.

It seems Nicholas can tell what she is thinking anyway. "There are a lot of things your husband doesn't know about," he says, and leaves the kitchen.

Alison gets drunk at dinner. It is the only way she can cope with the appalling thing that she has done.

"So ..." She helps herself to more claret. "What are you going to do next, Nicholas? Will you go back to Delhi?"

"That depends."

"On what?"

Nicholas looks directly at Stephen. "On what happens."

"Maybe we'll come and visit you in India some time," says Stephen in an insincere tone.

"Who knows if we three will be together again?" says Nicholas, and laughs his enigmatic laugh.

He is the only one of the trio who seems quite relaxed. Throughout the meal he has been paying provocative compliments to Alison as if he is drunk, but he is not. "Your wife is looking particularly seductive tonight, Stephen," he says as Alison serves the dessert. "If she weren't married I think I might fancy her myself."

Alison giggles and turns red, leaning toward Nicholas slightly.

"Oh, for God's sake!" Stephen pushes his chair back, throws his napkin onto the table, and walks from the room.

"It's disgusting."

Stephen rounds on Alison when she has followed him into the bedroom. "What on earth were you playing at, flirting with Nicholas like that? Behaving like a tart doesn't suit you. You're hardly the type!"

"And what's that supposed to mean?" Alison takes off her dress and flings it onto the bed. Her legs, encased in gray stockings, look thin and mottled.

"Nicholas was just trying to send you up, talking like that. And you fell for it!"

Alison flings on her robe and sits down heavily at her dressing table. There is a framed wedding photograph in front of the mirror, an image that she cannot bear to look at now. The dense black of the velvet dress that seemed such a free-spirited gesture at the time. The funereal lilies.

"No," she says. "That's not it. I'll tell you why you didn't like Nicholas flirting with me. You're jealous. Not of him. Of me."

Stephen puts down his jacket and walks toward her. "What are you implying?"

"I think you've ... got a thing for Nicholas."

Stephen opens his mouth to make some denial but thinks better of it. He sits down on the edge of the bed and stares down at his hands.

"Were you involved with him?"

"Yes."

Alison's hands start to tremble uncontrollably. "You mean ... lovers?"

"Yes."

"But not since we've been married?"

Stephen does not reply.

Alison spins round on her dressing stool, her face stricken. "Tell me, please! I can't bear this!"

"Once. But only once."

"Oh God!" Alison begins to cry. Noisy, uninhibited sobs leaving damp smears all over her cheeks, and her neck, and her hands.

Finally she straightens up and dabs feebly at her wet face with the hem of her robe. "Do you realize what's happened? Do you realize what's the most weird thing about this whole sordid episode? We had sex too!"

"I don't understand."

"I couldn't help it, it was as if he hypnotized me. And tonight ... this evening before dinner ... I let him make love to me. I'd been wanting him to do it since I first met him, but I also thought there was something not quite right, and when you said he was gay.... Perhaps it just made me want him even more, I don't know ..."

Stephen lies back on the bed, covers his eyes, and laughs a dry, joyless laugh. "Oh, Nicholas, you didn't! Jesus Christ, what a mess! What an absolute bloody mess!"

Stephen and Alison's parting is civil, even if it is not cordial. It proves difficult to be cordial with Sir Roland and Lady Delia pouring scorching reproach and invective down the phone. Stephen explains that his intentions were good and honest ones, even if he failed to live up to them, and Alison has to accept this. Nicholas has effectively proved that neither of them turned out to be as committed as they would have liked. They agree that the best course is to end their marriage as soon as possible, before further harm is done. Alison will keep the house, in her sole name, and Stephen will have their savings, which amount to a few thousand pounds.

He moves out of the house in Canonbury as soon as possible and returns to his Aunt Sara's flat in Beaufort Gardens. This is as good a refuge as any, except that it leaves him open to more reproachful phone calls, this time from his own parents. Sylvia is sad but fatalistic, Geoffrey brutally cold.

Then the moment Stephen has been dreading arrives. Nicholas telephones.

"Alison gave me this number."

"*Alison* did?"

"Yes, I thought that was very decent of her."

"Given that you've destroyed her marriage, it was, yes. I presume that's what you set out to do when you seduced her...."

"Seduced her! Poor girl was practically begging for it!"

Stephen hangs up.

The next morning he goes in search of the nearest travel agent and books a one-way ticket on the night flight to Kathmandu. He phones Alison to tell her of his decision and to ask her to come round that afternoon to sort out the final financial arrangements.

She's early, he thinks, when the doorbell rings, and then he understands why. Alison is with Nicholas, and she is not happy about it. Her face is pale and strained.

"I'm sorry, Stephen. He insisted. He said he'd follow me anyway if I didn't bring him."

Stephen feels himself tense as Nicholas strolls into the sitting room. The anger he feels only fuels his lust, and he remembers suddenly how it was when Nicholas first arrived at Maidenhurst, so exotic, so strange.... He longs to touch Nicholas so much that he feels faint. He is grateful for Alison's presence, without which he would inevitably weaken.

"So here we all are again, the happy threesome ..." Nicholas laughs. Then he catches sight of the open cases on the bed.... "What's going on?"

"I'm going to do some traveling for a while. Now, if you don't mind, Alison and I have some things to talk about."

Nicholas no longer seems aware of Alison. His olive complexion has turned a chalky gray color. "But you can't just go and ... I came back to you for Christ's sake! I came back and rescued you from your farce of a marriage. You can't just go again ..." He snatches at Stephen's arm. "You want me to come with you? Is that it? I can go and book on the same flight...."

"NO!" Stephen takes a deep breath. "I'm sorry, Nicholas, but I'm going alone. My life is in one hell of a mess and I just need to be on my own to try to sort it out. So please—just go. Alison and I have ..."

"In that case I might as well just end it all. If you don't want me then I've nowhere left to go." Nicholas fixes his glittering eyes on Stephen's face, exerting his hold on him. "I'll do it, Stephen. You *know* I will."

Stephen stares back at him, transfixed.

It is Alison who breaks the silence. Alison, whom they have both momentarily forgotten.

"Let him go, Nicholas," she says quietly. "We all know that you're not going to do anything so stupid, so just leave Stephen alone. All three of us have to accept that this part of our lives is over."

She goes to the front door and holds it open. Nicholas walks out of the flat without a word, pausing only to give Stephen a mysterious smile.

"But, Alison, what if ... ?"

"Look, just go and get on that plane. I'll deal with Nicholas."

T w e n t y - s e v e n

■

Though it might seem to an observer that the Maitlands' marriage is heading for disaster, to Jackie this is not the case. The structure has been dented rather than destroyed; it needs some patching and shoring up.

She arranges for the two of them to have a counseling session. During this session they are supposed to say how they really feel, but Jackie does not. She keeps those feelings well buried somewhere inside of her and merely says what she thinks she ought to say. However, the counsellor is more concerned with Gregory, and refers him for a course of psychotherapy.

Gregory's therapist is called Heather and lives in Chalk Farm. He attends with some reluctance at first, but after a while claims that the sessions are beneficial. He becomes fond of quoting Heather: "Heather says my aggression toward you came from a sense of threat imposed by your career." "Heather says that in taking for granted a level of success as high as mine, you are destroying the sexual role models that are part of my subconscious conditioning."

Jackie is sceptical about all this jargon, but the sessions seem to be working. Gregory stops hitting her when he is angry. Gradually he becomes angry less often. After a year of therapy, Heather tells him that he no longer needs her.

It is about this time that Jackie receives a major promotion at work. She is nervous about breaking the news to Gregory, and delays telling him for several weeks.

When she does, he looks worried rather than angry. "But what about you having a baby?"

"Well . . ."

"We'll have been married for two years this autumn. We always said that we would leave it about two years."

He wants me at home, thinks Jackie. That's what all this business about threats and role models is about. He'd rather have me here, making sure the house is run smoothly and there's a proper evening meal to come home to rather than something from Marks and Spencer's food hall.

"We could still have a baby. We'll just have to plan very carefully when it's born."

She fetches her personal organizer and opens it at the 1986 year planner. "The main factor we have to take into consideration is the launch of the new Munro shops."

This project is Jackie's brainchild, her own idea. Munro Willis is going to open a separate chain of high fashion boutiques, aiming particularly at business wear for the working woman.

"That's in June 1987, so whatever happened I'd have to be back at work by May 1987. It's February now, so . . ." She counts on her fingers. "If I get pregnant next month, the baby will be born in December, which will give me four or five months of maternity leave."

"Great," says Gregory, draining his coffee cup. "Why don't we start trying now?"

Jackie gives a self-conscious little laugh. "Well, I have to get to the end of this packet of pills first."

"Let's start practicing then."

Jackie is delighted when she becomes pregnant straightaway. Her success seems a vindication of good planning. She boasts to her friends at work about how fit and well she feels, how at this rate she will be able to stay at work until the week the baby is due.

All her spare time is spent choosing things for the nursery; pastel fabrics from Designers Guild to be made up into ruffled blinds and cushions, expensive hand-painted furniture. Then there is the nanny's room to be seen to. It needs decorating, and equipping with things like a kettle and a television. The modern nanny expects a television, so Jackie reads in the book she buys on the subject.

Jackie consults Gregory on every little detail, seeking his approval. Her deference irritates him. It is not in his wife's character to be animated or extrovert, but he has noticed that when she is with her friends and colleagues she is bright, confident. She is better at the art of friendship than she was in her teens, or when she first joined Munro Willis. She has learned to relax. But when she is at home with Gregory she is different. Quieter, more watchful. So afraid of making him angry.

Fearful of the effect that a baby will have on their ordered lives, the Maitlands also opt to streamline the operation of their home, to ward off the impending chaos. They have already spent a lot of their savings and their salaries are eaten up by the huge mortgage they have on their house, so they start to spend on credit. A new washing machine and tumble dryer. A microwave ("I read somewhere that you can warm babies' bottles in thirty seconds").

"I'd like a new freezer too," Jackie announces to Gregory one Saturday morning.

"We've got a freezer," says Gregory.

"That's a freezer *compartment*," explains Jackie. "We need to buy a proper freezer. Then I can freeze meals for us to save time, and stuff for the baby."

"And how are you proposing to pay for it? This baby has cost us several thousand pounds already, and it hasn't even been born yet."

"A lot of electrical stores have interest-free credit. We could spread the payments."

So they set off to their local white goods warehouse and stand around trying to look enthralled while the spotty pubescent salesman explains the merits of various identical white boxes.

"Now, if you're after a really good deal, this is the one you want. It's the most expensive model we do, but we can offer you interest-free credit. *And* it's got an auto-defrost button. I'll show you...." He opens the freezer door. "You just flick that button there, and it starts defrosting itself straightaway. No need to switch it back on again, because the thermostat controls it. When it reaches a certain minimum temperature it switches itself back on."

"Amazing," says Gregory drily.

"That looks good," says Jackie. "I think we ought to get this one!"

"I think that's just about everything," she pronounces when they have taken the freezer home and installed it. "Another six months before the baby arrives and we've done most of the preparation already."

"You can start knitting now."

"As if I have time!" Jackie takes a damp cloth and wipes out the inside of the freezer before transferring meat from her old freezer compartment. "Now I'm all set up, I can really concentrate my energies on the Munro stores project."

She does not notice that as she wipes round the freezer she presses the automatic defrost button to ON. The contents of the meat drawer start to warm up and melt. By the time the freezer resets itself, the meat inside has become contaminated.

Jackie is quite unaware of this the following weekend when she takes out frozen chicken to make a casserole. Within hours she and Gregory are stricken with diarrhea and violent bouts of vomiting. Jackie is particularly ill, so weak from dehydration that she cannot stand up. Gregory calls their GP, who diagnoses listeriosis. Jackie is admitted to hospital that night, where she miscarries.

After losing her first baby in the face of such stringent forward planning, Jackie panics. Her doctor advises her to wait several months before trying again, but she ignores him. After all, her body has just proved itself to be unpredictable, unreliable. What if it takes ages before she conceives this time?

She does so straightaway. The baby will be born in April.

"That's cutting it a bit fine, isn't it?" Gregory is doubtful. "You said you had to be back at work in May."

"It's going to be a bit rushed, I admit it, but we'll manage. Lots of women do it all the time. I'm always reading about them in magazines. Business women who are back at their desks two weeks after giving birth. It is possible."

"What if it's late?"

"I'll probably be early. Anyway, we're all prepared already, aren't we?"

Jackie makes it a priority to recruit a nanny well ahead of her confinement. She has so little confidence or experience that she elects to use the services of an exclusive domestic staff agency. They find her a nineteen-year-old from Australia: "Lots of experience, an absolutely super girl."

Apparently this girl has just been in Los Angeles looking after the offspring of a famous rock star. This makes her services more expensive. There will be a four-hundred-pound arrangement fee to the agency, then one hundred and fifty pounds each week. Gregory grumbles at the cost, but Jackie points out that they have little choice. They need her to be back on full pay as soon as possible, therefore they must have round-the-clock, reliable help.

"I'll just have to work harder, that's all. I'm due for another promotion next year, and that will mean more money. It'll all work out fine, you'll see."

He thinks I should stay at home. Well, I'm not going to. Not for him, and not for the baby either. . . .

When Emily Jane Maitland is born on April 20, 1987, small and delicately pretty, dark like her father, Jackie apologizes.

"I'm sorry, I thought we were going to have a boy first. I expect you wanted a boy."

Gregory holds the white bundle awkwardly, stroking a tiny hand. "I'm glad she's a girl. I think all men would like to have a daughter. Another female to make a fuss of them."

But I wanted a boy. I did. . . .

Jackie's feelings toward her daughter are a great muddle from the start. She had not expected to love her so desperately. But she had not expected to fear her so much either. This tiny scrap of flesh seems amazingly strong, powerful, to worm her way into Jackie's thoughts even when she is exhausted and wants to shut her out. She is watchful with Emily as she is with the child's father, afraid of what she will do next.

She tries to counteract this emotional chaos by being organized. But while the babycare manuals say that newborn babies feed every three to four hours, Emily wants to be fed every hour, sucking at Jackie's breasts until her teeth are set on edge. She tries to ease the strain by weaning her onto the bottle, but still Emily seems hungry all the time, and cries. Jackie even becomes so desperate that she telephones Pamela for advice, but Pamela is vague. She says she cannot remember very much about it. She, too, is disappointed that Emily is not a boy.

Jackie is relieved when it is time for her to return to Munro Willis, leaving Emily in the care of the athletic-looking Australian nanny, Leanne. But still she cannot switch off from Emily: her needs, her whims. She phones Leanne constantly from the office, giving her instructions, to which Leanne always answers, "Yeah, no worries."

Then she returns home earlier than expected and finds Leanne chatting on the telephone. She is probably talking to someone in Australia, but this is not Jackie's immediate concern. She flings her briefcase and mobile phone down in the hall and hurries to the foot of the stairs to listen.

"Leanne! Leanne put the phone down and come here."

Leanne hangs up reluctantly, after a convoluted good-bye.

"Leanne, Emily's crying! She's shrieking her head off while you're yakking away on the phone."

"No worries." Leanne thrusts her hands into the pockets of her jeans. "I've just put her down to sleep. She always has a bit of a cry before she goes off."

"How long has she been crying?"

"Dunno. Fifteen ... maybe twenty minutes."

"Well, that's too long! In future, I want you to go to her after five minutes."

In future there are to be yet more problems. There are the extortionate phone calls, and the other girls from the local nanny mafia sitting around in the kitchen drinking the Maitlands' tea and coffee and eating the contents of the larder. Then bottles of wine start to disappear. Leanne is moody too, stomping around the house, slamming doors, wandering up and down stairs in the middle of the night. Jackie begins to feel uncomfortable and ill at ease in her own house. She has no idea how Emily is faring. She is never at home long enough to find out.

Leanne has one weekend off in four. On the Sunday evening of her second free weekend, she phones Jackie and says that she will not be able to return until Monday evening. Jackie has no option but to take a day off work, canceling an important meeting of the finance committee. She tries to persuade Gregory to stand in for her, but he pleads ignorance of Emily's routine. He is even more afraid of her than Jackie is, mainly of the idea of getting sick on his suit, or his Hermès tie.

"This is no good," Jackie says at the end of a fraught day at home. "Leanne will have to go. I've got to have someone reliable, otherwise we can't get on with our lives."

"What will you do?"

"I don't know, but I'll find someone."

Jackie advertises in the local paper and finds Bridie. Bridie is a bovine Irishwoman, motherly in the extreme and with an ample bosom like the nannies in storybooks. She has raised five children of her own and she *loves* babies, she tells Jackie. She adores them.

Jackie is delighted. Here is someone who can give Emily all she needs and do for her all the things her mother cannot do. She goes to work with a clear conscience and a spring in her step.

When she returns home, she finds Bridie with her large bosom bared and one fat nipple thrust into Emily's mouth, breastfeeding her.

There is no quick and convenient solution to what is termed "the nanny problem," Jackie discovers after Bridie's rapid departure. She looks hard but she cannot find anyone suitable, and after the last two disasters she is determined not to compromise.

Gregory's suggestion is that she resign from Munro Willis and find herself another job when Emily is a little older. Jackie opts to take unpaid leave instead. And so, three and a half months after giving birth she comes home to care for the stranger who is her daughter.

She finds the task more difficult than she had ever imagined. Emily is a grizzly, restless baby, who seems to get bored very easily. When she cries it takes Jackie up to an hour to work out what she wants. Getting her to empty a bottle, then settling her for a sleep can take an indefinite amount of time, especially when she has to be picked up again and changed as soon as she has been put down. And she wriggles when she is being cleaned up. The cuffs of Jackie's dress-for-success blouses become covered in baby shit. After a while she ceases to care.

A whole morning can be wasted this way, achieving nothing at all. And it is impossible for Jackie to do anything for herself. If she starts to make a cup of tea, she has to abandon it without drinking it, or if she makes a phone call she has to hang up before she has been connected, because Emily has started to cry. She starts to feel a new respect for Leanne, who made caring for a baby look quite straightforward.

She misses the noise and bustle of the office, the conversations. Those ten minutes first thing in the morning, when she could have a quiet cup of coffee and chat with Pat, her secretary. Pat will still be there waiting for her, as soon as she can get out and find someone for Emily. . . .

Outings present further obstacles. They have to be squeezed in around Emily's naps and feeds, an impossibility in itself. Then all the right equipment has to be dragged along, nappies in case she is dirty, a bottle in case she is thirsty, the rain hood for the buggy in case it turns showery. . . . Sometimes Jackie hauls the carrycot into the back of the car and just drives around, as the motion of the car is guaranteed to put Emily to sleep.

But it is high summer and the car gets too hot, or sunlight falls across Emily's face, which makes her grumble. So Jackie parks the car, gets out the buggy and just walks. As long as she keeps walking, Emily stays quiet, so she plods along, up and down nameless suburban streets, mesmerized by the rumbling of the turning wheels. She does not go anywhere, the walking has no destination, no purpose except to make her feel more lonely than she ever has in her life.

And yet there are any number of women like her. She sees them everywhere, a silent army she had never noticed before, trundling buggies and prams. They are often dragging a small child by the hand, or lugging heavy bags of shopping. Whilst their husbands, like Gregory, sit in their air-conditioned offices sipping coffee and bantering with their colleagues. Even the well-heeled women of Hampstead seem like beasts of burden, hauling heavy folded push-chairs into their hatchbacks, struggling up the steps to unlock their front doors

•

with three bags of groceries in each hand, the baby under their arm and their handbag between their teeth.

They seem cheerful, or are they just resigned? Jackie will stand still on the pavement and watch them with awe before letting off the brake of the buggy and walking on, immersed in the loneliness of the long-distance mother.

T *w e n t y - e i g h t*

■

Matthew Pryce-Jones is looking at his face while he shaves. The face smiles back at him. Then it suddenly hits him that one day he won't exist, that there won't always be a Matthew Pryce-Jones. It does not seem possible. He is so real, so solid. It is *not* possible. He is going to go on living and getting richer for ever.

After he has shaved, Matthew gets dressed and switches his answering machine to "On." He does not tidy up—that will be taken care of by the cleaning lady—nor does he bother with breakfast, which will also be dealt with later. He grabs his car keys and bounds down the steps of his Chelsea house (bought a year ago for three hundred thousand pounds and now worth nearly half a million). He climbs into the front seat of his red Ferrari and roars down to the Embankment, heading east toward the City. Adrenalin is already flowing fast, and he sounds his horn impatiently at other drivers who are obeying the speed limit.

It is seven o'clock when he reaches Princes Street and the underground car parking space leased by his employers. He used to park on the pavement outside the office, but ticketing his car became the favorite sport of the local police, so he admitted defeat.

Matthew has worked at the investment bank Hanman Trust for two years. He is a Eurobond dealer, trading in interest-generating debts issued by large companies and governments. Since deregulation, the market is booming, outstripping the stock market in profits made. When Matthew joined Hanman Trust, the company only had two dozen Eurobond traders. Now there are fifty, and Matthew is one of their highest earners.

343

He joined at a salary of forty thousand pounds a year, twice what he would be earning as a senior doctor. A year later it had doubled to eighty thousand. This is only his basic wage. On top of this there is a commission taken from Hanman Trust's one percent of any deal they handle, and a profit-sharing scheme which more than doubles his salary. It is the sort of money that his parents' generation could only dream about, and here he is at the age of twenty-seven, earning it for the privilege of playing with other people's millions. Since he is single, and without dependants, it is expected that he will spend the money as fast as he makes it, and he does.

Matthew strolls into the dealing room, one of the first to arrive. He sits down at his desk, a sort of high-tech cubicle that houses his computer terminal and several phones. He calls a nearby delicatessen that does deliveries and orders black coffee, some almond croissants, and a round of cinnamon toast. Before hanging up, he has already switched on the VDU and called up the latest European exchange figures. He notes that the deutschmark has slipped slightly. He will have to do a bit of bullshitting if he is going to off-load the German issue he has taken on. The gilder's looking stable, on the other hand. Perhaps he'll put out some feelers in Amsterdam. . . .

He picks up the phone and begins to punch in numbers.

By late morning, the dealing room is a blur of noise and move-ment, dealers jumping up and down in their seats, gesticulating to one another, shouting instructions into the telephone.

Even though Matthew is as busy and pressured as anyone else, he does not stand up and he does not yell. He favors a laid-back style, which has become his trademark. He sits with his feet up on his desk, leaning back and swinging his swivel chair from side to side with a slow, regular movement. This has the effect of hypnotizing any of the other dealers who watch him.

"Hi, how are you?" He asks a potential buyer while the others screech and cajole like barrow boys. ". . . That's good. Listen, I've got a very attractive Eurodollar issue from a company in Thailand. The Far East is investing heavily in Europe right now; it's looking very interesting . . ."

When he stops for lunch at one, his position is healthy and he feels he has earned a little treat. He jumps into the Ferrari and heads straight for a champagne bar in Queen Victoria Street, where his date is already waiting for him.

"Pattie!" He kisses her an both cheeks. "You're looking gorgeous, as usual!"

"And you're full of shit, as usual." Pattie sits down and helps herself to a second glass from the bottle of vintage reserve she has already ordered. "The oysters look fantastic; when the waiter comes back, ask him to bring us a dozen."

"I'll order two dozen. They're an aphrodisiac, you know." He grins lecherously at Pattie.

"You wouldn't dare, Matthew, and you know it ..."

Pattie Destry is a financial analyst, ex-Harvard, working for one of the larger American banks. She and Matthew enjoy a friendly, slightly wary flirtation, and meet about once each fortnight so that Matthew can pick Pattie's brains about what is happening in the European markets. Matthew has never made a formal pass at Pattie, and has no intention of doing so. As well as being beautiful, in a big-boned American way, Pattie is fiendishly intelligent, and Matthew prefers his women brainless and amenable.

"I was surprised when you walked in here with a smile on your face," says Pattie, tweezing out her oyster with one deft, accomplished movement and gulping it down.

"Why on earth shouldn't I be smiling after the morning I've had? I've just off-loaded sixty million lousy German five-years, and I'm hot to ship a hundred and twenty five of that Thai issue you put me on to."

"I thought you might have heard the rumors."

Matthew pauses with an oyster halfway to his lips. "What rumors are these?"

"Word is that Hanman have overstretched themselves a bit with the bond dealing operation. In order to justify the salaries, you lot have to bring in at least seventy-five percent of their profit. The last couple of months' figures have been disappointing...."

"Okay, so we didn't do as well as we hoped with that Treasury auction, but we've caught up. Trade is steady. We're nowhere near as stretched as Goldstone White. They've got a hundred positions in their dealing room now."

"Exactly. You're all after a slice of the same pie. Is there going to be enough to go round?"

"It's first in, last out, in this business, isn't it?" Matthew takes a sip of his champagne, still smiling. "I've been working there longer than most, and I've earned Hanman more money than most."

Pattie shrugs. "In that case you're okay then. Now where's that second bottle got to?"

Matthew goes back to his desk with a smile on his face and the pleasant glow induced by lunch with an attractive woman (he saw the other diners looking at him enviously) and several glasses of champagne. However, he has cause to remember Pattie's words when he sees Stuart Fisher coming out of the manager's office.

Fisher is a twenty-year-old dealer who joined Hanman Trust as a school-leaver and worked his way up from the mail round to the dealing room by sheer cheek. He conforms with the new image of the City: cocky, loud-mouthed, a risk-taker high on his massive earning power. He wears heavy gold bracelets and crocodile skin loafers; drives a Porsche 911 with a Page Three model in the passenger seat.

He walks slowly back to his desk and thumps his fist down on it, hard.

"Fucking wankers!"

Then Fisher collects up his Mont Blanc pen, his portable CD player, and his bottle of Evian water and storms out of the room.

"Are we to take it that our friend Stuart has just left us?" drawls Charlie Lucas, one of the bank's Oxbridge graduates doing his obligatory stint in the dealing room.

"Been asked to leave, more like. . . ."

There are a few nervous glances in the direction of the door that Stuart Fisher so vehemently slammed. But the phones are still ringing and gradually the noise levels rise again, with Fisher's demise forgotten.

Matthew leans back in his chair, swings it to and fro, reflecting. Consolidation ... that is the word that springs to mind. He should consolidate his position. Make them realize that Matthew Pryce-Jones, of all people, is not one they can afford to lose.

He phones Bill Cartwright's secretary and tells her that he is popping in for a quick word. Cartwright is the senior manager whose job is to supervise and monitor the activities of the bond dealing room; a caustic Glaswegian with twenty years' experience in the City.

He twiddles his thumbs impatiently while Matthew enters on a long, persuasive spiel designed to remind Cartwright of the business he has brought to Hanman Trust over the years.

"Get to the point, laddie. I've got a lot on today."

"I thought you might like to consider upping my basic a bit. Just enough to take the pain out of the mortgage rate increase. The odd ten or twenty grand, say."

Cartwright grunts. "If you're not happy with us, laddie, then we'll just have to let you go."

"What the hell do you mean? Are you saying ... ?"

"It's like I just said: at the moment we can't afford to keep on people who are not happy with us."

"You're not going to sack me!" Matthew jumps to his feet. "I wouldn't give you the satisfaction. I resign!"

Twelve hours later, Matthew is leaving Tramp nightclub, feeling elated. So he resigned, so he has no job and a three-hundred-thousand pound mortgage to pay, so what? He's Matthew Pryce-Jones, he's got a marketable skill. He's hot property.

"I'm hot," he keeps saying over and over again to the blonde he has draped his arm around. "I'm just so fucking *hot!*"

He and the girl go back to his house. In a taxi. The Ferrari has had to be temporarily abandoned, he can't remember where. He will remember in the morning.

He tries to screw the girl, but he has had too much to drink. ("Screw" is the word he prefers; "making love" implies the presence of something that is not there, not ever.) She giggles (she has had too much to drink too) and falls asleep. Matthew leaves her lying on the bed and takes the phone into the bathroom.

"Hello, Pattie?"

"Matthew ...? Jesus, it's four o'clock in the morning!"

"I know. Listen, you were right."

"Matthew, please ... call me later, okay ..."

"About Hanman being in trouble. So I decided to get out while the going was good."

"Great. I'm pleased for you. Now could I please get some sleep?"

"All right, okay, sorry ... but can we get our heads together sometime tomorrow ... shit, that's today isn't it? I need you to tell me where's the best place for the most shit-hot bond trader in town."

When Matthew goes to start his new job, he does so on Concorde.

What the fuck, he thinks, now that I'm going to be earning half a million dollars per annum minimum, I can afford to blow a couple of grand on a plane ticket.

When he tells his mother about his mode of travel, he can almost hear Audrey concocting an excuse to drop in on her neighbors and pass on this piece of information. Perhaps it will be all the excuse she needs to hold a dinner party: "Have you heard from Matthew, Audrey?" "Oh yes, he telephoned me after he arrived in New York. By Concorde, actually ..."

Matthew even offers to fly her out on Concorde to visit him, but he knows he never will. He'll simply be far too busy.

Through a contact of Pattie Destry's, he has secured himself a job at Parker Brothers, one of Wall Street's top investment houses. They have a much bigger bond room than Hanman Trust (which Matthew is now prepared to dismiss as a tinpot little operation), and with a still-buoyant market there is unlimited opportunity for a trader with a good knowledge of the European market. In addition to a generous salary and bonuses, Parker Brothers are providing him with an apartment in Manhattan at a subsidized rent. He has kept his house in Chelsea but will not be letting it. He may want to hop across the Atlantic for the occasional weekend in London, and hell, it's not as if he needs the money.

A new city, he thinks, as the plane touches down. A new city for me to conquer. It's also a strange city where he knows no one, but that's not such a bad thing. London was getting boring.

He takes a yellow cab straight from JFK to the apartment block on the Upper East Side.

"How can I help you, sir?" asks the uniformed doorman, once he has helped carry Matthew's luggage into the cool chrome and marble lobby.

Matthew hands him a twenty-dollar tip. "Bring these up to my apartment in five minutes or so. I want to go up and have a look round first."

His apartment is on the twenty-third floor, with sliding glass doors onto a terrace that overlooks the East River. A quick glance confirms that the apartment is not up to much, but Matthew is not too concerned at this moment. He can get decorators in, or rent a bigger apartment. For now he is just content with being here.

He stands on the edge of the terrace facing south toward the financial district. It is starting to go dark and the gray silhouette of the Manhattan skyline can just be discerned in the dusk. Looking out over the lights that are beginning to pierce the dusk, Matthew feels quite invincible.

T *w e n t y - n i n e*

■

Carmen's friend Ros is getting married, and she asks Carmen to be her bridesmaid.

This will be the fourth wedding she has attended during the summer of 1987, including that of her younger sister, Sally. Sally didn't ask Carmen to be a bridesmaid. Instead she was attended by a friend from the insurance office in Hemingford where she works.

"When is it going to be your turn?" was all Jean Fox could say when she phoned Carmen to break the news about the impending family wedding.

"I have a career," says Carmen. "I thought you of all people would have understood that." Jean has just been promoted to regional manager.

"Women can do both these days," Jean says with great certainty. "Having a career shouldn't prevent you settling down."

Settling down. Even more people are doing it, dropping like flies. Most of Carmen's girlfriends are married now, some have babies. She heard from Ros that Jackie Maitland was expecting a baby. She does not see the Maitlands now. Jackie continued to make contact for a while but gave up when it was clear that her efforts were not going to be reciprocated.

"I don't care," Carmen tells her friends when they ask if she feels the lack of a permanent partner in her life. "My time is taken up with just having a good time."

At social gatherings she has developed a defiant flirtatiousness, a way of acting with the opposite sex that does not mean anything. She

350

knows it does not mean anything and the men concerned know it does not mean anything. She ignores the nagging sense of dissatisfaction and emptiness that she drags round with her everywhere. If she feels nothing for anyone she meets, she tells herself, it is only because she does not want to feel anything.

And as she tells her mother, there is her career to think about. A few months ago she left Thames Television for a small independent company called MediaWorld. She holds the position of junior producer, which is a significant step.

At the moment she is part of a production team who are putting together a talk show for Channel Four. At this stage it is nothing more than a collection of ideas tossed around endlessly.

"I think we all know what sort of show we want to make," the producer, Dan Watkins, says to the team at their next meeting. "We want something wacky, satirical, off-the-wall. Unconventional. We don't want the same string of famous faces waltzing in with the sole aim of plugging their latest book, or single, or film."

"And telling a load of fibs," says Carmen, sucking the end of her pencil. "What pisses me off about talk shows is the way the guests reinvent their life stories."

"I hate the way the interviewers always kiss ass," says one of the researchers. "Telling the audience how privileged they are to speak to this person."

"Okay," says Dan, a brisk, energetic Welshman in his early forties. "We've already decided we want a different format, and we don't want the show to pander to the guests' vanity. But the character of the show is still going to be influenced by the personality of the anchorman. We can't get away from that. So we need to pick our anchorman before we go any further. Any ideas?"

"No one well known," says Carmen.

"And no one too showbizzy."

"Is that agreed then?" Dan asks, looking round the circle of faces. "We want someone completely fresh. Someone inexperienced too, perhaps so that they don't fall into the same jaded old routines. What do you think?"

"I think it should be a woman."

"I think it should be Carmen."

"Me?" Carmen, who has been swinging back on her chair, jolts forward. "Get serious! I'm a producer, not a presenter!"

"You know, that's not such a bad idea," says Dan thoughtfully. "You've got plenty of style, Carmen, you've got the right sort of bold, hip look. And you're the same age as a lot of the yuppies that we would be hoping to attract with a late-night show."

"Yeay, Carmen, go for it! Media superstar!"

"No way," says Carmen firmly, pressing her pencil so hard that it snaps. "There is no way I'm going to appear in front of a television camera, alive or dead."

Dan Watkins gives Carmen twenty-four hours to make a decision.

"I'm not going to do it," Carmen tells Ros. Ros has come round to her flat for a crisis meeting, bearing a bottle of lemon vodka, which they are drinking frozen, out of sherry glasses.

"Oh, come on! Of course you are. It's the sort of opportunity most people in telly dream about. A chance like that only comes up once in a lifetime."

"But I wasn't looking for that chance!" Carmen jumps to her feet and begins to pace, her bare feet squeaking on the polished floorboards. "I never had any ambitions to appear on the screen."

"Didn't you?"

"Oh come on, Ros, you know I didn't!"

Ros pours two more glasses of vodka. "Okay, but look at it this way: what have you got to lose? You're only going to be signed up for a pilot show. Do the pilot show, which no one will watch anyway, and if you hate it, tell them you're not interested. But you might love it."

"I won't."

"Well, do it for the money then."

"Oh all right. People only watch talk shows for the guests anyway."

The pilot show is to be recorded in front of a live audience, at a small studio in West London. The set has been constructed as a pastiche of a conventional talk show set, with a huge squashy pink sofa, grotesque fake flower arrangements, plastic fruit, and a pale pink "princess" telephone next to the interviewer's seat. A pink stuffed poodle is fixed permanently onto the sofa.

Carmen herself has been taken to pieces by a stylist, a hairdresser, and a makeup artist and reconstructed. The new Carmen has her black hair in a chic, gamine cut, a flawless complexion and a severe black Jasper Conran suit with a very short skirt.

"Okay," says Scott, the assistant producer. "You're going to be sitting here, and you'll be able to read the autocue quite easily."

"I don't want to use an autocue. I told Dan that. I thought it was decided."

"Well, he changed his mind."

Carmen detects a note of spite in Scott's voice. He has been trying to get work as a presenter for years, and had hoped for the job of fronting this show.

"I've written you some notes to follow as well, to keep in front of you."

Carmen reads through Scott's script, which is made up of the things he would like to say if she had not got the job in his place. If she reads them, she will sound like Scott. Obviously this is what he is hoping for. Then he will be able to replace her when she fouls up.

"Okay, Carmen, just look this way for a minute will you. . . ." The disembodied voice of the lighting technician, followed by brilliant lights dazzling her. Her mouth dries up in response, so much so that it feels as though the insides of her cheeks have caved in and stuck together.

I'm not really doing this. This isn't real. . . .

Her legs and arms are like lumps of granite, she could not move them if she tried. The pit of her stomach feels as if it has been under the hands of a dentist, a shot of Novocaine spreading an icy numbness, followed by a drilling sensation. She does not dare even look at the audience.

"Okay, cue titles!"

The live studio band start playing the laid-back bluesy theme tune and the titles roll up: THE CARMEN FOX SHOW.

Carmen opens her eyes, blinks and starts reading from the autocue.

"Good evening, and a warm welcome to the Carmen Fox show. As you may have guessed, I'm Carmen Fox . . . Who writes this drivel?"

Her own voice returns from the place it has been hiding. The audience laughs. Carmen looks at them for the first time. She can't really see them properly beyond the blaze of the lights.

"The first thing on the agenda is this . . ." Carmen rips up Scott's script and flings it over the back of the sofa. The audience laughs again. "The second is a guest; actress Moira Howard."

Moira Howard is a doyenne of British theater, a woman of fifty-something (she can never remember her age) whose life story changes in detail each time she tells it. She is also immensely vain, fluttering her eyelashes at the audience as if she is playing the juvenile lead, speaking to the camera rather than Carmen's face. She has only agreed to come on the show because she needs to promote her newly published memoirs.

Carmen brandishes a copy of the book, *A Thespian's Tale,* holds it up so close to the camera that the title blurs.

". . . No doubt, Moira, the book is bursting with colorful theatrical anecdotes."

"Oh, absolutely! You know when I was in rep—"

"In that case, this is probably the best place for it."

Carmen tosses the book in the same direction as the torn-up script. The audience pull in their breath, titter slightly, then begin to laugh, a little uncertain. But Carmen is not so worried about the studio audience. She knows that the viewers watching television at home, feet up on the sofa, can of lager and packet of crisps in hand, will be laughing harder. It was a gesture tailored for the small screen.

As is the way she handles her next guest, a teenybopper's idol called Karl Wolf. Karl is all cropped blond hair and overdone suntan. He responds naively, eagerly to Carmen's flirting and giggly flattery, unaware that he is being sent up.

She brandishes a tabloid cutting at him. "It says here in this article entitled 'Twenty Things You Didn't Know About Karl Wolf' that you don't wear underpants. Is this true?"

"Of course, Carmen." Karl winks, hard.

"I'm not sure I believe that. After all, the press in this country are in the habit of making things up."

"I'll prove it, if you like," says Karl, as she hoped he would.

He stands up, turns his back to the audience and drops his fashionably ripped Levis. The cameraman has the presence of mind to freeze the frame and roll up the titles over Karl Wolf's chubby, suntanned buttocks.

The viewing figures for the pilot are disappointingly small, less than a million, but the show attracts a lot of press attention, not all of it favorable. The reviews use words like "refreshing," "naive," "uncompromising," and "infantile." But gradually the viewing figures creep up, chiefly because the show attracts big names as its guests. It seems that celebrities like the idea of appearing in something post-modern and a little outré, they even seem to relish the idea of being sent up and made to look foolish.

Carmen is naturally enough the focus of a lot of attention, because she is female and attractive and extremely young to host her own show (just twenty-eight when the first series is screened). There is a small piece in one of the serious Sunday papers, comparing the style of her show to other talk shows. Then other papers jump on the bandwagon, and the glossy magazines all run three-page features. She appears on the cover of *TV Times,* holding the pink stuffed poodle from the set. And finally one of the tabloids churns out "Twenty Things You Didn't Know About Carmen Fox." One of the twenty things is her real name: Carolyn Winifred.

"It says that your father is a biscuit-maker," says Jean when Carmen phones home. (Funny, how she still thinks of it as home, even though she has only been back to Hemingford once in the past two years, and has lived in London for more than ten.) "... Only that's not really true, is it?" Jean's tone makes it quite clear that she does not approve of any of this, especially not appearing on television. There are "better" (equals "safer") ways of making a living. "Just because he worked in a biscuit factory doesn't mean he makes biscuits. Did you tell them that?"

356

"No, Mum."

"Well, where did they get that bit from then?"

"I don't know. They dredge it up from somewhere. And what they don't know they make up."

Carmen is learning a healthy distrust of the press. One morning there is a photographer standing on her doorstep waiting to take her photo as she goes to the supermarket without her makeup. When she return from the same trip there is another stranger standing on her doorstep.

"I hate your program," he says. "I think it's shit." And he spits at her, the pellet of phlegm landing on her shoe.

She rings Ros.

"I can't handle this," she wails. "Can I come and stay with you and Pete for a while? It's awful everyone knowing where I live. I think I'm going to have to move."

"I don't know ..." Ros, like most of her friends has been wary of her since her new-found fame, probably afraid of seeming syco-phantic or impressed. "It's a bit late to get cold feet now, isn't it? You went into this with your eyes open."

"Thanks a lot! You virtually forced me into it!"

"But I thought you were enjoying it."

"I enjoy the forty minutes each week when the cameras are roll-ing ... thirty-five, say—I'm shit scared for the first five ... I hate everything else that goes with it."

Ros seems surprised by this. She pauses, then says, "But I've just read in one of those articles that you've signed up for a second series. Doesn't that mean it's too late?"

T *h i r t y*

■

Stephen has been on a small island off the south coast of Thailand for two months.

There are other Europeans staying on the island too, fellow travelers. In years to come he will remember their names but not their faces: Victoria, Jim, Marika the Dutch girl, Hugo. They live close to one another in beach huts and are on friendly terms, but know nothing about one another apart from Christian names. This anonymity suits Stephen very well.

When he left London he traveled first to Nepal, then on to India. He was fascinated by the subcontinent, but there were too many things there to remind him of Nicholas so he moved on again, going farther east. He stopped briefly in Hong Kong and Singapore, but they were too expensive for someone trying to live indefinitely off a limited amount of money.

And so he came to Thailand, traveling first to the forests in the north, and now to the southern peninsula. The island is the most primitive of resorts, with a few palm huts to rent from the owner of the local café and restaurant. The huts are only yards from the sea, underneath rustling coconut palms. There are rumors that the beach is dangerous; that local armed hoodlums patrol it, robbing and in some cases killing foreigners. Stephen has never seen anything of that nature, but it may explain why most Europeans prefer the larger resorts.

Today has brought a great treat: a letter from Alison. Stephen trudges up the beach to collect it from the café, which acts as his poste restante address. He sits on a bar stool on the shaded verandah,

357

sipping a glass of coconut water with the letter unopened before him. He only receives a letter once every two weeks, so he intends to spin out the pleasurable anticipation. The café proprietor watches him benignly as he dries glasses, grinning at Stephen every time he looks up.

Alison has been a faithful correspondent. She sometimes gives him news of Nicholas too, relaying his more eccentric or amusing escapades. At first he wondered whether they had become lovers in a bizarre pact to console themselves for his absence. But he quickly realized this was far from the case. Although she does not say so, he senses that Alison is disturbed by Nicholas's frequent visits. In her last letter she said that he had been pestering her for Stephen's poste restante address. She had refused to give it, and wanted Stephen to reassure her that she had done the right thing. Stephen wrote back confirming that she had acted in accordance with his wishes.

He is still not sure what his sexual identity is going to be, but he must be able to find out slowly, without pressure from anyone. The last thing he needs is Nicholas turning up here in Thailand, though he allows himself wistfully to imagine it; Nicholas strolling across the sand from the place where the twice-weekly ferry comes in. He would be amused, laughing as if his arrival here were some sort of prank.

Stephen sits at the bar for a while longer and has a second drink. He feels very thirsty today. Perhaps it is hotter than usual. Certainly the sun seems blindingly bright beyond the palm-fringed eaves of the verandah, making him screw up his eyes.

He decides on a swim to cool off before he reads the letter, delaying his treat a little longer. Putting it in the pocket of his shorts, he sets off to the end of the beach, to the sheltered lagoon that is his favorite place to swim. The water is cool and soothing, and he stays immersed for most of the afternoon, setting off back to his hut when the shadows begin to lengthen.

He sits on the steps of the hut, and with the wet towel still round his neck, takes out Alison's letter.

My dearest Stephen,
I am very sorry to have to be the bearer of such terrible news.
I am writing to tell you that Nicholas Pobjoy is dead.

It happened last Tuesday; they found him on the roof of the flat he'd been renting. He'd been lying up there naked, sunbathing, and had had some sort of heart failure. The post mortem apparently showed that he had taken a large number of tranquilizers, but it's not known if that was deliberate, or just an unfortunate combination with the hot sun. No note or letter was found. There will be an inquest but it's expected to return an open verdict.

I know that you will ask me what I think happened and I have to tell you, Stephen, that I'm just not sure. I know he drank a lot from time to time, and he used to take drugs sometimes, I think.

I feel dreadful, not least because of my part in all this. I felt responsible for him somehow, because of you marrying me and then our problems sending you off abroad, but lately it wasn't a responsibility I wanted. At first I did feel sorry for him. He told me some things about when he was in India, and how his family caught him having a gay affair with one of the servants. They rejected him completely, apparently, none of them spoke to him from then on. So he was all on his own in a way, but it started to annoy me that he did nothing about it. He just seemed to become obsessed with the past and his relationship with you, and I was the only remaining means of contact.

In the last few weeks his hanging around me all the time was starting to become a little macabre, and I have to tell you that I had my phone number changed and was seriously thinking about selling the house and moving up to Cambridge to get away. I was having paranoid fantasies about him following me up there, like some sort of evil genie.

I told him that in your letter you said you didn't want to give him your address, and the next thing I knew, he was dead. The police found a piece of paper with my old number on it by the phone, and they came to talk to me.

Stephen, I feel so terrible about what has happened. I only hope you can forgive me. And if it's any comfort to you now, one thing I am sure of is that Nicholas really did love you, it wasn't just sexual . . .

"Are you okay, Stephen?" Marika shouts a few hours later. Stephen is still sitting on the steps of his hut, with his towel draped over his head. He nods slowly.

Marika comes over. "Are you sure? You don't look very well. When you didn't move for so long, I thought . . ."

"I've had some bad news from home. A friend of mine ... he's just died."

"I'm sorry." Marika puts a hand on his shoulder. "Oh! You're burning hot."

"I don't feel too good. I've had a splitting headache all day. I think I'll go and lie down for a while."

Stephen switches on the electric fan and lies on the bed. He dozes for a while, but the pain in his head wakes him, the worst headache he has ever known. The sheet beneath him is drenched with sweat. He tries to stand, but cannot, his legs give way beneath him.

"Marika!" he shouts. His voice is feeble and he is afraid she will not be able to hear. "Marika!"

She comes eventually. "Oh my God, Stephen, you look terrible!"

"I think I've got a bit of a fever...."

Marika sponges him down, fetches aspirin and a thermometer.

"One hundred and four ..."

Hugo arrives, then the café manager. Voices become a blur. Stephen thinks they are saying he must go to hospital, on the mainland. He feels himself being lifted up and carried to a small motorboat, several villagers helping. He lies in the boat with his head on the lap of a young Thai boy. Above him is the moon, glittering, silver. Nicholas is dead and I am about to die too, he thinks. He feels utterly calm.

The only transport available to take him to the hospital at Muang Krabi is the same truck that acts as the local hearse. Stephen's body is severely jolted by riding stretched out on the back seat, but he is still alive when they arrive.

The doctor speaks some English. He explains that Stephen has a serious disease, but they must send off blood samples to the laboratory before they can start treatment. Stephen is only just conscious enough to take this in, but he understands from what isn't said that he may not survive until the results come back.

He is taken to the ward and settled into a narrow bed with hard rubber pillows. The nurses speak no English. The ward is crowded with the relatives of the other patients; whole families in constant vigil around each bed. The harsh fluorescent lights stay on all night and the only sign that night has come is the unrolling of mattresses by the relatives, who all sleep on the floor of the ward. Stephen drifts in and out of sleep to the sound of their alien chattering, and the *swoop-swoop* of the ceiling fans above his head.

Once his condition has improved slightly, Stephen becomes acutely aware of the discomforts of life in a provincial Thai hospital. There is no privacy, no escape from the constant chatter of the patients' families and the glare of the lights. Toilet facilities are limited to three holes in the ground shared between thirty-five patients, and squatting with a drip bag in one hand is an ordeal Stephen comes to dread. The menu is the same at every meal: salty rice and salt fish.

The food leaves him with a raging thirst, and he quickly learns to shout *"Nam yen!"* to the nurses—"iced water." The water must be boiled before it is fit to drink and it is still hot when the nurses bring it to the bedside. Not only does Stephen find it impossible to lift the heavy demijohn with a drip in his arm, but he is often forced to wait several hours for the water to become cool enough to drink. And as he waits he sweats, soaking the sheets and the thin cotton gown he is dressed in.

The Thai patients are more fortunate; they have their families to tend to their needs and carry out the tasks that the nurses are too busy to undertake. The teenage daughter of one of these families takes pity on Stephen and comes to sit at his bedside and sponge him with cool water, lifting a paper cup to his lips for him to drink. She visits every day and Stephen comes to long for the gentle touch of her hands and her sweet smile. He does not even know her name. He tries to tell her that he is called Stephen, but she is too shy to try saying it, giggling and hanging her head.

Further relief comes in the form of a visit from Marika and Jim. They manage to negotiate with the doctors and secure Stephen a single room. It is much more peaceful here, but his pale blond hair makes Stephen an object of great curiosity and there is a passing parade of local people, many of whom have never seen a Westerner before. They queue at the door, taking turns to stare at him.

Stephen's fever is still high; he does not feel significantly better.

It seems that his test results have been delayed because he had the misfortune to fall ill over a religious holiday. After four days the doctor visits him and confirms that he has typhoid fever. Another ordeal begins, a series of six hourly injections straight into his vein, which make his arm feel as though it is on fire.

He starts to improve, finally. He has no idea how long he has been here; time has been suspended. Years might have passed. He asks the doctor to tell him the date and finds that two weeks have passed since he first fell ill. It is May 3, 1985.

Beds at the hospital are scarce, and the staff have no wish for Stephen to prolong his stay once his recovery is certain. He is dispatched in a wheelchair to the nearby café, which has a phone he can use. A small Thai boy runs along beside the chair, holding up the drip, which is then hooked over the branch of a tree while he phones.

He arranges a flight from the local airport to Bangkok where he stays in a cheap hotel for a few days, resting and regaining his strength. Bangkok is dusty, noisy, polluted and he has no wish to remain there longer than is necessary. He will leave Thailand, and the Far East too. It is time to move on. At the travel agent's he runs his eye down the flight price list, picking a destination at random. He selects New York.

Stephen was prepared to like New York very much. Indeed, he does like New York. But he quickly recognizes that this is not the right place for him to stay. Everyone here is so hurried, so purposeful. He watches the traders and brokers scurrying down Wall Street like ants, the women striding quickly in their Reeboks, and he feels even more at odds with himself. This is not a city for someone who is uncertain and seeking to find some peace of mind. It is a city in which to step out with confidence. It is also too expensive.

Stephen spends three pleasant days being a tourist, then he enters yet another travel agency.

"Hi, I'm Sherry. How may I help you?"

"Er ... I'd like to book a flight."

"Certainly. And where would you like to go?"

Sherry holds red fingernails poised over the keys of her computer terminal.

"Um ..." Stephen looks around the room. In a magazine rack there is a copy of *Newsweek,* its cover proclaiming SAN FRANCISCO VOTED AMERICA'S FAVORITE CITY.

". . . I'd like a ticket to San Francisco, please. One way."

The sharp Pacific air fills Stephen with energy, he breathes it in in great lungfuls and strides up San Francisco's precariously steep hills with a vigor he has never felt before.

He falls in love with the city long before he comes to feel at home in it. This time he is sure he wants to stay for a while. He rents a room in a clapboard house in North Beach over Violet Lim's Beauty Salon and above a huge neon sign saying PIZZA—SAN FRANCISCO'S FINEST. After a few days of trudging around the streets he finds himself a job at a diner on Geary Street, serving the city's working population with their breakfasts of buttermilk hotcakes, hash browns, and other foods that are quite alien to his English tastebuds. He comes to recognize the regulars and to tell them to "Have a nice day" as they sip coffee and peruse their copies of the *Chronicle.*

In the evening, if he is not working, Stephen simply walks about. Sometimes he wanders through Chinatown, drinking in the exotic sights and smells, the rainbow of winking neon lights. Best of all he likes to go down to the Aquatic Park near Ghirardelli Square and sit with a carton of fresh oysters looking out over the Bay to the ocean beyond.

There is a certain satisfaction in being at the farthest point west, looking to the East. He sometimes imagines he can feel something of the mystical spirit of the Orient blowing in on the breeze. It is that same spirit that first drew him to Nicholas Pobjoy. If he closes his eyes he can hear Nicholas's voice whispering, *"We were free once, you and I...."*

T *h i r t y - o n e*
∎

"I think that went pretty well, don't you?"

Gregory and Jackie Maitland are cleaning up after a dinner party. Gregory gathers the plates together and starts to stack them into the dishwasher. Jackie throws the peach damask tablecloth and matching linen napkins into the washing machine and sorts out the remains of the food (globe artichokes, followed by angel-hair linguine with seafood and sun-dried tomatoes, fresh mango pavlova for dessert). Upstairs, nine-month-old Emily is sleeping peacefully in her cot.

"Alec and Joanna really are a pair, aren't they?" Gregory gossips amiably as he washes the champagne flutes by hand. His sleeves are rolled above his elbows and he is wearing an apron of Jackie's that just covers his midriff. "All that crap about organic food and minimalist interior design. Apparently they live in a converted loft in Limehouse and it's like the inside of a barn, with a few pieces of sculpture in it. And can you believe their children are really called Pansy and Clovis?"

"Amazing . . ."

"Are you all right?" Gregory turns round to look at his wife. "You've been pretty quiet all evening. Didn't you enjoy yourself?"

"Yes, it was fine." Jackie carries the tray of coffee cups and chocolate mints into the kitchen. "They seemed to like the food."

"Clever girl! I know I can count on you to do things right! With a little help from good old Megan, of course."

He bends down to bestow a congratulatory kiss on Jackie's forehead. There is no response.

364

"Are you sure you're all right?"

Jackie sits down at the kitchen table. "The thing is . . . I'm pregnant again."

"But you can't be! We were going to wait until next year. I thought . . ."

"I know. We weren't careful enough, that's all."

Gregory sits down opposite her, dish cloth in hand. "Oh, God. It's a bit soon, isn't it? How far gone are you?"

"Ten weeks."

"So Emily will be . . ."

"She'll be sixteen months. Nearly seventeen."

"Oh well . . ." Gregory forces a smile. "We were going to have another one anyway, weren't we? It's just a bit sooner than expected."

Jackie cannot accept the impending arrival of another child so readily. She and Gregory have talked about having a second child after two years, but Jackie was only paying lip service to the idea. She is not sure she wants more children at all, and certainly not for a long time. Emily is happily settled in the care of Megan, who comes in daily, but there are still times when the arrangement goes adrift and Jackie has to arrive at work late, or leave the office to go home, aware of the disapproving looks as she gathers up her belongings and rushes out of the door. And in addition to her job at Munro Willis she has to oversee the running of the house; ringing round constantly for available baby-sitters, chasing up plumbers and repairmen, cramming in visits to the supermarket and the dry cleaners and the chemist around her punishing work schedule.

She collapses into bed each night exhausted. When she has time to think, which is not often, she wonders what she did all this for: marriage, the house, motherhood. To try to have all of these things at once means to do none of them properly, to be in a continual race from one demand to the next, like a baseball player sliding from base to base, never touching down. . . .

She does not complain to Gregory, just as she never complained to her mother or her grandfather. She makes a point of not complaining. She told him she could do it all, and do it all she shall.

If her work suffers it is in small, almost imperceptible ways. She misses the occasional meeting and therefore knows a little less about what is going on. She comes up with fewer new ideas. With the help of Pat she keeps up, but it is a struggle rather than the pleasure it used to be.

This new pregnancy brings an added pressure. Jackie feels very sick, an intense, all-pervading nausea she has never experienced before. She is sometimes forced to leave the room and go into the ladies' cloakroom to vomit, washing her face and reapplying her lipstick before reentering the office as if nothing has happened.

Nevertheless she applies, and is short-listed for, the post of Senior Product Development Manager within the company. She is one of only three candidates and has far better qualifications than either of the other applicants, both men.

An interview is conducted by the managing director, but Jackie knows that it will only be a formality. The two of them talk about Jackie's involvement in the launch of the Munro fashion shops the previous year, and their successful turnover figures. As he talks, Mr. Barron, the MD, glances occasionally at Jackie's midriff, as though he is expecting some visible change in her figure during the timespan of the interview. The loose cut of her jacket hides her four months of pregnancy.

"And now to the question of hours ..." Mr. Barron says. "This upward step would obviously require an increased commitment in terms of your time...."

"That would be no problem," says Jackie firmly. "I'm used to working long hours. And I have plenty of domestic backup."

"I see. Good ... Would you care to wait outside with the other applicants, Mrs. Maitland?"

Jackie sits and waits with her two male colleagues. A few minutes later, Barron's secretary comes out and asks one of them discreetly to go back into the interview room. He has got the job.

Jackie waits until the formal business of offering and acceptance is over and the successful candidate has emerged. Then she goes back into the room.

"I know why I didn't get the job," she says in a calm, quiet voice. "It's because I'm pregnant, isn't it?"

Barron raises his eyebrows and his hands simultaneously. "*Are you?* I had no idea, really I didn't. Congratulations!"

He knew. I know that he knew. . . .

"The position should have gone to me. I have twice the qualifications of the other two."

"Well, obviously the question of family commitments is a significant one. And if you are shortly to go on maternity leave again ..." He raises his hands helplessly.

"If I thought that my sex or my physical condition prejudiced your decision in any way," Jackie says, still in that small, quiet voice, "I would consider taking you to an industrial tribunal."

But she does not; she just grows bigger, more uncomfortable and tired, and finally, at the end of August 1988, gives birth to a second daughter.

The baby is simply Baby Maitland for the first three days of her life while Jackie and Gregory, who had anticipated a boy, a Jamie, search for a name. They pick two names from the *Times* birth announcement columns: Alice Charlotte.

Alice is large and plain, with a lot of dark curly hair. She proves less demanding than her sister was in her first few months of life, but Emily is now going through an awkward, self-assertive phase and is jealous. It is she who wakes several times each night, screaming for attention. Sometimes both of them cry in concert, a noise that makes Jackie feel small and vulnerable. She would like to lie down under the kitchen table and cry like a baby herself, or run out into Compayne Gardens and disappear into the night.

Part of the problem is her physical condition; the birth was difficult and she lost a lot of blood, leaving her weak and anemic. She is not strong enough to return to work at the end of her maternity leave, and has to take further unpaid leave until she has recovered. Both children are crying as Jackie makes the phone call to the personnel manager to break this news. When she hangs up, she covers her ears and presses her face against the kitchen wall, hating them.

The interest rate on their large mortgage is rising, and with Jackie not earning it is impossible for the Maitlands to continue employing

Megan on a full-time basis as before. Jackie pleads and cajoles and makes economies, until Gregory agrees that Megan can still come to help for six hours each week.

Jackie lives for these few hours, even though she does not have the energy to enjoy them. She usually lies on the bed and stares at the ceiling and tries to will herself to get well enough to go back to Munro Willis on a full-time basis. They will not hold her job open forever. The thought of it falling from under her, of her office not being there any more, is terrifying. When Pat phoned her she said someone had asked discreetly if Jackie was suffering from postnatal depression.

When Megan is not there, Jackie reels from one protracted, messy mealtime to the next, living for seven o'clock when both of the children are in bed. Then she will clear up the smeared, sticky mess in the kitchen, pour herself a glass of wine and collapse on the bed. The daily struggle is much worse than it was when she had her first taste of full-time mothering. Alice is a placid baby, but then there is Emily too, willful and unmanageable, always whining for something. She does not undertake the endless walking this time. The double buggy is too heavy for her to lift in and out of the trunk of the car.

Gregory is only a distant figure in all of this. He works long hours, often attending meetings in the evening or seeing friends alone. Jackie is glad. She does not have the energy to devote to him at the moment. His presence is concerned and kindly but detached. Anyway, they are rarely both at home and awake these days. She does sometimes wonder how he sees her now, if she has really changed so very much from the confident, competent executive he first met.

One such occasion is an evening in February when Gregory returns home from work early for a change.

He finds Jackie in the kitchen, spooning tinned baby food into the girls. When Emily was a baby she used to prepare all her food herself, now she does not care. She is wearing bedroom slippers and a fuchsia pink tracksuit, the sort she saw housewives wearing to the supermarket and swore she would never be seen dead in. Her clothes are smeared with apple purée. There are a few strands of dried food in her hair.

"Oh, hello," she says, when Gregory appears in the doorway.

"Hi."

Jackie smiles at him a little uncertainly. She is not sure if she should get up, go over and kiss him perhaps? She never knows quite what he expects of her these days. The subtle art of relationships is one she does not understand. She has had such poor examples in the past after all: her mother and Billy, Norman Butler, silent Don Anderson.

She is also realizing that she did not know who Gregory was in the beginning anyway. In those days she was so busy not losing him that she never thought to find out. He was just a person in her fantasy family snapshot, "the husband."

"Hello, girlies!" Gregory bends down and kisses Emily on the top of her head, squeezes one of Alice's fat, waving paws.

"I haven't got anything in for supper tonight," says Jackie, pushing her hair back from her forehead with a sticky hand. "At least, I don't think so. You could try going through the freezer."

"It's all right, I'm not staying. I just came back to get changed. I'm playing squash with Alec tonight."

"Oh." After the conditioned response of relief, Jackie feels disappointment. It might have been nice, for once, to sit and have dinner together, after a reviving soak in the bath.

". . . Unless you don't want me to?"

"No, it's all right—you go."

She can still have the hot bath after all, followed by an early night. Another early night.

"Okay. If you're sure." Gregory watches Jackie tidy up, his arms dangling rather helplessly by his sides.

"Shall I . . . ?"

"No, it's all right. I can manage." Jackie forces a brisk smile.

"Right. I'll be off then."

After the children are in bed, Jackie toys with the idea of cooking herself an omelette but decides she is not really hungry. Fiddling with the children's meals all days tends to rob her of her appetite. She goes straight to the hot bath, and after climbing in and out of the water twice to settle Emily, collapses into bed.

\

There is a pot of moisturizer on the bedside table. Jackie smears it on liberally, then remembers Ros's warning about never being seen by one's partner with cream on one's face. She dabs off the excess with a tissue, but her skin is still greasy. Not that it matters now: by the time her husband returns, he's hardly going to notice.

The phone rings.

"Hello?"

There is a click, as the caller hangs up. After a few minutes she is drifting off into sleep when the phone rings again. The same thing; silence, then the sound of someone hanging up.

The third time the phone rings, Jackie says firmly: "Yes?"

"Is Gregory there, please?" A young woman's voice, young and petulant.

"No, he's not."

"Oh."

"The "oh" is surprised, put-out even, and the woman hangs up before Jackie can tell her that Gregory is playing squash with Alec.

T h i r t y - t w o

■

"Christ, what a day!"

It is Friday, October 16, 1987. Matthew Pryce-Jones and his friend
Cameron Vogler are leaving the high-rise building on Fulton Street
that houses the offices of Parker Brothers. All afternoon they have
been staring at computer screens and watching share prices slip lower
and lower following the failure of trade talks with the Germans and
disastrous U.S. trade figures.

"Let's get a drink." They sling their jackets over their shoulders
and trudge up Broadway to their favorite bar, which is full of people
like themselves; shell-shocked Wall Street traders and brokers gulping
down bourbon and watching the TV in the corner to see what the
evening news has to say.

"I don't believe it!" says Matthew, shaking his head. "The market
was looking so good. . . ."

"That's the whole point, buddy." Cameron extinguishes one cigarette and lights another straight away. "We've been riding on a bull
market for eighteen months or more. What goes up must come down,
it's the first law of the universe."

"But does it have to come so far down? I mean, on Monday,
when the market opens . . . if we continue slipping like this . . ."

"We're heading for a crash." Cameron shrugs. "Like I said, bound
to happen."

"You're being bloody cool about this."

"I've got my back covered, man! I can ride this out."

Cameron Vogler is Parker Brothers' star trader, known as "the
Prince." Son of a Waspie socialite and a Jewish property developer,

he left Princeton for Parker Brothers and after five years is making a million dollars a year. He owns a forty-room mansion in Connecticut where he has only spent one night. Most of his money is reputed to be invested in gold bullion, a safe commodity removed from the vagaries of the debt market.

Matthew shrugs too, laughs, orders another bourbon. The liquor traces a warm path through his innards; he starts to relax. So the market's going down. It will stay down for a while, and then it will go up again. It's bound to. There's so much momentum behind it, so much investment.

"What say we go and grab something to eat?" suggests Cameron. "Then go and see how much trouble we can whip up."

"Good idea. I'll call a few girls."

An hour and a half later, Cameron and Matthew are joined by two very pretty girls called Francine and Courtney. One of them met the girls somewhere, some time, but can't remember the occasion. The four of them go to dinner at the Canal Bar on Greenwich Street, where they consume three bottles of Krug, and then on to Nell's to dance and drink some more. Cameron overcomes the elitist admission policy by bribing the doorman with a hundred-dollar bill.

Francine and Courtney prove only the most lukewarm of companions, subscribing to the designer celibacy that is fashionable in New York at the moment. Sex has followed in the footsteps of cuisine, and in the nouvelle era less is more. Messy, sweaty or untidy sex is as passé as smothering your food in rich cream sauces. Smart girls talk about it, but are too busy with their careers to do it. And with AIDS, they have the perfect alibi.

Matthew's gaze wanders erratically around the room. After two bottles of champagne, he can only just focus on the girl who is dancing alone with delightful abandon. She has short hair dyed jet black and a gold sequinned bra top à la Madonna. Before long she is sitting beside him and offering him Ecstasy, which he declines. He talks to her, after a fashion. By the time he reaches the end of each sentence, he has forgotten how he started it; he scarcely even hears her replies through the noise of the music and the blur of champagne.

Then he and Cameron and Francine and Courtney are in the back of a cab, heading back to his apartment. The girl with the black hair is with them too. Someone switches on the TV and tunes into the Home Shopping Club. Cameron finds some Wild Turkey from somewhere, and some bagels, and they sit in a circle on the floor playing credit-card poker.

"I'll match your Citibank card and raise you a Diners...."

"... Raise you a gold AmEx...."

"... Bet you can't match this one!" Courtney is triumphant—or is it Francine? The card flung down declared that the holder is HIV negative.

Courtney and Francine leave, but the girl with black hair does not. She is lying on the bed, removing her mini skirt, stockings and suspenders.

"Which one of you guys want to go first?"

"Jesus!"

Matthew tries to make a move but is overcome with lethargy. He lies across one corner of the bed and half watches as the girl unzips Cameron's trousers and pulls them down as far as his knees. Matthew's eyes keep closing. The bobbing motion of the girl's dark head is soothing, hypnotic. In the background the saleswoman on the Home Shopping Club is still chattering away about *'kerwality items.'*

"Jesus!" Cameron says over and over again. "Jesus Christ!"

Matthew is not even aware that he has an erection until he feels the girl's hand on his fly, stroking him.

"No really ..." he protests. "It's okay, really, you don't have to...."

"Jesus, come on, Matthew!" Cameron is lying on his back on the other side of the bed. "What's the matter with you ...?"

The girl climbs on top of Matthew without speaking, and eases his penis into her. She rocks to and fro on top of him. When he opens his eyes he sees her magenta-painted lips parted in laughter, but she makes no sound. Cameron is laughing too, grabbing at the girl's breasts.

"Jesus!" This time it is Matthew who says it. "Sweet Jesus ...!"

■ ■ ■

"What a night that was!" Cameron says on Monday morning. "That was some night ... Jesus, will you look at this?" He points to the ring of computers that index trading prices. "Will you look at this fucking shit?"

By the end of Monday the nineteenth the average value of shares has fallen by five hundred points, the biggest single fall in its history. The stock market has lost twenty-two percent of its value. The Crash has happened; it is reality.

"The writing's on the wall for us now," Cameron says to Matthew at lunch time as they munch their hero sandwiches in front of the screens. He sounds perfectly cheerful. "They can't afford to keep all of us on, no way."

"They'll keep you on. They'd be fools to lose you."

"I'll quit anyway. It's not going to be any fun anymore. I'll take a long vacation, then I'll think of something else to do. Become an art dealer maybe. Or sell out and join Dad after all."

"It's all right for you."

"Hey c'mon! You'll be okay!"

But Matthew knows that he will not be. Last in, first out; that's the rule. The next morning he is one of the fifty who are called in and told, with regret, that there is no longer employment for them at Parker Brothers. The apartment will be paid for until the end of the month, but Matthew has no desire to stay around. He books a flight back, not on Concorde, but first class. I'm not going to slum it, he thinks, not while I still have money in the bank.

There will not be money for long unless he gets another job. When he bought the house in Chelsea he had no savings and took out a hundred percent mortgage, which now eats up several thousand pounds each month.

He phones Pattie Destry. "I thought I might give Hanman Trust another whirl. . . ."

"I wouldn't bother. Things over here are just as bad as they are in New York. Hanman just got rid of twenty-two people."

"Okay, so who else can I try?"

"No one's recruiting at the moment. Not at the sort of salary you would be hoping for. My advice would be to sell everything, get your hands on some hard cash. It's a valuable commodity at the moment. Then start over."

Matthew gets rid of the Ferrari, which is costing him a fortune in garaging. He financed the car with a loan, so there is no profit from the sale. The house should make him some capital though, after the mortgage is paid off. A hundred, maybe two hundred thousand.

"The market is quiet at the moment ..." murmurs the estate agent. "With the Crash, and the talk of a rise in interest rates.... It depends how quickly you want to sell."

"Quickly."

"In that case, you may have to drop the price a fraction...."

After several weeks with no buyer in sight, Matthew drops the price from five hundred thousand to four hundred and fifty thousand. He is offered four hundred thousand and accepts it. After the agent's commission is deducted and the mortgage and his credit card bills have been paid off, he is left with eighty thousand pounds. Enough to buy a small flat in an unfashionable area.

While he is looking, he rings a couple of his friends to see if he can borrow a room, but one is in the middle of moving, another is about to become a father.... So he rents a place; a small, dingy service flat in an apartment block near Sloane Street, usually let to tourists. From this uninspiring base he sets off to find himself a job.

London is awash with panic-stricken, unemployed whiz-kids. Door after door closes in his face, sometimes with a "Maybe next year ..." or a "You might try again in six months' time...."

"Join one of the professions" is the advice meted out wherever he turns. "Get yourself a professional qualification, something to fall back on in times like this...."

He applies to, and is accepted by, London's largest firm of chartered accountants. He will begin at the bottom, training alongside university graduates six years his junior.

He sits with them in a conference room on his first day at work and listens to the induction speech about hard work, dedication, and study. Matthew lets the words wash over him, he does not listen. He feels numb inside, disbelieving.

After the talk, the new recruits are sent to their allotted departments. Matthew and a gangling youth called Laurence are in the tax department.

"Right, first off ..." The departmental head hands them each a sheaf of papers. "I'd like you to copy these."

"I'm sorry?" says Matthew.

"I'd like you to take these to the photocopier and make one copy of each of these."

"You've got to be joking!"

"No, I'm quite serious. It's an exercise in familiarization with office routine."

Matthew and Laurence stand at one end of a long corridor with their sights on the photocopier, which is at the far end.

"Gosh!" Laurence laughs nervously, a glugging sound like water draining from a bath. "Got to start somewhere, I suppose ... are you all right?"

Matthew is staring far into the distance. He feels an icy coldness wrap itself round him and he shudders, as though he were standing in a draft.

"Yes, I'm all right," he says, and sets off slowly down the corridor.

At the weekend, Matthew trudges from one estate agent to another, looking for a flat for less than one hundred thousand pounds. He is staring at the window display of an agent in Upper Street when he notices a girl who is doing the same thing. He cannot help but notice her; she is tall and strikingly beautiful, with glossy hair lightly permed into a mass of sable curls. Graziella Buscowicz.

He does not want to talk to her so he moves away before she has a chance to recognize him. He hears her footsteps behind him and has to force himself not to walk faster.

"Matthew! It's me—Graziella."

"Hi." He kisses her on the cheek. "You look well."

"So do you. Are you looking for a flat round here?"

"Just toying with the idea. How about you?"

"I'm trying to find somewhere as soon as I can. I've just started as a registrar at the Royal Free."

"Congratulations. That's great ..." Matthew starts walking again, hoping his brisk pace will discourage her. But she keeps pace easily, falling into step with him.

"Are you busy? How about lunch?"

"Well, I am, sort of . . ."

"Oh, go on, Matthew. For old times' sake. . . ."

They go to Frederick's in Camden Passage. Matthew does not enjoy the lunch. Graziella's beauty and self-confidence make him feel embarrassed. He is waiting for the moment when she is going to ask him about being expelled from the medical profession. Or talk about how much they are both earning, which is an abiding preoccupation with everyone he knows at the moment.

But she talks about politics, food, and famine in the Third World, and then she asks if he would like to see a movie with her that afternoon. Matthew accepts, only because he cannot face spending the afternoon alone in his grimy service flat.

"So what did you think?" Graziella asks as they come out of the cinema. It has grown dark since they were inside, and much colder. Graziella links her arm through his and leans against him for warmth.

"The film? Oh, fine. If you like that sort of thing."

Graziella frowns at him. "Come on! I'm trying to have a conversation here! What is your opinion of the film as a piece of cinema, as entertainment?"

Matthew shrugs.

"You haven't changed, have you? Why is it so difficult for you to let me know what you think?"

"Look, *Doctor* Buscowicz . . ."

"You never did want to think about anything, did you? Nothing matters as long as you have a good time!"

"What the hell would you know?"

Matthew pushes Graziella's hand off his arm, turns on his heel and walks away.

On Monday, he leaves his office early and takes a bus from the City through Camden Town to Hampstead and the Royal Free Hospital.

Graziella is assisting in a clinic. Matthew sits outside with the patients and waits for her. He glimpses her every now and then through a half-open door, in her shining white, starched coat. He watches her give an injection, watches her calm a hysterical patient, help lift a wheelchair-bound one. He enjoys watching her. He quite enjoys being inside a busy hospital again. The familiar smell of it. He remembers.

"What on earth are you doing here?" she asks, when she sees him sitting in the waiting area.

"I wanted to apologize. I'm sorry I stormed off on Saturday. Will you forgive me?"

Graziella peels off her white coat and slings it over her arm. That makes him remember too. The feel of the syringes bumping against his leg. The thrill of it.

"I'll forgive you if you'll try and explain."

Matthew shrugs. "I'm having a hard time at the moment. Things aren't going very well."

There—he said it.

She smiles. "Apology accepted."

"Will you have dinner with me? If I promise to think before I say anything?"

The next time Matthew and Graziella go out, he is left with a powerful need to phone her as soon as she gets home, to make sure she is still there. This feeling intensifies with the next time and the next until it becomes overwhelmingly painful. He is dependent on her. He needs her. It is almost too much for him to bear. Why this? he thinks. Why now?

T h i r t y - t h r e e

■

The title music of the "Wogan Show" fades to a blaze of applause.

"... and tonight I'd like you to welcome a young lady whose rise in the world of television has been nothing short of meteoric. Less than two years ago, nobody had heard of her. Now she has just finished the second series of her own late-night talk show and is joining the BBC to present a new current affairs program.... Ladies and gentlemen, I'd like you please to give a big welcome to Miss Carmen Fox!"

The applause swells again and dies away as Carmen walks across the set in the Television Theater and takes her seat opposite Terry Wogan. She hopes her carmine pink Rifat Ozbek suit looks all right under the lights. Certainly she will be looking better to the viewers at home than she will to the studio audience. The producers of her new show told her to lose a stone before the series starts. In the flesh she now looks painfully thin; on screen she appears slim and elegant.

"Now, Carmen, there's been a lot of stuff in the media about your defecting from the other side to join us at the Beeb. Would you like to tell us a little bit about that?"

Carmen smiles as she prepares to answer the first question. The interviewer interviewed; it's a familiar twist by now.

After the show has finished, she is taken in a chauffeur-driven car straight to Television Center where there is a press launch for "Newsreel," the current affairs program that she will be fronting. There is a lot of champagne, a lot of hangers-on, a lot of popping flash bulbs. Carmen is required to stand next to her copresenter

379

Alexander Cairns and grin a lot while they are photographed. It is strange to be squashed up next to this man, to be treated as an equal after the way in which they met seven years earlier.

If Carmen grins more broadly than ever before it is because she is very nervous about the prospect of working with Cairns. It is not just because he is a well-respected and experienced journalist, and she is just an interesting newcomer, a televisual bimbo. She squints at his craggy face out of the corner of her eye as the cameras click and click again. Is he going to remind her of the way she cheated to try to get a job as his assistant. Or worse still, tell the press.

He does not. Instead he waits until the end of the session and says in a low voice: "I've got a good memory. You'd do well to bear that in mind." And throughout the first production run-through and rehearsal he makes a point of bringing her down, making her remarks look ill-considered or just plain stupid.

The first show includes an item on the acute lack of nursery care in Britain. It features an interview with a young working couple, as a real-life example of the problem. Carmen suggests that they get the couple to swap places for a day to see how their roles compare.

"Oh come on!" says Cairns. "Not that old chestnut! It's been done a hundred times a day; the housewife and the breadwinner change places. . . ."

"She's not a housewife!" Carmen sneers back. "That's the whole point. She's a working mother. And if her husband had to take the children several miles to and from the childminder's twice a day, get away in time to collect them and then feed them, as well as doing his own job, then it might give other men a new perspective on what it's like for women. Because unfortunately the government is made up of men—stupid men—and it's only the government who can change the childcare situation in this country!"

"Quite the little feminist, aren't you?" says Cairns drily.

"Listen, I know I've got a lot to learn, but at least I'm prepared to try!"

Carmen throws down her script and walks off the set, creating a frisson of whispers amongst the production team.

The producer likes her idea, however, and decides that Alexander

Cairns should be the one to introduce the film clip in the live show. The autocue breaks down by way of poetic justice, when he is halfway through his introductory piece.

Carmen is overwhelmed by the desire to watch him squirm in front of the camera, live. But her professional instincts take over and she steps into the breach, continuing as though a joint introduction was intentional.

"Thanks for that," Cairns says afterward. "You've obviously got a good memory too."

"I did have some input with that item," says Carmen, a little drily.

"So you did." Cairns smiles broadly, and his dour face changes. What nice teeth he has, thinks Carmen.

The next day Carmen is quite looking forward to seeing Cairns when she arrives at the studio, and finds herself watching him discreetly throughout the rehearsal, studying his interviewing technique. He is dressed in jeans and a sloppy sweater and looks younger than he does on screen.

Now that the first show has gone out—to good reviews—everyone is more relaxed, including Cairns. He smiles more, cracks jokes, though his sense of humor is so dry as to be brittle.

"Er ... Alexander, how about a drink in the bar?" Carmen asks at the end of the day.

"It's Sandy ..."

"Sandy ..."

"I'd love to, but I'm afraid I'd better get going. Lorna and I are going to the theater."

"Lorna?"

"My wife."

He's married; of course he's married. The interesting ones always are. Carmen puts Sandy Cairns from her mind and sets off to meet some friends at her favorite sushi bar in the West End. She is hungry. Life goes on.

She cannot forget about him because he is always there. They see one another every day, their photographs appear together in magazines, they go out in the evening with other people working on "Newsreel" ...

Sometimes, when they are on set together, lining up a shot, trying out a new approach, they touch. When this happens Carmen gets goose bumps. She sometimes wonders if it is intentional on his part. He is as patronizing as ever, but that is largely for the benefit of the others. He is attracted to her, that much is becoming obvious. She sees him looking at her sometimes. Apart from that, it's just a feeling.

No more married men. She promised herself that after Richard Kendrick, and then again after the Gregory Maitland fiasco. But who is there left, if married men are out of bounds? All the good ones have been taken.

The electric tension between the two of them builds until there is a palpable crackle when they are together. They start to be rude to one another again; their "friendship" breaks down. Then the end of the series is upon them and it will all be over for a few months. There is a party to celebrate.

Carmen avoids Sandy all evening, yet she knows she has worn her favorite white jersey dress for his benefit, and she knows she will be unable to leave without at least speaking to him and burying their particularly sharp-edged hatchet.

She leaves the party and goes back into the "Newsreel" office to collect her things. She has just switched off all but one of the lights when she hears someone come in and close the door that she left wide open. She knows without turning round that it is Sandy Cairns.

He walks up behind her. "I thought it was you I saw in here. It's that dress of yours; it glows in the dark."

Carmen laughs.

He puts a hand on her shoulder and turns her round to face him.

"I thought Lorna was invited. Did she not come?"

He shakes his head. "She doesn't like television people."

"Oh. I see."

Sandy pulls her toward him and they kiss. The idea of doing this here, in the dark, with Alexander Cairns, excites Carmen so much that she feels as though she is on fire. She responds eagerly, pressing herself against him. The weeks of tension have made her frantic for him.

The door opens and someone—one of the cameramen?—stumbles in.

"Whoops! Sorry!"

He goes out again.

"Come on," says Sandy, taking her by the hand. "Let's go somewhere more private."

Carmen knows before she does the test that she is pregnant. She has been pregnant before and she remembers how her body felt.

But if the sensations in her body are the same, everything else is different. She is alarmed, certainly, and a little frightened. She is also exhilarated and excited, overawed. The passage of time has brought an inevitable change. Then she was nineteen and penniless. She is twenty-nine now, and successful. Having a baby is something she can envisage.

But there is still Sandy. He will not want a baby, he could not. He and his wife have a daughter, now twelve. He says they are happily married, though Carmen is beginning to wonder what that means. When they parted after the end-of-series party he implied that he would be happy for them to resume their relationship when the new series began.

With the positive test still in her hand, she rings him.

"Carmen! What a nice surprise ...! I hadn't expected to hear from you so soon."

His tone is cordial but distant, as if she were any other member of the team who worked on "Newsreel."

She grits her teeth and ploughs on.

"Could we meet, please? I'd like to talk to you."

"Sure." She hears him flicking the pages of his diary. "It'll have to be about three weeks from now, only we're just off on a family holiday. To Ireland."

"No, it'll have to be sooner. Come round to my flat this afternoon."

She hangs up, in desperation, before he can argue.

He tells her that she cannot be having a baby.

"I'm pregnant. That's what it generally means." Sandy's tone is as dry as it was in the old days, when they were enemies.

"You may be pregnant, but you certainly can't go ahead and have the thing. It would be insanity."

Carmen's stomach contracts. "It's not a thing! It's our baby. Yours and mine."

"But we can't do this together, don't you see? I'm married, very happily as a matter of fact. . . ."

"Funny how men who have affairs always say they're happily married."

"And anyway, how can I be sure it's mine?"

Carmen stares at him angrily. I don't love him, she thinks, I don't think I ever did. It was just lust, a bit of friskiness brought on by the claustrophobia of the situation.

"Look, Carmen . . ." Sandy's tone is gentler and he attempts to put a hand on her shoulder but she pulls away. "It's not just me this would be disastrous for. What about you? Your career's on a high at the moment. We've got the second series coming up in the autumn, and if the word got out about me being the father of your expected child, we wouldn't be able to work together. It would be you the producers let go. And you'd have to take time off, which would mean missing out on auditions for the season after that . . . You'll be forgotten. Replaced. They can find another Carmen Fox anywhere."

Carmen turns away, looks out of the window at the leaves on the trees in the square, bending and sighing in the breeze. He's right; that's the bitch of it. He's right.

When Sandy has gone she phones the Marie Stopes Clinic and makes an appointment for a termination of pregnancy.

It hurts this time, much more than the last. She opts for a general anaesthetic because she does not want to feel the baby being pulled out of her. But the pain is still there, in her head and in her heart.

The anaesthetic makes her feel sick and weak afterward. She crawls back to her flat and hibernates in bed for the rest of the weekend. On Sunday morning she is woken by a frantic ringing on the doorbell.

Ros is on the doorstep, clutching a pile of Sunday papers.

"There you are! I've been ringing for ages . . . Jesus, Carmen, you look terrible!"

"Come in ..."

"I take it you've seen these, then?" Ros hands her the papers.

Carmen looks at the one on the top of the pile, a tabloid with a taste for sensational revelations about the love lives of the famous. TOP TV STARS IN SEX DRAMA blares the banner headline.

Carmen Fox and Alexander Cairns, copresenters of the BBC's top show "Newsreel" were discovered in a saucy romp at a TV party. "We all thought that Carmen and Sandy were hot for each other," a witness reveals, "but I didn't expect to find them making love on top of a desk!"

"Oh, no ..." says Carmen. "Is there more?"

"I'm afraid so. ..."

Carmen looks at the next paper.

After dramatic revelations about his affair with sexy young TV host Carmen Fox (29), Alexander Cairns (47) denied that he had any plans to leave Lorna, his wife of fifteen years ...

"It's not true, is it?"

"No! ... Well, yes, sort of ..."

The phone begins to ring. Ros answers it. "No—she's not here."

It rings again. Carmen unplugs it at the wall.

"Look, you'd better come and stay with us for a while. You'll be hounded here. I'll help you pack ..."

There is already a journalist on the steps when Ros and Carmen leave, and Carmen is photographed wearing dark glasses, with Ros's scarf draped ineffectually over her head. After twenty-four hours of relative peace, Ros's phone starts to ring.

"I can't stay here, Ros, it isn't fair to you and Pete."

"Well, where will you go?"

"It can't be anywhere in London; they'll find me. I don't particularly care where it is, I just want to be left alone."

Carmen goes back to her flat, packs some more clothes, and some books, then takes a cab to Waterloo. Buying a magazine for the journey turns out to be a bad idea. More banner headlines on the newstand, jumping out at her.

CARMEN FOX BONKED MY DAD!

  A former friend of Carmen Fox tells how she came back to the flat that they shared to find the saucy TV star in bed with her father. "Carmen was game for anything," reveals her friend, who did not give her name. "Booze, drugs, men. And it did not matter who they were ..."

Carmen squeezes her eyes shut, wincing. Polly. The bitch. Obviously the Kendrick family has fallen on hard times. I wonder how much they paid her?

Carmen does not buy the magazine after all, afraid that the cashier will recognize her. She sits on the train and looks out of the window, waiting for it to start moving and take her on the journey that she made in reverse eleven years ago.

"The train now leaving Platform Nine is the 11:14 for Hemingford, calling at Slough, Windsor ..."

I'm on the run, thinks Carmen, as the wheels heave forward and the train begins to slide out of the station. The idea would be amusing, only she has not done anything wrong. Except for making a complete mess of her life, of course.

Nothing has changed at 41 Tudor Avenue. Nothing except for the estate agent's board outside the house saying "Sold".

"It's nice to see you, dear," says Jean when she lets her daughter in. "Of course, you've been ever so busy, haven't you?"

Carmen can tell from her mother's face that she has read the stories in the papers but has decided to be tactful.

"I wondered if I could stay here for a while, Mum? A few problems, you know...."

"Of course you can, for a few days." Jean serves instant coffee in flowered cups and saucers, with silver coffee spoons and ginger-nuts to nibble. "Only ... well, your father and I are separating."

"Oh. I see."

"Yes, so we've sold the house ... you saw the sign up, didn't you? And the new people are moving in on Friday. That's why I'm not at work today. Packing up and so on."

"Why are you separating? Have you met someone else?"

"Oh, no dear ..." Jean takes the cups to the sink and starts to wash up. "No, it's not that. But after thirty-five years of looking after other people, I thought it would be nice to have a change."

Jean takes off her apron and sits down at the table again. She lights a cigarette and takes the first drag with a little shiver of pleasure. "The first one of the day is always the best...."

"You ought to give it up."

"You should talk!" Jean laughs. "You were forever nicking my cigarettes when you were little and thinking I never noticed."

"I know." Carmen grins.

"Your dad's in agreement about this, you know. About the move. He's got a lot of new hobbies—bowls, that sort of thing. We're splitting the money and we're each buying ourselves a little flat. In the same building, so we'll still see plenty of each other."

"That sounds a good idea."

"Only the flats are very small, dear, they've only got the one bedroom."

"It's all right, Mum. It's probably not a good idea to stay with you anyway. It would only be a matter of time before ..."

"You could always go to Sally's. Mind you, she's not feeling too bright at the moment, with a baby on the way. Did I tell you she was expecting?"

Carmen looks down at her hands, pretends to examine her fingernails. "A baby. That's nice."

"Yes, we're thrilled, Les and I. Most of her friends from school have got babies now, you know."

Jean's words give Carmen an idea. A very good idea. "Mum, have you got a Hemingford telephone directory?"

She makes a note of the address and calls a taxi to take her to St. Mark's, where Winnie Fox used to live.

T *h i r t y - f o u r*

■

Stephen first notices Heine Mueller when he is eating in the Mexican restaurant where he sometimes goes for supper.

He notices Heine because he is eating alone, with a book, just as Stephen is. Stephen often goes out to eat alone. He has made some friends in San Francisco. Yashiko, the Japanese student at Stanford who goes to the same t'ai chi class; Melanie, the secretary at the small wine importing business where he now works; Gary, who plays at the same racketball club and sometimes invites him back to Pacific Heights to have dinner with his family. But these three do not constitute a wide social circle and Stephen often dines alone in the evening.

He sees Heine the following week, and then again. They start to nod at one another and smile, and finally Heine comes over to talk.

Several margaritas later, they have told one another their life stories. Stephen finds his inbuilt reserve easy to overcome; he has been away from England for nearly three years now and there has been plenty of time to think. Ideas and emotions have tumbled over one another in his head: tentative explanations as to why things have happened as they have, but there has never been anyone to listen.

Heine is a good listener. He is only four years Stephen's senior, but has the manner of someone much older and wiser. Stephen finds his broad, Germanic face attractive, with its angular chin and sad brown eyes that droop down at the corners. His fine, mouse-colored hair is cropped very short and reminds Stephen of the coat of a well-groomed dog. He wears a sleeveless purple vest and a small gold hoop in each ear.

Heine is a second-generation American; his mother's family emigrated just before the Second World War and he was born and raised in the small town of Rexburg in Idaho. He moved to San Francisco in the seventies and is proud of his adopted city. He works at City Hall now, and owns his own home on the south side of the city.

"So how come you're able to work here legally?" he asks Stephen. "You got a green card?"

"The guy I work for told Immigration I was a European wine expert and got me an H-1 visa. It's got another three years to run.

"If you want to move out of that rented room of yours, you're welcome to come and share. I've got plenty of space; three bedrooms. I've set up a really neat den, with a desk and lots of books, and there's a pretty little yard. It's real tranquil."

"It's very tempting ..." Stephen remembers the home comforts of the house in Canonbury. "Maybe I could come over and take a look at it?"

"Sure, that'd be great. Here: I'll give you the address."

Stephen stares at the piece of paper Heine has written on. Eighteenth Street, Castro district. The heart of the gay quarter. He has visited it once out of curiosity and felt he did not want to go back there. He was uncomfortable at the sight of hard-core bars like The Bear on Castro Street, with its macho clientele dressed in leather biker gear, posing on the black leather banquettes, looking for pickups. The walls were also painted black and the interior was so dark that he could not see anything, he could only smell the place. It smelt of disinfectant and sawdust. And then there were the shops, selling fluffy slippers and high-heeled court shoes in men's sizes, and advertising "Leather, Latex, Lubricants & other male-oriented purchases."

"I know what you're thinking," says Heine. "But it's a good place to live, really. The scene's a lot quieter now since the AIDS scare, and everyone's real friendly. It's a community, a neighborhood. A good place to be—even if you're straight."

Stephen is something of an oddity in the Castro district. He refuses to make any concessions to the flamboyant style of its inhabitants and keeps up a rigidly English appearance, with his pale blond hair worn in a short back and sides and his face clean shaven. He wears neatly pressed trousers and shirts rather than tight jeans and T-shirts and the ubiquitous leathers.

He is happy. He enjoys the friendly atmosphere of the neighborhood, and he feels at home in Heine's house. His first impression of the place was of an extraordinary burst of color. The building is pink and blue Victorian stucco, like a birthday cake and has a garden overflowing with brilliant blooms. And on the steps of the house is a flagpole with a multicolored flag waving in the breeze, the rainbow stripes that denote gay allegiance. After passing the flag several times each day, Stephen ceases to notice it.

To begin with, he and Heine do not spend much time together. At least twice each week Heine goes out "doing the scene," drinking and dancing, indulging in soft drugs and occasionally having sex with casual pickups. He never discusses this with Stephen, sensing perhaps that the very idea of it disturbs him. Nor does he bring his lovers back to the house. When he is at home, he is calm, quiet, bookish.

Heine returns from City Hall one evening to find Stephen pacing the den, looking agitated. It is their custom for the first one home to wait for the other to arrive before having an early evening cocktail, but tonight Stephen already has a large scotch in his hand.

"What happened?" asks Heine. He flings his briefcase down on the rocking chair. "You look like something happened."

"It's Gary," says Stephen. "You know, my friend from Pacific Heights? The one I play racquetball with sometimes? He came round here."

"So?" Heine walks slowly to the drinks cupboard and mixes himself an old-fashioned.

"He ... propositioned me. You know, made a pass."

Heine sips his drink, frowns, adds a dash more of Angostura. "So. That surprised you."

"Well, of course it did!" Stephen walks over to the tray and pours himself more scotch. When he looks up, Heine's face is only inches from his own, his deep brown eyes inscrutable. A little amused perhaps. "The guy is an attorney; he's married with two kids and a third on the way!"

"It happens all the time. Guys from the bourgeois suburbs come down here looking for a bit of excitement. He must have thought you'd reciprocate. You live in Castro, after all."

"Yes, but it's not as if I'm . . ."

"Gay? Well, aren't you?" There is a tense silence. Stephen looks away. "You told me yourself about how you slept with that guy when you were at school."

"But that's different! That can happen to a lot of people who are confined in a single-sex school. It doesn't mean anything."

"Jesus, Stephen!" Heine puts his glass down with a thump. His face is pale with anger. "Why can't you just allow yourself to be a homosexual? It doesn't make you a bad person. All it means is that you enjoy sex more with someone of your own gender. Why is that such a terrible thing to you?"

"Because it's not just that, there's more to it than that . . . oh, I don't know!"

Stephen throws Heine's briefcase off the rocking chair and sits down in it, rocking to and fro so that the view of the garden outside rises and falls before his eyes, rises and falls. . . . The movement starts to calm him.

"When I was growing up I was made to believe that it was terrible. It was something you were not supposed to be. Adultery, infidelity, those were things you could sweep under the carpet but not this. And like I said, it's not a question that's so black and white to me. I loved my wife. I made love to her."

"But it didn't work. If it had, you wouldn't be here now."

"Okay, Okay . . ." Stephen closes his eyes. He feels suddenly tired, drained. "Maybe I am gay, I don't know. You can think of me that way if it makes you feel better."

Heine puts a hand on his arm. "I care about you a lot, you know that."

Stephen opens his eyes, looks down at Heine's strong, tanned forearm. The warm touch of his fingers feels so good. He feels tempted, oh yes, he feels tempted.

"I care about you too, Heine. I do. But whenever sex has reared its ugly head, things have gone wrong in my life. I didn't know what

I was getting into when Nicholas and I became lovers again. All I know is that he became depressed and he killed himself. So I'm going to stay celibate. Maybe I can be happy as a gay in a gay community, but I'm going to be a celibate one."

"Are you sure?" Heine's fingers apply the faintest pressure.

"Sure."

"Okay."

Heine is quiet and withdrawn over the weeks that follow, and Stephen knows that he is brooding on Stephen's decision. When he starts to refer to him as "the monk," Stephen knows the decision has been accepted. When he calls him "my English monk," with a faint smile, he knows that it is also respected.

Over the next year, Stephen and Heine settle into a comfortable routine. They behave like a couple, albeit a celibate one, and are accepted as such. With the devastating effect of AIDS at last writ large, monogamy is fashionable.

They travel around California, staying in old-fashioned bed and breakfast inns in Carmel and Marin County and the rugged northern coast near Ferndale. They take long, pensive walks and light fires on the beach and drink the state's best wine. Their friendship is both calm and intimate. Stephen feels happier than he has in years. In his letters to his parents (theirs are cool and distant; they still have not forgiven him for walking out on his marriage) he tells them that he might settle in San Francisco for good. They know nothing about Heine, they only know that Stephen is "in the wine trade," which is at least a respectable enough job to bear mention amongst their friends.

In the spring of 1988, Stephen and Heine plan their first interstate trip. They are going to Rexburg, Idaho, to visit Heine's elderly mother. Then Heine develops a rash on his back and ribs, rows of tiny blisters that burst, leaving raw, burning pain. The doctor diagnoses shingles and orders complete rest, so the trip is postponed.

"We can go in the summer, I guess," says Heine, but he does not sound enthusiastic.

Even after the shingles has cleared up, he is listless, dejected. At first he is simply withdrawn and Stephen leaves him a wide berth, seeing less of him than usual. Their relationship reverts to how it was in the old days; they are just roommates. Then Heine starts to lose his temper with Stephen, to indulge in angry outbursts and then sulk afterward. One evening when Stephen gets back late from work, he finds Heine in the rocking chair, with the house untidy and the breakfast dishes still on the table.

"Put the trash out," says Heine, without looking up from his book. "It's your turn."

The fragile reserve that Stephen has been holding onto breaks. He rounds on Heine.

"What the hell's the matter with you? I'm sick to death of you indulging yourself in your bad moods! You're a grown man for God's sake! Stop being so bloody immature and tell me about whatever it is that's bothering you!"

Heine's reaction is inevitably one of surprise; he has never heard Stephen raise his voice before. Then he buries his head in his hands and begins to weep.

"I'm such a coward," he mumbles over and over. "Such a goddamn coward!"

Stephen kneels beside him. "What's happened?"

"The doctor wanted to run some tests. He said that shingles in a man of my age suggests immune damage. The blood tests show that my T-cell ratio is way down the bottom of the scale."

Stephen stares at him. "What . . . ?"

"Shit, man, you know what that means! It means I've got ARC."

Stephen is familiar enough with the term; he has read about it often enough in the San Francisco press. ARC is AIDS-related complex. A health condition where some of the minor symptoms of AIDS have begun to appear, but which can be stabilized and might not necessarily develop into AIDS. At least, not for years.

He knows what this means, but still he can't take it in. Not Heine, he *can't* have. He said he was safe. . . .

"I don't want to die," says Heine, sobbing, whining like a child. "I don't want to fucking die, man."

"You won't," says Stephen firmly. "You don't have to."

■ ■ ■

For the next few months the two of them enter a terrible, dark place where they are stalked by fears, real and imaginary. Heine's state of health becomes an obsession with them. Is he stable? Is he symptom-free? The slightest cold spells disaster. In April he has one he is unable to shake off; it develops into flu, with fever and night-sweats and swollen glands.

Heine is dejected and Stephen finds his moods almost impossible to cope with. Particularly his obsession with alternative treatments. There *must* be a cure, he insists. There must be something that will work. He devours any information he can get his hands on and becomes very excited about Compound Q, a controversial drug from China that is undergoing tests at San Francisco General. Rumors abound that it is available (illegally) at some of Castro's alternative health stores.

"It sounds really something," Heine says, his pale face shining. "It sounds like it really might work. I ought to try it."

"No," says Stephen firmly. "It's too risky. You're not sick enough yet."

"How about this Ribavarin drug, then, from Mexico?" He brandishes a magazine. "A guy in this article has been on it and it helped rebuild his immune system. He's much better now. I ought to fly down to Mexico City and get some."

"You're not well enough at the moment."

"Okay, you go for me, *please*."

"It says here it has toxic side effects."

"Oh come on, Stephen, please! I'd get it for you, man, if you were fucking dying!"

Stephen hesitates. Suppose it does work. Perhaps they ought to try it . . .

"No," he says firmly. "No. For a start, you're not dying. You've just had a bad case of the flu and you're going to get better."

The effort of getting Heine well again leaves Stephen exhausted. He supervises a strict regime of good food, rest, and gentle exercise. They both stop drinking anything other than mineral water and herb tea. He bullies Heine into going to self-help classes in visualization and positive thinking, skills that will relax him and divert his energy away from anger and toward healing.

Gradually he improves. He gains weight again and his complexion loses its gray pallor. After several weeks of being symptom-free, he declares that he feels better than he ever has before.

"I think I'm up to that trip to Rexburg now," he says. "Feel like flying down for the Fourth of July celebrations?"

Stephen is too busy at work, but promises to join him as soon as he can. They go to the airport together and Heine waves from the barriers, jubilant to be on his way home.

On July 5, Heine develops a cough. When he mentions this on the phone, Stephen tells him he must see a doctor. He senses rebellion, though, and is not convinced that Heine will go.

A few days later he hears from Mrs. Mueller. Heine collapsed suddenly and was taken to hospital, where the doctors have diagnosed pneumocystis pneumonia. He is lapsing in and out of a coma. Three days later, as Stephen is preparing to fly down to Rexburg, Heine is dead.

Stephen asks the taxi to stop several yards from the house, so that they will not hear the engine and look out. He wants a few moments to collect his thoughts.

He carries his suitcases down the street and stands in front of the gate. The huge sash-windows in the drawing room glow golden in the darkness, lit from within. The curtains are drawn but he can picture what it is like inside. They will be reading, or listening to music. The fire will be lit to ward off the chill of a damp autumn evening.

And he imagines their faces when they see him, hears his father's voice saying, "Why have you come back? There's nothing for you here. . . ."

T *h i r t y - f i v e*

■

It takes Jackie some time to get into her tailored business suit; her waist is thicker since Alice was born and she has trouble fastening the zipper.

Alice is seven months old now and Jackie is feeling strong enough to go back to work; today is her first day. Anyway, she tells people she is feeling strong enough, but really the Maitlands are desperate for Jackie to start earning again to pay off the mortgage and all the credit they have run up over the past three years.

At least there is still Megan, who is coming back to work full time.

"Hi!" Jackie shouts down the stairs when she hears the key in the lock. Thank God. Thank God for Megan ...

She comes downstairs carrying Alice in one arm and her brief-case and papers in the other.

"Right ..." She fumbles around for her checklist. "I've got to get going ... they've both had breakfast. Alice has been up for a couple of hours already, so she should be ready for a sleep soon. You might persuade Emily to get her head down after lunch, but I wouldn't put money on it ... their lunch is in the fridge; puréed vegetables for Alice and macaroni and cheese for Em. Oh, and I've made up a couple of bottles for Alice, though she might prefer juice at lunch time. Also, it's Emily's afternoon at nursery, so perhaps you could walk her down there at two, and then pick her up at five-thirty."

"I'm afraid I won't be able to collect her this afternoon, Mrs. Maitland, I've got to go to the dentist at five."

"Oh God ..." Jackie hands the baby over and flicks frantically through the pages of her Filofax. "I've got a meeting at four-thirty, but I'll just have to cancel it.... Won't look very good on my first day back, but that's just too bad. So I'll go straight to the nursery ... no, that won't work if you have to get off at five ... I'll come here first and pick up Alice and then we'll go and get Emily ..."

There is a dull *clump* as the mail lands on the front doormat. Jackie picks it up and takes it with her on her way out to the car, flicking through it with one hand as she steers to the end of Compayne Gardens with the other. There is a white, handwritten envelope addressed to Mr. G. Maitland. A round, girlish script. She hesitates for a few seconds, then opens it as the car comes to a halt at the traffic lights on West End Lane.

"My darling Greg ..."

The letter is merely a confirmation of what Jackie has suspected for some weeks. Nevertheless she finds that her heart is pounding as she stuffs the letter back into its envelope. It is the boldness of the act, the cool defiance with which such a letter was sent to Gregory's home address. Why? Because the sender is hoping to be discovered, of course. Or perhaps Gregory was courting discovery by giving out his home address.

She holds the letter out to him when he gets back from one of his protracted squash matches.

"I opened this by mistake," she says. "Who's it from?"

The voice she hears coming from herself is quiet and careful, little-girlish. She recognizes it; it is the voice she used to employ when she was trying to prevent Gregory from hitting her.

"It's just from someone I know." Gregory takes the letter and thrusts it into his pocket. "It doesn't matter who."

"Are you having an affair with her?"

He hesitates; but only for the briefest moment. "Yes."

Jackie cannot think of an appropriate response, so she goes upstairs to check on the children. Alice is fast asleep with her backside in the air and her quilt wrapped around her head. Jackie straightens the covers and tucks her up, touching the fluffy curls thoughtfully.

Gregory comes into the room and stands beside her looking down at the sleeping form in the cot.

"We ought to talk about this," he says quietly.

"Not in here. Let's go downstairs."

They sit in the pretty pastel drawing room amongst their expensive consumer durables: television, video, and stereo. Images of family unity look down on them from all sides: the wedding picture, the girls when they were newborn, christening photographs, Christmas. In all of them Gregory personifies the ideal New Man, handsome, high-achieving, dynamic yet caring.

Jackie declines a drink, preferring to sit in the solitary armchair in the corner where she does not have to look directly into Gregory's face.

"I suppose it all started when I was seeing Heather," Gregory says. He sounds as if he is trying to be sad. "She told me that the reason I was threatened by your success was because I hadn't found my true identity yet. She said one way to find my identity was to explore new relationships."

"Don't give me that nonsense! Don't tell me you had to have affairs because your psychoanalyst told you to!"

"I'm not trying to shift the blame, I'm trying to explain!" Gregory's voice rises. "If you'd only listen. . . ."

"How many were there? You said you needed new relationships: how many were there? How many women?"

"There is only one! For God's sake, Jackie! . . . Well, two, if you count a very short fling I had a few years ago. But it was nothing, it never . . ."

"Who was it? The one you had a fling with. Did I know her?"

Gregory nods. "It was Carmen Fox."

Jackie laughs. "Carmen. My old friend. She always was a two-faced bitch, even when we were at primary school."

"Yes, well . . . it didn't mean anything."

"And what about this other one. This . . . ?"

"Jessica."

Jessica. A young name. Young handwriting. Obviously much younger than he is. Gregory has gray hairs now; she has just noticed them.

"What's going to happen with her?"

"I don't know," he sighs. "I really don't know."

Gregory does know really, he has worked it all out. He phones Jackie at her office the next day and tells her he is moving out, and can she tell him what time of day Megan and the children will be out so he can go round and collect his things.

When she gets back from work he is gone. Her husband is gone, reduced permanently to the smiling image in the snapshot.

Gregory has thoughtfully left Jessica's phone number so that Jackie can ring him if there is something wrong with the children. She does not want to ring him. She wants to get hold of his hair and shake him until his teeth rattle. She goes through his desk and finds that he has also left Jessica's letter, which contains Jessica's address. She makes a note of it: 5 Winchester Mews.

She sits for a long time staring at the digital clock on the video, silently pacing its way through time. Then, with a sudden surge of energy that comes from a hidden place deep inside her, she jumps to her feet and runs upstairs. Working quickly and methodically she puts cases out on the bed and starts to fill them with clothes and all the children's paraphernalia: toys, nappies and bottles. Then she reaches into the back of her dressing table drawer for her jewelry. Underneath the velvet boxes is a Christmas card, saved from last year, and addressed to the whole family: "Hope you are all okay. Things here are going very well indeed. Love, Rob." She hesitates for a second, then puts the card into her bag with the jewelry boxes.

When she has finished packing and the bags are downstairs in the hall, she lifts the sleeping Emily from her bed, wraps her in a blanket and takes her out to the car, where she straps her into her seat. Then she puts Alice into the carry-cot and secures her on the back seat next to her sister, then loads the cases and the buggy into the trunk.

Jackie drives slowly and purposefully through the suburban back-roads of Hampstead, following a route she has traced many times on her buggy-pushing excursions. She passes houses like her own, comfortable family homes with their curtains drawn and lamps lit, the flickering screen of the television glimpsed occasionally. It is raining

400

•

hard, and the monotonous sweep of the windscreen wipers calms her.

She drives into Winchester Mews and comes to a stop outside number 5 with the engine running and the wiper blades scraping from side to side before her eyes. There are no lights on. They have gone out, Jessica and Gregory. For a meal probably, or to the cinema.

Jackie climbs out of the car and stands in the beam of the head-lights. The same surge of energy courses through her and bursts over her in a wave and she realizes that it is anger, sheer, brutal rage. She picks up a milk bottle and hurls it at the window of Jessica's house, smashing it. Then another milk bottle, and another, and then, when she cannot find any more bottles, large stones. She bares her teeth and grimaces as she shatters each new pane, breathing out in a labored grunt, as if she is giving birth. The anger that she has held in her all her life is flowing out of her; anger at Billy for telling her nothing was too good for her, anger at Pamela for bringing her into the world and then losing interest, anger at Norman Butler for rejecting her, and most of all, anger with herself.

As the last pane of glass in the house is broken, a great sense of release comes over Jackie. It is such a pleasant sensation that she wonders why she never expressed anger before.

Emily has woken up and started to cry, neighbors are staring from windows and front doors are opening in response to the com-motion. Still high on rage, oblivious of her rain-sodden clothes and wet hair, Jackie jumps into the car and reverses out of the mews.

"Hey!" shouts one of the neighbors, running after her, but she ignores him, slamming the car into first and screeching away down the street. She drives out of London heading southwest, heading for Hemingford. She is tired now, exhausted, and the tiredness makes her forgetful. She drives first to 30 Wetherall Gardens, thinking it is still home. There are lights in Flat B; she sits for a few seconds and stares up at the window of her old room. The frilly pink curtains have gone, at last. Then there is nothing for her to do but drive away from the center of town to The Poplars.

"Oh dear," says Pamela when she opens the door. "Oh, Jackie, goodness!"

Jackie is standing on the doorstep with rain trickling down her face, a crying child in each arm. Pamela beckons her in and shuts the door.

"I need to stay for a while, Mum."

"Well, I don't know about that dear ... we're not really prepared for you, and there's not much space ..." She looks to Don for support.

Jackie's hands are shaking as she wipes the rain from her face, the water mingling with the tears that have come from that same buried place inside her. "Please, Mum, I need you to do this thing for me! Just be my mother; mother me—please."

Jackie is having a nervous breakdown.

She never allowed herself to cry when she was a child because she somehow knew that if she started she would be unable to stop. She cries now, incessantly, self-indulgently, for weeks, while the children are cared for by a surprisingly patient Pamela and a bewildered Don.

She thinks a lot about Gregory, the stranger that she married and who is now gone. She can see now how much of what happened is her fault. She put so much effort into *getting* Gregory, into marrying him and making a perfect home, creating a perfect family, that she neglected the task of getting to know him. All she saw, all she cared about was that he was eligible and handsome and intelligent. She wanted someone who would be strong. Norman Butler had been weak; she had recognized that, seen what it had done to her mother. But there was a lot more than strength to Gregory Maitland, a third dimension to her two-dimensional image that she did not care to acknowledge.

And she was greedy, too. The inbuilt emptiness of the rejected child sent her scuttling out into the world, grubbing around for everything she could lay her hands on, saying "This is *mine,* and this is *mine* ..." just like the two-year-old Emily marking territory with her toys.

Around the time that the crying stops, she gets a letter from Munro Willis saying she has lost her job due to unauthorized absenteeism. But she knew that already, and she finds she does not really care.

There is also a letter from Gregory's solicitor, telling her that a buyer has been found for the house in Compayne Gardens, and will she give her consent to the sale. She consents gladly, and a few weeks later receives a check for the proceeds of the sale, which Gregory is giving to her in full, to provide a new home for the children.

Jackie has no wish to return to London, so the new home may as well be in Hemingford as anywhere else. She finds a pretty converted Victorian cottage in the conservation area adjoining the old biscuit factory. It is in a quiet street, and many of the other houses have been bought by young families; even some other single-parent families, so the estate agent tells her.

Jackie does not care if there are other single parents or not; she just likes the place, likes the way it feels. She looks forward to the day of the move, relishes collecting the children from Pamela's house when their belongings are settled and taking them there for the first time.

"Is this going to be our home now, Mummy?" asks Emily.

"Yes," says Jackie firmly, closing the front door behind them.

T *h* *i* *r* *t* *y* *-* *s* *i* *x*

■

Matthew Pryce-Jones phones Graziella Buscowicz.

Come *on,* he thinks as he hears the ringing at the other end. Come on, Graziella, please be in! I want to talk to you. I want to tell you what a shitty day I've had in that shit-hole of an office. . . .

"Hello?"

It is a man's voice.

Matthew hangs up. He spends the rest of the night awake, pacing, in an agony of jealous rage. He leaves the answering machine switched on for the rest of the week and does not return Graziella's calls.

But on Saturday she arrives at his flat in her car, a convertible Morris Minor. It is March, the first warm spring day, and the roof of the car is folded down.

Graziella points to it with a flourish. "I thought it was time we took her out for a spin."

Matthew settles himself into the passenger seat with a bad grace. He does not like being driven by a woman. Especially with the memory of the Ferrari still so fresh.

"Who was that guy who answered the phone the other night?"

"Just a friend."

"Really?"

"Yes, really."

Graziella steers the car through the traffic of the King's Road and heads west, toward the M4.

"I thought we could go down toward Hemingford. That's where your parents live, isn't it?"

"Yes."

"So—we could go and see them, couldn't we? You said you hadn't seen them since you went to the States."

"But I don't particularly want to see them. They're not expecting us. Anyway, they're probably out."

Graziella shrugs her shoulders. "If they're out, they're out. If not, it'll be a nice surprise. It'll do you good, too."

Matthew ignores her sharp look, examining his reflection in the driving mirror. His hair is lank, his skin looks gray and tired and he does not know what to do about it. And there is another dilemma for him to consider as they head down the motorway. When he was at St. James's Hospital, he gave Graziella the impression that his family were grander, richer than they really are. What will she make of 9 Mount Rise and Audrey's pathetic social pretensions? What if it makes her go off him?

It is too late now, anyway. They turn off for Hemingford and when Graziella asks for directions he has no choice but to give them.

Audrey Pryce-Jones is flustered by the unexpected visit, but welcoming, charming. Even at fifty-five she is still emphatically trim, her body honed in aerobic classes, her hair permed and colored at Hemingford's newest salon. Ken is aging less well, his waistline bulging, and his head almost completely bald.

Audrey takes them out onto the patio, for drinks.

"We've just had the garden landscaped," she explains to Graziella, "and it is so lovely to sit out at this time of year, don't you think?"

Graziella responds happily to the questioning about her job.

"You've done so well to become a doctor, dear, hasn't she Kenneth? Because I gather it's much harder for a woman, even these days. . . ."

Graziella makes no comment when Audrey laments her son's decision to "give up" medicine. ". . . And then of course there's this business in the City, dreadful really . . ." She glances at Matthew, who stares fixedly into his gin and tonic. ". . . Now, our younger son, Tristram, is doing very well at the moment. He's a solicitor, you know."

"I hear you're an accountant, Mr. Pryce-Jones," says Graziella quickly. "You must be glad that Matthew has decided to follow in your footsteps?"

"Yes, well ..."

"I think we should go now," says Matthew, standing up. " 'Bye Mum. 'Bye Dad."

"I do hope you'll come back and see us again," Audrey kisses Graziella's cheek and murmurs. "You're exactly what poor Matthew needs at the moment."

Matthew and Graziella drive in silence to the steak house on the Hemingford bypass and order lunch.

"I thought your parents were very nice," says Graziella. "I'm glad I met them."

Matthew smiles back at her, his expression thoughtful. He picks up his tumbler of iced water and presses the cold glass against his forehead. "I've been so unlucky," he says.

"Unlucky?"

"Yes. The stock market crash coming before I had a chance to get established in New York, Getting caught the way I did at St. James's."

"The first of those things may have been well and truly out of your control, but in the second instance it was a case of making your own luck...."

Matthew gives her a warning glance.

"It's all right—I'm not going to lecture you. But I am sorry about it because I still think you would have made a fine doctor."

Matthew shakes his head. "No. No, I wouldn't. I never would have had the patience. I realized that the other day when I saw you at the Royal Free. That hurt. But do you know what was the worst thing about being there?"

"What?"

"It was being in a hospital and instead of having nurses give me saucy looks, they walked straight past me."

Graziella grimaces. "That sounds like the old Matthew Pryce-Jones."

"Yeah, and what an idiot I was. Professor Sadler told me that mistakes have a way of coming back to haunt you, and he was right,

I mean, look at me! Even my brother Tristram, who everyone had down as a dolt, is more successful than I am!"

"Hey, come on!" Graziella squeezes his hand. "You've got everything ahead of you! Once you're a qualified accountant, the business world will be your oyster. You'll get back on top again."

"You really believe that, don't you?"

"Yes, I do," Graziella looks serious.

"Graziella ..." Matthew takes hold of her hand again. "I think I love you."

"You *think* you do?"

"Yes."

She laughs. "That's a start, I suppose."

"We should buy a house together," says Matthew several months later.

Graziella, who is half submerged in a sea of medical journals, case notes, and textbooks, looks up at him over the rim of her glasses.

"Hmm. Maybe."

"It makes sense if you think about it. We're both looking for flats in the same area, and we're virtually living together all the time anyway."

"Okay, yes. If you put it like that ..." Graziella picks up her pencil again and returns to her work.

"Well, you might try showing a little more enthusiasm! It wouldn't hurt you to appear interested!" Matthew begins pacing the room, a habit he has recently acquired.

"I said 'okay.' Let's get a house."

"Just like that?" Matthew throws his arms wide in exasperation. "Don't you see, for once in my life I don't want things to happen just like *that*." He clicks his fingers. "This isn't about instant gratification, it's about the future, about making plans."

"Matthew, I agree with you, honestly. We'll make plans, just not now. I have to write up these discharge summaries before tomorrow."

A week later, Matthew lets himself into Graziella's flat before she has returned home. There is nothing unusual about him arriving before her: she often works late at the hospital. Tonight she is even later than usual, but Matthew's annoyance takes second place to his excitement.

"Look at this!" He thrusts a printed brochure under her nose as soon as she has walked in.

Graziella glances at it; it is a set of estate agents' particulars.

"I've found the perfect house! It's in exactly the right location and it's exactly the right size. . . . And I went to the building society today and filled in all the forms for the mortgage. It should be through in a few weeks. So . . ."

His voice tails away. Graziella has put the brochure down without looking at it.

"I was at a meeting this evening." She falters slightly, then clears her throat and goes on. "That's why I'm back later than usual. My consultant called me in to see him after the ward round." She looks up, meeting Matthew's angry, bewildered gaze. "He wants me to apply for a new job that's come up. At Leeds General Hospital."

"Leeds? But that's at least two hundred miles away. You can't live here and work there!"

"No, I know. I won't be living in London any more."

"But Graziella . . ."

"Matthew, this is a really big chance for me. It's one of the best hospitals in the country for surgery. They have a brilliant team and I ought to take the opportunity to be part of it."

Matthew breaks into a grin. "Well, it's simple then, isn't it? I'll move up to Leeds too. To tell the truth, I'm getting a bit sick of London. It's dirty, noisy, expensive. The traffic's diabolical, it takes hours to get anywhere. . . ." He rips the brochure in two. "There are several big accountancy firms in Leeds; I shouldn't have any trouble finding something."

Graziella stands up and crosses the room, resting her forehead against the window pane so that Matthew can't see her facial expression, just her finely chiseled profile. "I don't think that's a good idea."

"But why? I thought we were . . . together."

"We are. But that's because we both happen to be here. We bumped into one another again, we were both unattached, so . . ." Graziella shrugs.

"And we would be together in Leeds. It would be exactly the same except for the geographical location. I don't see what the problem is."

•

"Relationships just don't work that way, that's all. You'd be there because of me, and that would make things different. Uprooting yourself, moving to a city where you know no one but me . . . and I'd be working to a pretty, unforgiving schedule. It would put too much pressure on us."

Matthew comes to stand immediately behind her, stoops to kiss the back of her neck. "And what if we made it permanent?"

"What do you mean?"

"Marry me. I want us to get married, Graziella."

She lets out a long, shuddering sigh. "No."

"Why not?"

"Because I don't want to marry you, Matthew."

"But why? I don't see . . ."

She turns round abruptly. "You want the truth? You really want to know?"

"Of course."

"Okay then. It's because you're not the sort of man a sensible woman would want to marry. Oh sure, you're very good-looking, very charming . . ." She smiles slightly. ". . . Very good in bed. Great to have an affair with. But women don't necessarily want that for the rest of their lives. They want other things—dependability, fidelity, unselfishness. Trust."

"You don't trust me? But Graziella, I love you."

"Sure you do. For now. But I remember how things were last time. The minute I achieved something you couldn't deal with, you were off. Straight into the arms of someone else."

Matthew backs away in a panic, stumbles around the room, treading on her books, bumping his shin on the coffee table. "Jesus, that was ten years ago! I've changed—I'm different now. I mean . . . this is crazy, goddammit! The things that have happened to me these last two years, they've changed me!"

Graziella shrugs. "Maybe. But finding out isn't a risk I can afford to take at this point in my career."

"Your bloody career, Christ! . . ." Matthew manages to control his anger. "Look, you've got to believe that I've changed. I *swear* it! What do I have to do?"

Graziella becomes impatient suddenly. She pushes past him and starts to go through the contents of her briefcase. "Nothing. I've made up my mind and I'd be grateful if we could leave the subject now."

"So that's it, is it?" Matthew twirls her round angrily so that she's forced to look at him. "You're just writing me off. Not prepared to give me the benefit of the doubt. Just when I'm getting my life back into some sort of order you turn round and kick me in the balls. What do I do now, eh, answer me that?"

"That's your problem, Matthew, not mine."

Matthew removes his belongings from Graziella's flat by the end of the week. A month later the rental agreement on his own flat expires. He takes a shabby bedsit on a temporary basis and returns to his search for a flat to buy with his dwindling piece of capital.

The one for which he offers in the end is smaller and more expensive than he had originally wanted, but by now he is desperate to get away from the stale-smelling bedsit at the top of its dank flight of stairs, with his belongings littering the floor in suitcases and cardboard boxes.

A week before contracts are to be exchanged, the estate agent telephones him and tells him that another purchaser has made a higher offer for the flat, and he must match it or pull out. Matthew cannot match it. In rage and despair he bundles his possessions into the back of a taxi and takes them to his parents' house in Hemingford, the only refuge left to him.

T *h i r t y - s e v e n*

■

In the center of Hemingford a noise can be heard above the hum of the traffic; rumbling cement mixers and clanging girders. The bingo hall behind the shopping center has been torn down, and a conference center is being built in its place. The developers hope to exploit the new electrified railway line to London, which has cut the journey time to twenty minutes.

Opposite the shopping center is the hair salon that used to be Snips and is now called Akido. The interior is decorated with tatami matting and minimalist black and chrome; the stylists all wear pseudo-Japanese black workwear. Jangles nightclub has become a video rental shop and the old fish and chip shop two doors away is now a Burger King and is doing a thriving trade. Polystyrene burger boxes and chip cartons drift along the pavement, carried by the spring breeze.

Carmen Fox notes all these changes as her taxi takes her through the town center and out again round a complicated one-way system. The shops become fewer and further between, they pass small factories and business units on the new industrial estate, a huge DIY superstore. Then the familiar outline of the biscuit factory looms ahead. The taxi turns left down one of the streets where the factory workers used to live. The flat-fronted cottages have been bought privately and gentrified now; they all have neo-Georgian doors and carriage lamps, ruched blinds and repointing. Window boxes and tubs planted with spring flowers; polyanthus, tulips, and daffodils fill the street with color.

The taxi stops outside one of these houses and Carmen rings the doorbell.

Jackie Maitland answers the door. When she sees Carmen she is visibly taken aback, paling slightly.

"What are you doing here?" She stares angrily at Carmen's suitcases.

"Jackie, I'm in a bit of a fix ... Ros told me you'd moved back down here and ... I wondered if you could put me up for a while."

"You've got some nerve!"

"Oh, I see ... May I come in?"

Jackie stands back and beckons her silently into the house.

"You've obviously heard about Gregory and me...."

At this point Emily Maitland provides a temporary distraction, trotting up to them and inspecting the suitcases. Carmen bends down to show her how the locks fasten. Jackie stands next to her, waiting.

"Look, Jackie ... there's not a lot of point to my apologizing, but I would like to explain."

"All right. Come into the kitchen."

She leads Carmen through the sitting room to the back of the house, where a modern extension has been turned into a kitchen with sliding doors onto the small garden. She puts the kettle to boil and they wait in silence until Emily has run off and busied herself with her crayons.

"Gregory sort of blackmailed me ... he kept coming round to see me and he said that ... being with me prevented him getting angry and slapping you around. I believed him."

Jackie nods, looks thoughtful as she stirs two mugs of instant coffee.

"I know that's pretty feeble as explanations go; believe me I'm not proud of myself. And it's really no excuse, because I *did* find him attractive and I did want to ... you know."

"It's okay," says Jackie quietly. "It was just as much my fault as yours. I obviously drove him crazy. I must have been a real pain to live with."

"Now come on, Jackie! You mustn't start blaming yourself for what *he* did! You wanted the marriage to work, didn't you?"

"But it didn't."

"No, well … we all make mistakes." Carmen smiles over the rim of her coffee mug. "Between us we're a right pair, aren't we?"

"I heard about the business with you and that TV presenter." Jackie gives an embarrassed smile. "What I mean is, I read about it in the papers. Will you go back and do another series of 'Newsreel'?"

Carmen shakes her head. "No. I'm going to have to resign. Which doesn't bother me all that much, in fact it's rather a relief. But I didn't want to stay in London, or go away to some strange place where I was completely isolated. My parents can't put me up, so I thought I'd ask if I could stay here."

"Well …" Jackie gestures around the four walls of the room. "What you see is what you get. It would be a bit cramped. I could put the girls in together, I suppose, but the third bedroom is really tiny."

"I'll pay my way, of course. And I could give you a hand with the children. Give you a chance to get out a bit."

Jackie looks thoughtful. "I can't deny that I could do with some baby-sitting. And some extra money would come in handy…."

"You know, Jackie, we've known each other twenty-five years and we've never become more than friendly acquaintances. Do you think we could become friends?"

She smiles. "I suppose it's about time we did…."

"So that's what you've been doing all these months since you've been back from America!" Geoffrey Noble paces to and fro on the same small patch of library carpet until his hand-stitched brogues work up static. "Sneaking out in that shifty way without saying where you were going! Your mother and I thought you must be looking for a job."

"We thought you might be seeing Alison again," says Sylvia quietly.

"I mean, why Hemingford, for God's sake!" Geoffrey rubs at his neck, which has turned dark pink around the edge of his collar. "Hemingford doesn't need that sort of place…."

"It's called an AIDS Advisory Center, Father." Stephen keeps his voice quiet. "And one reason I'm setting it up here is because Heine stipulated when he left the bequest that the center was to serve an area that didn't already have that kind of facility. A small town, like the one he grew up in. The other reason is that I wanted to come back here and show everyone that I'm not ashamed of who I am."

Geoffrey ignores this. "This town doesn't have that sort of person; it's not like London, or San Francisco. People from around here are decent, clean-living sorts."

"But I'm from Hemingford, and I'm gay!"

"Stephen, darling, please!" Sylvia shoots a warning look in the direction of his father.

"Well I am, to all intents and purposes! It's taken me five years to come to terms with it, so now I'm just going to be honest about it...."

Geoffrey sits down at the desk and buries his face in his hands.

"I haven't got a lover, if that's what you're afraid of. But I know I'm never going to have a normal relationship with a woman, either."

Geoffrey looks up abruptly, shouts: "Get out! Go on, get out! You disgust me!"

Stephen goes out onto the terrace and stands at the edge of the pool, watching the reflection of lights in the water. The heavy, sweet scent of flowering jasmine catches at his nostrils.

Sylvia comes out onto the terrace and stands beside him. She shivers in the night air, pulls her arms closely around herself.

"I've been speaking to your father. He's just upset...."

Stephen looks down at their two pairs of feet, his in grubby tennis shoes, his mother's long, elegant feet in navy blue Russell and Bromley loafers with gilt chains across the instep.

"Try talking to your father again, Stephen, please. You've been away for so long.... Neither of us wants to lose you again."

Stephen returns to the library. His father is standing by the window with his hands in his pockets, looking out over the garden.

"Father ..." He puts his hand on Geoffrey's arm, half expecting him to pull away. He does not. "I know that my being gay hurts you, and I'm sorry, I really am. But I can't change it."

Geoffrey nods.

"If you don't want me to stay on in this house, I'll make arrangements to leave."

"No, don't go!" Geoffrey's voice catches sharply, he clears his throat. "That would upset your mother terribly."

"All right, I'll stay."

Geoffrey wipes his fingers across his eyes before turning round again. "I suppose I'm just not very good at this sort of thing. Wasn't brought up to be."

"Neither was I."

Stephen gives his father's hand a brief squeeze before leaving him alone again. He knows he has had the best apology he is ever going to get.

The Hemingford AIDS Advisory Center is run from a suite of rooms in the old Victorian building that used to house the offices of the town council. The service answers telephone enquiries, sends out information, runs counseling sessions, and the staff of three are very, very busy.

Stephen occupies the position of director and senior counselor. He feels stretched, tested for the first time in his life. The academic world seems dim and distant; this is happening and the problems are real. Their urgency gives him vitality and he is experiencing for the first time how it feels to be successful. The Hemingford center becomes the model for others that are opening across the country. Stephen and his work are featured in the media; the local radio station and television network send reporters to interview him.

He works every day of the week, going in at weekends to check the answering machine for urgent messages. One Saturday morning in the summer of 1989, he locks the door of the office and steps backward into the path of a familiar figure.

"Matthew! How lovely to see you again."

Stephen smiles broadly, extends his hand.

Matthew is frozen to the spot. His eyes stray up to the brass door plate engraved with the legend HEMINGFORD AIDS ADVISORY CENTER.

"I work here," says Stephen with a reassuring smile. "I'm director of the center."

"Oh . . . great." Matthew proffers his hand slowly.

"It's all right, you won't catch anything."

"It's not that, it's just . . . well, you're looking so good. You really do look terrific."

Stephen hesitates. He was about to make a similar response but realizes that it wouldn't be true. Matthew does not look well. His face is gray, drawn.

"So, what brings you to Hemingford?" he asks instead. "Visiting your parents?"

"I'm living with them, actually. I'm training to be an accountant, so I commute up to London every day. Saves on the rent, you know. . . . At weekends I study mostly."

"Well . . . that's good."

"It's only temporary, of course. Until I can buy a place of my own. But with interest rates soaring . . . you know."

"Yes, well, stay in touch . . ." Cautiously, Stephen reaches out and gives Matthew's shoulder a pat. "It would be good to have a proper talk."

"Okay," says Matthew, forcing a smile. "If you like."

Matthew sits in the kitchen that evening, watching his mother clear up. She is fully engrossed in this task, which means that she isn't talking at the moment. Matthew is relieved to have a few minutes' silence. His mother is a habitual chatterbox. Ken no longer listens to her, so Matthew has been cast as resident recipient of her endless confidences and trivial gossip about the neighbors. She keeps asking about Graziella, too, predicting that the two of them will get back together again. She cannot understand how any woman—even a doctor—could fail to accept her son's offer of marriage.

"See anyone you know in town?" she asks absently. Acquaintance-spotting is one of her many meaningless pastimes.

"Yes I did, as a matter of fact. I saw Stephen Noble."

"Really?" Audrey pulls on her rubber gloves with a snapping sound and picks up the bottle of disinfectant. "What's he doing these days?"

"Running the AIDS Advisory Center in town."

"Oh." Audrey purses her lips in disapproval.

"He's doing pretty well, actually. He seemed happy. And I've read that the place is a real success . . ."

Audrey turns back to the sink.

". . . which is odd, if you think about it. I mean, I would have put money on me being the success and soppy Stephen Noble being a no-hoper. He was always such a Mummy's boy at school. We all used to laugh at him. But now it's the other way round. Stephen's got his life sorted out and I've come running home to Mummy...."

"What, dear?"

"Oh, for fuck's sake, will you stop doing that and just listen to me!" Matthew's voice rises to a hysterical note. "I'm trying to tell you that I've fucked up my life. Literally!"

"Matthew ..." Audrey starts to cry. "Don't say that!"

"Why not? It's true, isn't it? Otherwise why the hell would I be here, in this bloody place, at the age of thirty?"

Ken has heard the raised voices from the lounge and has come to stand in the doorway. "What's going on?"

"*You* did this to *me!*" Matthew shouts at him. "Both of you. The way you carried on when I was young made me think it was clever to go and fuck lots of different women. To be always looking out for something bigger and better in life. And now I'm on my own with no roof over my head, no professional status, and I've lost the only woman I ever cared about because she thinks I'm bad husband material!"

"Now wait a minute!" Ken takes a step forward. "If you think you can blame us because you were too greedy, or too stupid, or too dishonest ..."

Matthew raises his hand and stands there with it poised inches from his father's temple. Then he lowers it slowly and hangs his head.

"You're right, Dad, I'm sorry. I screwed up all by myself. And it's not your fault I've dumped myself on you because I've got no home to go to."

Audrey puts her arms around her son and kisses him. "But that's silly. You have got a home...."

"She's right." Ken tries, awkwardly, to hug the two of them. "I know it's not what you've been used to, but you'll always have a home here."

T *h i r t y - e i g h t*

■

It is Christmas Eve 1989, and Jackie Maitland has just been combing the Yellow Pages for the names of places selling Christmas trees. When she finds somewhere that still has trees left, a pet shop that sells them as a seasonal sideline, she bundles the children into the car and sets off.

It is already dark, and as Jackie parks the car, the children are attracted by a blaze of color and light opposite the pet shop. It is a showroom selling luxury cars, decorated festively with colored lights round the window and a tree trimmed with glittering baubles. Jackie stares up at the proprietor's name in gold letters above the string of lights: ROBERT JONES OF HEMINGFORD.

So Rob is doing well, as he said. The cars parked in the expanse of window are Rolls-Royces and Porsches, gleaming just as brightly as the Christmas lights. There is carpet and potted palms and squashy leather furniture. And this is one of two branches; Jackie passed the one on the other side of town when she was house hunting.

On a sudden impulse she pushes the door open and goes into the showroom. There is a woman sitting behind the reception desk, but no one else in sight.

"We're just closing, dear."

"Is Mr. Jones here?"

"Neither Mr. Robert nor Mr. Gareth is here. Would you like to speak to Mrs. Jones? She's in the back office."

"Mrs. Jones? Rob Jones's wife?"

"Gareth's wife. Robert isn't married."

417

418

"Oh."

"I could take a message for him."

"No, it's all right." Jackie hesitates. Emily is staring at the Christmas tree, transfixed. She remembers how she used to love seeing the decorations and lights in town when she was little. They never had a tree in the flat in Wetherall Gardens. Pamela said what was the point, with just the two of them?

"Er, yes, I will. I will leave a message. Will you say that Jackie Maitland called, and that he can find my address and number in the Hemingford directory. Say it's under my maiden name because I'm divorced."

"Excuse me, aren't you Carmen Fox?"

Carmen is sitting in the wine bar in Hemingford, surrounded by her bags of Christmas shopping.

"I recognized you from your TV show. I don't suppose you recognize me?"

Carmen looks at the face of the young man in front of her which is just—but only just—familiar.

"I'm Matthew Pryce-Jones."

"Of course! Well, well, well ..." Carmen laughs. "As I recall, we didn't exactly part friends last time we met."

He seems smaller than she remembered, paler. Less golden.

"Will you let me buy you a drink, by way of a very belated apology—or have you got more shopping to do?"

"No, I've finished. And I'd love a drink, thank you."

They have several drinks and talk until the shops across the street close their shutters and all the shoppers go home. Carmen tells Matthew about her brief career on television, and the press witchhunt. She thinks her story sounds quite tame after Matthew's. She is intrigued by him.

"You know, there was a time when after an evening like this I would automatically have made a pass at you," she tells him.

"Me too." He smiles at her as he drains the last dregs of champagne from the bottle. "I would have expected you to jump into bed with me."

"But we're not going to, are we?"

He shakes his head. "Nope. We're not."

"I'm glad you had the guts to come over and say hello." Carmen looks thoughtfully into her empty glass. "You know, it's funny how when we're in the middle of making a mess of our lives, we think we're the only ones doing it. When in fact it's going on all around us."

"I feel better for knowing that. But I had to come here to get things into perspective. Back to Hemingford. I never thought I'd end up back here."

"Neither did I."

Carmen sighs, looks around her vaguely for her bags of Christmas shopping. "So, what do we all do now?"

"We start again. With the new decade ... which reminds me, there's a reunion for the alumni at Albert Road Mixed Infants. On New Year's Eve. Stephen and I thought we'd go along for a laugh. Why don't you join us?"

"I will," says Carmen firmly. "And I'll bring Jackie along. You remember Jackie Yardley, don't you?"

"Of course. She'd never let me kiss her when we played Kiss Chase in the playground."

"How do I look?"

Jackie presents herself for inspection, wearing a strapless dress made from midnight-blue velvet, sheer stockings, and suede court shoes.

"You look very nice. You need something round your neck, though. Here—borrow my pearl necklace."

"But you don't think it's too smart, do you? I mean it's only Albert Road ..." Jackie views her reflection critically. "I wish I knew what everyone else was going to be wearing ..." She catches herself out, and laughs. "Silly, isn't it, the way we still care about these things."

"If we look a bit flash, so much the better. No point going back to the old dump unless we're going to do it in style. Now, what do you think ...?"

Jackie swivels round on her dressing stool, puts her head on one side, looks Carmen up and down. "Hmmm ... I think the black's a bit too sophisticated. I think your red dress would be better. You look nice in red."

Carmen accepts this advice, and when she has changed, peers at her reflection over Jackie's right shoulder. Then she sits on the end of Jackie's bed and the two of them apply their makeup in companionable silence.

Living together for the past nine months has worked out better than either of them could have imagined. Being different is an asset; they complement one another. And Jackie now has someone with whom she can share her children; both the good moments and the bad. She never shared them with Gregory.

Carmen is doing some free-lance media research, Jackie some free-lance retail consultancy. They coordinate their work so that there is always someone on hand to mind Emily and Alice.

Of course, they both acknowledge that this is only a temporary situation; the house is too small for all of them. Carmen talks frequently about buying a flat of her own, but somehow her plans have not materialized.

The phone rings and Carmen answers.

"It's for you," she mouths, with her hand over the receiver, "someone called Rob Jones?"

"Hello?"

"Hello, Butterfly."

"Rob. Hello."

"I ... I just wanted to ring and wish you a happy new year. Are you going out somewhere?"

"Yes. Yes, I am."

"That's good. Well ... It would be nice to meet up some other evening. Could we do that?"

Jackie smiles. "Yes, please," she says.

The assembly hall at Albert Road Mixed Infants runs along the south-facing edge of the smaller playground. It is here that pupils once said their morning prayers and pretended to be trees during Music and Movement.

Now the hall is hung with balloons and streamers and packed

with those same pupils, wearing a uniform of party dresses and tuxedos, smoking cigars and drinking glasses of sparkling wine. Above the lectern where the headmistress used to stand is a colored banner saying WELCOME BACK TO A.R.M.I.!

"There are Matthew and Stephen, over there!"

Carmen takes Jackie by the hand and pulls her through the crowd, treading on the toes of the people she passes, her puffball skirt catching against their legs. It is so hot in the room that she can hardly breath, and a thick cloud of smoke hangs in the air like fog.

"This is impossible," Stephen shouts above the music after their attempts at conversation have dwindled. "I can't hear myself think!"

Matthew wriggles one arm free of the crush and points to the doors. "Let's go outside. . . ."

The four of them spill out into the playground, drinking in great gulps of frosty air.

Carmen sniffs. "Still smells of sick."

"Isn't that old Rudd's classroom over there?" Matthew points to the windows on the other side of the playground. "Someone's left the lights on."

"Perhaps Miss Rudd's in there!"

"Let's go and have a look. . . ."

The four of them re-enter the classroom where they learned to add and subtract, to divide and multiply, twenty years ago . . . It has the same smell that it had then; chalky, sour. The Naughty Chair is still there, and the shoebox of pencils on the desk. There is still a Behavior Board with the pupils' names listed in Miss Rudd's meticulous hand.

"Old Cruddy Rudd. What a bitch that woman was!"

"God, I hated math!"

"Me too."

"So did I."

"She tried to put me in detention on my birthday," Matthew remembers.

"I was in detention that time too."

"And I was!"

"We all were."

Carmen walks slowly round the room, looking at the pictures on the wall. The form project for the last term was an environmentally conscious one named "Saving Our Planet." She stops in front of one picture, a girl's face with mouth turned down and tears running down it. The caption, in childish hand, reads: "We must change the things we do or else we can't save the world and there will be no future for us."

Matthew is on his hands and knees, rummaging around at the bottom of a cupboard.

"Rudd used to store old exercise books in here ... look." He pulls out a pile of faded blue books. "Nineteen sixty-nine."

"Let's have a look ..." Carmen flicks through the books. "I don't believe it, this is mine; Carolyn Fox—Class Two."

"Here's mine," says Jackie. "And yours, Matthew. And Stephen's."

"I'll tell you what ..." says Matthew. "Why don't we have a little celebratory bonfire!"

"I'm not sure that's a good idea." Jackie looks round the room. "There's a lot of wood in here. It would be terrible if it got out of hand."

"Just a little one. A contained one."

"I think it's a brilliant idea." Carmen is already piling the books onto Miss Rudd's desk. She holds her cigarette lighter to the corner of her own exercise book, and when it is alight, puts it on top of the pile. The paper is very dry, and after smoldering for a few seconds the other books quickly catch fire, sending up a small column of flame.

The four of them—Carolyn, Stephen, Matthew, and Jackie—stand round the fire in a ring, Matthew holding a fire extinguisher at the ready. The strains of "Auld Lang Syne" float across the playground from the assembly hall.

As they stare into the flames all four of them think of their former selves, who yearned to leave this place, to go out and show the world who they were. And now they are all back here again, with the process of knowing themselves only just beginning.

"Here's to all of us!" Matthew tosses his book into the blaze.

Stephen follows suit. "Here's to our generation!"

"And the next!" says Jackie with feeling. "And the next. . . ."

Acknowledgments

Grateful thanks to my editor, Caroline Upcher, and my agent, Vivienne Schuster, for their continuing help and support. And most of all to my beloved husband, Ian, without whose patience and encouragement this book would never have been completed.